Contents

Introduction

In 1858, when Gracie Tipton left Nashville, Tennessee, on the long trail to The Pinery in the Guadalupe Mountains on the Texas and New Mexico border, she had no way of knowing how her life would change. Within two years, she was a wife, a widow, and expecting a child.

After coming to tell her of her husband, Jedediah's death, her father-in-law, Hurricane Bailey, left in the dead of night, before Gracie could tell him of his soon to be born grandchild. What would happen to Hurricane after losing his son to an Indian arrow? Would he turn into a bitter old man and go back to the alcohol which had sustained him all of his life? Where would the abusive man find the peace, he'd needed? Was there any such thing in this world? He had to find the answer. The Black Hills of Nebraska Territory were calling him.

Because of his concern for his daughter, during her pregnancy, Jonathan Tipton schemed with Preston Stockton, a man Gracie and her father had admired on the trip West, to take her to his ranch, The Glory B, in the Glass Mountains for the baby to be born.

Realizing she loved Press Stockton, but not willing to say it, even though he'd once declared his love for her, she left with her father for the Davis Mountains, and the new Butterfield Station established there. Press came for her, and they were married.

~

Over twenty years have passed since the marriage, and some of Gracie's children are grown up and leaving the Glass Mountains. She decides to go on another trail, this time a longhorn drive to Abilene.

We'll join Soot, the lead longhorn and the Carter twins with Caleb's handsome son, Thomas. The Stockton's travel along with their children and cow-boys as they drive the herd from The Glory B to Abilene, Texas. Planning to retire from cattle drives, Press has given his oldest son, Jonathan, the important position of trail boss on the journey. What problems will he and the drovers have to overcome on the way? Will Gracie survive the trip?

Waiting in Abilene is Doctor Sarah, Gracie's friend from Nashville. Ruby Eliza is her nurse, and the ruggedly handsome new superintendent of the Texas and Pacific Railroad, Grant Bailey.

~

First, we follow Hurricane as he leaves The Pinery, and then we'll go forward with the herd of beeves, and the Stockton family to Abilene.

THE GLORY B

A Sequel to *Butterfield Station*

REBA RHYNE

Chapter One

The Day After New Year's Day, 1859

On January 2, 1859, Hurricane Bailey led his horse quietly and stealthily from the stockade at The Pinery—a station on the Butterfield Overland Stage Line through Texas. The sun hadn't risen on El Capitan's face nor did it shine in the cold valleys of the snow-capped Guadalupe Mountains, where the pines' elongated shadows graced the canyon's floor. He dropped the reins of the bridle to the ground.

"Hold still, Old Girl," he whispered to his horse, knowing she would stand quietly, even if he didn't tell her to. This horse was a new ride for him—bought at El Paso for the trip to The Pinery. This was after the raid by the Indians in Arizona which took his horse and the life of his only son, Jedediah.

Tugging at his saddle, which was harder to do in his early-fifties, he slung it over the horse's back, positioned it, and tightened the cinch underneath the horse's belly.

In the cold darkness, he went back into the stockade, pulled his saddle bags from a wooden peg on the wall, and picked up his bedroll from the fresh hay where he'd slept during the night after turning down a warm spot by the kitchen stove. Rolling his bedroll up as he walked back out, he passed a white bundle, sleeping by the wooden stockade door.

Wooly raised her head, disturbing Ticksy, and eyed him for a brief moment. She returned to her sheep dreams, as the cat snuggled against her in the frigid night air.

The old man didn't notice. He walked to his horse and attached his saddle bags and bedroll.

His intention was not to arouse any of the sleeping inhabitants. Especially his deceased son's young wife, Gracie, whose words, "You make me sick," still rang in his ears.

Although later, he had to admit, she'd added, "I hold nothing against you." The old wagon trail master and tracker found her words hard to believe. Forgiveness was something he didn't know much about and didn't cotton to.

At this stage in his life, he really didn't care one way or the other. He'd killed everyone in his life he should have cherished. Now, he was alone—the very thing he'd dreaded for as long as he could remember. Alone.

Instead of mounting up, he pulled on his fur-lined leather gloves, buttoned his coat against the incessant Texas wind, and walked his horse as soundlessly as possible to the main road, where he continued for several hundred feet toward the east. His moonlit shadow walked along with him. He stopped. Looked back at the faint light arising from the stronghold he'd just left.

Finally, with his foot in the stirrup, he grabbed the pommel, pulled up, and slung his leg over the animal, resting his tired body, as comfortably as possible in the chilly saddle. He shivered for a few seconds on his cold seat and then nudged his horse forward.

Anyone looking at the forlorn shape of a man in a rough coat on horseback, would notice his hunched back and lack of enthusiasm for life—his misshapen hat mashed on his bowed head. Hurricane Bailey didn't care if he lived or died. Losing his only son in an Indian raid, had sucked all the want out of him. He just didn't care.

For several days, he plodded on toward Fort Chadbourne, one of his old stomping grounds. He pulled his horse off into the brush or the entrance to an arroyo when he saw the distant dust of the Overland Stage heading for The Pinery or other wagons with pioneers on the road. He was in no mood to greet anyone, as he followed the stagecoach route east, at least not in Texas. He avoided the fort.

Late one afternoon, he turned off the main trail and headed north toward the Red River.

Why north? North was Oklahoma and above that state, the etched-out territory of Kansas. Why go to Kansas? Because he had memories there and a place he wanted to visit. Also, he had a confession he wanted to make to the person he had prized the most in the world. The one besides his son.

Hurricane could take care of himself. Had since his father died when he, as a young man, was twenty-six years old. Being alone was something new. The older man was a hard drinker and taught his son all of his vices, just as Hurricane had tried to teach Jedediah.

But Jedediah, his only son, had resisted those temptations, preferring to remain sober so he could take care of his drunken father. He had often hauled him from saloons in the primitive West where they made their meager living, guiding wagon trains, tracking Indians, or game to sell or eat, or doing odd jobs they found around stables, bars, or stores.

The shock of his son's death had altered Hurricane forever. He hadn't had a drink since, and he didn't intend to take another. But being sober meant he had to face the demons in his life, some of which were ingrained and hard to confront. Could he change? He had vowed, over his son's grave, to do so. But how do you change after leading a hard-drinking, hard-riding life?

He hadn't told Gracie that. First, he wanted to make sure he did. Would he ever see her again? He didn't know, and at this time, he didn't care.

~

Two months after leaving The Pinery, he sat in the cold, on the banks of the Red River, looking at the Last Chance Saloon. A wisp of smoke oozed from the chimney. He noticed the door had been repaired and now hung correctly in its frame. *Business must have picked up*, he thought.

He'd gotten drunk here as Gracie and her pa traveled the rough Texas frontier road to The Pinery. He vaguely remembered Gracie's scorn and their conversation as he tried to mount his horse, fell off, and landed in the Texas red dirt. Not the first time he'd fallen from his horse in a drunken stupor. Inside the building were two kinds of warmth. He decided to leave both alone.

Pulling the collar of his coat around his neck, Hurricane gave a short-disgusted chortle, nudged Old Girl, and rode onto Colbert's Ferry which had no one but him for the short trip into Oklahoma.

Around one-and-a-half years had passed since the former passage, when he and Jedediah had taken over the scouting for the Tipton wagon train headed for the Guadalupe Mountains.

The ferry nudged the opposite bank. Lines were tossed to waiting men who wrapped them around poles to hold the boat against the river's swift current. Hurricane guided his horse up the riverbank, just as the boat's owner walked outside his mercantile store's door to collect any money owed for the crossing.

Seeing Benjamin Colbert, a Choctaw Indian, the older man stopped to talk and buy a few supplies at his roadside store. Colbert was a talker and Hurricane needed to catch up on current happenings. Part of his father's tracker training was knowing the happenings on the road ahead.

"Hurricane, haven't seen you in a while. Where you headed?" Benjamin stood outside the door of his establishment in a buffalo robe, munching on a large piece of corn pone—a staple of the Choctaw and Cherokee Indians' diet. In between chews, he smoked a pipe full of tobacco which was raised on his plantation, mostly by slave labor. Benjamin was rich by Indian standards.

Hurricane dismounted, his mouth watering as he eyed his companion's fare. "Headed toward Leavenworth in Kansas Territory. I need some supplies," was his short reply.

Colbert noticed the tired eyes wandering over his repast. "Are you hungry? Come on in. Today, there's corn pone aplenty."

The interior of Colbert's establishment was dark but warm, with only a couple of lamps burning to drive away the gloom and brighten the space. Colbert went to the stove in the rear. Taking a cloth, he grasped the handle of a large iron skillet, pulling it from the hot surface to a table nearby. A knife swiftly cut Hurricane a large chunk of corn pone from the portion in the metal pan. He offered the warm piece to the forlorn man who stood rubbing his cold arms with his hands.

"The stove warmth sure feels good. Thanks. Ain't had nothin' but jerky fer days. Gits a little tiresome after a while. What do I owe you, Colbert?"

"Aw, don't worry about it. Are you still leadin' wagon trains?" The wealthy Colbert wiped his mouth on his sleeve, took a long draw on his pipe, and let the smoke out in a puff which circled in the air above his head.

The one characteristic, passed from Bailey fathers to sons, was the distinctive ability to track men or animals or lead wagon trains as scouts on trails across the West. The three men excelled and were widely recognized as being the best.

"Nope. I'm just driftin' at present. Any news of the area?" Hurricane said through a mouthful of cornbread.

"Kansas and Oklahoma—and maybe further north—still unsettled. The government's permanent Indian settlement is a pipe dream. The Osage are causing lots of trouble. Even the Cherokee are fightin' amongst themselves. Not only that, but in the mix, in Kansas there's real trouble over slavery. Did you hear about Fort Scott? Are you headin' that way?"

"Don't hear much, if you're diggin' dirt and rocks from the road fer the Butterfield Stage. What's happened?" He could have added and if he was drunk most of the time when he wasn't working.

"I guess you knew they closed the fort and auctioned it off. Turned it into the town of Fort Scott. Well, from what I've heard, the town's been invaded with people from both sides of the slavery issue. Several people have been killed and the military comes and goes to restore law and order. They no more than leave town and the fight between the factions starts again. Amazing ain't it. The Indians don't cause trouble now, but the people find something else to fight about." Colbert shook his head in disgust.

"I was sorta planning on ridin' through there. Maybe I'll change my plans."

"I would if'n I was goin' that way. Thar's two hotels in Fort Scott—one pro slavery and one agin it. On one raid into town, a man named Montgomery, who is agin slavery from what I hear, tried to burn the hotel which housed those who were fer slavery. One man ridin' on the Butterfield Stage showed me a newspaper from back east callin' that part of the country *'Bleeding Kansas'*."

Hurricane wiped his mouth on his sleeve. "Guess I'll buy a few supplies and head north." He walked over to a counter and started pointing out items he wanted to purchase.

"Will you be back this way?" asked Colbert, after the old man had paid for his supplies.

"Ain't fer sure. If'n I do, I'll stop in. Say hello."

Hurricane walked outside, slung his bag of supplies over the pommel, and mounted up.

His horse had taken a few steps from the store when Colbert remembered and called, "Where's your son?"

Hurricane threw his hand up, rode harder, and didn't answer. He headed northeast on the old wagon road across Oklahoma. As he traveled, he considered changing his mind, and did, deciding to journey on through Fort Scott as he headed for Leavenworth, Kansas.

As the days flew by, he headed for Fort Gibson, and into Kansas, encountering the mostly flat Military Road which ran straight north along the boundary of the State of Missouri. He hoped to bypass most of the trouble in Kansas. He had enough to think about without getting involved in a conflict which he wasn't sure of the side he was on.

It was in May before he reached Fort Scott. At the former military outpost, he paused long enough to buy more supplies. Even so, he heard more details of killings in the area.

"Are you continuin' on the Military Road?" asked the clerk of the supply store in what was the old Post Headquarters of the military fort.

"Yep, at least till I reach Leavenworth," explained Bailey, who'd been on the road many times.

"Then you'll pass *Marais des Cygnes*." The clerk nodded his head. "Better watch out. Thar may be ghosts 'round the area."

"What's so important about the place?" asked Hurricane, remembering a deep ravine and trees crowding the trail leading from the dirt road.

"The massacre, that's what." The clerk finished filling the old man's saddle bags, giving them a final pat and shoving them in his direction across the wooden counter.

Hurricane reached out his hand to take the leather bags and paused, "I ain't heard of it."

"Happened last year. Some pro-slavers crossed the state line, rounded up some Kansas free-staters, took them to the ravine, and shot them all. Tried to kill 'em, but five men survived the massacre to relate the story. The free-staters go into Missouri keeping things stirred up, and doing their own killin'. Tit for tat so to speak. We're hoping things will settle down a bit later this year."

"I've been through and know that area well. I'll keep my eyes peeled for trouble." Hurricane hefted his saddle bags to his shoulder and left the store. He didn't believe in ghosts and didn't expect any trouble.

Several days later, he bypassed Kansas City, Kansas and rode on to the outskirts of Leavenworth. Following the high bank of the Missouri River, he soon came to a place where he could see through the brush and briars covering the hillside. These shrubs, some flowering, continued in profusion into the delta or floodable lowland. The Missouri was wide at this point with sandbars dotting the watercourse's expanse.

On the other side, the proslavery state of Missouri started with Kansas City just south of where he stood and St. Joseph to the north. He'd been both places many times at the start of wagon trains heading West—most from north of the fledgling Kansas City area where they crossed by ferry to start the long trek to future homes. He had signed on as lead tracker, looking for problems with Indians, or struggles with the road ahead, or good water where the future settlers could overnight.

At the Rockies, he would turn back, never wishing to go farther than the foothills, although his father had ridden with Jedediah Smith into Oregon Territory and to the Pacific coast. Drunken talk around the campfire always turned to yarns about those years when Smith trapped furs on both sides of the Rockies. He'd told them so many times, he was believing it was he himself involved in the various escapades.

With a deep sigh, he dismounted Old Girl and with leaden steps continued on, not relishing the actions he would take next. He pushed through the underbrush, walking past tall sycamore and oak trees as he headed upriver. Lofty cottonwoods grew in the valley, closer to the river's edge in the wetlands below.

Months had passed since he'd left The Pinery, and the trees and bushes had green leaves. Hurricane hadn't noticed as he traveled north, except when crossing a shallow river where the willow's foliage brushed his arms or legs.

Spring was gone, and summer was on the way.

Ruby Eliza Bailey wasn't buried in a regular cemetery, but alone, in a cleared area on a nearby hill next to a tree behind the log hut they'd lived in. Hurricane had dug the grave himself, and he was sure he could find the spot, because he'd left a stone to mark it.

But he encountered some difficulty, because the area had changed with other houses and dirt roads crisscrossing the bourgeoning area—the town was growing. Slogging through the dense undergrowth, he came upon a slight, grassy mound of earth which had a large round stone at one end.

He'd made his son stay at the house until he buried his Ma in her pine box. Finding a rock to use as a head stone, he'd called to Jedediah, and the young lad had helped him roll it to this exact spot. In this manner, the boy could find his mother's grave in the future. Each time they'd been close to Leavenworth, he and Jedediah had come to the grave and spent a day or two in their old home.

Hurricane Bailey pulled a few weeds and sat upon the stone, turning at right angles to the grave, still looking in the direction of the river, where his mind could wander from the task ahead.

A distant ferry, plying the silently moving water below, blew its horn in short bursts. This faraway sound reaching distinctly across to the Kansas hillside where he sat. The craft floated east toward the distant smoke plumes of Missouri, with its steam-run paddlewheel churning the river water into a white turbulence behind it, and leaving a wake which splashed against the shore below.

Although there was noise and movement around him in the brush, the man who sat on the stone took no notice. Finally, gathering courage, he turned and spoke to the mound of earth.

Taking off his hat, he placed it on his knee, and clearing his throat, he said, "Ruby Eliza, our son is dead. I kilt him." And, for the second time since the Indian raid in Arizona, he sobbed his heart out—terrible, deep, guttural sounds—his face changing, his body shaking with the emotions he was feeling.

"I'm not worth killin," he moaned through his falling tears, and that was all he said.

When the tears no longer came, he stood up, and pulled the weeds from the mound, and mashing his hat down on his head, he said with a sigh, "I'll be back."

Then he walked off the hill and went in search of his old home.

~

If Hurricane expected the house to look the same as when he left a few years ago, it did not. The elements had taken their toll, but he placed his bedroll and supplies inside. On looking around, he decided he could patch the roof holes, stay for a few days and rest, until he decided to move on. This activity would take his mind off his problem, the one he must solve. If he was restless before, now he itched to be on his way—run, run as fast as he could from thoughts which pursued him.

As he worked, his reflections were of Nebraska territory—Nebraska, an Indian word meaning, 'land of flat waters', and the Oregon Trail. No, he wasn't going to Oregon. He'd heard there were places where you could lose yourself on this side of the Rockies—the Black Hills or Badlands of the Dakotas, the vast Wyoming prairies, or even the low-rolling western hills of Kansas where he could rest for a bit.

Which place could he best escape his feelings? Clear his mind? He was in agony and the only way for his mind to be at peace was to run away from Texas and Kansas, places fraught with memories he needed to forget. Even his sleep did not quiet his opinion of himself as a worthless person. He had nightmares, waking in gut-wrenching sobs or weird, disjointed screams. Surely there was a place he could go, and he must find it. This was what he was searching for—a peaceful place. He had to find it or lose himself in drink again. But where? The Nebraska Territory went north for hundreds of miles.

The hot Mid-west summer was in full swing as he mounted Old Girl and headed northwest. He did not join one of the wagon trains traveling on the Oregon Trail, but rode by himself. He would go to the Land of Flat Waters. If he did not find peace there, he would continue on until he did.

Behind him, on the mound of earth with the round rock at the end, a bunch of freshly cut black-eyed Susans rested in the early morning sun with drops of dew glistening on the petals.

Chapter Two

Hurricane Stops at Fort Kearny

The Platte River snaked through the lowlands of the southern part of the Nebraska Territory. From Hurricane's perch on a slight hill overlooking the unobstructed silver thread below him, the stream looked shallow and easy to cross. Although he would rather have avoided the heavily traveled area near Fort Kearny, he needed supplies after some weeks on the road, and this was the closest place to get them.

Fort Kearny was easily recognizable on its slight rise in elevation with the shallow Platte River flowing from the west to the east. Wagon trains accessed the Oregon Trail here, after converging from numerous paths approaching from Kansas or Missouri. They stretched or circled on the north and south sides of the Platte River, surrounding the military fort on all sides. Their inhabitants resting, restocking supplies, and sending messages home, while bracing for the final, arduous climb up and then down the Rocky Mountains.

Hurricane was familiar with the expensive Conestoga wagons, although most of the conveyances on the plains before him were only glorified farm wagons with a makeshift cover. Most were not very solid, but were entrusted with the settlers' hopes and optimism in making the journey to the western side of the Rocky Mountains.

Unusual were the tents of gold seekers, dotting the flat land area. These men, heading for the newly discovered gold fields of Wyoming, were camped in small groups, here and there. They only stayed a night and moved on. With riches in sight, their goal was only a few days or weeks away. Unintended consequences of this invasion were the building irritation of the Sioux Indians living in the area.

Because of the never-ending wind blowing the grasses on the prairie, smoke reached his nostrils from the continuous campfires in the area. A lone dust-devil whirled to the west of the fort and spun toward the east, indicating the dry, sunny days he'd just ridden through. This did not bode well for his future journey.

The travelers on the Oregon Trail joked that the Platte River was "a mile wide and one inch deep." In most cases this was true, except when the snow melted in the spring or heavy rains in the mountains raised the depth, causing massive floods in the lowlands. In dry spells, there were places where the water just disappeared underground. Digging, in the river's pebbles, caused puddles to form so horse and man could drink.

Hurricane reminded himself to get several canteens full of water—some for him and some for Old Girl just in case. Water might be scarce ahead as he traveled west and then north, and these he would keep in reserve.

He planned to follow the Platte River until it divided from the South Platte and became the North Platte, but not all the way into Wyoming Territory.

There was an area known as the Black Hills in Nebraska Territory. His father had talked of it, because he'd been there on a quick side trip with Jedediah Smith as they'd roamed the eastern face of the Rocky Mountains trapping beaver. The mountainous hills sounded like a good place to lose yourself.

At least, at this present time, this was his destination.

A short distance and just west of Fort Kearny, Hurricane spotted a small settlement known as Dobytown which had sprung up since he'd last traveled in the area. This rowdy place was known along the way west and east by the freight men who were returning supply wagons loaded with buffalo hides or furs to sell in Kansas or Missouri. They had warned him about it being a wild, rough frontier town, home to a number of unruly inhabitants. Every unsavory aspect of a military town, such as gambling, liquor, and disreputable men and women were its main attractions. He could find provisions there, but he would also find the terrible whiskey known as tanglefoot which he was very familiar with. No, he would avoid the delights of Dobytown at all costs.

Nudging Old Girl in the hot, sweltering noonday sun, he rode off the hill and into the fort compound. The fort wasn't surrounded by walls, but was open to the prairie. He passed two-story officers' and soldiers' quarters, stables, military storehouses and the headquarter buildings. These were both frame and adobe-brick, positioned around the usual central military parade grounds. From the front porch of one somebody shouted, "Hey, Hurricane. Where you going? Wait up."

Reluctantly, Hurricane pulled back on Old Girl's reins, turned, and looked at a man, which although it was hot and mid-summer, sat clothed in a long overcoat which fell to the side of the cane back chair he leaned against the porch wall of the building where he rested.

There was a clunk of the chair as the man stood and walked to stone steps which led off the porch. Grasping the wobbly step railing, he descended and headed toward the man sitting on the horse. A buffalo hunter, Walton Bowie walked with a slight limp caused by a fall from his horse in a difficult and wild buffalo chase while pursuing a large herd.

"Bowie, what're you doin' in Nebraska Territory? Last time I saw you was in Fort Chadbourne, Texas. You and the boys had sold yer hides and were restin' after following a large herd of buffalo as it headed north. You're a fer piece from thar."

"I might ask you the same question, my friend. You were working for the Butterfield Overland Stage," stated Bowie, grabbing Old Girl's rein. No one ever called him Walton, just like no one called Hurricane by his given name—Henry.

"Where's the rest of your party?" Hurricane asked, although he felt sure he could have made a good guess as to where the buffalo hunters were taking a breather.

"Ah, they're over at Dobytown, gittin' drunk on their hide money, I guess. I've got enough of a headache without addin' to it. Why don't you git offen your horse and sit a spell? We'll catch up on recent times."

Hurricane hesitated, but replied, "I'm jest here to stock up on supplies." He made no attempt to dismount his horse.

Bowie could read the tea leaves. From where he had been sitting, he had recognized a hunched over Hurricane as he rode off the low hill into the fort area. Something was wrong with the man. "Are you heading north? We'll be going in that direction as soon as the boys quit restin'," Bowie blinked in the blazing sun as he looked up at the older man. "Why don't you join us? Make some money on the way."

"Don't think so," Hurricane responded. He knew there'd be hard riding in the buffalo chase and plenty of just as hard drinking around the campfire. At the moment, he didn't feel up to such activities. "Is thar a large herd in the area?"

"Yes, and they're payin' more for hides, meat, and dried buffalo jerky to make pemmican because of the long wagon trains and gold seekers usin' the Oregon Trail headin' west. We aim to fill our pockets with as many silver dollars as possible."

"If you've got some extra jerky, I might need some of it."

"We'll find some, my friend. We've got several racks dryin' right now at camp. Are you goin' north?" Bowie asked again.

"Yes. But I'll follow the North Platte River after it separates from the Platte for a ways before I turn north."

"You headin' for the Black Hills?"

"Thinkin' in that direction." Hurricane nodded his head. "On the way here, I heard the Sioux aren't too happy with the United States Government at present.

Have you heard anything?" Hurricane was headed into Sioux territory when he turned north.

"Lots of rumbling, 'cause the government ain't honored their treaties. The Indians, could be the Sioux or Ojibwa, are losin' faith because of failed promises. Between them and the unrest in the south, things is gittin a little unsettlin', wouldn't you say?"

"Yes. I come through Bleedin' Kansas. Hit's in the throes of change. I hope all will be cleared up without the further spread of bloodshed. Lots of people are sayin' the word war."

"I heard the same as we came through."

"Not heard of any Indian raids, have you?" Hurricane hoped the answer was a resounding no. As a lone rider heading north, he couldn't take on a group of enraged braves.

"A week ago, thar was a rumor went through here like a Wyoming wind. We didn't git many details, so I can't say. Hit may have come from Western Minnesota Territory. Course thars rumors all the time. Who knows if they's true?"

Chill bumps stood out on Hurricane's arms as a strange foreboding filled him. "Good to see you, Bowie."

"Sure, you don't want to come with us?"

"I'm sure. Thanks. You men ride careful. There may be more to that thar Wyoming wind than you know." Hurricanes sixth sense was saying this same thing to him—be careful.

He nudged Old Girl to head for the sutler's store. Stopping her, he turned and called back to Bowie who stood watching him leave. "I'm in need of a pack mule for my trip north. Do you know of one for sale?"

"Thar's messages posted at the sutler's store—inside on one wall. Look there." Bowie pointed in the general direction. "When you need that buffalo jerky, I'll be sittin' here on this front porch."

Hurricane threw up his hand and continued on the path by the parade field. He did need more supplies because he was headed into an isolated area, where stopping at a home or passing others on the trail would not be helpful in case of emergency. He'd thought about buying a mule earlier, but houses were not totally scarce along the path he'd ridden coming west. They would be soon.

The fort's sutler's store, where he could stock up on supplies, was busy. Future settlers of the West were lined up outside the entrance. If they didn't have the money to buy, the government would give them a stake to continue on their way. This same action could happen at the next fort, although not all of them supplied the migrants on their journey west.

Dismounting his horse, he tied Old Girl to a porch railing and pushed his way into the building to the angry stares of some of the hot, sweating men. Once inside, he looked for a place where notices could be attached. A distant wall next to a window looked promising.

On approaching, he saw tacks and a hammer on a rough table positioned underneath several hanging pieces of paper. Instructions for writing and attaching messages stood out plainly above all. One suggestion, he noticed, was to include the date on top. A calendar hung nearby, turned over to June. Rummaging through the variety on the wall, he found a promising one and taking one of the hammers, he pulled the tack from the wood, and detached the paper.

"Mister," called a man from the line inside the store. "Are you looking for a mule?"

Hurricane turned around and stood looking at an unshaven man in a clean but faded blue shirt. "Yep. How'd you know?"

"That's my paper you hold in your hand."

"Well, then. Let's talk," encouraged Hurricane, waving the paper and heading for the door. The man left the line and followed him.

Walking outside the building, the two men found a bench under a porch in the shade. The man who wanted to sell his mule turned out to be a talker.

"I'm Daniel Dyer from Tennessee. My family lived along the Mississippi River."

"Are ya goin' to Oregon or California, Mr. Dyer?" Once over the Rockies the trail split with one section going to California.

"I have a brother who went to Oregon. In a letter we received last November, he has endured much difficulty and his health is failing. He begged us to come." Daniel paused and took a deep breath. He plunged on, "We sold everything, and I quit my work. So here we are, at Fort Kearny. I'm hoping we'll be in Oregon before the snow starts falling."

"My name's H-henry." Hurricane stumbled over his given name, since he almost never used it. He paused for a second, wondering if he should volunteer any more information. He decided not to. Then he continued, "Why'd you want to sell yer mule, Mr. Dyer?"

"Call me Dan. I hope I can call you Henry."

Hurricane or Henry nodded. "Yep, do."

"It's a long story of several hundred miles. We had trouble with our first wagon and had to buy another. That took a lot of our savings. Then, Henry, there were the rains which caused major flooding on the roads we needed to travel. We spent lots of time digging the wheels of our wagon out of the mud. This delay depleted our food and proved to me that mules would be better than horses to pull our wagon, since we were going over the Rocky Mountains—another expense. Our horses wouldn't make it. When we arrived here at the fort, my funds for the trip were to the point I knew they wouldn't last to Oregon. After all, they tell me, we aren't halfway through. I'm not used to taking handouts, although the government would help. My wife and I decided to sell the mule. Stubborn is a good animal, even if she's a bit ornery." Dan flashed a quick grin after his last sentence.

"You don't need her to finish your trip?" asked Hurricane.

"No. She's a small mule and my son's pet, and he wasn't inclined to come with us if his mule didn't come. He would have stayed with his grandma. Now, since we've had so much trouble, he's offered Stubborn to help. It's a sacrifice he's willing to make. We all have losses, Henry—some big, some little." Dan seemed to apologize for selling his son's pet.

Henry couldn't answer immediately. Instead, he nodded his head in agreement. "You seem schooled. You talk real good." It was a question for Dan to answer and to change the subject from one he didn't want to think about.

"Yes, I was a schoolteacher in Tennessee, and I'm planning on teaching when I get to Oregon. My brother says there's interest where he lives. And, if I can supply room and board to those who live too far away to come each day, others within the area will send their children to learn. My wife is agreeable to the idea of boarding students. She loves children. So, once we get there, my family should be safe and our success secured."

"You should do well," observed Henry.

Then Dan continued as they shared the porch's shade. "Being able to teach didn't make me a success story on the way west. It's obvious I'm an inexperienced covered wagon immigrant, because I overestimated the sturdiness of the wagon, chose the wrong animals, didn't have enough supplies, and didn't plan on the much-needed repairs of driving on a rough road."

"Most of us gain from suffering, Dan. Yer a seasoned settler now, ain't you?"

Dan chuckled. "Yes, I suppose so."

"Do you have a pack saddle fer Stubborn?"

"I made something which works, but not a normal one. She's not had to carry a load."

"Your price is acceptable. Whar's the mule?"

"At the encampment where the wagon train is circled. Do you want to go and see her?"

"Yep. Whar's your horse?"

~

The late afternoon sun was beginning to cast shadows on the prairie, as Dan and Henry arrived. Dan's wife and two young girls sat in the shade of the wagon's canopy, using their aprons to fan their faces. Nearby, a fire with a spit and kettle held something cooking over the coals.

Hurricane noticed at least eight children in the area, playing some kind of game. He wondered how many of them were Dan's and how many were his youngsters' playmates.

As the two men dismounted, the woman in a blue-flowered dress got up and greeted Dan. "Did you get a piece of meat and some apples, dear?"

Dan shook his head. "No, the line was very long, and I met Henry here, who might want to buy Stubborn. He's come to look her over." Dan paused and introduced his wife. "Henry, this is my wife, Deborah."

The two acknowledged each other with head nods.

"Pleased to meet you, Henry."

"Same here, Mrs. Dyer. Something smells good."

"It's my vegetables cooking—potatoes and carrots and cabbage. Guess it'll be soup without any meat. We haven't had meat in days. Most of the wagon train is without. We couldn't move for two weeks because of the rain, making the rivers too high to cross, and for some reason there were no animals to kill and eat. I'm beginning to crave meat." She looked sadly at her husband.

Before Dan could respond, Henry said, "I have a little buffalo jerky. You could cut it up in pieces to put in your soup." Henry headed to his saddlebags and pulled out a small package wrapped in a cotton cloth. Walking back, he handed it to the woman. "This is the last of my stash, but I deem there's enough."

"Thank you, Henry. Stay for supper and eat with us. We don't have much, but you are welcome to what we have. And the jerky, smoked over a fire," Deborah raised the package to draw in a deep whiff, "will give my soup a better taste." She smiled at Henry.

Henry started to decline her invitation, but Dan joined his wife in insisting and suggested, "Come on, and let's go meet Stubborn while my wife fixes one of her delicious meals." Dan winked at his wife, gave her a quick hug, and turned to head toward some undergrowth nearby.

The two men walked to the other side of the covered wagon, where Dyer's animals were staked several feet away in heavy, but short undergrowth along the river. Because of the wagon train traffic, vegetation was in short supply and never had time to grow very high.

There, in the underbrush, lay a small charcoal-gray mule, her legs, underbelly, end of nose, and a ring around each eye light gray with the rest of her body a dark gray. Stubborn had eaten into the dirt an area large enough to hunker down. She rested in all the shade she could find which included a small, bushy willow tree about three feet high. Most of the leaves were gone.

If Henry could have seen the brown eyes in her dark face, he might have turned around and left immediately, taking his jerky with him. But he could not.

Stubborn's eyes narrowed almost imperceptibly as she looked at the unfamiliar man coming toward her. She sized him up. Was he a friend or foe? She, of course, could not know and did not bother to get up as she often did when Josiah came around, because he sometimes had an apple core, carrot stem, or another treat for her to eat. One thing she was positive about, the new man did not have anything in his hand.

She realized the men were pointing and talking about her. She turned her head, ignored them, and closed her eyes, lowering her nose to the ground. The nose just barely touching the willow tree which partially shaded her head.

"When will you need to pick up Stubborn?"

Hearing her name pronounced, Stubborn's ears twitched slightly, but she made no other movement.

"I haven't settled on a place to camp. I jest rode into town with the intent of stockin' up on supplies, stayin' the night, and then I was headin' on upriver until my cutoff before Scotts Bluff."

"Why don't you camp out near us—be part of our family until you leave?"

Henry thought about Dan's suggestion. He had had no intention of interacting with anyone socially at Fort Kearny, since he intended to go straight on following the Oregon Trail at a distance. Maybe, it would be nice to be around people for a day. Could that interaction keep his mind off his problems? He nodded and replied, "Tomorrow, we could go together into the sutler's store for supplies. I'll take you up on that offer."

Dan and Henry turned around and headed back around the covered wagon. A young boy, maybe twelve years old, approached as they neared the cooking fire. He stood eying the two men as they talked.

"Where are you going from Scotts Bluff?" asked Dan.

"Headin' straight North toward the Black Hills in the Dakotas."

Interrupting the men's conversation, Josiah asked timidly, "Mister, are you buying Stubborn?" He was the oldest of the Dyer children, long limbed, and dark headed.

Henry looked over at the young lad who had edged closer as the men talked. "Yes. I gotta have a pack animal for the trip into the unsettled territory whar I'm going. Thar, I won't be able to stop at a hut and ask fer help."

Dan introduced the man to Josiah. "This is Henry." Then he paused and added, "I don't know your last name, Henry."

"It's Bailey—Henry Bailey."

Josiah looked up at him with sorrowful eyes. "Mr. Bailey, will you take good care of her? She's my best friend in the world."

What could Henry honestly say to those unhappy eyes? Looking over at Old Girl, he replied, "I'll certainly do my best."

"Something smells good, Henry. Let me get you a chair. Better yet, Josiah will you get our visitor a chair to sit in. How about yours? You can sit on the quilt with your sisters."

Josiah headed for a chair hanging on the side of the covered wagon. He lifted it off its hanger and brought it to Henry who sat down.

Dan pulled his chair up alongside but didn't sit down.

Instead of heading toward the quilt where four girls now sat awaiting their early supper, Josiah hunkered down next to Henry, almost touching his knee. "Mister, Stubborn's a good mule. She really is. She likes apple cores and berries and carrots." He could have added the mule was always hungry and ready to eat.

"I see, Josiah. Is there anythin' else you can tell me about yer mule?"

"While you two talk, I'll help Deborah with the food." Dan went toward his wife and the cook fire.

Henry had no idea this would open the floodgates for the boy to talk about his mule. "When Stubborn senses danger, she makes a peculiar noise, and she stops immediately. That's how she got her name. We used to call her Sally. That changed when she saved my life by alerting me to a copperhead snake where we lived in Tennessee."

"She alerted ya to danger?"

"Yes, I was riding her bareback when she balked and stopped on the path to my grandma's. She almost threw me off over her head she stopped so abruptly." Josiah was grinning at the experience. "I slid off and tried to urge her on, but she was determined not to change her position. So, we both stood there, making no headway, until I saw a movement in the weeds next to the trail. When the snake left, she continued on. After that experience, I let her lead. She knew where my grandma's house was, and there was no reason to guide her in that direction."

"That's some story. She has an eye for trouble. I'll remember to be alert to 'er moods."

"Henry, here's your bowl of soup. I think you'll like it." Dan held a pottery bowl full of soup so the old trail master could take it. "Josiah, go get our guest a spoon."

The following morning the two men stood in line in front of the sutler's store, awaiting its opening. "Dan, I'll be leavin' around noon, so I'll need to load up Stubborn with my extra supplies. The only hitch is Josiah. I know he's goin' to be sad."

Dan stood considering the dilemma. "Henry, I realize you want to be on your way. Stay tonight, and leave tomorrow before Josiah gets up. We won't keep the fact that you'll leave in the morning from him. He'll have today to say goodbye. Don't you think this is a better plan?"

The teacher's words sounded good to Henry. "I agree. One day won't make much difference to me, but it will to him." The wagon train master did not realize he was getting a heart which could be soft to a young boy's hurt.

"I'll help you with loading Stubborn in the morning."

"Thank you. After we get our supplies here, we'll look up my old friend, Walton Bowie. He's findin' buffalo jerky for me, and if'n I know him, there'll be plenty for you, and he owes me, so there'll be no money to exchange. This will help you on your funds to continue on over the mountain."

After getting sack loads of provisions, the two men mounted their horses and headed toward where Henry had last seen Bowie. The conversation continued.

"Henry, I have to tell you the truth. I think the Lord led you to me, because you have been an answer to my prayers."

"Wall, I don't know about that. Don't consider the Lord or the Bible much. None in my family never did." Henry was telling the truth about that. "When the preacher married me and Ruby Eliza, that's the only time I seen the Good Book as some calls it."

"You should consider it as you say. Every time we've had trouble on this trip, someone to solve it has been provided. God and his son, Jesus Christ are the Good in the book. I perceive you have a problem. I don't know what your trouble is, but He can help."

Henry rode along pondering Dan's words. No one had ever talked to him about God and Jesus Christ. He was saved from Dan asking more questions or having to volunteer more information about himself by another summons from the front porch where Bowie had sat the previous day.

"Hey, Hurricane. I've got yer buffalo jerky." Bowie patted a large sack beside his chair. He got up and hefted the cotton bag over his shoulder and was soon off the porch and staring up at his friend.

"That's a whoppin' sack full!" Henry exclaimed.

"Thought you might need a sack full," he grinned, handing the jerky up to his old friend. "Afterall, I owe you."

"Thanks Bowie. I plan to share some of it with my new friend here. His name's Dan Dyer from Tennessee. Dan this here's Walton Bowie."

"Pleased to meet you, Walton. Any friend of Mr. Bailey is a friend of mine," announced Dan.

"No, don't call me Walton. It's just Bowie. Everyone knows me by my last name. How do you know Hurricane? Must be a story thar."

"No, there's no big mystery. My son has a mule Henry wants to buy."

"Henry!" Bowie looked startled and then he laughed, slapped his hip, and asked, "Have you reverted to your first name, Hurricane?"

"I guess I have." He did not look his friend in the eye but looked across the parade ground at a group of military men grooming their horses.

"Why?" a curious Bowie looked up at his old buffalo-hunting partner. What had happened to make Hurricane use his given name?

"Just thought I would." Hurricane or Henry didn't feel it necessary to explain his need for privacy or obscurity. Right now, he didn't want to be anybody, least of all Hurricane Bailey.

Realizing no answer was coming to his original question, Bowie asked, "Did you find the supplies you needed at the sutler's store?"

Dan replied, "Yes, and then some. Henry, I'd better get back to camp so my wife can cook some of it for supper. Are you coming?"

"Yes." Henry turned to his old friend, "Maybe we'll see each other along the trail, Bowie. I'll be lookin' fer you." With that he threw up his hand and followed Dan.

"I'll be lookin' fer you, too, Hurricane," Bowie called after him.

~

When Henry caught up with Dan, the teacher asked, "So, your name is actually Hurricane Bailey."

"No. My name is fer sure Henry, but those who've known me fer a long time call me Hurricane."

"How'd you get the name Hurricane."

"I don't rightly know. My father always said that if'n I could get out the door of the house, I'd get gone and lost as quick as a hurricane. I guess that stuck, 'cause he always called me that and others just picked it up from him."

As the two rode into camp, Josiah approached them. Was there a hint of red in the young boy's eyes? Had he been crying? "Poppa, did you find some apples at the store?"

"Yes, I bought some for your mother and Henry bought some to take with him when he leaves tomorrow."

"You're going tomorrow, Mr. Bailey."

"Yes, early in the mornin', I'll be on my way."

"Henry, I'll find Deborah. She must be over at our neighbor lady's wagon. I think they were going to cook the noonday meal together so we could share. I'll be back soon."

Josiah stood looking up at Henry. "Would you like to meet Stubborn, officially?"

"Sure. That can work both ways, specially with mules. She might want to meet me. Come to my tent so I can stash my goods, and we'll go take care of your offer."

Henry had camped away from the circled wagons. A piece of a tree with a few leaves so high the wagon train animals couldn't reach them, provided a bit of shade. He slid off Old Girl and placed his supplies out of the sun. "Let's go."

"No," said Josiah. "We need an apple and you should cut it into pieces."

"Do you want it peeled?" asked Henry with a hint of a smile.

"No, it's for Stubborn. She likes apples, and don't worry about the seeds. She likes those too."

"Oh, I see." Henry searched for the bag he'd placed in the shade of his tent, and Josiah watched him pull out his pocket knife and quarter the red apple. "Is that good enough?" he asked, handing the pieces to Josiah.

Josiah nodded, "Now we're ready to go."

Stubborn didn't appear to have moved a muscle from the day before. She lay in the same depression in the ground with a few willow leaves shading her. But on hearing Josiah's footsteps or smelling the fragrance of the quartered apple as it floated in the wind, she slowly rose to her feet.

"Come on girl. We're going for a walk."

Stubborn followed her master without harness or bridle.

Josiah headed toward an ill-defined path next to the river with Stubborn on his heels. The path was rough and sometimes the two had to jump over wet places to avoid deep holes filled with water embedded in the river bank.

Henry followed behind them. Obviously, these two had been on this path before.

"Where're yer goin', Josiah?" asked Henry as they continued to walk by the river without slowing down.

"There's a place where the river is deeper, and Stubborn can get into the water up to her belly. I think people have dug it out so their animals can do the same. She'll be able to cool off and eat her apple. She enjoys doing this."

"I wondered when you were goin' to offer 'er the apple. Reminds me of a story I heard of the donkey and the carrot. The farmer put a carrot on a stick in front of the donkey far enough away so the animal couldn't reach it. This made the animal walk and plow the ground at the same time. Yer walkin' to the front of Stubborn to get 'er to follow you, ain't you?"

Josiah didn't have time to answer, because the mule hurried off the bank, splashing water in all directions, straight into a small pool of muddy water where another mule was standing.

This was the fastest Henry had seen her move. He couldn't help but smile at the mule's antics.

Josiah waved at a friend who was holding a rope tied to the harness of his mule. "Hi, Benjamin." The two mules touched noses, as Benjamin pulled on the rope to encourage his animal up the bank. Stubborn sent her friend a goodbye heehaw.

Benjamin's mule brushed by Josiah, sniffing at his clothing. Where were the apples? Then it disappeared with its owner into the willows on the river's edge.

"This is the place," announced Josiah, squatting down on the bank, watching Stubborn wade in and bury her nose in the cool water.

"Do you feed 'er the apples now?"

"No, Mr. Bailey. You have to think like a mule. When I want her to come out, that's when she gets the delicious red apples."

Henry grinned again. He should have known the boy was smart enough to figure out Stubborn.

~

In the morning darkness, Henry hurried around quietly in his camp. He remembered another recent time when he'd left before daylight. He'd felt better around the Dyers, but remembering brought back the reason for his current trip north. He sighed and looked up as Dan approached.

"Good morning, Henry." Dan spoke in a low tone so as not to wake the sleeping family.

The horse was saddled and Stubborn was loaded when Dan came. "Good morning. I'm ready to go," Henry whispered back.

"Are you loaded up?"

"Yes. Thanks for helping me, Dan. I need to be on my way. Tell Josiah goodbye, and I'll take good care of Stubborn as promised."

Did the mule know she was getting ready to leave Josiah forever? There was no way of knowing. He had a quartered apple in his pocket just in case he needed it. He was sure she could smell it. He'd learned something from Josiah, even though he was just a boy.

"Maybe we'll meet again."

The two men shook hands.

Henry walked his horse away from the Dyer wagon, not knowing two eyes watched his best companion disappear into the night. A small muffled sniff meant Josiah was crying.

Chapter Three

Finally, Henry Heads North

Although a traveler didn't realize it, the Oregon Trail gradually rose in elevation until you confronted the slowly developing majestic heights of the Rocky Mountains. It was there the settlers realized the magnitude of the next stage—conquering the vast towering Rockies.

Having been here years ago with his father and then with Jedediah Smith, Henry rode along, reliving memories of the scene appearing around him. He knew he was close to Scotts Bluff when he passed the Chimney Rock, a famous pinnacle which poked into the sky. It was located about a day's ride from his cutoff. Layers of eroded rock were mounded around its base, as it did when you passed all the sandstone formations in the western territories.

He smiled when his thoughts turned to Jedediah's attempt as a young boy to crawl up the steep rocks to the ascending peak. He'd fallen and skinned both knees. When Henry had buried him, the scars were covered by his well-patched breeches. The pain of Jedediah's death descended upon him with these thoughts. He rode along with less enthusiasm for the trail ahead.

"O-o-h," escaped from his lips with a large sigh following. He needed to get away from these areas of memories. The Black Hills of the Nebraska Territory was the perfect place—no memories of his son there.

In the afternoon he stopped and made camp next to a small stream running into the bigger river. He realized tomorrow might be the last time he'd be near the North Platte River.

He was tired and dirty after riding in the dust-laden wind all day—some of it caused by the wagon trains going west on the trail—an identifying plume in the air of ground movement below. He lowered his dusty bandana and looked around for a good place to establish his overnight camp.

Henry chose a place with running water. He unloaded Old Girl and Stubborn of their burdens, watered them, and tethered them in a grass-filled hollow nearby where he could watch their movements and any movements around them.

The sound of water rushing over rocks and downed trees in the smaller stream was too pleasant to resist. Henry removed his clothes and gradually entered the running creek, being careful of some jagged rocks on the bottom as he walked. Sitting down in a hollow filled with pebbles, the water came to his waist. He splashed handfuls over his head and shoulders, sending droplets into the air. They glistened in the afternoon sun.

The red, ragged scar from an Apache arrow stood out plainly on his shoulder. He'd received this reminder when he and Jedediah, along with others, had rescued Gracie Tipton and another girl from

Indians on the trip to Pine Springs in the Guadalupe Mountains of Texas.

Upon getting out, he let the constantly blowing plain's winds dry him.

Donning a new outfit from his saddlebags, he washed his old one, spread the wet pieces out to dry on the rocks, and then prepared his supper. Within a small fire, started from dry wood he'd gathered beside the creek, he placed three rocks. He opened a can of beans and suspended them between the three rocks, intending to warm his supper. Taking a metal spoon out of his saddle bags, he stirred the warming food. A few pieces of buffalo jerky completed his meal.

His variety did not change much each day, except for some ripe blackberries and currants picked along the way—those he didn't share with Old Girl and Stubborn. He sat spooning his meal from the can. Once he was finished with his meal, he cleaned his spoon in the creek and placed his metal utensil in his saddlebag. He'd learned long ago to put things he used back in their proper place. Losing a spoon, knife, gun or other necessary part could mean the difference between life and death in the West.

Returning to rest next to his fire, he noticed Stubborn was acting uneasy. She kept moving on the tether and eyeing something up the creek. Remembering what Josiah had said, Henry craned his neck in that direction, noticing a movement in the brush next to the water.

Coyote. Probably only one, because they only formed packs in the winter when game was scarce. He picked up a rock and slung it in the coyote's direction. It slunk off into the woods.

Henry yawned, looking up at the Nebraska sky, where the bright stars were appearing. He was ready to stretch out and catch a few winks. But instead, he arose and went in the direction of the disappearing coyote to assure himself that it would not be a problem. After walking in continuing larger circles, he found no evidence of the animal.

Back at his camp, he moved his horse and mule closer to his tent and stretched out on his bedroll.

Sleep came quickly under the stars.

Scotts Bluff was a well-known location looked for by settlers traveling on the Oregon Trail. For decades, whispers of the death of its namesake had fascinated those traveling the area. Hiram Scott's demise was shrouded in mystery, although his death, verified by a pile of human bones, happened here, lending his name to the area. The high rocky hill, tannish-gray protruding starkly from the grassy plains below, was easy to spot from several miles away.

It was here Henry would turn north and make his way to the Black Hills where the Lakota Sioux and Cheyenne lived. He estimated another day's ride would take him close enough to his intended cutoff.

He set off from the Chimney Rock before the sun came up. Old Girl was an easy ride, and Stubborn hadn't caused any trouble. They'd moseyed along at an even pace. Henry wasn't in any hurry.

The smell of apples and the opportunity to munch on one had pacified any idea of Stubborn balking on the trail. Even a piece for Old Girl was pushed in her direction at times.

For several days, he'd been shadowing the wagon trains as he rode west. They'd been driven steadily alongside the North Platte River—the oxen and mule teams plodding along.

It was just past noon, according to the overhead sun, when he noticed several wagons had circled along the North Platte not far from the bluff's base. The white canvas of the prairie schooners was blinding in the overhead sun, although clouds were building over them toward the foothills of the Rockies. Rain was coming before nightfall.

Henry shaded his eyes to look closer.

Strange, he thought. Wagons never stopped in the daytime, preferring to travel as far as possible in the daylight and circle the wagons in late afternoon. He wondered if there was a problem. Maybe a wagon had broken down. Could he lend a hand? Wagon repairs had always been a specialty of his, especially if he didn't have a hangover from drinking too much—not a problem at this time in his life. He rode toward the train.

Seeing a small crowd at the wagon closest to him, he decided to head in that direction. Before he got there, he heard a woman's high-pitched screams.

The sobbing woman coming from inside the wagon held a naked child in her arms. "Pa, he's dead. Our perfect son is dead."

Her husband helped her to the ground and threw his arms around his wife, who was holding the limp child. Others stood nearby to comfort the distraught couple.

Henry went to the nearest man and asked quietly, "What happened?"

"We don't rightly know—maybe cholera. Them's the symptoms," he said, shaking his head. "Only two days ago, the child played hide and seek with my children."

Henry looked at the haggard man standing next to his wagon, holding onto his distressed wife. He could help dig a grave, but other than assisting with moving some dirt, he was powerless to help, and there were plenty of people standing around who could lend aid in burying the young lad.

"Did you treat him with camphor or laudanum," he asked the man who stood watching.

"Yes, both. Didn't help." The man thought for a moment. "Cholera is a killer."

Henry nodded in agreement. "I've seed it doing its dirt afore. Don't know what causes the fever, nausea, pain and cramps. Hit's a terrible way to die—poor child."

The old wagon master knew the next few days would see a terrible crisis occupy these people. This sinister fever could run through a whole wagon train, and many people might die before the disease abated. Sometimes, almost half of the people got the sickness and were buried in shallow graves with no marker.

He looked at the man standing next to him, knowing he might be the next one clutching his crying wife, holding a sick child. That's the way the illness worked.

The whole situation brought back fresh memories of another time and another death. He needed to leave now, before he got the fever, and since there was no reason to stay, he made the decision to ride north.

He wasn't out of sight of the wagon train when something started nagging at him. Slowing down, he turned his horse, and with Stubborn, he retraced most of his steps, heading back down the rim of the gulch he'd chosen as his guide north. In this hollowed out depression in the ground, he might find water for his animals, and he could drink the liquid he'd stored in his canteens at Fort Scott.

He retraced the path from the direction he'd just come, planning to stop short of the wagon train on the North Platte River. He'd wait here for Dan to arrive, warn him, and those with him of the disease ahead.

Topping a slight rise, Henry looked to the west. A streak of lightning, went from a dark cloud to the ground. The burst of lightning was so far away, he heard no thunder. In the distance, water fell from the sky in gray blankets with the sun shining intermittently through—making a line of thunder showers. Henry suspected the air would turn cooler with the coming rain. There might even be hail from the sky. He'd seen enough of prairie storms to know he wouldn't have to worry about tornadoes or high winds. There would be wind, but nothing destructive.

What he didn't know was this rain would be a blessing in disguise for the wagon people, washing the fever on down the Platte and giving those on the train a better chance of survival.

The old scout needed a place where he could rest in the dry, because by midnight or before, he estimated the rain would come down by the bucket full. From experience, he knew it wouldn't last long, but long enough for the narrow gulch he rode through to become a raging creek for a day. He'd considered making camp alongside. Now, he must change his mind.

Searching for a dry camp wasn't easy. There were no trees anywhere to be found except down along the creek bed, exactly where the water would come. He rode on. The mouth of the creek fanned out onto the flatland before it ran into the North Platte.

As he rode south, the banks had slowly diminished except on the western side. He settled on this side where a rocky face, around ten-foot-high, with a washed-out overhang would provide some protection from the coming storm and from the rising waters which would soon come. The stream bed had eroded, throwing most of the current onto the eastern side bank.

He put up his tent, something he didn't always do, and tethered Old Girl and Stubborn in what he hoped was a safe place nearby. His animals would face the full force of the storm in the open. He patted the rump of his horse as he removed the saddle. Dust flew. "Guess you're going to get a well-needed bath Old Girl," he explained, as he gave his mule the same treatment, and said, "Watch those ears, Stubborn." Mules did not like water in their ears.

Stowing his supplies and saddle in the tent, he returned outside in the open, sat cross-legged, and ate his can of cold beans while sitting on the horse's saddle blanket—no open fire tonight.

His camp afforded him a clear view of the surrounding area. He watched as a herd of antelope—maybe twenty—made their way to the river. Any other time, those on the wagon train would probably shoot one for fresh meat. Today, the travelers had other things on their minds.

He reached for his Hawken rifle, which was always close. He took aim, but did not fire. He'd wait until Dan showed up, and then provide fresh meat for him and his family. The herd would be easy to track in the mud left by the rain.

When the sun set behind the clouds in the west, he felt the first sprinkle on his bare arm. Making sure his possessions were in the dry, he went to check on Old Girl and Stubborn.

The mule nudged his pocket. "You're right, Stubborn. Thar's one piece of apple left." He pulled it out, broke it in two pieces, and gave parts to both animals. "I can't leave out Old Girl. She came before you," he explained to the mule as she poked his pocket again. The sprinkle turned into a drizzle and then a downpour. He entered the tent and got back as far as he could to the rock wall. "Let it rain," he mouthed to the world. "Thar's nothing else I can do at the present to stay dry."

Not knowing how long it would take for the Dyers to arrive, Henry waited, warning other travelers as they appeared from the east of the pending danger ahead.

In the afternoon, on the third day, he was sure he saw the wagon train in which the Dyers were included. He saddled Old Girl and rode in its direction. Before he got to the line of white-canvassed prairie schooners, he saw Josiah running toward him.

Although he was out of breath, when he reached Henry, the young lad called, "Mr. Bailey, where is Stubborn?"

"Stubborn's at camp. I come to talk to your dad about somethin' really important. Here climb on behind." Henry reached down his hand and pulled Josiah up on Old Girl. They rode toward the Dyer wagon, with Josiah clutching his shirt.

"Hello, Henry," called Dan. "Didn't think I'd see you here."

Dyer couldn't stop his wagon, since he was part of the moving group.

Pulling up to ride alongside, Henry said, "Dan there's trouble in front of you. A wagon train with cholera is camped just ahead on the North Platte. Your people must avoid it at all costs, or you will have the fever in yer midst."

"Are you sure it's the cholera?"

"Yes, that's what I was told, and some people have already died."

"Josiah, jump down and bring my horse around." Dan's horse was tied to the back of the wagon—saddle on.

Minutes later, Dan and Henry approached a younger man—the wagon master, and after introductions they delivered Henry's message. The three didn't talk long before an order was given to another man on a horse who'd joined the conversation.

"We'll stop here for the night," said the man with the authority over the others. "Circle the wagons," he shouted to his trail guide.

"Thank you, Mr. Bailey. We'll stay here tonight and continue on in the morning—drive around the other train. Do you think we should see if we can help them? We have camphor and laudanum we could share."

"They have some, but if you go, keep a distance. This fever is powerful. I've seen it afore on this same trail and the Santa Fe Trail in Mexico."

The wagon master frowned and asked, "Were you a guide?"

"Tracker, guide, and scout until the end of last year."

"Is your name Hurricane?"

Dan responded, looking at his friend with a question on his face, "Yes, his name was Hurricane."

"The famous Hurricane Bailey, as I live and breathe—a legend in the west," exclaimed the wagon master, an incredulous expression on his face. "Never thought I'd meet you."

"Like I said, be careful if you go over there," the famous Hurricane Bailey nodded toward the west where the other wagons were parked.

"Don't worry. I'll be sure and be careful."

Hurricane turned to his friend, "We'd better go Dan. I'd like to take Josiah antelope huntin' if'n you don't mind. I've tracked a herd, and we can have fresh meat fer supper tonight."

"If you get one, bring me a piece," called the wagon master as the two rode off.

Dan threw up his hand and turned toward Henry, "Deborah will be pleased." He wanted to ask more questions, but decided against it. "We'll ask Josiah when we get back to the wagon."

~

"Mr. Bailey, are you sure the antelope will be here?" asked Josiah after he and Henry had been sitting for a while behind some bushes near a puddle of water.

They were up the creek from where the old man's camp was set up.

"Josiah, call me Henry," returned the old tracker. No one ever used Mister with his name.

"Oh, no sir. Mom and Dad would never let me do that. They're adamant about respecting your elders."

"Are you calling me old?" Henry asked.

"No sir, I mean..." Josiah stopped, totally confused.

Henry gave a little chuckle, the first one in several months. Something about interacting with this young boy was helping mend his heart. "Obey your parents, Josiah, and yes, the antelope will be here, but we must be quiet." Henry put his finger to his mouth. "Sh-h-h."

The two sat silently for several more minutes. Suddenly, Henry put his hand on Josiah's shoulder, squeezed, and pointed. Six antelope stood watching the approach to their drinking water. Putting the Hawken Rifle to his shoulder, Henry aimed and pulled the trigger.

One of the smaller animals fell over. The rest ran for their lives, although running wasn't necessary. The Hawken was a muzzle-loading gun, and even though Henry was fast at loading it, the herd had plenty of time to leave.

Josiah jumped up. He said excitedly, "You got it!"

"Yes, let's go get it. We need to dress it and get it ready to cook."

"Dress it? What do you mean?"

"Hasn't your mother ever killed a chicken, plucked its feathers, and gutted it so she could cook it?" Henry asked as they walked toward the downed animal.

"No. Dad always brought them home ready to cook. He bought them from the parents of his students."

"Hum-m. Well, someone had to kill it, pluck the feathers, and gut it, in other words dress it. You're ready for a new experience, one which a boy your age should already know. Here, carry the rifle." After cutting the animal's throat and waiting to let the excess blood drain out, Henry hoisted the antelope to his shoulder and headed for the Dyer wagon.

Dan met them and pulled out a small table for dressing the antelope. Henry wasn't sure if Josiah appreciated watching the animal become meat, but Dan took it in stride, and fixed a spit to roast the animal. Soon the smell of cooking meat permeated the air.

Henry and Deborah cut the cooked antelope into sections while Dan and Josiah distributed them among their friends, including the wagon master. Then the family sat down to roasted antelope meat, boiled potatoes, and cooked apples. Josiah ate as much as the others.

The next day, Henry Bailey said his final goodbye to the Dyer family. Josiah walked with Henry to his horse, patted Stubborn, and before Henry could protest, gave him a hug.

"I'll miss you, Mr. Bailey."

"I'll miss you too, Josiah. Don't worry about Stubborn. She'll be in good hands." Henry meant it.

Henry mounted up and rode north toward the gulch he'd started along on his first trip north. Just before he rode out of sight of the Dyer wagon, he turned Old Girl to take a last look at his new friends. Josiah stood almost where he left him.

Both man and boy waved.

Chapter Four

Henry Sees a Light

When Henry headed north, he was in new territory. Although he'd been over most of the West, he had avoided the Dakota region. He pondered this as he rode along.

He spoke out loud to Old Girl, while Stubborn flicked her ears. "There was really no reason for it. I just hadn't had a yearning to discover its attractions."

He was quiet for a few minutes. Then he started again, "Maybe avoided ain't the right word. But what other purpose could thar be? Will I soon find out? Was the reason a part of my conversation with Bowie at Fort Kearny or not? Were thar words of my father which brought me here?" Henry was trying to remember something, but he just couldn't pull it up. Years of drink had erased old memories.

He shook his head. "Better to enjoy the scenery around us, Old Girl." He stretched out his arm and patted the horse's neck. Turning around, he said, "You, too, Stubborn."

~

Days passed as he rode the surface of the slowly rising prairie. Finally, in the distance, he saw the first rolling hills. The sighting didn't last long until he was climbing sharply up steep rocky hills, or following buffalo or elk trails into the forests of evergreen trees.

Although the air was sharply cooler and autumn was in the air, the tree leaves hadn't changed in color, except the short, scarlet-leafed sumac growing along the sides of the animal trails. They were always the first to change.

His momentum was reduced by the steepness of the climb with switchbacks, going up and down, meaning he wasn't making much time. He was covering lots of ground. He just wasn't getting anywhere.

Animals were in abundance. He could now include in his diet a rabbit or squirrel shot with his rifle and roasted over a warm fire. He was a good shot with his Hawken rifle and in former days often bragged about his skill, especially when he'd had too much to drink and always before his son had died. Bragging and drinking were both castoff after Jedediah's untimely death at the hands of the Apaches in Arizona Territory.

He stayed away from birds. Plucking feathers was a hard, nasty job. But, if he found a goose or wild turkey nest full of eggs, he cooked them in boiling water and ate them on the trail. Any change in diet was always welcome.

He got into the habit of keeping the flames of his campfire going into the night, by rummaging around the area and piling dead limbs in a stack, to place them on the embers when something woke him in the night—a coyote or wolf howling, or large animal poking around in the brush. The area contained grizzly bears, dark brown buffalo, or herds of elk getting ready for the fall rut. He kept Stubborn close. She was an excellent alarm as she nervously pawed the rocky ground when she sensed danger.

Since it was autumn, he often picked ripe persimmons or wild plums to eat, giving Old Girl and the mule their share. The apples had been long gone, and no chance of any in the near future.

In late autumn, he rode across another low plain, still steadily climbing toward another range of mountains in the distance. He was sure the Sioux called them *Paha Sapa* or "hills that are black," because they appeared flat and black in the distance, especially with the dusty air he was looking through. He wondered if the forests on the distant Rockies were on fire to the west of him. This wasn't unusual with thunderstorms in the area.

Indians. He didn't have much use for them … any of them … after Jedediah.

Years ago, his pa had related the story of the Sioux when he was wagon master on the Oregon Trail. The Black Hills were sacred and considered the womb of Mother Earth. They often returned during the year to conduct ceremonies and burials. He'd have to keep a watch out for them—although they were at present mostly peaceful.

According to his pa, they weren't the first Indians to live here. The Crow, Kiowa, and Pawnee were earlier tribes living in the area. They were driven out by the Cheyenne, and the Cheyenne overcome by the Sioux, who had arrived from the east of the Missouri River. The Sioux now claimed the land for themselves.

As he traveled north, he could expect to see bands of them as he rode through, on their ponies with a feather in their braided hair, wearing buckskin and loin cloths—fierce warriors who defended their territory with their lives. He would avoid them.

Others he might see were prospectors looking for gold. After finding the precious metal in California streams in late 1849, men started panning many of the streams of the Rocky Mountains, and soon there was a strike in the Western part of Nebraska Territory. Henry expected to see some prospectors nosing around in this area. At Fort Kearny, he'd heard there were isolated settlers bunching together up streams with sluicing operations for taking gold from the waters.

The trees of the Black Hills gave the area its name. Sitting on Old Girl on top of one of the mountains he'd climbed, Henry noticed tall Ponderosa Pine, White Spruce, and other pine trees which appeared in groves up and down the mountains and gave the forest a dark color. He picked Pinion Pine nuts and ate them along the trail.

Mounds and peaks of granite rocks poked through the trees making ridges of stone, standing out starkly in between the groves of dark-colored trees.

Nudging Old Girl, he continued down the mountain, riding through valleys of Quaking Aspen trees whose white bark and golden leaves were making streaks of yellow up these hollows. There were other oak and ash trees in the process of developing fall colors.

He had ridden for ten days in these vast tree-covered mountains, when suddenly Stubborn balked as they rode down a long steep trail for a flowing creek at the bottom. In the many miles they had covered, she had followed peacefully along.

He pulled on her lead, but she would not move.

He knew better than to ignore her. So, he dismounted Old Girl and went to the mule. "What is it, Stubborn?" he asked, stroking her neck.

Of course, she couldn't answer, but she was nervously looking in one direction ... up the creek and to the north.

There was a thicket of brush above them on the side of the mountain where they had stopped. He would secrete his animals there and check out the area. Something was wrong. He needed to find out what.

Tying his horse and mule to the bushes in the brush shield he'd picked, he looked around for someplace to sit and survey the vast area unhindered. A flat rock above their hideout provided a place to see the area below and above him. He would take his loaded rifle, sit there not moving, and observe the area.

It didn't take long for him to see movement along the creek they were soon to cross. A large four-hundred-pound grizzly with two yearling cubs moseyed down the stream on a direct collision with the trail he'd been riding on. She could have spelled major trouble if she felt the need to protect her cubs. He was downwind of the large animal, and therefore safe from the bear's detection, but Stubborn had smelled her and sensed danger.

Henry watched the bear as it padded in and out of the stream, turning over rocks, and dodging the trees growing on the creek bank. Once, it turned in his direction. He froze and watched closely as it stood on its back legs and smelled the air, turning its head to test the odor coming to its nose. The wind, making noises in the trees, covered sounds but brought all kinds of scents. Was there another bear in the area? A male grizzly? A threat to her cubs? Was that the reason for its testing of the air?

Henry watched the bear retake its position on the ground. Whatever the problem was, she and her cubs hurriedly moved to the south of him, where he could see them no more. He waited several more minutes, observing the forested area.

There was no movement except birds flying in the trees, including an eagle, soaring on the air currents. Suddenly, it plunged toward the ground, and then it reappeared with some kind of rodent in its talons. He watched until it flew out of sight.

Pushing off the rock, he joined his horse and mule.

"Ready, Stubborn? Thanks for the heads-up." He gave her a good scratching behind her ears, went to Old Girl, replaced his rifle, and mounted up.

Henry kept his eyes moving to his right and left as he traveled down the rocky hill. The grizzly had made him cautious and careful. He wanted out of the area. Although he normally picked a campsite in late afternoon, he kept moving until it was almost dark before starting to look for a flatter place. None appeared.

Still more downhill, he thought, looking ahead through the darkening forest and out through an open break to the landscape below. The rocky hills did not look very well-suited for a campsite.

He was bone-tired and bleary-eyed as he rode further, reined in Old Girl and sat in silence, trying to decide on a course of action, realizing he should stop and rest. The sound of gurgling water meant a small steam was ahead. Maybe, there?

No, none there. He started across the small rocky creek, carefully picking his way.

On the other side, Stubborn balked again. Henry turned in the saddle. "What is it now, Stubborn?"

"Hello there, rider."

Totally startled, Henry jerked around with his hand immediately on his rifle. Below him was a man carrying a very sooty lantern and a rifle. Where had he come from? Why hadn't he seen him?

"Who're you?" Henry asked, in the gloomy dark of the bearded man who held the lantern up over his head, sizing him up. The lantern gave off little light.

He must have passed inspection, because the man added, "I saw you up on the mountain, riding through on one of the bald spots, and knowing the trail, realized you would be coming this way. I have a place just down the creek, if you'd like to stay the night. It's not much, but it's better than sleeping on the steep hill, and there's fried rabbit and beans if you're interested, and room for a bedroll by the fire."

If Henry had known the man better, he might have laughed with relief at his timely and welcome suggestion. Should he be ill-mannered and turn down this offer of hospitality?

Instead, he dismounted Old Girl. "Thank you, kindly. I'll take you up on yer offer. I'm tired, and none of us have eaten since morning. Saw a grizzly with cubs and decided not to stop until dark. Get out'en her territory. A camp wasn't to be had. It's so steep and rocky."

"That grizzly, I've named Flower. She pokes around here occasionally." The man headed for Stubborn. "Here let me lead your mule."

"The mule's name is Stubborn, and this here's Old Girl. My name's Henry, Henry Bailey."

"Pleased to meet you, Henry. I'm Jason Douglas. My lean-to is just ahead to the right of the creek. There's a small corral where we can put your animals with mine. Not much in the way of fodder, but we can take care of that tomorrow. Watch your step." Jason cautioned, still holding the sooty lantern above his head and stepping gingerly himself.

Henry followed a tall man, slightly taller than he, who from all he could see in the darkness was fairly young with light brown hair. He wondered and asked, "Why do you trust me?"

Jason chuckled, "Not many bad men lead a mule behind them, and certainly not many scratch one behind the ears, as I could tell you were doing."

"That's where Stubborn balked when the grizzly came down the creek," exclaimed Henry.

"Yes, Flower has been known to inhabit that area. She probably went down the other side of the mountain, if she followed the creek."

"She had two cubs with her."

"Born last year. She'll probably have two more this winter. We're almost there."

A hundred more feet down the creek and a rough log hut appeared attached to the bank of the hillside. "It's not much, but for now it's home," the man said of his ramshackle shack.

A makeshift door and what appeared to be a fireplace, which was the nicest part of the whole, made up the rest of the dwelling, if it could be called that. Lumpy chinking filled many of the holes in the logs along the sides and front of the abode, making the inside easier to heat. Obviously, Jason had hurried to erect a place to live.

The two men walked the animals to the corral. Jason's animals consisted of a mule and a goat. "I milk the goat," said Jason, pointing to his black and brown on white spotted specimen. "Keep the jug in the stream."

"Where do you go fer supplies?" asked Henry as he took off his saddle, bedroll, and grub sacks, so Old Girl and Stubborn could be free of their loads.

"Mostly just eat off the land, since you travel for around twelve days to the nearest fur trading post at Cherry Creek. And it's about the same to Fort Laramie. You never know what will be available when you get there. I brought the staples in large bags, since I didn't know how long I'd be here. One person doesn't eat that much, and I forage among the trees for the rest."

"How long have you been here?"

"Since spring."

Henry wanted to ask more questions, but decided getting better acquainted might be the better step. He made sure his two animals were comfortable, before they headed for the hut. The men carried his saddle and supplies with them.

Once inside, Henry leaned his rifle up next to the wall, noticing the backside of the hut was dirt, dug out to make the floor, which was covered with bark chips and pine needles.

He was amazed that the fireplace worked. It seemed Jason had taken more pains with its rocks and mud mortar than any other part of the building. The fire felt good. He went to warm his hands and turned to observe the rest of the room.

A makeshift table with two stools was the kitchen area. Logs framed a bed on the dirt floor, opposite the fireplace, with deep pine needles for a mattress, and a hollowed-out place where someone had been sleeping. The place was rough, looking like someone didn't intend to stay very long, or had other things on their mind which didn't include agreeable living conditions.

"Henry, the rabbit and beans are on the table. Help yourself," volunteered Jason. "I'm going to get another large log for the fire."

"Thanks. I believe I will. I'll help you find another rabbit or squirrel tomorrow."

~

The sun was shining brightly when Henry stepped outside the following day. He stretched his arms toward the sky.

What time is it? he wondered.

Jason was nowhere to be seen. Henry walked around to the corral to see his animals.

"Good morning, my friend," greeted Jason. He sat on a log, milking the goat. "How about eggs and corn pone for breakfast? There's cold milk in the stream, and with the two pieces of rabbit left from yesterday …"

Breakfast wasn't bad at all, and Jason talked most of the time about life back East.

Henry had had every intention of leaving, but as the day went on, he found he was fascinated by this man. He was interested in his life and his words.

Chapter Five

Who was Jason Douglas?

Jason Douglas had been in the Nebraska Territory for at least six months. As he told Henry on day two of their acquaintance, he was looking for the answer to his family's disappearance and for peace. This struck a chord with the old wagon train master. Their life difficulties seemed the same. Henry didn't want to be alone, and he certainly needed peace. He wondered should Jason solve his problems, if that answer could resolve his own?

The third morning, after looking around at the rickety lean-to and corral, he asked, "Jason, are you goin' to stay through the winter?"

"Yes. My idea is to stay until sometime next year. At present, I have no plan to leave."

Henry asked another question. "Jason, could I stay with you fer a while? We'll build on to yer hut and expand yer corral. Make you a proper home—safe from the winter snows and animals," he suggested. He figured a heavy snow would bring this hut down on top of the man. "Can't promise about the Indians, drifters, and gold seekers—the two-leggers as I call them."

Jason laughed. "I wanted to ask, but I was afraid of your answer. Of course, stay as long as you want. I like you. I think we'll make a good team."

Other than the Dyers, no one had had much good to say about or to Henry. Jason's comment was welcome. An indication of the changes going on in his life.

The first decision they made as a team, was to start anew and next to the lean-to, leaving it attached to the new dwelling. Since winter was not far away, they'd keep the fireplace side. By closing the present opening, removing rocks and mud from the back side for a new opening, it would heat the newly attached home, and Jason wouldn't have to build another. This change they would save for last after the walls and roof were built.

They would also add a short open loft. Since heat always went up, they would have the option of moving their beds into the warmer attic, during the coldest days.

"Henry, I haven't been here in the winter," Jason explained, standing on the vacant ground where the new home would be. "If we get the house built and stay through this winter, the animals could use the lean-to for protection from the weather. We can store hay in the loft over the animals, to eat, and to sleep on. During bad storms they would have food, and water will be close by. As we build, the animals will be easy to take care of."

Henry nodded, "Hit jest makes more sense for us to winter here together."

Jason was walking around, gesturing as he moved. "Let me show you more of the area." He pointed down the creek. "We'll take the animals with us."

Jason led Henry down the creek to a meadowland in a hollow where the trees were few and grass grew abundantly on the hillsides.

They had to force the animals to walk on, because they wanted to stay and forage the area for grass. Several feet later, he pointed out another area. This one was almost devoid of trees, which could be used as pasture—a large flat land on the creek, including several beaver dams with backed-up ponds, and plenty of cleared meadow up the adjacent hollows. Here, the animals could graze. Small pockets of grass appeared elsewhere in the wooded area surrounding the beaver colony.

The animals headed for the grass as the men walked from the beaver ponds to where the stream formed a short rapid with a sparkling waterfall at the end. Standing there, the view was magnificent, with rolling hills giving away to vast prairie lands many miles in the distance.

"Surely God's hand was in this," commented Jason, viewing the scene before them.

Henry looked at him, wondering at his comment. *What did this man know about God?* He would soon find out.

~

The two men set out to build onto the hut, evaluating each tree, and cutting down ponderosa pine, skinning off the limbs, cutting to size, and shaping them for walls. The ring of their axes echoed in the forests. The work was time-consuming.

They used Old Girl and the two mules to snake the logs down the mountain and help with dragging them into position.

Jason advised, "We should build a rock foundation, but with winter almost on us, a trench to position the first run is the best idea. This will help to level the prospective floor of the new dwelling." Soon notched and stacked logs were placed in position and braced so they wouldn't fall.

The next day, Jason stood before the evolving cabin. There was some progress with two rungs of logs in place. Sitting on the top course, Jason suggested they take a breather and hunt for game to roast and smoke over the fire in their fireplace. "Today is Saturday. Tomorrow is Sunday, when we will rest."

"How do you know it's Saturday?"

"My mother taught me this poem about the months and days in the month, and I have the notches on the log in the lean-to." The two went into the old sleeping place and next to the chimney were Jason's notches.

"What is a poem?" asked Henry, totally fuddled.

"A poem is a few or a lot of sentences about one idea or subject. Songs are poems. In this case, the one I know goes like this,

> *Thirty days hath September, April, June, and November.*
>
> *All the rest have thirty-one, save February left alone.*

"How many days does February have?"

"Twenty-eight normally, but every fourth year you add an extra day."

Henry shook his head at such nonsense. He went over to scratch Stubborn behind the ears and pat Old Girl on the rump.

~

On Sunday, Jason pulled a book, covered in black leather, from his belongings and went to sit on one of the stools at the cabin's table.

Henry had gone outside to carry firewood inside and put a couple of logs on the fire.

"Henry, I'm going to study the Holy Bible this morning," he advised. "Do you want to listen in?"

Henry turned from the fire and saw the black book on the eating table. He thought about it. "I've never heard anything taught out'en the Bible. So, I guess I would. Can't hurt, can it? Don't people call it the Good Book?"

Jason smiled and turned the Good Book's pages and then closed it. "I haven't told you of my life, Henry. Because I think you should trust a man before he knows your story."

"I can agree with you there. I ain't shared mine with no one."

"I was trained as a preacher back east. When Minnesota became a state last year, my wife and I headed west to be Christian missionaries to the Indians, thinking the opportunities to share would be great in the new state, or even farther west. We headed for booming St. Paul, crossed the Mississippi River and planned to settle in Minneapolis around the Fort Snelling area. We soon found out that most of the Indians had moved on West, spurning the developing area which included crowds of fur traders and timber people. Since they had left, we moved on with them.

Our tribe was a little known and small offshoot of the Sioux. We settled down, built a cabin, taught them English, and learned the language of the natives living around us. They were receptive to the message we brought." Jason paused to listen to the distant howl of a coyote. "Time for the coyotes to form packs," he mused.

Henry took advantage of the pause to say, "I've never been thar … to Minnesota. Only as far as St. Joseph, Missouri."

"Lots of prairie, up there my friend—flat land or rolling hills covered with grass and lots of buffalo." Jason shook his head and continued, "Besides being a preacher, my trade is in using rock and mortar, which I learned from my father, as you can see from my chimney." He threw his hand toward the fireplace.

"I wondered about that," said Henry, letting the man continue speaking.

"When a new cabin was built in the area where we lived, I was always called to build the chimney. Mine always drew air. They worked. There's lots of limestone blocks in Minnesota and constructing a chimney isn't nearly as hard as irregular rock, as the one here. I received a notice that a fine two-story home was to be built in the Minneapolis area, and I was wanted. It meant money that we needed, but it also meant I would have to be away from home for at least a week. My wife was expecting our first child." Jason stopped and put his head in his hands. "I shouldn't have gone," came the muffled words.

Henry realized he'd come to the hard part of the story. "You can skip the next part."

"No, I can't. I need for you to know what happened. I finished the job. When I came back home, my wife was nowhere to be found. The house was in perfect order. It was as if she'd just walked out the door and intended to come back. At first, I thought she'd be at one of the many Indian homes. Maybe someone was sick. She was wonderful when someone needed nursing. I went to find out. But I checked all those and found nothing."

"Did you search the river banks?"

"Yes. I searched the river banks in the area—for miles around. I followed information the people suggested. Nothing. Nothing turned up. I noticed some of my friends started to stare at me as if I'd done something to her. I loved my wife. She was my earthly inspiration.

"Everyone started to avoid me, and I noticed them whispering behind my back. I was always about, because I'd kept nosing around the area—hoping, just hoping. Henry, I almost drove myself crazy. I guess I searched for over six months. That's when I decided to sell out and leave, leaving the people I'd come to serve. To find a solution, I've walked across Nebraska Territory with my goat and my mule, pulling the sled. My wife is gone. We would have had a little one by now. She's not coming back. I need to move on, but I need a reason. I think it's here." Jason tapped the Bible. "I've avoided this Book. But it's never let me down. I just need to get into the Word and find the answer."

Silence reigned in the room. The old wagon master had no idea what Jason was saying about an answer out of a book, and the one on the table meant nothing to him.

Jason felt the need to ask a question. "Henry, have you ever loved anyone?"

"I've been married. Isn't that love?"

"It should be. But love can also be just an attraction—a want to fulfill your desires—to use someone to satisfy your own needs. To really love someone, a person has to be responsive to their necessities, almost before their own. The Holy Bible says 'First, we love ourselves. Then we can love others likewise and in the same manner. Love is many things as explained in I Corinthians in the Bible. Chapter thirteen talks about love. We can talk about love as explained therein. What was your wife's name?"

Henry did not understand the talk about love, but he answered the question. "Ruby Eliza."

"I've been studying in I John, where the apostle Paul says 'God is love.' This is the first principle we must understand. Love is all through the Bible. God created the world in love and for people to love and for us to love others. For a brief period, love was perfect. Then sin came into the Garden of Eden."

Henry was totally mystified "I don't understand God. Most of the people I know curse someone they call God. They yell loudly his name when they are upset or angry or even excited."

Jason looked at Henry in surprise. "Has no one ever told you about how the earth was made and who made it? That God knows everything? He's in everything? He's right here, right now?"

Henry shook his head, but didn't offer any more information.

"My friend, will you let me teach you about the Bible? We'll go slow." Jason thought for a minute. "A few minutes by the fire each night. How about it?"

What could it hurt? Henry thought. Maybe this God was the answer to finding peace in his jumbled-up life. He was tired of running from his thoughts, and this last week working with Jason had helped. He nodded his head. "Okay. I'll listen."

Jason's face lit up, and he smiled. "Good. We'll start tomorrow at the beginning—the Old Testament as it's called or as I've named it—God's Plan, Jesus."

Henry stood up and put on his heavy coat. "Jason, you study the Bible, and I'll take the animals to the pasture. Can't afford to leave them by themselves with the coyotes and wolves runnin' around—not to mention Flower. I wonder if she likes mule flesh?"

"Thank you, Henry. We'll eat the rest of the rabbit we shot yesterday when you come back. Do you know how to make a trap for catching game? Sure would save us bullets and powder for our rifles."

"Hadn't thought about it. I'll work on it while I wait for the animals to feed. Do you mind if'n I take your axe?"

"Of course not. Don't cut your leg off," he called after Henry as the door shut behind him.

On Monday, Tuesday, and Wednesday of the following week, the men continued to cut trees and dress them to make logs for the house. This time they piled them away from the new walls which they would start building upward. The last two days of the week, they notched and placed the new logs on the developing walls. They continued this same schedule each week, adding a window in two of the walls.

At night, Jason gave Henry a condensed version of the Bible, starting at Genesis. At first, Henry just listened. Soon, he was thinking about Jason's words and asking questions.

Chapter Six

The Babe at Christmas

Work progressed on the new cabin, as the two men started to call it. Even though a two-inch snow fell to hamper their progress and muddy the ground, on the first week of December, the walls built of think logs were finished.

"I am thankful for the mules and Old Girl," said Henry, as they stood looking at the finished walls, after walking the outside perimeter.

"Me, too. They've made our work much easier."

Since it was so close to winter, they decided not to make a gabled roof, which would take days or weeks longer. They would use another angled covering like the lean-to. This top they could build in a week with smaller and lighter timber, some of it already cut from the bigger trees which were down on the ground with the limbs cut off. The back of the roof, toward the bank behind the home, would be higher and the front slope toward the creek. This meant the runoff from rain or snow would be turned to the downside or creek side of the cabin, where the entrance door was located and where they now stood.

"We'll have to figure out something to turn the water away from the door or we'll get soaked when we go outside in the rain," advised Jason, checking out the opening. "Maybe a wooden gutter."

"Look for a hollow log. One of those might work—at least over the door or we could build on a porch. I was also thinkin', we'll need to keep our firewood dry, so there's another shed, here close to the door. H-m-m-n—more poles, shakes …"

"Whoa, whoa. First things first."

Henry started laughing. "I agree. We can leave the firewood stashed in the present lean-to and stay dry. Hit's only a few steps away."

"Our cabin is taking shape. Do you think we'll be able to use it by the end of December?"

"Before, if you work hard." Henry chuckled. "But I was wondering', how are you goin' to cover the windows? We don't have glass or anyway of making a see-through opening."

Jason walked to a covered bin at the back of the lean-to, one he'd pulled on the sled coming from Minnesota. "Will this work?" Opening the lid, he pulled out two buffalo hides and brought them to the table. "We'll nail them up for the winter, and open them up for summer."

"I'd sure like to see the sunlight, especially during the winter. One day we'll do something about having the sun shining into the cabin."

"Henry, did you see the Red Cedar tree which was next to the last Ponderosa Pine we cut down yesterday? It would make wonderful and easy-to-cut shakes for the roof. Why don't we cut it and saw chunks from the trunk? We can cut the shakes at night as we rest from the day's work and study the Bible."

"You are a glutton for punishment," stated Henry, using a new word he'd learned from the nightly studies he was beginning to enjoy. Even the way he pronounced some of his words was changing—the *ings* were coming back. Without realizing it, Jason was teaching him read*ing*, writ*ing*, but not arithmetic—point*ing* out different sentences or phrases in the Bible and mak*ing* sure he could read them.

No one would recognize the old Hurricane with his newfound knowledge of the Bible and this man, a minister, as a friend. He still hadn't shared his life story with Jason, although the need to was getting greater. It was almost a year since Jedediah had died, and he wondered what Jason would think of him should he learn the truth of his existence.

Was the attack only a year ago? he thought. It seemed like years.

~

Henry didn't know it, but Jason often wondered when he looked at his friend, *what would open Henry's heart to tell the experiences he'd been through?* He was sure the man needed Jesus in his life. But, since he was in the throes of a personal problem himself, could he help another person with problems?

~

Because the men didn't have a crosscut saw, it took most of a week to cut the Cedar tree down with a handsaw and remove some blocks out of it. They got rid of the loose bark with Jason's hatchet, and he found a wide chisel in his tools to split the wood.

"If'n I'd known I was going to build a house in the Black Hills, I'd of brought different goods," sometimes

Henry commented, as the two did everything the hard way. He set about making shakes for the roof, while listening to Jason read and talk about the Bible stories he'd chosen.

Standing the about eighteen-inch-long piece of wood on its end, Henry took the chisel and made several incisions in a straight line along the diameter of the wood. Then he inserted a piece of flat oak, with a sharply angled side he'd whittled with his knife, into the cross cuts. He hit this wooden wedge with a short wooden mallet, he had carved from a tree limb, and grinned as an almost perfect shake, split and fell to the ground. He picked it up and sighted down its length, nodding his head.

"What do you think, Jason?" He held the piece up so his friend could see. "Of course, I'll have to clean the sides up some so they'll fit together properly."

Jason looked over at him and grinned, "Amazing isn't it, if you don't have the proper tools, the human mind can always improvise."

The process was time consuming and sometimes he lost one, but slowly, his stack of shakes was getting larger and larger. While the shakes were being readied at night, the roof was taking shape during the day.

The smaller tree trunks were in position on top of the notched log walls. Jason climbed up on the unfinished roof. With a small hatchet he dressed the limbs as flat as he could get them. Without sawn lumber, this was all he could do to make a flatter surface for the shingles.

At the end of each day the men were exhausted. There was no need of a lullaby to put them to sleep.

When Henry pronounced his job good enough, Jason started putting the finished shakes on the roof, covering each joint and making a dry cabin interior. Since the shakes were large, the area was almost covered by the end of the week.

Henry made the rest of the shakes, while Jason started opening up the chimney so a fire could heat the new home's interior. Both men were getting excited. Their new home was almost done.

The week before Christmas, the shakes were on and the fireplace finished. They built a fire on the new hearth, tacked the buffalo skins over the two windows, moved their beds, and spent the first night in their new home.

~

"We'd better see if there's grass for the animals in the meadows," suggested Henry, the next morning.

"Is that more important than chinking the holes between the logs? You haven't forgotten this chore, have you. Even with the logs on the fire and the heat radiating through our home, I felt a cold draft on my face last night. My nose turned into an icicle like the ones hanging from the roof shakes."

"I was hoping you wouldn't remember the chinking. Playing in cold mud isn't my idea of working." Henry had realized this part of the home building was coming, and he'd thought to get his suggestion in first.

"Wait until you've done it all day, my friend."

"Chinking is more left to the young." Henry was smiling now, as he protested because of his age.

"I tell you what, you go cut the grass, and I'll work at chinking the logs. After all, it's not much different from building a fireplace with mud. I'm good at that."

"And, you are much younger than me," Henry returned to his younger theme. "Climbing the ladder and poking mud in the log walls will be easier for you."

The young man laughed, "Take the wooden sled and attach it to my mule. She's used to pulling it. You can cut and transport more fodder." Jason was shooing him on the way.

"I was going to ask you about letting him help."

"I'll help you store the cut grass when you come back." Jason picked up the water bucket and opened the door.

"What part of the house are you going to chink?"

"I'm only going to work on the outside of the logs, and later I can do the inside. When the sun ceases to shine on the house, I'll have to quit. My hands will become too cold to work properly, even if I use warm water to work the mud."

"I'll come back before dark." Henry shouldered his rifle, walked out the open door, and went to hook the mule up to the sled. When he was ready to leave, he took a short-handled scythe to cut the grass, and loosed Old Girl and Stubborn so they could follow along behind.

As he headed for the goat, Jason appeared around the house carrying the bucket. "Leave the goat in the pen. I need to milk her."

"She won't be happy."

"I'll leave her loose. She'll follow you to the fields. Don't let Flower get you."

Henry shook his head, laughed, and threw up his hand. Meeting the female grizzly was the last thing he wanted to do, especially since she had two cubs.

~

"Henry, tomorrow is the celebrated day of Jesus Christ's birth." Jason was sitting on one of the stools at the table with the open Bible. It was Bible study time. "This is the direction the Bible has been heading for in the chapters we've studied. Remember me saying the Old Testament could be called, God's Plan, Jesus?"

"Yes, I remember. You helped me memorize a verse in the ninth chapter of Isaiah, pointing to this same notion."

"Can you say it?"

Henry grinned, turned from the blazing fire, and said, *"For unto us a child is born, unto us a son is given: and the government shall be upon his shoulder: and his name shall be called Wonderful, Counsellor, The mighty God, The everlasting Father, The Prince of Peace.* I still don't understand all the meaning of the verse," he confessed.

"There's a lot of people in this world in those same shoes, but I'm praying you will, Henry. Much of the Bible must be taken on faith, especially after an experience of salvation when one starts to believe in Christ. We can't ever know the total mind of God. He's infinite, complete, and perfect."

"Wall, I certainly don't understand. I ain't never seen a perfect man."

"No, and you never will. But God doesn't see each man the way we do. That's another story we'll get into in a few months. That's where love comes in." Jason hesitated and cleared his throat. "Since this is the evening of the Child's birth in the verse you memorized, I'd like to go to Luke in the New Testament and read up to the day he was born. We'll finish the rest tomorrow."

"Sure." Henry came from the fireplace and sat on the other log stool opposite Jason, giving the scripture reader his full attention. He fidgeted on the wooden seat, until he got comfortable. "My friend, one of us needs to make chairs for the table."

"If we get comfortable here," Jason tapped the wooden table top, "We'll just get fat."

"Hey, I'm older. A back, other than the one I've got, would be welcome."

"Work on *your* stool. I'm sure you can come up with something."

"I'll give it some thought. It looks like snow out there for tomorrow. The last time I got wood for the fire, the sky was a striking orange-red above the clouds. I bet we have the same color in the morning." He looked over at Jason who was smiling. "Go ahead and read."

"These verses are found in Luke's gospel, chapter two, verses one through six. *"And it came to pass in those days, that there went out a decree from Caesar Augustus that all the world should be taxed. (And this taxing was first made when Cyrenius was governor of Syria.) And all went to be taxed, every one into his own city. And Joseph also went up from Galilee, out of the city of Nazareth, into Judaea, unto the city of David, which is called Bethlehem; (because he was of the house and lineage of David:) To be taxed with Mary his espoused wife, being great with child. And so it was, that, while they were there, the days were accomplished that she should be delivered."*

"That was a long time ago, wasn't it?" Henry said in a hushed voice.

"Almost two thousand years." Jason closed the Bible. "A very long time, indeed. How old are you, Henry?"

"I'm fifty-two years old. Most of them hard living ones."

"I've been wondering." Jason would never have guessed that his friend was that young, although there was a bit of the handsome man he must have been still in his weathered countenance.

"You wouldn't like me, if I told you of my previous life."

"Henry, why don't you let me be the judge of that,"

"Alright, I will. Up 'til a year ago, I was always a hard-drinkin' man. I don't even recall not drinkin'. My father was that way, and his father. I guess it run in the family."

"Drinking can jump from one generation to another. I've seen it in the East and the West. The Bible also recognizes this fact, when it talks about generation to generation."

"My Pa run after women and had a bad temper, and so did I. At least, until I run up against a good-looking woman in Kansas. Her name was Ruby Eliza Linkford. When my father died, I rode back East, and we got married. We got married, because I never did like being alone. Don't like being alone now. Guess that's why I'm building a cabin in the Nebraska wilderness."

Jason nodded his head. "Did you and Ruby have children?"

"Yes, a boy. I named the young'un, Jedediah, after one of my scoutin' buddies, Jedediah Smith. I didn't stay at home much. I'd be away fer a year. One time, I came home from scoutin' and another man was thar. We had a fight, and I run him off. Ruby and I got into an argument over him, and I took my anger out on Ruby. I hit her. She fell off'en the porch and hit her head on a rock. She didn't move. I kilt her, Jason." He stopped to see how his friend was taking this and then rushed on. "All this time, Jedediah was watchin' out'en the window. I don't know what he thought. I buried her in a grave on a rise behind our house. Then I took Jedediah, and we headed West."

"That was a long time ago, Henry. Ruby's death was an accident. I find it hard to believe you acted in anger. I've not detected any in you while we've worked together."

"No. I've changed some. The rest of the story took that from my life. I tried to make my son into the man, thar's some question about that, I was—hard drinkin' and hard livin', but he never took to that kind of life. I even tried to knock it into him. Didn't work either.

"The last wagon train we helped scout, about two years ago, there was a young girl named Gracie Tipton. He was taken with her—drawn into her presence. Gracie was a spitfire. We butted heads. I tried to keep them apart, but one day he defied me and left for a Butterfield Overland Mail Station in the Guadalupe Mountains called The Pinery. Thar, she was helping her father work a stop on the stage line. They got married. I heard about hit from some of the drivers on the stage. I'd tried to put down some shaller roots at Ft. Chadbourne, and I'd started work on the roads fer Butterfield in that area."

"Had you ever stayed in one place before, Henry?"

"No. Once a job was done. I'd stay drunk for a few days and before the money run out, I was on the road. Fort Chadbourne was a chance to stay in one place for a while. I'm sure Jedediah knew hit wasn't permanent. Hearing of the marriage, I set out to prove to Gracie Tipton that blood is thicker'n water. I knew exactly what to say to my son. He'd leave her. Come with me. I was willin' to bet on it."

"Henry, I'm going to get a couple of logs to put on the fire. I'll be right back."

"Hit is gittin' cold in here."

When Jason returned with the logs, Henry stood by the fire—his hands stretched out to warm.

"You were right about the snow. There are flurries outside right now. The moon can't be seen and the stars aren't out. The wind is sighing and moaning in the tall pines."

"We may have a big un in the mornin'. The clouds looked heavy today," nodded Henry. "Several inches I'd say. If'n we were in a wagon train, I'd say it was time to circle the wagons, build fires, put the stock in the circle, and wait."

Both men stood, watching as new flames climbed upward from the hot coals. Within minutes the fire was blazing again and radiating its warmth throughout the room. Henry went back to the table and sat on his log stool. He looked around the room. "We built a really good cabin, my friend."

Jason followed. He sat on the opposite side and asked, "Did Jedediah leave Gracie?"

"Yes, he did. We went on to a stretch of road in Arizona Territory. It paid well, because Apaches were raiding in random attacks, no one else wanted to go there and work. They'd already killed some unprotected settlers. The men on the stagecoaches told us they were around. We'd been working several days and hadn't seen a one, but that changed. One night they raided us.

"The men I hired were drinkers like me, and nighttime was when we tied one on. By the next morning, the alcohol's effects had worn off, and we worked hard until the night and drank again.

"When the attack happened, we were all locked in drunken sleep. Jedediah must have woke up when they started stealing our horses. He fired a shot and hit one. The wounded Indian's blood-curdling cry woke the rest of us up. The Indians started circling our camp and shooting arrows at anything moving. The only one who could fire a gun and aim properly was Jedediah. I could barely hold my gun up, let alone aim it. My son hid behind a stack of supplies, trying his best to defend us all. Hit was just a matter of time before an arrow was in his back. He was dead before I could get to him. I kilt my son, too." For the third time since Jedediah's death, sobs racked the man. He put his head on his hands which rested on the table. The table shook as his eyes ran with tears.

Jason realized he was alone in his sorrow—the one thing that Henry dreaded.

He got up and went to the man. Kneeling on the floor, he reached up and put his arms around him, clasping him tightly.

Henry turned, put his head on his friend's shoulder, and started to cry even harder, mumbling when he could finally breathe. "Now, you hate me. I hate me, too."

"No, Henry. I don't hate you. The Bible says *let him who is without sin cast the first stone.* I cast no stones at you."

Henry finally collected himself. He sat back up and pulled out his bandana as Jason went back to his stool. "I'm sorry. Hit's just when I think of Jedediah's dying … well, the sorrow's great."

"Do you remember when we talked about King David?"

"Yes, I remember he'd done a lot of bad things, but God gave him His heart. I guess God loved the king even though he couldn't be right or do right all the time."

"So true, Henry. All you have to do is admit your sins, ask for forgiveness, and invite Him into your life and heart." Jason paused to see if there was a response. He continued because Henry was silent. "When we talked about sin, I said according to the Bible all have sinned. That means me. That means you. Tomorrow, when we read the rest of Luke, we see what God did to take care of getting rid of sin. I'm tired. What about you?"

"I'm ready to sleep. I'll go get more logs to go on the fire and put some on the hearth." Henry pulled on his coat and disappeared out the door. When he came back, he shook snow off his shoes at the door. "A dusting on the ground already, Jason."

"I declare tomorrow a day of rest. It's also a day to give gifts, and I have one for you. What do you say, Henry?"

"I agree to being tired, and a good rest will be welcome. I'll have to think about a gift."

Chapter Seven

A Week of Rest

The next morning, Henry pushed the door open and took one step outside into the open-air. The snow came to his boot top, the wind was blowing, and the cold air cut into his skin. He wondered just how chilly it was outside. A quick look toward the stream gave him his answer. A light skim of ice covered it, at least where the snow didn't—the air temperature was somewhere below freezing. He reached for an icicle hanging from the roof. It snapped off, and he put the end of the spike in his mouth to melt.

Back inside, he walked across the wood chips on the floor and headed straight to the warm fire. "Whew," came from his lips as he visibly shivered.

Turning his back, he looked over at the other occupant in the room.

Jason was wrapped in his blanket with the tip of his head showing, snoring softly, and in deep sleep. Hard to believe he'd known the man only three months—long enough for them to become fast friends and share their life stories. He would give his life to help Jason, and he felt like the younger man would do the same for him.

Pulling in a lung full of air, he started for the door again and stumbled over his feet. His movement woke Jason.

"Good morning, Henry. Did we get snow last night?" Jason stretched his arms over his head and sat up, rubbing his face to wipe the sleep away.

"Yep. Enough to ensure we won't be doing anything but sittin' here in the cabin for the next few days. Instead of a day, it looks like a week of rest."

Jason smiled, "Unless it snows again." He got up and opened the door to a white world. "How cold is it?" he asked as a blast of wind blew through the open door, to where Henry stood. Jason shut it.

"Below freezing. Thar's ice on the stream and icicles hangin' from the roof. I was thinking we'd better check on the animals and bring more wood into the cabin. You never can tell how cold it'll be tomorrow or how deep the snow will be. I started outside but headed back to the warm fire—decided to warm up some more, before tackling the outside again. No place better than here. Your chimney puts out good heat."

"Let me put on my boots, and I'll go with you. I have a surprise for you." Jason walked across the wood chip floor in his wool socks to retrieve his boots. Coming back, he pulled his log stool away from the table, sat down, picked wood shavings from his wool socks and threw them back on the floor. All this, before he pushed his feet into the shoes.

Henry watched from his place before the fire. The log stool—a plan formed. They might be consigned to the cabin, but he had an idea. This was the celebrated day of Christ's birth. Since it was customary to give gifts, he knew just exactly what they both needed.

Jason stood up and walked to the milk bucket, taking it from a nail in the log wall. "Can't forget the goat. She'll need to be milked this morning."

Since the dry wood was stashed in the old lean-to, the two broke a path through the snow to the door which they had decided should remain open in the daytime and closed at night. This way the animals could go outside into the corral to sun should they wish.

Flower would be no problem to them, because she would be denned up somewhere with her cubs.

"You pull some feed from the loft, and I'll break the ice on the water bucket," suggested Jason. "Then I'll show you my surprise."

These chores were accomplished in record time. The animals pushing them aside to get to food and water.

What was Jason's surprise?

Henry watched as Jason went to the back of the fireplace, knelt down, and pulled a section of rocks and mud mortar from the bottom. A puff of heat could immediately be felt coming into the cold room.

Jason placed the water bucket nearby. "My gift to the animals. Don't think the water will freeze again soon," he stated. "Of course, there won't be enough heat to warm the room, but maybe it'll keep their hooves warmer," he laughed.

"Old Girl and Stubborn will be the first to enjoy the heat and the water."

Henry was wrong.

The goat nudged her way to the warmth and stood, facing the opening while Jason milked her.

"I sure hope we've got everything covered," Henry looked around, after the milking was over. "Are you headed back for our drawin' room?" he asked, jokingly.

Jason chuckled and nodded his head, "Yes I am. Are you coming, Mr. Bailey?"

"Shortly, Mr. Douglas. I have an errand to make. Won't be long."

With that the two men separated. Jason went to the cabin with the milk, and Henry went to the woodpile to check out timber for making two backs to their stools.

~

Late in the afternoon, Jason took his Bible and sat down at the table. He opened the book and started to read.

> *And she brought forth her firstborn son, and wrapped him in swaddling clothes, and laid him in a manger; because there was no room for them in the inn. And there were in the same country shepherds abiding in the field, keeping watch over their flock by night. And, lo, the angel of the Lord came upon them, and the glory of the Lord shone round about them: and they were sore afraid. And the angel said unto them, Fear not: for, behold, I bring you good tidings of great joy, which shall be to all people. For unto you is born this day in the city of David a Saviour, which is Christ the Lord. And this shall be a sign unto you; Ye shall find the Babe*

> *wrapped in swaddling clothes, lying in a manger. And suddenly there was with the angel a multitude of the heavenly host praising God, and saying, Glory to God in the highest, and on earth peace, good will toward men. And it came to pass, as the angels were gone away from them into heaven, the shepherds said one to another, Let us now go even unto Bethlehem, and see this thing which is come to pass, which the Lord hath made known unto us. And they came with haste, and found Mary, and Joseph, and the babe lying in a manger. And when they had seen it, they made known abroad the saying which was told them concerning this child.*

The fire crackled on the hearth, as Jason read this scripture in a low, reverent voice.

Henry laid aside his woodworking, sat forward, and listened attentively. Never in his life had he heard this story. The old Hurricane Bailey would have scoffed and left the room for another drink of tanglefoot.

If it hadn't been for Jason becoming his friend first, he would not have listened to him. Jason had said many times, this was God's Plan, Jesus. He was beginning to wonder if there was more to the story. After all, men were born, they lived, and they died.

"Henry, all the words of the Old Testament point to this fleshly *Word*, Jesus. In the Book of John, we read—*and the Word was made flesh, and dwelt among us, and we beheld his glory, the glory as of the only begotten of the Father, full of grace and truth.* But that's not the end of the story."

"I thought so," replied Henry, shaping a piece of wood with his knife.

"We'll study the rest during the winter days. I don't guess there'll be much outside activity for us to do, except get wood, milk the goat, and feed the other animals."

When Jason finished talking, he got up, walked to the fireplace and started singing in a clear tenor voice.

"Silent night! Holy night! All is calm, all is bright. Round yon virgin mother and child! Holy infant, so tender and mild, Sleep in heavenly peace! Sleep in heavenly peace!

Silent night! Holy night! Shepherds quake at the sight! Glories stream from heaven afar, Heavenly hosts sing Alleluia! Christ the Saviour is born! Christ the Saviour is born!

Silent night! Holy night! Son of God, love's pure light. Radiant beams from thy holy face, With the dawn of redeeming grace, Jesus, Lord, at thy birth! Jesus, Lord, at thy birth!"

"That's a pleasant song."

"Yes, I used to sing it with my wife. We would harmonize as we sang it. It's been over a year. I miss her." The man bowed his head and watched the leaping flames of the fire.

From where he sat, Henry thought he saw a tear glisten in his friend's eyes. "Jason, do you know the word I dwell on from hearin' your verses?"

Jason raised his head to look at Henry, "No. What is it?"

"It's peace. That's what I'm after—peace. Peace over Jedediah's and Ruby Eliza's deaths, and I reckon over my life, too."

"Remember we talked about the world being perfect for a period of time until sin came into the world. There was perfect peace then. Now we can't have perfect peace except with the knowledge that God loves us and that his son, Jesus, came to save us from our sins. Our sin is what haunts us."

"I don't for sure understand all you're talkin' about, again."

"We'll be doing more reading and more studying." Jason walked over to a leather bag hanging from the wall and secured something from inside. "Henry, I have something for you." He walked over to the man and offered him a book. "This was my wife's Bible."

Henry held up his hand, "Jason, no. I can't take this. It's your prized possession."

"If she were with us, she would hand it to you herself. So here, you need this. Then, you can follow along as we study God's Word, with your own Bible. I can't think of anyone I'd rather have it." Jason smiled as Henry accepted his gift.

"I don't have anythin' to give you back, but I'm workin' on your surprise. We'll both have chairs with backs before long, my friend."

"Henry, let's say your verse together as a prayer."

The two men stood before the fire, with its light dancing around the room and flickering on their faces. They repeated, *"For unto us a child is born, unto us a son is given: and the government shall be upon his shoulder: and his name shall be called Wonderful, Counsellor, The mighty God, The everlasting Father, The Prince of Peace."* Jason added, "Thank you, Father for your Son and give Henry and me the peace we each long for."

There was silence as both men pondered what had just been said. Henry because this was the first time in his life he'd prayed, and Jason because he was thankful for knowing God, during his time of distress.

Jason added, "Well, the Prince of Peace has been born. I'm praying that you find him, and my friend, we both need peace—the Peace that passes understanding, which comes from God. Jesus is our way of understanding Him, as much as our simple minds can grasp."

Chapter Eight

Henry Leaves the Cabin.

Jason and Henry survived the winter. In April, when they could go outside to warmer weather, they passed a new woodshed they'd built at the front of the cabin and stood under a porch to turn the rain water from the front door.

"Henry, let's both take the animals to their pasture. I can't wait to sit and let the sun warm me, and I need to see something besides cabin walls and trees."

"Come on. The grass is startin' to green up, and the sun will feel good. I've been meanin' to talk to you about somethin' I need to do."

They rounded up Old Girl, Stubborn, and Jason's mule and goat and headed out down the trail to the beavers' dams. The trail was sharply defined, because of all the traffic of the men and animals back and forth. Finding a good place to sit close to the waterfall, they basked in the warmth of the overhead sun while looking out at the distant flat land embedded in the Black Hills.

After several minutes, Jason asked, "What did you want to talk about, Henry?"

"I've been thinkin' I might need to move on."

Shocked, Jason looked over quickly at his friend. "Are you upset? Did I say something to offend you?"

"No," Henry shook his head.

"So, why do you want to leave?"

"Do you remember me tellin' you about not stayin' in one place for long?"

"Yes, but I …"

"You were hopin' I'd changed. I think I have, but … somethin' is pushing me to explore further into these Black Hills. I can't account for the feeling," Henry finished lamely. How could he explain something he didn't understand himself?

"Better to follow your hunch, my friend. I'd like to ask you to stay through next week. We'll be studying the final days of Jesus' life. I think you need to hear about what happened to him before you go." Jason was not a pushy preacher. He let the words of the Bible reach into his listener's heart, and Henry did not know the full story.

April the eighth was Easter, and he'd purposely counted the days and taught his friend the Word, leading up to this day. He continued, "Not only that, but the weather will be a little warmer for you to travel."

~

"For with God nothing shall be impossible," Jason's audible prayer, from words of the Bible, mingled with the sighing wind in the tall spruce and pine trees. They followed Henry as he rode on Old Girl up the main trail, from the place where they had originally met.

Before he was out of sight, Henry turned and waved goodbye to the only true friend he'd ever had in his life. This leaving was different from his last one—the one from The Pinery in Texas.

This time he sat straight in his cold saddle, took off his hat, and waved it in the air. He had a reason to live and a decision to make on his future life.

Jason had left him with this choice. He knew he must make it, and he knew this choosing would give him peace. Why couldn't he make it? Why was he hesitating? Had he lived so long in one way that he couldn't change? He pushed his old hat down on his head, turned Old Girl, and rode out of sight.

But Henry found he could not ride away from his thoughts. The one preying on his mind and that he couldn't run from was in last week's Bible study, when Jason read and talked about the lost sheep. When he asked if he was important enough for the God of the universe and his son, Jesus, to come for him, Jason's answer was yes, yes, always yes.

And then, Jason had explained and read about Jesus's last days on earth, where he willingly died for all sinful men. Jason had explained, "When we profess faith in Jesus, God sees us through Jesus's blood. He cannot and does not see our sin through this red curtain. If not for his death, and his shed blood, we couldn't go and dwell in Heaven with the Triune God."

It was Jesus's words on the cross which broke Henry's heart. *"Father forgive them; for they know not what they do."* Yes, he now understood he needed forgiveness.

~

One week later, after riding up a long switchback trail, Henry sat on the top of a mountain. Looking across the wide, deep valley before him, he was startled to see movement in the distance. A string of untamed horses followed their wild mustang leader in single file, moseying down the side of an arroyo into a creek flowing alongside the embankment. They stopped, scattered, and standing midstream, dipped their heads for a drink. Henry counted. Almost thirty were grouped together.

Giving Old Girl a nudge, he headed down the mountain, keeping the animals in sight.

Suddenly, the leader, a beautiful solid black horse raised his head, shook his long black mane, and with a snort loud enough for Henry to faintly hear, pawed the ground, and started to run in the man's direction. What had spooked him?

Henry pulled up Old Girl so quickly that Stubborn bumped into her. Scanning the horizon, he soon saw the reason for the mustang's rapid departure. A band of Indians rode pell-mell down the steep side of the arroyo, in hot pursuit of the black beauty. The rest of the horses scattered across the valley, as the band rushed through the creek with water flying in all directions.

As the leader, one Indian in particular seemed to stand out from the rest. He was lighter skinned with hair not black. He sat his horse as if molded to it, riding with grace, his long hair flowing in the rushing wind of his chase.

Realizing the horse and Indian band were coming his way, Henry quickly dismounted Old Girl and pulled her and Stubborn behind some prominent rocks next to the trail. If the group slowed, they were sure to see him, but as they rode headlong after the horse, he was safe. He watched the progress of the horse's flight, as it went up the valley and finally crossed over the edge of the arroyo away from where Henry had hidden. The Indians followed closely behind.

Henry let out a huge sigh, realizing he was a little disappointed he hadn't witnessed the end of the chase.

His bet was on the horse.

He stopped for several minutes and waited. They might come back for the other horses. He needed to be sure, before he exposed himself in the valley, where he'd decided to stay the night.

~

The following morning, Henry headed up stream and topped the arroyo where he'd last seen the Indians in their mad gallop after the black beauty. To his surprise, the horse stood there, grazing with several of its companions.

He laughed, telling Old Girl and Stubborn, "I just knew black beauty was smarter than a human." He rode on, skirting the herd.

Seeing the Indians had made him more wary of animals or travelers he might encounter on his ride north. His eyes wandered continuously over the flat or mountainous areas he rode through, checking trees, rocks, and strange shadows.

Two days later, a whiff of smoke was his reward for being careful.

"Now what?" he said out loud, not expecting so much human movement out here in the wilderness of the Black Hills.

Sniffing the air and checking the wind, he decided to see if he could find the source of the smell, which could carry some distance in the atmosphere. He needed to know if this odor came from a forest fire, which was unlikely or a human presence in the area. Would he need to avoid the source or confront it?

"Girls, let's find out where this comes from." He gave his horse a nudge, and they were off, on the trail of the scent.

In the late afternoon, a few miles distant, he came upon the source of the smoke he'd been tracking. Appearing in the trees, near a creek, were several fires from an encampment of a mounted rifle regiment, or cavalry, of the United States military. Time to make a decision. Should he reveal his presence or ride on? His stomach decided this question. It growled, because within the smoky smell was the odor of cooking food. Could they have some different government rations he could eat? Riding through a closely growing stand of aspens, he approached.

Catching brief flashes of something moving through the trees, one of the cavalry men in his green trimmed uniform, which was closest to Henry, grabbed his rifle musket and aimed it toward him.

"Whoa, I'm a friend," yelled Henry, who saw the man's actions and held up his hands to show he was unarmed. He continued into the camp.

"Sorry, I couldn't see much of anything but movement," apologized the young man when Henry stopped and dismounted at his cooking fire.

"What makes you so uneasy?" asked Henry, who was not laughing. Several other young men started gathering around to see this roughly clad intruder.

"We've been tracking Crazy Horse and a band of Indians riding with him."

"Crazy Horse, who's he?"

One of the other men, introduced with the last name Johnson, a Lieutenant by the stripes on his sleeve, answered, "A young Sioux. He's gathering wild horses and some say stealing them, also. We don't know, but according to the Captain, we're just making sure he knows we're around and that he's heading for the Sioux reservation."

"What does Crazy Horse look like? I saw a band two days ago, includin' a Sioux with lighter hair down to his waist, tracking a black horse."

"That sounds like him. Let me take you to Captain Smithfield. He'll want to talk to you," suggested Lieutenant Johnson. "Follow me." He turned on his heel and headed for the largest tent in the area.

The startled Captain looked up as the two men entered. He was eating his supper. "Lieutenant, who is this man?" he asked as he picked up his napkin, wiped his mouth, and stood.

Henry answered, "My name is Henry Bailey, Captain Smithfield."

"Why are you here, Mr. Bailey?"

Henry wanted to say, your officer brought me, but he didn't. Instead, he said, "I've been checkin' out the Black Hills, just gettin' a feel for the territory. Haven't been here before."

"Are you looking for gold?"

"No, not gold. Just peace, I reckon."

"Peace may be a hard thing to come by, Mr. Bailey, from what I hear back East. But I guess you're in the best place to find it. Have you had your supper?"

"No, sir. Somethin' sure smells good."

"Lieutenant Johnson, take Mr. Bailey to your fire and feed him. While you're at it, send the boy in to me."

"Yes, Sir." Johnson saluted.

As Henry turned to leave, the Captain called, "Mr. Bailey, we'll talk after you've satisfied your hunger."

Henry nodded and followed the lieutenant to his camp fire. An enlisted man dipped food out of an iron pot into metal pans. Henry pulled out a glove and put it on so the hot food wouldn't burn his fingers. Provided with a spoon, he began eating a stew containing fresh vegetables—potatoes, carrots, and onions—and sliced bread.

Oh! He savored every bite.

Before sitting down, the lieutenant went to the door of his tent and called, "Boy, come out."

Henry watched as a young boy of four or five appeared from the tent's interior. What was he doing in this military encampment?

"Go to the Captain's tent. He needs to talk to you," instructed Johnson, pointing.

The young boy nodded and headed toward the tent indicated.

Seeing the question in Henry's eyes, the lieutenant explained, "Found him hiding at a campsite a few days ago, and we've been taking care of him ever since. We searched the area, but his family was nowhere to be found. He hasn't spoken two words to any of us. No telling what trauma he's been through." The lieutenant shook his head slowly in amazement at what he was saying. "How often do you find a child in the wilderness, eating the last of his food? If we hadn't come along ..."

"How long have you been on patrol?"

"Two weeks, and we have several more weeks to go with lots of ground to cover. The Captain has expressed concern over the boy's presence, slowing us down, or becoming a problem should we be involved in a confrontation."

Henry finished the man's words with his own thoughts. *The boy could be a problem to them, fer sure.* After eating his last bite, he wiped his pan with a piece of bread, scooping up all the juices and stuffing the tasty portion in his mouth. The enlisted man came for his plate.

"That was the best food I've had in months," he told the man.

"MacDonald is a good cook. He cooks for all the officers. Henry, why don't you pitch your tent here next to mine."

"Thanks fer the offer, but I prefer to stay apart a bit. I'm thinkin' over there under the large oak. I might find enough leaves to make a softer bed under my bedroll. Thanks anyway."

"Before we go back and talk to the Captain, would you like to take care of your animals, or I can get MacDonald to help you with them."

"No, I can care for them." Henry headed over to the oak tree which was outside the main camp. He unsaddled Old Girl and pulled the packs off Stubborn. Taking their leads, he went to the stream for water, and then he turned them loose in the corral the military men had built for their horses.

~

His talk with Captain Smithfield was full of answered questions about his experience with the Indian party and his last few months in the Black Hills. When he said he'd helped to build a cabin in the foothills, and his friend was a minister from Minnesota, the officer seemed particularly pleased with the answer.

"Are you going back there?" he asked.

"Yes, I think so. It's in the back of my mind," answered Henry.

The Captain nodded his head. "You saw the young boy we've found at his family's campsite. We know nothing about him." He walked over to a table beside his cot and came back with a book. It was a Bible. "This we found at their cabin—no names or even notes inside. He is a mystery, and he hasn't said a word since we found him."

"It seems I'm followed by this kind of happening." Henry related his full experience with Jason, including a mention of his Bible lessons.

Regarding this man in a new light, the Captain had a slight, knowing smile on his face. "Our regiment will be moving at a fast pace the next few weeks, and a young child will slow us down. Henry, would you take the young boy back with you? As far as we could ascertain, he has no family and no home. You can make him your own son, or maybe the minister would take care of him—the child who wasn't born to his wife."

"No, sir. I don't have a good history with a family or children." Henry did not tell the man why.

"Think about it," asked the Captain, who yawned discreetly.

"The answer is no, Sir. Thanks for the food. Guess I'll turn in."

Henry left to raise his tent. His feet were like lead as he walked. Why was he so tired?

"Henry, come here," the Lieutenant called as he passed. The young boy sat by the warm fire, using a stick to write in the dirt. "I'll send MacDonald over to help you set up your tent."

"Much obliged, my giddy-up-and-go is gone," said Henry, saying something he'd heard his father say. The old man used it after riding in the saddle all day and before his usual trip to a local saloon or the bottle he kept in his saddle bags. He wasn't tired enough to push into his bedroll and rest.

The cook came over and they raised the tent in record time, sheltering his saddle and supplies inside.

"Thanks, young man and thanks for the grub."

Henry crawled inside. Exhausted, he went to sleep. His deep-sleep dreams were of eating good food, men riding horses, and a young boy at his campfire.

When he woke, it was still dark. When he had groggily crawled out of his tent, he found out what had flowed through his mind in the night wasn't a dream! The men were gone. At the lieutenant's campsite, the light of glowing coals was all that was left. How had they managed to leave the area without waking him?

He walked to the corral. Old Girl came trotting over, and Stubborn stood with another pony. He wondered, why the pony? His suspicions were immediately aroused.

Rummaging around back at his campfire, he found a bag each of potatoes, carrots, and apples, for which he was grateful—MacDonald or the lieutenant, he smiled.

Becoming serious, he looked toward his tent. He hadn't bothered to do anything but stumble into the darkness when he'd left. He walked over and stuck his head inside. The sound he heard didn't surprise him. The young boy lay to one side of his tent, mixed in with his saddle and the mule's packs and covered with an army blanket—fast asleep. Now, what? This responsibility he hadn't asked for—had actually declined.

In shock, Henry went back outside. He searched for pieces of wood at the abandoned campsites, found some, and came back. He put two pieces of wood on his fire, and hunkered down. He needed to think. What decision should he make? Go on, or go back? He sat and thought until the sun's light started to reveal tree shapes in the night sky.

Was this the reason he needed to come north? Could this young boy be his second chance? He put his hands over his face.

Shaking his head, he prayed, "Why do You want me? Why have You come for me?"

Was it as Jason had said? God was not through with him. Now, he was sure this was true. The One who'd made the universe, the stars above him, and the earth where he sat, wanted him as his child. With this realization, tears flowed as he asked his Heavenly Father to forgive him. "I believe," he said brokenly. "I believe. Do with me as you wish. From now on, I believe in your Son and the Spirit which now dwells in me."

Henry got up and went to the tent. He looked at the sleeping child. This young boy would need a father just as he had needed one.

Love flowed from his heart—a feeling unknown to him. He was so astonished at its presence, he put his hand over his heart, expecting—he knew not what.

More thoughts came in quick succession. On his trip into the North lands, he'd found what he was looking for and more. The greatest love, God's love, forgiveness, and His peace which passes understanding—a second chance.

There was great relief, and a great weight lifted from off his shoulders. Back at the tent, he carefully extracted his saddle and walked to the corral to saddle up Old Girl. On a log in the corral rested a saddle for the pony.

He got everything ready. He would not wake the young boy but wait until he woke of his own accord. They would have a talk and then leave to head back to the cabin. Henry put more wood on the fire and sat down to wait as the sun came up over the Black Hills.

He would head back to Jason, so the minister could teach *his son*.

Chapter Nine

Saturday, March 17, 1883

Twenty-three Years Later. The Glory B Ranch

The Glory B Ranch sat on the side of the northern Glass Mountains, looking visibly much as it had since Gracie and Press Stockton had married. Unless you knew where to look, it was almost indistinguishable from its background, except in the winter when smoke from the chimney isolated it from its surroundings. The trees had grown taller and the unseen part of the house had enlarged. Even the bunkhouse, below the main residence, had disappeared into the vegetation.

Several miles to the north of the Glory B Ranch was Fort Stockton at Comanche Springs. This fortification, along with others, had effectively blocked the annual late autumn raids of the Comanche tribe into Mexico.

The Indians' pathway had split at the Glass Mountains, going to either side and combining at the south end, toward The Big Bend in Southern Texas. This merger was just before Persimmon Gap. Riding through the Gap, they encountered the vast hot Chihuahuan desert of the Bend region and mile-high

Chicos Mountains, before crossing the Rio Grande River to raid in Upper and Central Mexico.

On their ride through The Big Bend, sharp conical peaks attested to the violent, fiery nature of former times. Now, when the Comanche rode through, the peaks were silent.

Their raids netted slaves, to keep or sell, animals, and food for the long difficult winters. Not much was left of a Mexican village when they attacked.

Fort Stockton was only one in several lines of forts built to make settlers, trails, and other movement safer in the West.

For a period of time, in the early 1860's, an uneasy peace settled in the lower Midwest area, but this didn't last long. The start of the Civil War soon involved the new settlers, forts, Union and Confederate troops in Texas, along with most Indian tribes.

The possession by each military of the many forts on the frontier seesawed back and forth between the North and South sides, and so did the many Indian tribe's allegiance.

When the Civil War was over, the unease in Texas continued. Agreements made with the tribes by the United States government were soon broken. There was no money or excess goods to honor the treaties made between them. Depression settled into the state.

From the reservations in Oklahoma, Indian raids across the Red River into Texas netted captives for the tribes. These were held for ransom. Within Texas, and especially The Staked Plains, the Apache, Comanche, and other tribes kept up raids for captives, horses, or food. This ended with the command of William

Tecumseh Sherman, the general in the Civil War who burned Atlanta. He stopped the raids for captives.

General Sherman was *for* the buffalo hunter on the vast prairies. With the mass killing of the plains buffalo, at first for food and then for profit, the Indian's daily existence became dire, especially in the winter. They decided to attack the buffalo hunters. This brought in Sherman's military. As the months passed, many members of the different tribes perished. They died of bullet wounds, disease, and starvation. Finally, realizing their situation must change, they returned to the reservations in Oklahoma.

After this bewildering period of time, with losses on every side, the new residents of Texas slowly overcame their mourning, realizing they could devote their time to building the newly developing state. Instead of living in fear and conflict, they could increase their own personal resources by rounding up herds of longhorn cattle and driving them to market—first to Missouri, then to towns in Kansas, and finally outlets in Texas for shipping East.

The West was even more open to settlement, because of the rapidly expanding network of railroads. This mechanical miracle, moved by water, heated by wood or coal to steam, hauled everything from cattle, wood, visitors, and supplies back and forth to the East. By 1881, its whistle could be heard across the rolling hills and waving grain into Abilene, Texas. Two years later, most Texas cattle drives were headed to Abilene, instead of north into Kansas, or to Fort Worth.

"P.T., do you want to ride over to the Johnston Ranch with me? You'll have to take your sleeping bag, because we'll be gone three days—three days of continuous moving in a cold saddle." The older man hunched his shoulders and shivered at the thought.

Press Stockton, Jr. looked at his fourteen-year-old son, Preston Stockton, III or P.T., as everyone called him, who was helping carry horse tack to the front of the barn.

The two had just come from a ride to one of their holding areas where the wild longhorn cattle were corralled, rounded up for a coming drive to market in Abilene, Texas. This last enclosed area was rapidly filling with cattle from the scrub brush and hilly area to the west of the ranch house, being one of three or four which would be combined in the near future for the trip. The ride had taken most of the day.

Press and his son stood in an open-front shed which was new and located nearest the ranch house on the hillside. The wooden barn, with its lean-to attachment, held the equipment and animals the family used on a daily basis, making going downhill to the bunkhouse area unnecessary.

From the barn for animals, P.T.'s new horse, Star, whinnied at him, pushing her head through an opening in her stall. He had dismounted only minutes ago and removed his saddle and bridle which he was in the process of stowing.

Press grinned, shaking his head. "She's definitely taken to you. What have you been feeding her?"

"I just give her an extra pat on the head, Poppa." He didn't add the apple slices from the cellar under the ranch house didn't hurt either.

"Yeah, and an extra lump of sugar no doubt." Press shook his head as Star whinnied again. "Do you want to go, Son?"

"Oh! Poppa. Yes!" P.T. skirted a two-seat buggy and hung his bridle on wooden pegs behind it.

His father hefted a saddle onto a rail, which ran alongside the buggy, leaned against it and rubbed his cold hands together. "This year when we round up the cattle, we've planned to go to Abilene, Texas to take the cattle to sell. The new railroad and stockyards outside of town provide a shorter cattle trail. That's a switch from our customary trail to Fort Worth. The Johnstons usually join us with their drovers, and this lets us take both herds together. We can leave more men at home to work the ranch."

"How many beeves are you taking?" P.T. walked toward his father, brushing a few stray pieces of hay from his pants in the process.

Press watched him come, noting that P.T. was almost shoulder to shoulder with him. His son was *sprouting up like an unwanted weed*. He grinned at the thought.

"Our herd is about two thousand longhorn cattle—the most we've trailed in a long time. Combined with the Johnston's we should have four to five thousand animals."

"How many men does it take to drive so many beeves to market?"

"Usually, twelve to fourteen drovers. Combining herds makes life easier for all of us. The last time I talked to Harry Johnston, and that's been awhile, he indicated he wanted to do the same this year—go with us when we go to Abilene." Press shook his head. "I haven't heard anything from him since. He usually sends one of his boys to follow up on arrangements."

"When are you plannin' to start our cattle drive?"

"After Easter. The time is close. I'm concerned somethin' may have happened at their ranch. I need to find out." They had moved to the front of the buggy, listening to the chilly wind whistle around the building. "I can't get over this continued cold. Usually, our weather has warmed by the first of April."

"What do you think has caused this cold spell?"

"It's not a cold spell, we just haven't gotten over winter. Our trip will mean chilly ridin' in the saddle."

"I'll go with you to the Johnston's. For sure. I can handle this weather."

"I don't doubt that a bit." Press stopped talking for a minute to sniff the air. "I think I smell Maria's cooking—cabbage soup. I'm hungry. How about you, Son? Let's head to the house and get a bite to eat. Race you!" Press clapped P.T. on the back and ran from the stable toward the front steps of the Glory B. Getting a head start, he outdistanced his son.

"Not fair, Poppa. You shoulda warned me."

"Sorry. I'll do better next time." He paused and grinned as P.T. caught up.

"When are we going, Poppa?" P.T. asked.

"Not tomorrow, but the next day. You need to start gettin' ready. The weather may be cold, snowy or rainy. Pack your clothes for any possibility."

"I will." P.T. hopped up the steps of the ranch house, grabbed the door, and opened it wide. "Here, let me hold the door for you."

From somewhere in the house a familiar voice was heard.

"Hurry in, you two," Maria called loudly. She had insisted on a small window in the hot kitchen. She usually kept it ajar even in the winter, causing a draft when the front door was opened. "I feel cold wind on my old bones."

"Hey, Maria," P.T. called, ignoring her comment and closing the door to the house. "What's for supper?"

Maria appeared at the kitchen door, waving a stirring spoon at him. "Never you mind. You clean up— *Señor.*" She demanded and made a face at her favorite charge.

Press laughed and headed for the parlor at the back of the house, giving Maria a quick sideways hug as he went by her. "We won't be long, Maria," he whispered.

~

The early morning mists hung in a wet silvery layer over the wide plains spread out below the porch of the Glory B. The tops of trees or cacti or large rocks appeared to float unattached to the earth if they poked above the thin white line. Somewhere, underneath this cold blanket and in the distance, a dove cooed, "good morning," to its mate.

Below, from the bunkhouse, the faint sound of men rising to start the day's chores, was heard. These worked close to the house in the garden and fields, or took care of a herd of horses used by the cow-boys, making sure they would be ready for the trail. Each man had a string of personal mounts he tended or which needed to be tended. Their whinnies along with the dove broke the quietness of the morn.

Intensifying from the east, the sun promised to warm the earth and dry off the damp ground, plus the low-lying fog. This couldn't come too soon for the small group standing by the porch steps of the house in the Glass Mountains.

"Gracie, where's P.T.? He's late. It's too cold to stand here and wait very long. We need to be moving." Press wasn't noted for complaining, but time was important for this trip.

"He said he's on the way. Wouldn't let me in his room. Said he'd taken care of packing himself. I have no idea what he's taking." Gracie clasped a long fur coat to her body. A crocheted hat hugged her head and covered her still unruly curls. "We could go back into the parlor by the fire," she suggested.

"Ooh!" Press shivered. "Maybe I should go see. Here take the reins of our horses." Press took the front porch steps two-at-a-time. Opening the front door, he almost knocked his son over.

P.T. had two large duffle bags which he dragged behind him. Jonathan Tipton Stockton, his oldest brother, followed.

"Son! What have you got in those bags?" Press looked incredulously at the bulging, brown sacks. He closed the front door before Maria could complain—then opened it and told Gracie to come in.

"I—I did what you said. I packed for any possibility."

Press might have laughed, but P.T. looked so earnest, and he'd genuinely tried to do what he'd been told.

Press looked up as Gracie joined them.

Looking over the situation, she stepped over the bundles and decided to let her husband handle it.

"Poppa, I tried to tell him he couldn't take all the gear he put in there, but he wouldn't listen."

"All right," Press said, noting the hurt expression on P.T.'s face. "Let's drag these back in the parlor and see what we can leave behind."

It took twenty minutes to sort through and reduce the contents into half. Not bulky, the ties would be easy to place over his saddle pommel.

"Now, P.T., we'll put what we've saved in both the bags. When you hang them on Star, they'll be balanced," said Jonathan, packing away and feeling sorry for his little brother. Tying the bags together, he demonstrated his words by putting them over his shoulder. "Here, I'll carry them for you. You get your bedroll and extra blanket." Jonathan put his arm around P.T. and walked him outside and down the steps. A smiling Press, with his arm around Gracie, feeling affection for his two sons and shaking his head, followed.

Maria stuck her head through the kitchen door, spoon raised, prepared to complain again. Seeing no one, she shrugged her shoulders and disappeared.

Outside, the group gathered around the two horses.

"Guess I learned something today. Won't do that again," P.T. said, after tying his bedroll and blanket to the back of his saddle. He stood putting his wool-lined leather gloves on.

"I did the same thing when I was your age when Poppa let me pack. Get on Star, and I'll hand the bags to you."

Press and Gracie stood by in amazement and watched this display of brotherly love between two siblings who were usually picking at each other.

While one brother helped the other, Press put his arms around Gracie and said goodbye. "Sorry to leave the clutter in the parlor, but we need to head out."

"I'll clean it up." Gracie nodded, putting her arms around his waist. "Actually, I'll just pile it in his room, and he can take care of it later."

"We should be back late Wednesday night."

"Be careful, dear. It's so cold. Are you going through town, picking your way down the Glass Mountains to the Johnston ranch, or ride down to the old Comanche Trail and follow it South?"

"If we had time, I'd go down the Glass Mountains and pass our old hideaway, but the Comanche Trail is the best choice—safer this time of year with no leftover ice and snow to worry about." Press kissed her.

"If you don't come back on time, we'll send someone to find you."

Press nodded. "See you in three days." He walked around and mounted his horse. Father and son set out down the hill toward the weathered bunkhouse. At the wooden structure, Winky Hall, P.T.'s best friend, stood leaning on the corner to send them off.

"Watch out for rattlesnakes, buddy," he laughed as the two riders came near.

"Yeah, I'm real worried." P.T. gave a smirk. "Rattlesnakes don't bother me," he said, turning in his saddle to wave goodbye to his mother.

"Winky, we'll see you in three days." Press rode off, leaving the two friends to say goodbye.

"Think you can make this trip without me, P.T.?"

"Aw, Winky. Go eat your breakfast." P.T. suggested and nudged Star. Squaring his shoulders, he rode after his father.

Chapter Ten

The Trip South and the Rattlesnake

From Fort Stockton, which was north of the Glory B, the old Comanche Trail split at the Glass Mountains. One part went to the west side and another traveled east following a rough road Southwest. The two parts connected again where the mountains ended before the Big Bend's Persimmon Gap. Their trip would not take them to the vicinity where the parts connected, but would stop short where the plains were flat and prairie dog towns inhabited the fields, below the five-thousand-foot-high mountains.

Bundled up in heavy coats and leather gloves, Press and P.T. urged their horses down the clearly seen path.

The way was rough and barely suitable for a horse pulling a sturdy wagon. Deep holes meant frequent stops or at least slowing down to just barely moving for a cart to traverse.

Press grinned, remembering the past when he and Gracie had left The Pinery on their first trip home. He had loved her the minute he'd met her and having her close was a dream he'd almost come to doubt. But circumstances changed all that. They hadn't driven this road, but the one they were on was just as bad. He'd made her a bed in the back of the wagon, because she was expecting her first child—not his, but her first husband, Jedediah's. Press grinned again and looked over at his last child. Gracie had given him some wonderful children.

He and P.T. rode side-by-side for several miles as the strong, cold wind blew sporadic clouds eastward across the blue sky and whipped dust in their eyes and faces.

"No way to get out of the wind. My nose feels like it's frozen," said Press, slowing his horse to a walk and pulling his bandana to his face. He wiped the dust from his eyes with the ends of the cloth.

P. T. did the same and asked, "How far is the Johnston Ranch, Poppa?"

"About twenty-five miles as the crow flies."

"What do you mean by, *as the crow flies*."

Press laughed. "It means, if I could fly like one of those black birds, I'd cover twenty-five miles in a flash, but since we must take a round-about method it's longer." After wiping the dust from his eyes, he urged his horse to walk a little faster.

"Oh." P.T. thought for several minutes before asking, "How much longer will we ride today?"

"There's a high cliff about five miles away on the right side of our ride. We'll stop there. The rock wall will give us protection from the chilly wind and the overhang will keep water off should the skies drop rain, sleet or snow." Press looked upward. "No clouds now. Are you getting tired, Son?"

"Oh no, Poppa. Just keeping up with the plans."

Press nodded. "That's always a good idea, when you're riding on a trail, to know the current day's plan—and the next day's plan," he added. "So, we'll be in the saddle most of the day tomorrow—part of it on the way to the Johnston ranch and part as we head back home."

"Poppa, we haven't passed a single house, today. Where is everybody?"

"Hopefully, one day, there'll be ranches all along today's ride. But not now. Once we get to the Johnston ranch, we'll be close to Peña Colorada Springs. When your grandfather first came here, this watering hole was a preferred stop for the Comanche. They used it when they rode through to The Big Bend on their way to rob the Mexicans."

"Why did they rob the Mexicans?"

"Because they were easy pickings. That's most of the reason."

"When did they quit going into Mexico?"

"They quit their raidin' maybe twenty-five years ago. Not too long before your mother and I were married. The arrival of the settlers and military forts, especially Fort Stockton and Fort Davis, upset their normal method of livelihood."

"Did you see them as they rode South?"

"No. My father did. He and the rest of the families at Mountain City, tried hard *not* to catch their attention as they rode though. Of course, Mountain City wasn't much then. There wouldn't have been enough of them to fend off a thousand Indians intent on a rampage for winter supplies. I've heard that recently, there's been an encampment of the United States Army at the springs."

"Will we be going to Fort Peña Colorada Springs?" The prospect of seeing men in uniform grabbed P.T.'s interest.

"Nope. We'll stop a few miles short."

"What's the Big Bend like? Have you been there?"

Press huffed a chuckle. "Yes. I've been there with my father. Come to think of it, we went a lot of places together." He nodded, thinking back. "P.T., the Big Bend is a desert, full of cacti, javelina, and the Chisos Mountains. The Chisos Mountains are two thousand feet over a mile high. It's hot in the summertime! Down in the desert you burn up, and in the Chisos you need a fireplace. Course the way the weather is this year, I doubt you could ride a horse or climb to the top. The trail is probably covered with snow and ice, if they've had any rain at all."

"I've never been that high—over a mile high? Poppa."

"Yes. Our Glass Mountains come fairly close. I remember My father and I walked our horses to Boquillas Hot Springs on the Rio Grande. I could use a little dip in the spring water right now. Might warm us both up. We passed symbols painted on the cliffs, like someone had been there many years ago. And, at the springs the rock is hollowed out so you can sit in the hot water and rest your weary bones from a day's riding."

"Do you think we can ride there together some day, like you and your father did?"

"Let's plan on it, Son. Maybe, we can camp out and see lots of coyotes and roadrunners."

"Now you're talking. Poppa can I go with you on the cattle drive to Abilene?"

The abrupt change in subject caught Press by surprise. He smiled remembering Gracie's observation, '*where his father goes, watch for P.T. to be his shadow.'* He immediately realized asking this question and anticipating the answer had been on P.T.'s mind for several days. "I've been thinking about the trail drive. Let's wait and see what's happened to Harry before I answer you."

"I'm ready to go help you."

"I know you are. Look! That's the cliff I was talking about." Press nudged his horse to the right and walked it about a half-mile, along a narrow path, lined by cacti and creosote bushes. The base of the imposing overhang stretched both north and south along the trail. Ashes from the fires of other campers lay in piles along the bottom edge.

They both dismounted and tied the reins of their horses to a scrub bush nearby. "Let's scout for firewood and get a fire going—warm up, before we unsaddle the horses. Can't see any wood close. Looks like we may have to go out into the bushes to find some."

"Which way do you want me to go?"

Press pointed to the trail beneath the cliff. That route seemed the safest. At least he wouldn't get lost, since most of the area looked the same. "Stay along the cliff. Watch for cactus spines."

P.T. headed out.

"And, P.T." Press called after his son, "look for a pocket of drinking water for the horses. That break in the cliff face," he pointed. The split went top to bottom, and he knew it wound several feet into the rock face. "Check it. It may be the best place to find water. I've found water there before. The sun doesn't hit the bottom of the passage and dry it up. Do you understand where I'm pointing?"

After seeing P.T. nod, Press headed for the rough road they'd just come from, walking across to look for kindling. He rummaged through the prickly pear cactus, watching out for scorpions and poisonous snakes—snakes with rattles.

Several minutes later, he walked back into their campsite with an armload of wood. P.T. hadn't returned.

Star whinnied and pawed at the ground.

"What is it girl? Do you miss P.T.?"

Press dropped the wood on the ground. Bending over, he picked up some small pieces, pulled out his knife, and whittled tinder to start a fire. From a small box in his saddle bag, he took a match and lit it. A few sticks later, he had a blaze going.

Star whinnied again, pawed the ground, and pulled at her reins tied on the bush. "Star, is something wrong?" he asked, knowing horses can sense danger. Was his son in trouble? "Okay, I'll go look for him. He's probably forgotten what I've sent him for and is poking his nose into nothing we need." Still, P.T. wasn't likely to veer from his mission. Press eyed the area where his son was last seen. Nothing moved.

Putting some larger pieces of wood on the flames to bank the fire, he decided to go look for P.T.

After walking several feet, he cupped his hands to his mouth and yelled, "P.T. Where are you?"

No answer.

Press walked to the mouth of the break in the cliff. "Son, are you up there?" His words echoed off the high walls.

Walking further in, he called again. This time he heard a faint, soft cry, "Yes, Poppa! Hurry!"

What had happened? Apprehension gripped Press like a vise as he hurried toward the sound of P.T.'s voice. What was wrong? Had he fallen and hurt himself? Then, another, more ominous sound came to his ears. He'd heard *that* many times before. He slowed his walk, knowing he needed to make less noise.

Rounding a curve, within the deep break in the cliff, he saw a sight which made him quickly suck in his breath and stop dead in his tracks. His son was backed up against the rock wall.

Making plenty of noise, a large rattlesnake was coiled up opposite him. A puddle of water lay between.

"I found the pocket of water, Poppa."

"Yes, you did and you *found* something else too. Be very still, while I think of a way to get you out of this. One quick move and that snake will strike." At the sound of his voice, he saw the snake's head dart quickly in his direction and jerk back toward his son. The rattles on the end of its tail moved faster, if that was possible.

Press's mind raced as he looked for a possible solution to the problem at hand. He put his hand on his gun which was still in its holster. Shooting the varmint wasn't a good idea. Bullets ricochet against rock. He might kill the snake, but he could also hurt P.T. or himself.

"I'm going to move slowly backward toward the mouth of the break."

"P—Poppa," P.T.'s voice broke. "You'll hurry back?!"

"You won't even know I'm gone. Pray hard, son."

Slowly, Press backed quietly down the rock corridor so he wouldn't disturb the snake. Out of the snake's sight, he turned around, noticing a stone ledge or shelf that protruded from the rock wall. It angled upward, going higher and higher into the cleft in the rock. The shelf started close enough to the rock's opening, so he could step on the surface. If he was careful, he could slowly inch his way up toward P.T. and the snake. He followed the ledge with his eyes. Increasing in height, it angled up the rock and continued as far as he could see.

If he could carry a rock up that ledge. *If* the rock was big enough to kill the snake or at least attract its attention until P.T. could run out of danger. *If* he could position it over the snake's head. *If* he did not lose his balance on the narrow ledge and fall himself—*if* was the question!

Gaining the entrance at the rock split, Press looked around for another solution. No wood to throw. He'd ruled out his gun. He didn't see any other way.

"You still all right P.T.?" he called loud enough for P.T. to hear.

"Yes, Poppa. But, hurry. I'm getting a cramp in my leg," came from the hollow. "It's starting to hurt, really bad."

"I have an idea, and I'll hurry as fast as it's safe." SAFE! P.T. could be bitten at any moment. Safety was not a question. Several rocks lay in the area, most too big to pick up. Selecting one he could just carry, Press headed for the ledge.

Next problem. The ledge wasn't very wide and the stone would pitch him forward. He took off his thick coat and threw it over the bushes at the entrance. He stepped on the rock shelf. With his back arched sharply against the cold, sometimes jagged wall, he tested the path, and started inching his way toward his captive son. The rough wall pulled at his shirt, and he felt it tear his flesh, but he couldn't stop.

Holding the rock off-center to his side, Press kept watch on his feet. Moving slowly, slowly, and deliberately, on the uneven surface of the rock, he was afraid to look up. Hurry, hurry! His heart said to his feet, but he couldn't. A cold sweat crept down his forehead, threatening to enter his eyes. He shook his head vigorously, hoping to sling the water off. This action made him instantly dizzy. Stopping, he closed his eyes, pushed his torn back against the wall and stood still for a moment.

"Poppa, I can see you," he heard P.T. say. "Be careful."

When Press opened his eyes, he wasn't too far from his endangered son and the angry rattlesnake. Just a few more careful steps in that direction.

"How's the cramp?" Press called. He started moving again, watching his feet.

"No worse, but no better either. Oh! Poppa be cautious." P.T. sucked in his breath. He slowly let it out as he added in clipped words, "The ledge looks crumbly above the snake."

To punctuate his son's words, some pebbles fell to the ground below and behind the reptile, which adjusted its striking position.

Growing more threatening, the snake jerked its head upward and back toward P.T. The snake's rattles shook more vigorously. The snake wanted out of there, and as far as it could see, that path lay through

P.T. The least little movement and the incensed snake would …

Press steadied his hands.

Time to implement the plan. He was directly over the enraged rattlesnake.

"Son, I'm going to drop this rock on the snake's head. I hope to kill it, but that may not happen. When it hits the snake, you run like greased lightning toward the mouth of the corridor. Remember, don't move until you see the rock hit the snake's head or body! I'm going to count to three and drop the rock. Ready?"

"Yes, Poppa."

"Here we go. One—two—three."

The rock fell vertically from Presses hand, followed by more pebbles from the ledge. The minute it hit the snake's head, P.T. took off and ran as fast as he could away from the snake, toward the entrance of the break in the rock.

Press sucked in a lungful of air and let it out in a loud rush. "Thank you, Lord!" he exclaimed, raising his arms and almost losing his balance. Without warning, more rocks fell from the ledge. He quickly moved down the rock path to where he could jump safely to the ground below. Standing there, he realized he was shaking from his son's close call with almost certain death.

P.T. ran to him, embracing him in a bear hug.

"Ooh, Poppa! I thought I was going to die." P.T. held on for several seconds. Then he ran for Press's coat.

Press put it on, not wanting his son to see his torn, bloody shirt. "I'm not surprised. I wouldn't want to be in a situation like that. But you were so calm. You handled yourself like a real cow-boy."

P.T. stepped back, waving his arms. A tear or two ran down his face. He brushed them away. "I saw the puddle of water and ran toward it. I wanted to see how deep it was. The snake was stretched out at the base of the ledge. I didn't notice it, until it moved and coiled into a strike position. My only hope was you, Poppa. I kept praying you'd come the whole time. That's the reason I was calm."

"You did right and now it's over. How'd you like fresh, rattlesnake steak for supper," he asked his son.

"That would be better than cold beef jerky, but I'm not sure I want to go into the rock opening again."

"Oh, come on. We're safe now, and we can go slowly since we know where it is. We'll face the danger together."

Press put his arm around P.T., and the two walked carefully back up the rocky path and approached the still twitching snake. The rock rested on the snake's head, holding it firmly to the ground. Press did not move the rock but took his hunting knife from its sheath on his belt.

"Why am I not moving the rock, son?"

P.T. looked at him and realized he knew the answer. "Because a snake can still strike you, even if it's dead."

"So, true. Many a man has lost his life because he didn't remember that one fact." His hand still shaking noticeably, Press cut the snake's body off where it went under the rock. Suddenly, the snake's tail quivered. Its rattles made noises, and its body curled tightly around his arm. A startled Press, pulled the snake loose an threw it hard against the rock wall.

P.T. jumped back.

The two stood there and watched the snake twitch. Press chuckled. "I don't understand why, but they still move for a while, even if they're dead." Reaching down he expertly cut off the rattles, handing them to P.T. "A souvenir," he said, "to show to Winky. Let's go back to our campfire."

"Are you going to take the snake?"

"Of course. It'll be a pleasure to roast rattlesnake steaks over the fire." Press bent and picked up the snake, letting it dangle from his hand.

The walk back to their camp helped both of them settle down.

"Ah, our fire has burnt down to just a few glowing ashes," observed Press. "Why don't you take care of it, and I'll work on the snake."

While P.T. put more wood on the coals and nursed the flames back to life, Press skinned the rattlesnake and dressed it. Using a small iron skillet as a cutting board, he cut steaks from the widest parts. "There's nothing better than rattlesnake cooked over an open fire, Son. Before we roast our supper, we need to take care of our horses."

The fire was blazing as they walked to the horses and took off the saddles, stashing them on flat rocks next to the cliff. Leading the horses by their bridles, they watered them in the pocket P.T. had found, avoiding the snake's head and remains.

Walking back outside of the opening, a flat area let them stake their rides to munch on the winter grasses.

"Time for us to eat, son. Go get us some sturdy mesquite sticks to hold our supper while it roasts."

Soon the smell of roasting rattlesnake permeated the area. With water from their canteens the two had no difficulty eating several pieces.

They ate their fill and wrapped the extra pieces in cloth to save for Sunday travel.

"P.T. let's stretch our canvas for our bedrolls first, and then we'll bring the horses closer to the fire." Press pulled a small hatchet and a piece of folded canvas from his saddlebags. He tossed the canvas on the spot where they would sleep, and the two headed for small trees nearby. Two poles of similar length with a notch on top would hold a rope stretched across. Stakes cut from the trees would anchor the poles. The canvas was stretched over the rope, an extra part to the front. The back touching the ground. The frontside was open to the fire. This way the fire would reflect off the canvas, keeping those inside a little warmer through the night. Being expert in making this makeshift shelter, the actual building didn't take long.

Satisfied with the results, the two went after the horses.

"Son, Star warned me earlier that something was wrong."

"She's a good girl, aren't you," P.T. said, stroking his horse's neck and soft, velvety nose.

The two walked back to the fire. "Why don't you choose a place to stake them. And do I have to tell you to be careful?"

P.T. laughed. "No, although it is getting darker and trouble may be lurking in the scrub brush." He winked at his father, chose a spot, and went to stake the horses.

While P.T. did this small chore, Press banked the fire with some large logs, and the two, fully clothed with coats on, burrowed into their bedrolls. P.T. started laughing. "Wait 'til I tell Winky what happened. I think I'll give him the rattles, and what will Momma say?"

Press replied, "Son, if I want this told, I'll tell it."

"Yes, Poppa," the corralled son answered.

"No use in stirring up a hornet's nest and worrying your mother.'

~

Before noon on Sunday, Press and P.T. rode up a long incline into the hills of the lower Glass Mountains, arriving at the sprawling Johnston ranch. Press knew everyone should be home, because there were no churches or other families nearby.

"Go knock on the door, P.T."

Press walked the horses to the hitching post next to the grey-planked barn. He stood there, looking at the expansive view of distant mounts, some looking like volcano tops, and the empty lower fields. Something was wrong. It was quiet, too quiet.

He walked back to P.T. and arrived just as Mrs. Johnston answered the door. Her daughter looked out behind the elderly lady. Emanating from the doorway was the smell of fried food cooking.

"Press, I been hoping you'd come. Did you know Harry died?"

"Oh, no! When?"

"About a month ago. He just took sick, and he was gone. We was all so busy after he died, trying to run the place and get the cattle ready to drive to Fort Worth. I couldn't break anyone loose to ride over your way to tell you. I'm sorry. I know you two was good friends." She dabbed at her eyes with her apron.

"Mrs. Johnston, I felt something was wrong. That's the reason I'm here. Where are your longhorns."

"Harry, Jr., Luke and Charlie decided to leave with some of our cow-boys about two weeks ago, so they could get back by my birthday." She grinned. "I told them you and Harry usually made plans to drive the beeves together. Not knowing what you two planned, and being in such a hurry, they went on. I hope they don't run into trouble. It's still awful cold outside."

"Leaving two weeks ago is a little early to drive the cattle to market." Press nodded, agreeing with her. "Snow melt from the mountains swelling the rivers and not enough new grass to maintain the cow's weight are the two biggest problems—although rains have been scarce so far this year. One thing's for sure, we've had enough cold weather."

"I know," she said. "And I've worried about that. Harry always said, *'either too much rain or not enough rain. Why can't it be just right.'*

She opened the door wider. "Won't you come in and eat. We've got plenty and your company will be appreciated. Is this boy P.T.?" She stood aside to let them pass.

P.T. nodded as he walked through the door.

"My, you've grown, Son," noted Mrs. Johnston. "You was just a little lad the last time I saw you, pulling a toy wagon your Grandpa Tipton made fer you.

A fire burned in the parlor fireplace. Press and P.T. headed for it. They took their gloves off and held their hands out to thaw.

"Rebecca and I'll set two more plates. We've got fried chicken for today's meal. Fresh kilt today. Come on to the table when your hands are warm."

~

"P.T. let's take a shortcut." Press said as they left the Johnston farm with their bellies full. "The detour cuts off a few miles. We may have to walk our horses, because we'll be going through a prairie dog town. It's new ground for you to see. We'll make camp a few miles after that. Late tomorrow afternoon we should see home."

"I'm ready, Poppa. I hope we don't see another rattlesnake."

"Me, too. Remember what I told you last night." Press shot a look over at P.T. who nodded. "Before the Johnstons bought this land, my father and I along with our cowhands would ride all over these hills. We rounded up longhorns, horses and any other animal he wanted to keep. That was before I married your mother."

"How did the cows and horses get here?"

"From what I've heard, the earliest ones were brought into Texas by the Spaniards from Mexico. The cattle and horses stocked their missions. When the missions closed down, the cattle were let loose and allowed to roam free for hundreds of years."

"Is that the reason for so many longhorns and wild horses here in Texas?"

"As good of one as I know. Course, I don't know everything. When the Stockton's and others started rounding up cattle, there were millions in Texas, like the buffalo. Now, the buffalo are gone."

"Are you saying the longhorns will be driven out?"

"I think we'll have to start a way of growing herds instead of rounding up wild ones."

"I still think there must be millions of longhorns."

They rode some minutes in silence.

"Will there be a problem starting our drive since the Johnstons have already left?"

"No, I hope your brother, Jonathan, will be through with the roundup when we get back and all the branding done. The longhorns should be ready to move from Bull Elk Hole northeast to Abilene. We're taking a few gentle cows to Abilene for Ruby Eliza and Sarah. I think Chester, their handyman, will take care of them."

"Am I going to get to go on the drive, Poppa?"

"Looks like it, son. We'll need all the help we can get since the Johnstons won't be going with us."

"Yippee," yelled P.T.

Press looked over at him and grinned. This youngster had no idea what he was getting into—how hard it was to move about 2,000 head of stubborn beeves to market—the dirt, smell, mud, cold …

"A cattle drive sounds like fun, but you'll find out it isn't."

"I understand, Poppa."

Press just shook his head, remembering himself as a young boy several years earlier. He'd gotten his experience the same hard way.

This was the year Press had determined to put Jonathan in the lead as Trail Boss. At twenty-two, he was capable and experienced. He'd started at the same age as P.T. and had eight years of trail riding under his belt. During this time, he'd experienced everything the trail could throw at him. At least, Press hoped so.

Chapter Eleven

March 25, 1883, Easter Sunday

"Gracie," called Pastor David Ormand. "I may be a little late for dinner, today." Sunday dinner at the Stockton's was a weekly given.

Gracie turned around on the top step of the church portico and waited for him to catch up. His slow forward movement told of his advancing age. A noticeable limp came from a bullet wound in the Civil War which damaged a muscle.

Gracie took his outstretched hand and hugged him. "Pastor, you can be late anytime. If necessary, Maria will keep your food in the warmer. Is someone sick in the congregation?"

"No. My cat had kittens this morning before I left for church," he grinned sheepishly. "I need to check on her and her litter."

"I understand. Are these some of Ticksey's descendants?"

"Yes. Do you want one … *please*?"

"I might. That means Ticksey has great-grandkittens." Gracie laughed at the idea. She added more seriously, "You preached a wonderful sermon this morning."

More people left the church, saying goodbye as they bypassed the couple on the steps.

He nodded. "Jesus's death means life for us, doesn't it? That's the amazing hope I have, since I'm getting up there in years."

Gracie hugged him again. "You've got many more years, Mr. Ormand."

"Only God knows." He nodded. "Jerusalem, during the first days of Easter, wouldn't look anything like this beautiful, sunshiny Texas day—not until the tomb was empty," he said and added, "which was on the third day, of course."

Gracie took one step down, looking at the blue, cloudless sky. "No. Today's not anything like the Bible depicts of that evil time. Jerusalem's darkest hour and the darkest day on earth was when the Savior hung on the cross, dying for the sins of everyone who's ever lived in the world."

"Yes, and He died for those who'll never acknowledge Him, too. I grieve for them."

"I'm so happy He gave me a chance to know Him."

"Not only do you know Him, but He's given you a wonderful husband and six lovely children who have experienced His love. You have a lot to be thankful for, my dear."

"You're right." Gracie looked toward the road in front of the church. "Speaking of husband, he's sitting patiently in the buggy waiting for me. I'll head on. Come when you can, Pastor." Gracie waved as she walked away, thinking she'd never get used to calling him Pastor. He'd always been Mr. Ormand to her, ever since their fateful meeting at the Harpeth River outside of Nashville, Tennessee. She was following her father at a distance, determined to go to Texas with him. She sighed, but that was a long time ago—over twenty-five years. Her life had changed since then.

Press called from the buggy as she approached. "Is Jonathan coming?" he asked, motioning toward the church.

Gracie looked around for their oldest male child.

Jonathan stood on the top step she'd vacated, talking fervently to the Pastor. His girlfriend stood waiting at the bottom. What were they scheming? David Ormand was explaining something. Then he nodded and turned to lock up the church. Jonathan hopped down the steps and took his girlfriend's hand, heading for the waiting buggy.

"Poppa, sorry I held you up," he said, taking Joanna's gloved hand and helping her into the buggy's back seat. "Where's P.T.? He told me he was going to ride with us."

"No. He, Winky, and Benjamin are in a footrace toward home. The rest went ahead with Mary Elizabeth and her husband, Peter. If we don't hurry, they'll beat us." Press answered. He flicked the horse's reins and they were off with a jolt.

~

"Dinner's served *Señora* Gracie," Maria said. She turned and left the sitting room, walking much slower at sixty-two years of age. Yesterday, Press had encouraged her to go home and rest, telling her there were plenty of women to cook our Easter dinner. But she had refused. "*Señor* Press, no messin' with my kitchen!" and she meant it, often running anyone *messin' with her kitchen* out with her favorite wooden stirring spoon, waving in her hand.

Gracie watched her go and smiled. She loved Maria. Without her she couldn't have raised the six children, sitting around the parlor. Wait! She was missing one. Where was Benjamin?

"P.T., where is your brother?" she asked.

Preston Stockton, III or P.T., looked over at her. They hadn't intended to name a child after Press, but when the little one was born, with the same tiny, facial features, they couldn't resist. He was the youngest child at fourteen.

"Probably in the library with his nose stuck in a book." P.T. said this with a little bit of brotherly disdain in his voice.

"Nothing wrong with book learning or reading, son. You could use some more yourself." Press got up from his chair and waved. "I'll get him, sweetheart." His cow-boy boots echoed down the hallway toward the library.

"Is no one hungry in this house?" At Gracie's question, everyone got up, including her oldest son Jonathan and his girlfriend. They all headed for the dining room. The smells coming from Maria's kitchen were causing everyone's stomach to grumble.

"How was your trip from Abilene?" Gracie asked Doctor Sarah Cobb, her long-time friend from Nashville. She was a doctor in the growing town, aided by Gracie's daughter, and first born, Ruby Eliza Stockton. Ruby Eliza was her nurse. Since moving her practice three years ago from Fort Worth, Sarah always came for Easter.

Sarah walked across the room and linked arms with Gracie. She was followed by her name-sake and shadow, sixteen-year-old, Sarah Susannah Stockton.

"I'll be absolutely thrilled when the railroad decides to go in different directions, although I do hear the section to Marathon is complete on the Western side of the Glass Mountains." She shook her head, laughed and continued, "The stagecoach from Abilene to Fort Stockton and beyond hasn't improved its ride much over the years."

"No, it sure hasn't," agreed Ruby Eliza, grimacing. "The potholes seem to grow along with the scrub brush and cacti."

Doctor Sarah frowned at Ruby Eliza and continued, "But, unlike Ruby Eliza, I think the one saving grace is the prairie. It's so beautiful in the spring. The grass is turning lime-blue green, waving in the wind, and stretching as-far-as-the-eye-can-see." She laughed, again. "That's why I love spending Easter with you at the Glory B. The scenery takes my mind off the bumpy road, and the fact that I can't go home to Nashville. You are my family."

From behind her, Ruby Eliza joined in, "And the pillows we sat on helped a lot, didn't they boss."

"Now, Ruby Eliza, you didn't have to give that secret away." Sarah grinned.

"I suppose your patients will miss you." This from Gracie's daughter, Mary Elizabeth, who sat at the table with her husband, Peter. Mary was expecting a baby in September—the first grandchild.

"Yes, maybe they will. But it's been a quiet winter for medical problems—no cholera, smallpox, or yellow fever to speak of."

"We did have a sickness we couldn't identify, didn't we Doctor Sarah?"

"Yes. The illness caused a high fever and rash, but all our patients pulled through. Thank goodness we had no deaths from it, although we came close," Doctor Sarah said, as she pulled out a chair to Gracie's right and sat down. "Sarah Susannah, sit here," she said, indicating the place next to her.

"That one was a puzzle. We couldn't connect it with anything in our medical books," commented Ruby Eliza nodding as she sat down to Gracie's left.

Doctor Sarah leaned over and whispered loudly. "I think I'll have another doctor or nurse in my office in a few years." She patted her seat mate's arm.

Sarah Susannah smiled. "I wish it were tomorrow," said Gracie's youngest daughter. Why she liked blood and runny noses Press and Gracie could not fathom.

Press and Benjamin arrived. Press sat at the head of the table and Benjamin went to the last vacant seat.

This was Maria's signal. She entered the room and poured chilled tea into the glasses on the table. Next came the rolling cart, with plates of food and her sliced canned peaches in dessert bowls. She busied herself with placing the food, with a flourish, before those seated at the table.

There was no way to be choosy with her. The family ate everything she brought or suffered the consequences—a gentle tongue lashing in Spanish.

The cart disappeared back through the kitchen door, the chatter continued, and everyone started to eat.

The table was full except for the empty chair belonging to Pastor David.

Ruby Eliza cut off a slice of peach. "I assume Poppa will be heading North with the beeves soon." She forked the piece into her mouth. "Yum! Yum! There's nothing in Texas like Maria's canned peaches."

Those at the table nodded, agreeing with her.

Answering her question, Gracie replied, "Monday week, Ruby. He'll be on the trail. He's bringing the milk cows you requested."

"We can use them. So many people are coming into the area because of the railroad extension west of Fort Worth. Puts a lot of pressure on the town's resources. Abilene's really grown in the last three years," she responded. "The expansion of the Texas and Pacific Railroad causes towns to pop up everywhere.

Jonathan joined in the conversation. "The roundup's over and the branding's done. We've been getting everything else ready for several days. Looks like we'll be taking two wagons besides the chuckwagon this year." He pulled out a large piece of paper from his pocket. "Because of the cold weather, we're loading dry wood and kindling into one, plus extra food supplies and our tents. We don't want to get caught without a fire and shelter in wet, freezing conditions."

"At least going to Abilene, Texas, instead of Dodge City or Abilene, Kansas or Fort Worth, will make the drive much closer and safer." Gracie added this because she was always happy to see the men in their group come back in one piece.

"We can't go to Abilene, Kansas, since they passed the law making it illegal to drive longhorns to the railhead there," Press added, forking a piece of tender steak into his mouth.

Mary nodded, agreeing with her father. "Poppa says it'll be the whole state next. Thank goodness for the Texas and Pacific Railroad in Texas," she said, echoing Sarah's words.

"Yes, Momma." Jonathan looked at Gracie, knowing she worried until the droving crew returned. "I'm figuring on about ten to fifteen miles a day. We'll arrive in the town about thirty-five or forty days after we leave. That is, barring problems on the trail. Since it's closer, we won't have as much time to get into trouble."

"There's talk of fences being built north of here. Have you heard anything about them?" This from Mary's husband Peter.

"No, not a word," answered Jonathan.

"Did you hear from Caleb?" Gracie asked Press. Because the Johnston's weren't driving their beeves with the group, they needed more help. One of the twins from the Butterfield Overland Mail had stayed in the Fort Davis area with his family. A letter sent on the stage asked for his help.

"Yes, he's coming and he's bringing his oldest son, Thomas. They'll arrive here next Thursday."

"I can't wait to see him again, and I know Cephas will be overjoyed to know his brother will be here to help," Gracie replied.

Cephas came to work at the Glory B after his brother had married.

Gracie looked around the table. Her family was here. Most of it. She dreaded another long cattle drive. She never felt easy until they were out of harm's way, and back here on the ranch at the Glory B. She started eating, listening to the friendly talk around the table.

The continuing conversation was interrupted by the appearance of Pastor David Ormand, who was now minister of the church in Mountain City—the new name for the town. Maria appeared with drink and food as soon as he sat down at the table.

Pastor David greeted everyone. He looked across the table at Jonathan and his girlfriend and said bluntly, "Are we going to have a wedding soon, children?"

Jonathan, the most serious cow-boy in the group, scraped his chair back from the table and stood to his feet. Being addressed so directly, his face reddened, and he stammered when answering. "P-Pastor Ormand and everyone here, the answer is yes. We will have a wedding as soon as we return from the cattle drive. Joanna said yes!" Now it was Joanna's turn to be embarrassed.

Stunned, at the quickness of this announcement, Press and Gracie stared at each other.

When he recovered, Press stood and congratulated Jonathan, reaching to shake his hand. "Son, I'm proud of you. I think you've made a great choice for a wife." He nodded and beamed at Joanna who smiled back.

Only a few steps and Gracie was around the table to give Joanna a hug. "I can't say this wasn't expected," she told her. "But, I'm so glad it's official." She gave the girl a kiss on the cheek. "You'll be a welcomed member to our family, and we'll have a wedding to plan."

Gracie returned to her seat and sat down, realizing in the excitement her hunger pains had vanished. She picked up her fork and picked at her food.

Looking around, she remembered the first time she'd sat in this room. The peaceful painting of the horses grazing by the flowing river still hung on the wall. Today, the freshly polished silver tea service wasn't the only item on the cherry-wood buffet. She'd placed the brown crockpot with her wooden and metal serving spoons beside it. Both of these heirlooms were from grandmothers she never knew—one from New York on the Stockton side and one from Cades Cove in the Smoky Mountains on the Tipton side.

Thoughts came quickly. There were missing faces. But, this day at the table, was for present family. Tears stung her eyes as she looked at each person. Press caught her eye. He smiled and winked. She wondered if he was thinking the same thing.

The table was full—full of everything a family should enjoy.

Chapter Twelve

A Walk Down Memory Lane

Easter was always a glorious time at the Glory B Ranch. Even though the weather could be cool or downright cold, small green leaves were out on the hardwood trees. Yellow daffodils flourished in patches around the ranch house, sometimes in the midst of snow. And the fruit trees—apples, pears, and peaches were full of pink and white blossoms against the green of the pine tree forest.

With the addition of six, rambunctious children, the house had expanded over the years. Press had added a library and six small rooms, in a new wing—one for each of the brood. Privacy, for their children, was important to them. Now some of them were empty.

"Wife, are we going to take our customary Easter afternoon walk?" Press asked. They'd taken a nap after their Sunday dinner. After rising, she had walked back to check on their guests who were playing checkers and cards in the library. He sat in her rocking chair pulling on his boots.

"Yes," Gracie yawned. "I'm ready to go."

Press looked around the bedroom. "Do you miss the cradle that used to sit in this room?"

Gracie's eyes opened wide. "*Don't* get any ideas, Mr. Stockton."

"Oh, no." Press laughed and held up his hand. "I was just thinking maybe we'll have use for it again—soon."

They were walking out into the bright sunlight which shone over their private patio as Gracie answered. "You mean we may be keeping Mary and Peter's, as grandchildren."

"Yes." He answered, as he stepped off the patio. "We might fill up the empty rooms with *grand* children."

Gracie laughed. "Do you miss the patter of little feet?" she asked, knowing he loved children.

"Yes, I miss them running down the hall to our bedroom and jumping into the middle of our bed. I miss them playing outside on our patio, laughing and yelling. I miss them sitting quietly while you or I read a story or the Bible to them."

"We may have more, when Jonathan gets married."

"The sooner the better." He started laughing again and continued to walk in the direction of Mountain City. "I thought Jonathan was going to melt onto the floor. What about David being so direct? It's not like him."

"No, it's not." Gracie replied. "I don't have an answer, but I do think it's about time those two decided to tie the knot."

Press stopped and entwined his fingers with mine. "Have I told you lately that I love you, Gracie Tipton Bailey Stockton?"

"Not today, you haven't, and you've not kissed me this afternoon either."

Press took care of the kiss. "I love you more than the day I married you. I think in the Bible, it's called a maturing love."

As he held her, Gracie realized she still thrilled at his touch. "You're the only man I've spoken love too, except my father. I think God was in our meeting and match."

"I think He's been with us for many years, my love."

"Twenty-four years in October," Gracie sighed, standing back and looking at him. "Really, would you do it over?" she teased. At forty-nine, he was as handsome as the day she had walked out of the church on his arm. Now, he had just a touch of gray at the temples and a few more well-deserved wrinkles from squinting in the Texas sun. She put her arms around him, gave him a firm hug, and put her head in the nape of his neck.

"Ouch. Careful of the back."

"Sorry. Is it better?" She released her hold somewhat.

"Yes. And to answer your question—every day, maybe twice a day," he grinned.

"I love you, Press and I love our family—the beautiful children you've given me—the shelter of this home and our church. This is what I wanted as a sixteen-year-old girl, heading west from Nashville. I couldn't have dreamed *this*, even if I'd tried."

Hand-in-hand, they continued their walk toward town. Each year, the path went down main street and around the church—in a walk of remembrance. They returned on a trail in the midst of the pines to the back patio.

Why? To see what, if anything, had changed during the year and to talk yearly things. Out of the corner of her eye, Gracie looked at her husband. He reminded her so much of her father …

Thirty minutes of strolling and they stood in the heart of Mountain City.

"Let's go to the church," Press said.

But he made a detour.

Walking on beyond the church was an enclosed area where those deceased in Mountain City were buried. They came to the cemetery, opened the gate and went inside. There were no new graves, but Gracie knew where he was going. Press's father had died a year before hers. They stood for a few minutes in silence.

"We were privileged to have great fathers, Gracie." He bent and pulled some weeds from around his father's tombstone.

She nodded. "I miss both of them. They should have lived to be a hundred."

A few more steps brought them to her father's grave. Tears burned in Gracie's eyes. "Pa always said he wouldn't fight in another war. I guess he did in a way. Runnin' supplies as a teamster to Fort Davis from Fort Stockton to help the Union. It wasn't the Confederates that shot him and Mr. Ormand. Renegades, an off-shoot of Quantrill's Raiders, they say, shootin' at anything Union, scavenging off the land and people."

"Too bad the Raider's didn't remain in Missouri and Kansas. Texas didn't need any more trouble. At least, when they did come, *most* of them stayed in East Texas."

"I call them bushwhackers. The group here in southwest Texas didn't have allegiance to any side. They just killed for the sake of killing. Yes, they killed Pa and left Mr. Ormand for dead."

Press and she didn't notice David Ormand until he spoke. "Whenever their bellies needed food or anything else, they took it. Course the settlers fought back and got murdered in the process." Now thinking, he rubbed his upper hip. "Gracie, I played dead. That's the reason they didn't finish me off."

Sensing the fact, we were watching him, he grinned self-consciously. "Just thinkin' back to that time, the old wound aches. I miss your Pa, Gracie. We were good friends—best friends. I'll see him again someday," he nodded, relishing the thought.

"Great sermon, Pastor. If not for Easter, there'd be no second seeing," Press answered.

"So true, Press. Guess I'll mosey on to the house. Just saw you two in the cemetery. Thought I'd join you for a moment. I left the children playing checkers. Benjamin was reading a book, as usual. See you at church tonight."

Press and Gracie continued past Pastor Marshall's and Julia's grave. "So many of the older ones are gone," he noted. "So many who shaped my life."

Gracie remembered thinking Julia was the mother she needed, during her first stay at the Glory B. She'd always love and be grateful to her. She had helped birth all their children.

Press laughed. "I'll never forget Julia asking about morning sickness when you were expecting Ruby.

When you said you hadn't had much and she said, *'Then you're going to have a little girl.'* You asked her how she knew."

"She said, *'because boys make you sick,'* and Pastor Marshall exclaimed, *'Julia!'*"

"She tried to explain her comment and finally gave up. When you two went to the bedroom to discuss things further, we both laughed and laughed. Course the pastor was somewhat embarrassed at the whole exchange."

Press and Gracie laughed again, remembering the conversation.

"Do you ever wonder what happened to Hurricane? He left in the dead of night after coming to tell you of Jedediah's death."

"Occasionally, he comes to mind, but only when I look at Ruby Eliza. I wonder if he's still drinking? Will we ever know? I continue to pray for him."

Press just shook his head.

We resumed walking to the back of the church to a marker saying, WOOLY and one saying TICKSEY. What more fitting place for them to lay than in the cemetery where those who loved them were placed. Press had made little boxes for them, and we'd buried them with the children present. P.T. was only a baby during this time.

"Lots to think about Gracie."

Gracie nodded, with tears burning her eyes again. "Pastor Ormand has new kittens—some of Ticksey's descendants. Should we get one?"

"That's entirely up to you, Sweetheart."

We headed back through the pines toward the Glory B, strolling slowly, hand-in-hand. We passed the trail to Moses Mountain. "What do you think, dear," Press said, motioning toward the path.

"I *think* we'd better get back home and eat supper. We'll just have time to get to church."

~

Jonathan stood on the patio as we approached. "I wanted to explain the Pastor's comments at dinner," he said.

"Good!" His father replied. "We've been talking about his abruptness."

"After church, I told Pastor David that Joanna and I were to be married and there'd be a wedding after the cattle drive. I explained I didn't just want to get up at dinner and tell everyone—would he ask me if there was to be a marriage so I could respond. I realize he could have been gentler about the question. Anyway, he got the job done."

"I'm glad to know why his words were so blunt. He's so composed and kind and not like that at all." Press nodded. "Your mother and I think Joanna is a really nice girl. You two get along really well. We'll be happy to have her as our daughter-in-law."

"Have you decided on a place to live?" Gracie asked.

"I was hoping Poppa would let me build a house over in Panther Hollow, above the fourth watering hole. You remember, we talked about how the place was level enough with a view of the cattle fields below. It would be easy to watch a large herd from there."

"Good choice, Son. When we get back from the cattle drive, we'll ride over and check out the ground. Take a look-see. You mother and I want you to own the land. We'll designate the area and make a deed. Do it up proper."

"Thanks, Pa. I'd like to own part of the Glory B Ranch. I think Granddad Stockton would like this too."

"I agree with you, Dad would be glad to have his grandchildren own his ranch. There's also something I've been meaning to tell you. I want you to take over the trail drive this year as boss. With eight years of riding herd, I think you're ready."

"I am ready, Poppa. And, I'll make you proud. You're going, aren't you? I might need some advice."

"Oh, yes, I'll be around should you need a voice of experience or encouragement, *and your mother also*." Press raised his eyebrows and looked at me. "Will you go, Gracie? I'll fix you a comfortable bed in one of the wagons we're taking. It'll be like reliving your ride to The Pinery, years ago."

"What!" she said, astonished at his words. Gracie had never been on one of the cattle drives. Young children had kept her at home.

"Gracie, we'll need every hand we can get. How about it? You can help Jorge. He's getting old and slowing down. He insists on going this time. I think this is his last trip on our drives."

"Let me think on it. We'd better get washed up and head for supper or we'll be late for church."

Jonathan left to tell Joanna of his new position on the drive, and Press went to tell the others in the library.

Later in church, Gracie wondered. Could she actually go on a trail drive? Riding on a horse for several hours a day or on a wagon seat did bring back memories of years back when she and her Pa had left Nashville for The Pinery in the Guadalupe Mountains. Those were fun days. Yes, and hard days. She was older now—forty-two didn't seem too elderly. *Why not? Yes, Gracie. Why not!*

Chapter Thirteen

Reinforcements Arrive

It was late afternoon when Caleb and Thomas Carter were spotted riding up to the Glory B. P.T. came flying into the back parlor to announce their arrival.

"Go get Poppa and tell him Caleb has arrived, Son." Gracie instructed P.T., motioning him, with a wave of her hand, back down the hall toward the front of the house. "Run to the bunkhouse and tell Cephas, also."

Cephas was Caleb's twin brother.

Since the two were expected, everyone had stayed close to the ranch house, so they would be around and greet them when the arrivals appeared.

The bang of the front door meant P.T. was on the way. Gracie headed to the front of the house, opening the door she stood on the front porch, watching her visitors as they rode up the hill to the house.

When they got close enough, she called, "Caleb, I can't believe it's you."

"I'm not a ghost, that's for sure," he said back as he dismounted his horse and tied it to the hitching rail at the front of the house.

He took the front steps, two at a time and gave Gracie a big bear hug.

"And who's this?" she asked.

"This here's Thomas. At eighteen, he's my oldest." Caleb beamed at his son. Thomas was a tall, thin young man with wavy, brown hair. He looked more like Cephas than his dad.

"How many more are there?"

"Three more, and we're hopin' for another before Christmas. We're still trying for twins."

Gracie had to laugh. "A Christmas gift, huh?"

"Yes. That'd be nice." He nodded his head. "A young boy who said he was P.T. passed us. Said he was headed for the bunkhouse."

"Yes, he's our youngest, and he's gone to get your brother and Press. The others are out in the fields, herding longhorns." Gracie opened the door. "Come on in. We have a fire in the fireplace."

"Thank you, Gracie. It'll be nice to warm up a bit, won't it, Son?"

Gracie closed the door and indicated two chairs for their comfort. She sat down in another, facing them.

"It's been a long time since you were at the Glory B."

"Twelve years, I guess. Brought Cephas and took home a milk cow. Some exchange, if you ask me." He laughed. "How is my brother?"

"About the same. He's found one of the ranch hands to hassle. Reminds me of the good days at The Pinery. Great memories."

Caleb nodded, agreeing with her. "Yes, and you haven't changed a bit, Gracie. Still got that curly hair. Are things pretty much back to normal here? The Panic of 1873 lingered on in the Fort Davis area. Thank goodness for a garden and the milk cow you sent us.

Off and on, I made a little spending money at the fort. Blacksmithing and helping with shoeing the horses, when the military was there. Things are much better now. I set up my own blacksmithing shop, and my wife sews for people on a Singer Model 13. We bought it from Col. Seawell's wife before they left Fort Davis. She sews all our clothes and some for others as well." He pulled at the shirt he was wearing. Obviously, he was proud of his wife.

Gracie nodded. "Longhorns brought little money during the depression. Prices are higher now. Press hopes the drive will be more profitable this year."

"I'm running a few myself. Brought 'em with me."

The door opened before he could say more. Pulling off his hat, Press entered the front parlor with Cephas and P.T. following on his heels.

"Caleb, so glad to see you." Press extended his hand. "How was your trip?"

"Great." Caleb arose and shook hands.

Press stepped back to give Cephas a chance to greet his twin.

Cephas opened his arms and gave his brother a hard hug, lifting him clear off the ground.

"Whoa, brother," Caleb protested, struggling to get down. He pulled in the air his brother had just squeezed from his lungs. "I'm not made out of rock."

"I'm just glad to see you, brother. Don't complain." Cephas stood back at arm's length and looked his brother over. "You've not changed much; except you've lost most of your hair."

"I wondered how long it'd take for you to comment on that. I told my wife not more'n five minutes. I think you beat my estimate."

Everyone in the room roared with laughter. These *were* old times all over again.

"Please, sit down, everyone." Gracie waved her hands at chairs in the room. They all found a seat. P.T. went to put another log on the fire.

"Press, this is Thomas, my oldest child. He's been ridin' herd with me in Chihuahua. And, we've been practicing with my small herd, haven't we, Son. I think he'll make us a good hand."

Thomas stood, crossed the room and shook hands with Press. "Good to meet you, sir."

"We're glad to have you join us, Thomas," responded Press.

At that moment, Sarah Susannah came into the room—hat on and riding gloves in her hands. "Anyone for a ride into Mountain City?" she asked, looking around at the new visitors. Her eyes lighted on Thomas. She smiled at this handsome lad with the dark, curly hair.

He greeted her. "Hello, I'm Thomas."

"I'm Sarah Susannah."

P.T. broke into the conversation, if you could call six words a conversation. No way was his sister going to take away a potential pal. "Thomas, how'd you like to go see my new horse, Star? Poppa's planning on me riding her on the drive."

Thomas looked at his father.

He nodded. "Go ahead, Son."

"P.T., why don't you take Caleb's and Thomas's horses with you and put them in the barn in the stalls next to Star. Unsaddle the horses. Make sure all the animals have feed and water."

"Okay, Poppa. I'll make sure everyone's fed and watered," replied P.T., as the two boys rushed out the door, followed by Sarah Susannah.

"Be back at dark." Gracie called just as the door slammed again. "Supper will be ready." She wasn't sure if they heard her or not. "No use in preachin' about slamming doors around here." Gracie sat wondering what the conversation was like outside between the young people.

Press laughed and got up from his chair. "Caleb, let me show you around the Glory B. We may ride over to see the longhorns. It's not too far, because we've got them all corralled fairly close. My son, Jonathan, is with the herd. He'll be trail boss this year. I've retired." Press grinned. "Cephas, go with us. You two can catch up on old times." Press put his hat on and headed for the door. "If we hurry, Caleb, we'll catch the boys before they unsaddle your horse. Gracie, I promise we'll be back before dark."

"You'd better," Gracie pointed her finger at him.

"Be careful that thing might go off, my love. Come on, Caleb. I sure am glad you're here. We've not changed much since …"

Press shut the door softly as he went out. At least, Gracie had trained one.

~

Catching up at dinner was fun with Cephas and Caleb trading jabs at each other.

"Ruby Eliza was here on Sunday for Easter. She and Doctor Sarah Cobb left on the stage for Abilene the next day. The doctor couldn't be gone long from her patients, and Ruby is her nurse. Do you remember me talking about Sarah Cobb? She was my friend from

Nashville. She has a practice at the new railroad town."

"You mean there's women doctors now?" Caleb asked. "I bet she was the first."

"No, no," Gracie replied. "Sarah said there's a few more. Sarah went to Geneva Medical College in New York State where the first woman doctor graduated. Her name was Elizabeth Blackwell. Blackwell graduated head of her class—a very smart lady. Sarah saved her money and went to the same school. She wanted to be one of the best doctors around."

"I just can't believe there's women doctors," Caleb shook his head.

"What's wrong with women doctors," Cephas asked. He was on Sarah's side because she'd given him a tin of salve for a burned arm. He'd burned it on a red-hot horseshoe which slipped from his tongs and flipped from the anvil when he hit it with a hammer. He didn't have a scar.

"Nothing, I guess. I-I've just never seen one," his brother replied.

"They ain't any different, brother. Gracie's daughter, Sarah Susannah, has a hankerin' for the same profession," Cephas informed his brother a bit haughtily, indicating his subject and his devotion by waving his hand in her direction.

Sarah Susannah sat a bit straighter in her chair. Press often said she was a chip off the old block—meaning Gracie. Of course, most of the children were. Leaders everyone.

After Easter, with their visitors gone, they'd played the game of changing seats at the dining table. Jonathan was riding herd at Bull Elk Hole, so he wasn't present, nor was his intended, Joanna. She was with her parents.

After checking those sitting around the table, Gracie looked over at Sarah Susannah who was smiling, *rather pointedly,* across the table at Thomas. Her single daughter sat almost straight across the table from him. *He was smiling back!*

What was this? Gracie was speechless—unusual for her. The conversation continued, but it lost her.

She caught Presses attention and rolled her eyes with a small nod toward their daughter.

A slight nod and grin meant he saw what she saw.

Gracie sighed. Wasn't there enough happening without dealing with a daughter being attracted to a young man she hardly knew? *Alright, Gracie. Could your Dad have thought the same thing when he realized you were attracted to Jedediah? Sarah Susannah is the age you were when you left Nashville with your Dad, and she's soon to have a birthday! Just like you did!*

Gracie sat thinking. She sure was happy her daughter wasn't going on the drive.

Chapter Fourteen

Talking Strategy for the Trail Drive

On Sunday afternoon, instead of their usual walk to town, Gracie and Press hauled their boxed clothes and personal supplies outside and packed them into a wagon for the trip from the Glory B to Bull Elk Hole, where the herd waited for the start of tomorrow's drive.

P.T., Thomas, Caleb, and Cephas did the same.

Remembering something he'd forgotten, Press headed quickly down to the shed closest to the house. Everyone stood milling around, waiting for him to return.

At the last moment, Maria came running from the ranch house and down the front steps with a picnic basket full of cooked items.

"Fried apple pies, *Señora* Gracie, I fixed enough to last two or three days," she said, breathing hard and handing the heavy carrier over to her mistress. The smell of cinnamon, apples, and butter-fried pastry floated through the air.

"Thank you, Maria. I wondered what you'd been cooking the last two nights, and I can't think of anything tastier on a long cattle drive, especially while sipping coffee sitting around a campfire."

"Yeah, Maria," said Cephas, sniffing the air. "My mouth is already watering."

"Ah, brother, your mouth is always watering at something to eat. Look at your belly."

"Ok, boys. Enough said. We'll all enjoy them tonight—mouth, bellies, and all."

Maria stood smiling at the banter over her specialty.

Gracie walked over to put her foot on the hub of the wagon wheel. Before she could step onto the wheel, Cephas interrupted her.

"No Gracie, I'll put them in the wagon." Cephas offered to help. He hefted the heavy basket of pies and put them under the wagon seat. "They'll be safe there. Safe from you know who." He sneaked a look at his brother.

Everyone was laughing as Press came up the path from the shed. Seeing Maria, he walked to her and gave her a hug, "Take care of the place until we get back. We won't be gone as long this year."

"Si, *Señor* Press. Maria will take care of the Glory B. You no worry."

From the house, Sarah Susannah came out on the porch to wish everyone a safe trip. "Maria and I'll take care of the house," she nodded at her father.

Press looked around. "Is everyone loaded up and ready to go?"

There was a course of yeses and just as the group prepared to mount up, Pastor Ormond appeared.

"Hello, everyone. I came to see Caleb," the pastor said, walking over to his old friend from The Pinery. "You are a sight for sore eyes."

"Mr. Ormand, good to see you," was Caleb's muffled answer as he was embraced in another bear hug by the delighted pastor, but one which didn't lift him off the ground.

"I heard you were coming. I missed you at church this morning, and who's this?" He noted the young man standing next to Caleb.

There were introductions to Thomas.

"You couldn't have a better father, Thomas. I've known him many years."

"Thank you, sir. He's taught me a lot," Thomas agreed, while flicking a glance toward Sarah Susannah, who was still draped over the front porch rail, watching the goings on below.

"Everyone, we'd better mount up and head for Bull Elk Hole."

Those riding horses walked to them, and Gracie and Press headed for the wagon seat. Their horses were tied to the backboard of the wagon.

The pastor, Sarah Susannah, and Maria stood waving at the group as they went down past the bunkhouse and out on the open prairie for the ride to the watering hole.

~

Heading for Bull Elk Hole the day before the trail drive actually started, would let the participants go over Jonathan's preparations, make suggestions if need be, and spend the first night getting acquainted, before the drive started with the drovers. If something was lacking, one of the cow-boys could still make a rushed trip back home before they left the next day.

Press and Jonathan went over the young man's list for the fourth time. Everything was in order. The trail drive would start in the morning around daybreak as scheduled.

After supper, Jonathan, Press, and Caleb took time to discuss the pecking order on the drive. Gracie poured coffee for them and sat down on a box to listen. Jonathan pulled a list from his shirt pocket. It detailed who would have each job, according to who was best qualified for the position.

Caleb was to ride as point. He would lead the herd and pick someone to spell him or ride with him. His position at the front of the cattle drive could be dangerous, especially if the longhorns stampeded. He and the front drovers would be the ones to turn the herd, getting the animals to form a tight circle, and quit their pell-mell rush toward certain injury.

All agreed on Cephas as wrangler of the one hundred or so horses or *remuda* as the cow-boys called the bunch. Each man needed six to ten extra mounts to keep horse fatigue from being a problem. Some of the cow-boys would change their rides three times each day. Others less, depending on how long the daily drive covered and the herds tendency to stray.

"Cephas can throw a rope with the best of them. This is important with horses, barely broken to ride." Caleb gave his brother credit for his lassoing ability. "From the back of the horse, I've seen him nestle a rope behind a horse's ears and let it fall over the nose, completing the whole operation fifty times and never missing. He's real good."

This was important because horse selections were made each morning for the day. If the wrangler wasn't accurate, He could excite the horses, causing them to run through their makeshift corral of rope and stakes.

Six men would ride flank or as swing men. These outriders would take opposite positions down the sides of the drive. These six men kept the cattle in a line and made sure all stayed in the drive. Stragglers and wanderers were, as quickly as possible, brought back into the herd.

Two would finish at drag or follow to the rear. Drag was the least desired position. These men ate dust, rode in the deepest mud if it was wet or rainy, and the smell—well, you wouldn't want to use it as perfume. Normally, the greenest or newest ones to drive a herd were assigned this position.

Jorge was the cook, and Gracie his helper. Thomas and P.T. would drive a wagon and help where necessary, especially with the *remuda* which would be driven just behind the lead wagons.

As trail boss, Jonathan made sure they all did their jobs, solved problems of horse, men, and wagons. He made sure supplies for food and repairs were on hand, and the longhorns got to Abilene. He or Thomas would spell anyone sick on the drive. And, he would referee any arguments or fights.

"I think we're ready to go," Jonathan said, checking off the last item on his list and drawing in a sigh, because the responsibility weighed only on him personally. He stood from his position around the campfire.

Gracie knew he was feeling the heavy obligation for men and cattle, and she had to grin at his list. He reminded her of her father and his numerous lists on their way to a new home in Texas.

"Caleb, let's ride over and check on the herd." Jonathan and Caleb mounted their horses and rode away.

Press came over to sit by Gracie, reaching for her hand. "I've made a good choice for a trail boss."

"I agree," said Gracie.

"He reminds me of your father. His lists." Press laughed.

"I was thinking the same thing," she laughed with him. "Those were good times, Press."

"Yes, I fell in love with a feisty lady. I'm sure glad the Comanche and Apache didn't get you—and that I did. Remember Wooly's flight from the stockade and that crazy ride you took in the barrel?

"Yes. I miss my lamb," Gracie returned with sorrow in her voice.

Not wanting for his wife to dwell on events in the past, he asked, "How about a ride?"

"Yes, of course. It's pleasant out here tonight with the lowing of the cattle and cooing of the doves." Gracie stood up. "Let me get my coat and hat."

As Gracie approached the wagon she would be driving, a noise of something falling came from within. She reached for her hat and coat, looked around but couldn't see anything. The noise wasn't loud, so she dismissed it.

Press and Gracie took a leisurely ride around the gathering of longhorns. She marveled at the many colors of the herd—beige or black with large and small splashes in all shades of these two colors. The deadly looking horns varied in length—none on the Glory B's cattle were over five feet, end-to-end. These longhorns were a sturdy breed, with tasty meat and not much fat.

"Do you see the solid-black longhorn feeding next to the large clump of prickly pear cactus?" He pointed to a lone animal feeding near a patch of grass.

"Yes. What's his problem? Doesn't he have any friends?"

"He's a leader. His name is Soot. When we move out tomorrow, Caleb will make sure Soot's in the lead. This'll be his second year to be at the head of our drive. There're also one or two others who will follow closely behind him. These few will lead and the others will follow."

"Makes a trail drive a bit easier with a trail blazing longhorn as a leader, I'm sure."

"Yes, and we have a mixed herd," Press said, as they stopped to look over the rest of the beeves. "That'll slow us down some." Mixed, meant bulls and cows. They would use the cow's milk to drink, make bread, or soup.

Gracie nodded. "Are any of the cows going to give birth on the drive?"

"It's possible, but I sure hope not. Even with our slower pace, calves just don't have the stamina to keep up. They usually die enroute. Let's head back to camp. This has been a long day." Press yawned. "Jonathan may want to talk to the men about their responsibilities before they bed down for the night. I hope I can stay awake."

"Don't tell me old age is slowing you down."

"What do you think?" he grinned.

Gracie grinned back and shook her head. "Maybe in another ten years." They dismounted and walked arm-in-arm to the campfire.

Before bedtime and around the campfire, as those on the drive came back for a final cup of coffee, Jonathan gave his expectations about the responsibilities of each person on the drive.

After instructions to the rest, he turned to his Momma and Jorge. "You'll rise very early before light, each morning to make breakfast for the trail hands. Those on the drive will head out after your fine meal of scrambled eggs, chuckwagon chicken (bacon) and sourdough bullets (biscuits) cooked over an open fire.

"Is that all we can cook for breakfast?" asked Gracie.

"Momma, I was joshin' you," returned Jonathan, giving her a wink.

Finally, it was bedtime, and Gracie was ready. She and Press sat on the back of her wagon for a few intimate minutes with arms around each other. He would not sleep in the wagon with her.

"Good night, my love." With a kiss, he headed for the tent of Jonathan and disappeared inside.

Gracie sat watching as the golden sun went slowly down in the west. The orange globe fell behind the hilltops, silhouetting their tops in the distance.

Shadows flicked on Jorge's chuckwagon and inside the canvas tents where lanterns or candles gave a soft glow. Silhouettes danced around the campfire area as the men got ready for the night, rolling out bedrolls, and climbing in to sleep, until called for their shift of tending the cattle.

In the distance, those horseback riders, who were working the first two hours of night shift, sang in low voices to keep the beeves calm. A whippoorwill joined the soft crooning of the men, making its own distinctive call join with theirs. She wondered if the bird was singing its own version of "Home Sweet Home," like the men were singing to the cattle.

Gracie climbed in the wagon, pulled on her gown, and stretched out on her cot.

The music lulled her to sleep.

~

Gracie rolled off her cot and put her feet on the floor of the covered wagon. Press had built two small cots, one on either side of the wagon bed. A canvas stretched across the open rectangle made a softer bed with blankets or bed roll on top. He'd said the other bed might be occupied by anyone who got sick on the trail. He intended to sleep with Jonathan and Caleb in their tent or if it didn't rain, on the ground by the fire. Gracie could tell he was enjoying renewing his trail drive skills.

She'd slept tight and warm with blankets wrapped under and over her. She couldn't gripe about her first night on the trail not being comfortable.

"Whew! The April night air is cold," she said, as she rubbed her arms to warm them up.

The interior of her wagon was full of extra supplies. These included horse blankets, bedrolls, and horse tack—even saddles. It smelled of leather and sweat and something else she couldn't identify. What was that smell! Mixed in with these distinctive odors, was the faint smell of smoke. Her stomach started growling.

Gracie's back, she thought.

Then it hit her. The breakfast fire was burning! Was she late? Jorge was supposed to wake her up.

She scooted over and looked out of the wagon flap. It was pitch-black outside, which it should be. Silhouetted in the campfire light, Jorge moved around, going back and forth between the campfire and the main chuckwagon. He'd placed two large iron skillets on the fireplace grids which were positioned over the coals. She watched as he dipped lard from a large tin pail into one skillet.

"Hey, cow-boy," she called, even knowing this might disturb some of the sleeping men who were closest to the tent campfire. "Why didn't you get me up?"

"We thought on the first day, we'd let you sleep in," he explained, grinning and waving the lard spoon in the air.

Gracie wondered who the *we* were, and quickly looked around the firelit area. Seeing nothing, she shook her head and let the flap fall.

After putting the cloth canvas back in place, she hurriedly pulled on her britches and cotton shirt. There wouldn't be a long skirt on this trip. She intended to be one of the trail hands, and she intended to be comfortable and dress like one. After getting into her trail duds, she climbed from the back of the wagon. Someone grabbed her as she hit the ground.

"Good morning, sleepyhead," said the other part of *we*. Press wrapped his arms around her, giving her a quick peck on the cheek and whispering in her ear, "I missed you. My feet got cold." Then louder, "You'll have to get up earlier than six o'clock, if you're going to help Jorge. Look! The sun's starting to glow slightly in the east." He threw his arm out in that direction—fingers extended. "Even the roosters are crowing."

Gracie looked where he pointed and laughed. He had a good imagination, she thought. There was no evidence of a sunrise and certainly no chickens to make any sound here in the Chihuahuan Desert.

"It's not my fault. Someone didn't get me up," she complained, laying the blame on the cook by the fire.

"Jorge, is that any excuse?" Press gave her a real good morning kiss and let her go.

"Ah. I forgive her on her first day on the trail. It's my fault, boss."

"I don't know whose fault it was. I think it was a conspiracy."

Gracie went over and gave her cooking buddy a hug and looked into the skillets. One they would use for cooking the bacon and eggs. In the other, they would bake the sourdough bullets. After the bread browned on one side, they'd turn them over in the pan, so they could brown on the other. The lard had melted, just covering the bottom of the pan. Gracie pulled it off.

"Jonathan said we'll eat in two shifts," Press said. "The ones who slept in camp will eat first. They'll spell the others riding night shift. As soon as everyone's eaten, Jorge, you and Gracie will head out before we get the herd up so you can find a place for us to noon. You'll need to be on the road at daylight."

Jorge and Gracie decided her morning responsibility was to stir up the biscuits and bake them over the fire. This mixing would be done by the light of a lantern hanging on the chuckwagon. She went over to get her mixing bowls and the bread ingredients.

"Gracie, the recipe is on the side board. The one that lets down so we can serve the crew. I thought you might need it. It's been a long time since you cooked for this many."

"You're right. Maria has spoiled me. She practically swats me with a mixing spoon if I enter her kitchen. By the way, where are the mixing spoons?"

She heard Press laugh. "You two. I'm going to start rousting everyone. Get a move on." Jonathan had assigned him this responsibility, because he was an early riser. He headed for three tents positioned around another campfire.

Gracie whispered to Jorge, "He'd better get out of here before I *hit* him with a spoon I can't find."

"I heard that," came from the darkness.

Jorge and Gracie laughed. He came to point out the utensils and other supplies she needed and returned to the fire to turn the sizzling bacon.

"I'll know where everything is in the morning," promised Gracie.

They got busy making the cow-boys a hearty breakfast.

While Jorge and Gracie washed the breakfast dishes and pans, P.T. and Thomas hooked up the three wagons. When everything was back in its place, Jorge, Gracie, and the boys started out at dawn to find a good place to noon. They would soon be followed by Cephas and his horses.

The whippoorwill was back in the bushes, singing its morning song while the beeves bawled their displeasure at being forced into a standing position. From somewhere a ladder-backed woodpecker looked for bugs in the bark of a tree. It's rat-a-tat stood out starkly against the other daytime sounds.

A morning fog made it difficult to see the trail ahead. Gracie was glad her fellow cook knew the way. She often saw these white sheets of fog from the hillside at the Glory B. The valley would be hiding from view, and she felt like she was in a castle, suspended or floating above the white cloud below. The mist always melted away in the day's, warming sunshine.

Jorge chirped to the mules pulling his wagon. Gracie followed with her team. The boys fell in behind. Gracie had time to think, since her mules followed the leader without urging. She couldn't help but remember the many days Jonathan Tipton and she'd climbed aboard their small Conestoga wagon on their way West to The Pinery.

Big Red pulled the wagon along with the other mules. There were fun times, hard times, and scary times. She missed Pa and swallowed a lump of sadness in her throat.

Just before noon, the procession stopped at a small creek. P.T. and Thomas pulled their wagon to the north of Gracie's and Jorge's. They jumped down from their wagon, pulled two axes out of the back, and headed for a small stand of trees upstream. Returning with two arm loads of wood, the young men built a cook fire—part of their responsibilities.

Gracie handed them two pails. "I'll need water to boil the potatoes," she explained.

"What kind of potatoes are we having for noon meal, Momma?"

"Steaks for meat and chunks of boiled potatoes in cream sauce."

Yesterday, during the final part of the roundup, a longhorn had stumbled into a gopher hole. With its leg broken, the animal couldn't walk. The men had shot the unfortunate creature, and Jorge had dressed it and spent most of the day cutting off choice parts, and roasting some of the larger pieces of meat for today's night meal. The rest of the fresh meat was given away to the families from Mountain City who had visited to tell their loved one's goodbye. The bones were hauled into the desert for the coyotes or other scavengers.

Today at noon, we were having steaks and boiled buttered potatoes with cream gravy—a fitting noon meal of celebration for the first day on the trail. Of course, there would be biscuits to sop the gravy and eat with the quart jars of honey and bowls of butter for dessert.

Gracie put the sideboard down and retrieved a mixing bowl and knife from a shelf inside.

She walked to the back of the chuckwagon. The potatoes, along with carrots, onions, and cabbage were packed in straw in several wooden boxes at the back of the chuckwagon. She counted out twenty-four large potatoes.

"Enough for seconds, if anyone wants them," she told Jorge, tipping the bowl so he could see it was full.

Pulling a stool hanging on a peg from the wagon side, she sat down to peel potatoes. The boys appeared with the water.

"Momma, the horses have arrived. We're going to help Cephas with the *remuda*."

"Did Poppa tell you to help with the horses?"

"No, Jonathan did."

"Go on, then. Do exactly what Cephas tells you." Peeling the potatoes, she watched them head over to a herd of horses—about ten for every rider on the trail.

Jorge watched them go. "If the drovers rotate their tired-out horses for fresh ones during the day, we don't have as many accidents from stumbling or slipping." Jorge continued, "A fresh horse is always best should the beeves decide to stampede. The drovers ride at breakneck speed to turn the crazed animals and stop their headlong flight. It's a dangerous happening."

"I hope *not* to see a stampede this trip."

Jorge poured water into a kettle. "Longhorn cattle are strange creatures, Gracie. They'll stampede at the drop of a hat or any sudden noise." He placed the kettle on a hook hanging on a spit over the fire and pointed. "Water to boil your potatoes."

Gracie watched him as he rummaged around in the chuckwagon, where he found two long metal skewers for grilling the steaks. She saw him poke both metal rods through each steak. The meat would be evenly cooked by turning it over, but still, medium to rare in the middle. The hungry drovers wouldn't care. They'd wolf it down—hardly chewing it. Longhorn steaks could be a little tough but very tasty.

Gracie rinsed the potatoes by pouring water in her bowl and draining it. Getting up from her stool, she walked over to the kettle and dumped the peeled and quartered potatoes inside the boiling water. Later, she'd add a slurry of flour, milk, and salt. This would make gravy to eat with the bread she'd mix up. She went to the chuckwagon to get the ingredients for the gravy and biscuits and started to measure them.

Soon Jorge said, "Gracie, there's a large can of peas to add to the potatoes on the sideboard."

Sure enough, there was. "I'll need your help opening them. Don't you think we should cut up some of the extra meat and start cooking it for stew? You have an extra hook and kettle. We can eat it for noon tomorrow. We'll have potatoes, carrots, and onions to go in the pot and cook enough for supper, too. My mouth's already watering. Cornbread—yum, yum."

"And butter." Jorge said. "How about brewing hot tea to go along with the coffee. Our drovers will have a choice. They don't get that often."

A female voice came from the front of the wagon Gracie had been driving!

"Honey, on the cornbread! Momma," it exclaimed. "I can't stand this talk of food. I'm starved! Are you making more biscuits for dinner? I'd sure like one."

Sarah Susannah Stockton stuck her head out and grinned at us. "I can't wait any longer. I need food or I'll faint." She put her hand to her forehead, but they could tell she was eyeing them through her fingers.

Jorge and Gracie looked at each other in astonishment. They were stunned!

"W-what are you doing here? Where have you been? Wait until your father hears of this!" Gracie was almost speechless. She was so astonished.

"I'm hungry," Sarah said, climbing down to the wagon's wooden tongue and bouncing to the ground. "I haven't had food in a whole day."

"Answer my questions," said her mother, "and I may find a biscuit from yesterday for you to eat. What are you doing here?"

"Everyone else in the house is here—everyone but Mary and Peter. Why should I stay at home?"

Gracie pushed out an angry lungful of air. "Why? Because you were told to stay, *maybe*." Gracie put emphasis on the maybe.

"It wasn't fair, and I can ride with the best of your riders *out there*," she emphasized the last two words and jabbed with a pointed finger toward the dust cloud that was approaching.

Gracie raised an eyebrow, realizing she was probably right about that. She could sit a horse as well as any drover *out there*. But there was danger in riding with a herd of agitated longhorns. "Where were you last night?"

"I hid underneath the blankets, bedrolls, and saddles. Wasn't I quiet as a mouse?" She grinned. "You didn't know I was in the wagon with you, did you, Momma."

So, last night, the other smell was a whiff of her perfume, because Gracie could smell it faintly now. "Where's your horse?"

"With the rest of the extra horses in the corral."

"Is Cephas in on this?"

"I'm not telling. Can I help?"

A grinning Jorge had remained out of the discussion until now. "Sounds just like another spunky lady I know about." He laughed, bending over and slapping his knee, while putting the first of the steaks over the fire. "Gracie, we're gonna need those biscuits soon and the gravy. I think I hear the beeves bawling already. Them cow-boys ain't goin' to want to wait."

"I can't believe this, and your father's not going to believe you're here either. And, yes, I'm making biscuits. You'll need to help. I don't have time to search around for a biscuit." There were no free rides, so to speak, on a trail drive. Everyone was expected to pull their own weight, including her.

With the biscuits ready for the lard, Gracie put a dollop in and told her daughter to cut it in with a fork. She placed the milk nearby to be added. "Let me know when you're ready to add the milk, and I'll pour it in." Then she started mixing the milk gravy for the potatoes.

With Sarah Susannah's help everything was ready when the beeves arrived.

Press was not amused when he came in from the drive at noon. Gracie heard him pull in a lungful of air and push it out his mouth. "I should send you home this afternoon, but Jonathan can't spare anyone to take you to the Glory B."

"Poppa, I can ride. I can herd cattle as well as anyone." Sarah Susannah was begging for the opportunity to remain in camp on the drive.

"But can you obey orders? Sure, doesn't look like it." Press was not happy with his youngest daughter.

Sarah Susannah went to stand before her father. "I'm sorry, Poppa."

"Riding trail is a dangerous business. The cattle aren't accustomed to being herded all day long. Most don't like being pushed or prodded to keep moving."

Press stood nudging a pebble in the dirt as his heart softened.

"Please, Poppa?"

Gracie heard Press sigh again. "Are you willing to take on any job Jonathan or I assign to you?"

"Oh, yes. Anything. Give me the toughest, dirtiest job you've got."

"That's exactly what I'm going to do. You can help by riding drag." Press turned to Jonathan. "Sorry, I didn't mean to barge in on your authority, but this is a family matter. I needed to tend to it."

"I understand, Poppa."

The discussion was over. Gracie wondered if her daughter realized what riding drag meant—eating blowing hoof dust for ten or twelve hours a day. Plus, the smell would definitely cover up her delicate perfume fragrance.

"Are the steaks ready, Jorge?" Jonathan asked.

"Yes, sir." Jorge gave instructions to the cow-boys milling around. "Everyone should get their steak and bullets on the sideboard and dip your potatoes out of the kettle over the fire. I'll bring a few more pieces of meat in a few minutes. They're cooking now."

The cow-boys crowded the side board. Food appeared on tin plates as if by magic. One or two steaks, hot biscuits slathered with honey and butter from a jar and bowl, and a ladle full of potatoes with peas mixed into the cream gravy. Hungry, no one complained about the peas in the potatoes. The men sat cross-legged on the ground, eating their grub.

"Brother, we oughta get up a game of horseshoes after we eat supper tonight." Cephas sat close to Caleb whose son sat knee-to-knee to his father. "I brought the shoes and stakes in the wagon P.T.'s driving."

"Are you hankering for a beating?" Caleb punched his son on the leg. "Thomas knows I can play. Don't you, Son?"

"I wouldn't get too huffy-puffy. I can remember you losing—several times, the last time we played."

"Well, *you* didn't beat me."

"Maybe, I didn't, but I'm better now."

"Okay, horseshoes it is. What I'd like to know is, where did you buy the storage tank." Caleb pointed to Cephas's oversized canteen, from which he was drinking water in gulps.

"Don't talk about my water bottle. You'll be wishin' you had one before this drive is over. There's lots of places where springs and clear streams ain't available, and the water isn't fit for humans to drink."

Jonathan cut in. "Speaking of water, I've been noticing some extra clouds floating around late morning. Hope we don't have rain tomorrow. Droving is really hard to impossible on muddy ground, especially if we have a downpour." He looked over at his father.

Press rested on a wooden box with P. T. on the grassy ground below him. The other men hunkered in an arc around the campfire. "Of course, we need water for our herd,"

Benjamin sat on a large piece of wood with a book in his hand. "There's never a happy medium when you're riding the trail." He added to the conversation.

"Yes, Son. It's either too hot or too cold, too wet or too dry."

Gracie looked over at her son who took after her for his interest in reading books. His clothes were dusty and an unusual shine rested on his head—grime from the trail. Benjamin glanced her way and wiggled his fingers in a *hello*. He raised the book so she could see the title, *The Expedition*. Gracie nodded, knowing he was on two trails; theirs, and the path with Lewis and Clark, the great explorers of the West.

Chapter Fifteen

Day Three and The Threat of Rain

From the southwest, the clouds grew thicker, heavier with moisture, but the rain held off for another day. Somewhere on the distant mountains, buckets and buckets of water had hit the earth. With this prospect, flooding in the coming days could be a problem the advancing herd and drovers would have to address. Jonathan grew increasingly concerned.

The prospect of threatening rain changed the method of positioning the Glory B's wagons for cooking. At noon two days later, Gracie put hers side-to-side with Jorge's, leaving a space large enough for them to walk between and access supplies from his cupboards.

After unhitching the mules pulling the three wagons, P.T. and Thomas got two canvas covers from theirs. They helped as the smallest canvas tarp was pulled tautly between the wagons, and another large tarp was attached to the back of the chuckwagon and Gracie's wagon. When pulled outward, it would shelter as best as possible the fire, those cooking, and the squatting drovers from the rain. When positioned like this in the future, this area would give the cowboys a dryer place to sit and eat—and dry out as the drive continued toward Abilene.

While the men ate their noon meal, Jonathan's words about rain proved true. A rush of wind blew dirt and ashes everywhere. On the wrong side of the fire, men jumped up swatting at burning embers on their clothes and coughing in the smoke-filled air. Everyone knew the rain wouldn't be far behind, because over the wind, you could hear it pounding the ground.

"Wouldn't you believe it!" exclaimed Jonathan. "We haven't had rain for two weeks, and the third day on the trail, drops come from the sky." He threw the rest of his coffee into the wind which blew it several feet in an arc, and dropped his empty plate into the wash kettle's hot water.

At the first few scattered drops which bounced as they hit the earth, Cephas got up and put his plate and cup on the sideboard. Running for his slicker tied on back of his horse along with his coat, he pulled two leather strings and retrieved both. He put on his coat and then his slicker. Returning to the fire, he led his horse closer to the tarp.

"What's wrong, brother? Will you melt?" Caleb called to him across the fire. He laughed, along with some of the other men.

Cephas ignored the comment and the laughter.

As soon as the laughter died down, the angry, leaded skies opened up with a deluge of rain. Quickly loaded with water, the tarp shot a sluice of water from its top. Hitting the ground, it splashed mud under the canvas. Coarse, brown blobs splashed on those who'd just laughed and anyone who remained under the awning on that side. Even the fire hissed when drops hit the coals.

As the others wolfed down their food, got rid of their plates and cups, and ran for their horses to retrieve their rain gear, Cephas threw his rain slicker over his shoulders. He gave a low chuckle. His white teeth showed in his ear-to-ear grin. Calmly eating the rest of his food, he placed his plate with cup in the wash kettle to be cleaned.

"Thanks, Jorge and Gracie," he said. Walking out from under the protection of the canvas, he mounted his horse and rode toward the *remuda* to tend his horses.

Gracie wanted to hug him.

She and Jorge started cleaning the cooking utensils, plates and forks. They loaded the chuckwagon, putting every piece back where it came from. By the time they were finished, she sure wished they had throw-away plates. But the tin metal plates and cups were too expensive to throw away.

The large tarp was taken down, but the fire which had been under it still glowed. She and Jorge stood with hats and slickers on, warming their hands, while P.T. and Thomas, hooked up the mules for pulling the heavy wagons. The small tarp was removed, folded, and packed in P.T.s wagon along with the extra dry wood they'd been hauling. It sure looked like they might need to use some of it for the night meal.

The chuckwagon and its reinforcements were always the first to leave the temporary camp and the first to stop at noon or supper. The *remuda* followed a close second. This gave Cephas a chance to rope the cow-boy's reserve horse and put on the extra saddle and bridle located in Gracie's wagon for the afternoon ride.

Jorge asked, "Is everything clean and back in the chuckwagon?"

"I think so, but how will we maintain a fire for supper? All the wood will be soaked." Gracie said, looking at the coals, now spitting only steam from the barely glowing embers of the warm fire we were leaving.

"P.T.'s wagon has enough kindling to start several fires and some large logs. We'll manage by adding some larger dry wood as we need it."

"I hope you're right." She did not look convinced.

"I'm always right, Gracie." Jorge winked at her.

They both laughed.

"When you need them, you'll find more food supplies with the wood in his wagon."

"I'll check out the provisions the next time we stop."

"You ready, Thomas?" Jorge called.

"Yep," came the reply from the seat on his wagon.

"Then let's head-up and move out."

Press and the other cow-boys were rounding up the few stray longhorns who had scattered during the first onslaught of the storm. He rode over for a private conversation with his son while the last of the animals were rounded up. "What are you going to do since it's raining, Jonathan."

"The grounds still dry enough, so we'll try to make some more miles today. If this doesn't let up, there's no reason to move the herd tomorrow. Travel will be dangerous for the men, horses, and the longhorns. Even if the rain quits, the ground will have to soak up the water before we can move. Do you agree with me?"

"Yes, I would've made the same decision. Your men won't be happy riding the rest of the day in the pouring rain."

"No, they won't, but they won't be happy sitting anywhere in the rain, either. I hope we don't catch up to another herd on the trail before us. I've had my suspicions. We'll be trying to walk through hoof-plowed ground, mud, and who knows what else. Dangerous territory and only clumps of muddy grass for the beeves to eat."

"Just say the word, and I'll scout out new terrain to cover. Maybe we can miss the herd in front of us and find good grass or at least enough for our beeves to eat."

At the slow pace of a cattle drive, the longhorns always found time to nibble the prairie grass or edible bushes along the way.

"Thanks, Poppa. I may take you up on that."

The drovers had finished the roundup of strays. They waited on their horses, slickers on and bunched in the rain, for the rest of the day's orders. Press was right. None seemed particularly interested in sitting on a wet saddle even for half a day.

Jonathan shouted over the roar of the rain, "We need to make a few more miles today, if possible. If we decide to call a halt, I'll wave my hat, as a signal. Does everyone understand?"

Several grunts of approval came as the men turned their horses toward the herd. They were happy to know what the boss had decided. Their slickers were big enough to cover man and saddle, but they did little to add warmth to a rainy ride. Every man there would be glad for a warm fire and food at the end of the trail this day.

"Don't push the cattle. Let them mosey at a slow speed." Jonathan suggested in a final instruction to the men. He watched them ride away.

Press and Sarah Susannah mounted up and left.

Minutes later Jonathan rode toward his father and called, "I'm goin' to go ride ahead. Catch up with Jorge. And see what's out there."

Press nodded, waved, and continued on to ride drag with Sarah Susannah.

Jonathan turned his horse and after some minutes caught up with Jorge. As the two continued on without stopping, he explained his concern. "No need in you worrying about a good spot. Soon as I find one, I'll mark it and ride back to inform you. Look for my red bandana." He looked up at the sky and shook his head. "I probably shouldn't go too far. The trail will soon become impassable. Follow my horse's tracks." He waved goodbye and rode slowly toward the road leading northeast. Riding faster than the chuckwagon could go with its team of mules, he was soon out of sight.

As he picked up speed, he noticed an arroyo on the left side. Tall cottonwood trees and hackberry bushes identified the waterway in the ground. He followed it for five or six miles. The dip in the earth soon turned northwest, and he urged his horse across the shallow impression which was devoid of water. On the other side he paused to check out the location. On a tall spine of an ocotillo cactus, he tied his extra red bandana. They would cross the arroyo and stay here for the night.

~

Jonathan rode on. The grade slowly increased. This would slow Jorge and the others down considerably. He hoped the heavy covered wagons wouldn't get stuck in the muddy ground once they resumed travel.

A few miles later, he confirmed his earlier suspicions. There was a herd being driven ahead of his. Where they were from, he had no idea, but this group of cattle must have joined up with his chosen trail a day earlier than his longhorns. He couldn't spot them in the distance, but from the looks of the ploughed-up ground, this group was much bigger. He wondered briefly which ranch had so many cattle. This was a puzzle he couldn't figure out.

He sat on his horse, checking out the possibility of another trail to Abilene. Ahead, something dark was moving. He hadn't intended to go further, but decided to check out the activity.

As he rode closer, he realized a stray longhorn was in trouble. Trying to get up on all fours, the creature kept falling down on its side. It was exhausted and lay there now, covered in the knee-deep mud. He rode over to the animal which still moved to rise as he approached. Something was wrong with its leg or hoof. He looked around, trying to ascertain how the accident had happened. As with the longhorn at the beginning of his drive, a broken leg or foot problem meant sure death for a large, heavy animal.

Who would leave a live longhorn in such a cruel situation? He pulled his rifle from its holder and shot it. There was no way his crew could drive the longhorns this way. The danger of someone besides an animal getting hurt was too great.

Why are these people continuing? He wondered. The fields would be a waiting disaster for anyone coming behind them.

Not noticing a lone rider observing him on top of a hill to the west, he turned his horse and started back for his herd. He hoped Jorge had seen his bandana or that he hadn't gotten to it.

When he got to the shallow arroyo, Jorge wasn't there. He felt even more sure that the drive didn't need to go any further until weather conditions improved, and besides, the arroyo was the perfect place to stay. Already there were puddles of water in the deepest parts and probably more on the way from the west where the rain had pounded the earth. There would be water for the animals, washing cooking utensils and clothes, and maybe up the soon to be creek, a muddy bath. Drinking water would come from the barrels installed on or in the approaching wagons.

When Jonathan saw the chuckwagon, he'd only ridden minutes from the arroyo.

"Hey, Jorge, we'll stop just ahead in a clump of trees. You'll see my bandana on the northern side of the arroyo. Make a more permanent camp and use the large tarp for shelter and to cover your fire like you did at noon. With this rain, doesn't look like we'll be moving anytime soon."

"I hear you, boss. We'll make camp, put up the tarps, and start cooking. The drovers will want food when they get here. Hot soup and hot coffee, I think. Do you want the boys to set up the drover's tents?"

"Good idea—the tents and the cots. Make sure the extra small tarps are placed over the tents. We might as well be as comfortable as possible in this downpour. Get Thomas and P.T. to start stretching them and when Cephas gets here, he can help. Dig trenches to drain water around the tents if you have time. Make the area as dry as possible."

Jorge nodded as Jonathan continued. "If I don't run into Cephas, you can tell him he needs to corral the *remuda* in the taller grass down below you." Jonathan pointed in the general direction. "You'll see what I mean when you get there. It backs up from the arroyo to the low hills beyond to the south. The grass will be good for horse and longhorn alike. The boys can help him."

Jonathan rode over and stopped to talk to his mother. "Momma, we're at a stop until the rain lets up. Get comfortable and cook plenty of good food. No one's goin' to be happy the next few days with this going on."

Jonathan waved at Thomas and P.T. as he passed.

He continued on and encountered Cephas with the *remuda*. "Jorge is just ahead. We'll not be moving for a day or two. There's a grassy spot below the position of the chuckwagon and along the arroyo. Fix your makeshift corral for the horses there. Leave enough distance from the chuckwagon and the herd. I'll see that the longhorns are below you."

"Will do," Cephas replied. "How is it up ahead?"

"Muddy and messy, for sure. Help the boys put up the tents. I gave instructions to Jorge."

Jonathan rode another two miles. A softly blowing wind brought the smell of wet cattle to his nostrils.

The rain on its nose made his horse snort.

He bent over the horse's mane and patted his neck. "It's okay boy. We'll soon be done for today." Seconds later, around a curve, he met Caleb and Soot at the start of the herd.

"Have you had any trouble?" He asked his point man, turning his horse to ride beside him.

"None to speak of. How about you?"

"There's a mess ahead. Another herd's been in front of us. They've plowed the ground up pretty bad—enough until I think we need to break a new trail. At least try to miss them. Looks like we'll be in camp a few days until this blows over and the ground dries up."

"I figured as much. Those of us in front have the easiest ride today." Caleb looked up at the clouds and the sky. Water ran off the back of his wet hat onto his rain slicker. The slicker covered him and his saddle. "Sure wish I could predict the weather. At least, there's no thunder, so the beeves aren't likely to stampede from the noise."

"I'm wondering who the people are driving the herd ahead of us? They left an injured longhorn beside the trail. I had to kill the poor thing."

"No one does such a harsh thing." Caleb answered, shaking his head.

"Someone did. I'm going to ride back and see Poppa. I need some expert advice on how to proceed from an old-timer."

"Hey, I wouldn't let your father in on that statement." Caleb threw after him.

Jonathan turned in his saddle. "That's true. You're not too far behind the chuckwagon. I'll see you there." He waved and continued on.

Instead of riding straight down the line of moving longhorns, Jonathan urged his horse to the top of a slight rise so he could observe the progress of the shuffling, bawling herd. From his perch he could see the end of the drive and the two riding drag.

When he looked to the front of the herd, he saw Caleb and ahead of him in the distance and across the arroyo Jorge and the wagons were already in their camp with a warm fire burning. Below the campfire was the *remuda,* where Cephas was actively spreading a little hay. This would keep the horses in the area until he would build a makeshift corral. Cephas hadn't gone for P.T. and Thomas to help with stretching the ropes and driving the stakes. The area where the beeves were going was below the herd of horses in a grassy area next to the low hills on which he was atop. He turned his attention back to the long line of cattle before him.

Beeves, on a drive, do not travel in a bunch but strung out in a long line. He saw the natural leaders of the group were in the lead. This included Soot, the acknowledged general or trailblazer. The strongest cattle were behind them and the weakest or laziest or hungriest nibblers, looking for the tastiest morsels in the rear.

The drovers on drag kept up with nibblers and wanderers. They were also responsible for the milk cows who weren't used to being trailed for long distances.

These longhorns were usually the ones walking into the scrub brush to find a tasty morsel, and the ones needing to be watched the closest. They sought their days feedstuff from naturally low areas, where they usually foraged. Especially when driving a herd through a lot of short shrubby bushes, it was easy to leave the stragglers behind.

Most ranchers weren't interested in losing one animal on a drive.

His herd of longhorns lumbered along beside the arroyo and a low bunch of hills on both sides, which included the one he sat on. Jonathan resisted the urge to wave his hat at his father, riding instead down the hill to greet him.

"Where's Sarah Susannah?"

"Ah, she's looking for one of our stragglers—one of our regulars." Press laughed.

After filling his dad in on the details of the cattle drive ahead of them, he asked, "Any idea who's moving this herd?"

"None," Press shook his head. "Must be a new bunch who don't observe the rules of the road. As long as the longhorns don't have a brand, anyone can round up a herd on open range, use a red-hot iron to verify the ranch's ownership, and move them to market. Was there a brand on the animal you shot?"

"I didn't think to look for one. Actually, the longhorn was covered with mud and finding one would have been really hard."

"I see. Sounds like the road ahead is a muddy mess. Do we need to check out a new route?"

"Not now. It's too late to start today, but in the morning if this keeps up—yes."

"Okay," said his father. "We'll start out in the morning after a good night's rest." He sniffed the air. "Is that smoke I smell?"

"Yes. We're close to the chuckwagons. I think Jorge has some kind of soup for tonight's meal. It can't come too soon for me today."

"Yes. I'm hungry, and I can't wait for the warmth of the fire. It will feel good after riding in a cold saddle all day."

~

Under a huge cottonwood tree on the bank of the arroyo, Cephas stood looking at the three tents Thomas and P.T. had erected. With the continuing rain, the canvas needed to be stretched tight, the ropes taut, and the stakes driven at an angle, deeply into the ground. He walked into the nearest tent to look around.

"Good job, and the ground isn't soppy with water," he said, nodding his head. "Aren't there extra tarps—small ones we can use to cover the tent tops? That'll help keep the rain from sifting through during the night."

"Yes. We didn't know what to do with them." P.T. munched on a leftover bullet from breakfast—one he'd put in his coat pocket. "I'll go get them."

"After we finish with the corral, I guess we'd better try to hang them over the tent area. The boys will need something to keep them dryer. Canvas doesn't keep off all the rain, and," he looked at P.T., "your Momma will tell you a mist comes through the cotton and wets everything, including a feather mattress. There's nothing worse than sleeping on a damp feather mattress."

"Are we gonna help you set up the corral?" Thomas ventured.

"Yes. I put down a few piles of hay to keep the horses happy until I checked on you. I can use good help. The stakes and rope are in Gracie's wagon. Go get them and meet me next to the other big cottonwood tree down yonder." He pointed. "We'll start there."

Gracie was stirring the vegetable soup as she watched the two go by. She stopped and watched as Cephas marked spots with the toes of his boots for the young men to drive stakes into the ground in a large circle. She estimated about an acre was enclosed, knowing this would be moved as the herd cleared the area of grass. The group tied rope from stake to stake, leaving an area open where the horses could be herded inside. Then, the boys and Cephas herded the horses into their new corral. Tomorrow morning, Cephas would let the cow-boys pick their mounts for the day, and Cephas's rope would catch their first ride.

Gracie smiled as she watched an operation which had taken place in Texas for decades. After coming from Tennessee to Texas years ago, she had embraced her new state with her whole heart.

"Gracie, are you going to make the apple pudding for dessert?" asked Jorge. "The water is boiling, and you can put the dried apples into it."

She jumped at his statement. "Yes, Jorge. I was just reminiscing about coming to Texas and meeting Press. So many years ago. I'll get busy and see that we have apples cooked with sugar, cinnamon, and nutmeg."

"You know, he loved you from the first minute he saw you. We all kidded him about his fascination with you."

"You shouldn't have," stated Gracie.

"Yes, we should," replied Jorge. "We wanted you too."

Chapter Sixteen

Sarah Susannah Makes Two Friends

The next morning, the water kept coming from the leaden, gray sky. The need for a fresh trail grew greater with each hour of drenching rain.

Jonathan stood under the big tarp which stretched from the chuckwagon, drinking the rest of his second cup of hot coffee. As was his usual habit, he threw the final sips and dregs into the air. Walking over to some cow-boys playing cards while sitting on crates from the supply wagons, he stood thinking of his next moves.

"Who's winning?" he asked but not paying much attention to the response. He continued, "You know the order of riding herd today?" he asked.

There were several grunts of approval as one of the cowpokes threw his cards on the makeshift table. The man got up and gave his seat to another willing participant.

Jonathan went over to Sarah Susannah who was helping his mother clean up the breakfast dishes. "Sarah Susannah, get Cephas to saddle your horse and mine, and I'll meet you beside the corral. On second thought, tell him to saddle up Golden's horse, too. We'll all check out the herd. Make sure they are safe and being tended as I've planned."

Sarah Susannah started for the corral.

Jonathan called to her. "Instead, bring the saddled horses back here. We'll leave from the chuckwagon. I might need another cup of hot coffee."

Golden, as everyone called him because of the color of his hair, had been Jonathan's playmate and friend for years. After looking around camp, the trail boss found him sitting on his cot in one of the tents.

"Hi, boss," the drover greeted him with a smile.

Jonathan sat down beside his friend. "How're you making it, buddy?"

"I've seen worse, but I can't remember when," laughed Golden, who was known for his jokes on people and his sunny attitude. His comment was a standard or common reply from him.

"Why are you sitting here all by yourself? Is there a problem?"

"Aw, I'm just concerned about Martha. She wasn't feeling good when we left. I hope she's all right."

Jonathan tried to reassure his friend that his wife would be fine. "Come on. I need you to ride with Sarah Susannah and me to check on the longhorns and milk cows. Caleb told me he needs help today, and he suggested you. You can't sit here moping all day." He urged Golden to get up, knowing that action rather than inaction was better when confronted with a problem.

Golden put on his rain slicker and hat and the two left the tent just as his sister arrived with the horses.

~

The rain eased somewhat as the three rode toward the milling cattle. The drovers on the morning shift were moving the herd to a grassier area as the three arrived.

Jonathan waved at Caleb, and Golden went to join the point man for instructions to help in relocating the herd.

Arriving at the drag position which hadn't started moving yet because it was behind the others in the drive, Jonathan and his sister counted the milk cows going to Doctor Sarah at Abilene. "Looks like we lost a cow during the night," Jonathan observed.

"I counted one less too. Where do you think she's gone?" asked Sarah Susannah, looking around at the tall scrub brush and hills on both sides of the arroyo.

"Hard to tell but would you check those low hills to the west and see if you can find her? Don't go too far. In other words, don't get lost."

"I don't get lost," stated Sarah Susannah, her feathers ruffled.

Jonathan held up his hands. "Okay, okay. I'll ride back to the chuckwagon and bring Thomas to ride drag in your place. We're not going but a short distance with the herd today. Just getting them to a little better grass Caleb found yesterday afternoon."

Sarah's heart did a little flip-flop when Thomas' name was mentioned. She'd only been around him to say good morning or good night. They'd been so busy the two had only bypassed during the day, and at night he'd stayed with P.T. and the other men. There'd been no interaction at all. Maybe this would give them a chance to talk.

Sarah Susannah craned her neck toward the western sky, noting several qualifying hills that were close. "Sure, I'll look. Where exactly?"

Jonathan pointed to a series of short protrusions and gave thorough details of several hills. "If I was a cow, I think those would be on my list to visit," he declared. And then he added, "Be careful."

As Jonathan rode off for camp, the rain slacked to a drizzle.

Sarah Susannah urged her horse forward. Looking at the hills which her brother had pointed out, she chose one with a prominent rock on top. Riding northwest, she headed for the first low mounds of earth. It was necessary to cross these and the dips beyond to get to the distant hill she had selected.

Most cows did not make new paths but followed ruts already in the ground which were traveled and carved out by wild animals. The cow she looked for could be anywhere in the vegetation or not in the area at all.

She picked her way over a rugged trail made by wildlife in the area. Numerous tracks in the mud meant the path was used by all kinds of wild animals in the brush. There were no hoof marks that she could see.

"A needle in a haystack," she murmured to her horse as she rode up the first hill.

She picked her way through creosote bushes, whose shiny, olive-green leaves were made more vibrant by the yellow flowers blooming on its long stems. The creosote was accented by the purple blooms of the sage with its dull green leaves—its first bloom of the season.

Still enjoying the beautiful flowers, she traversed a valley and turned her horse west to climb the first rocky hill. Suddenly, her horse reared at movement on the ground. Grabbing the horse's mane and clutching the saddle horn, she managed not to be thrown off into a clump of prickly pear cactus. A black-tailed jackrabbit ran down the trail in front of her. Scooting at break-neck speed, its long ears lying flat along the fir on the top of its head. Three baby rabbits or kits followed.

Alarmed, she yelled at the intruders, "Get off the trail." The rabbits continued on, until with a long jump, the mama disappeared under a large flat rock, her kits scampering to follow.

Sarah Susannah shook her head, amazed at how quickly disaster could strike. She patted her horse's shoulder. "Thanks for not bolting and running in this rocky area."

Topping the crest, she descended and rode along the valley floor northward, between two rows of squatty hills. The sparse vegetation was short and seeing a lone cow should be easy. After riding a mile, she topped the hill to her right. Down below, the scattered herd milled in an area watched by the drovers.

Cold and wet were the words for this day, she thought, as she looked the herd over.

As if he sensed her, Thomas looked up to the ridge where she sat.

Her heart jumped as she recognized him. She pulled off her hat and waved to him.

He waved his hand in return.

She was mystified by her fascination with the young man. She was drawn to him at first glance, and although she'd thought and thought, she couldn't figure out why. He wasn't anything more than the cow-boys working for her father, but … he *was* different and she couldn't explain her attraction.

Turning, she went back down the hill, crossed another and in the next depression she started south in the opposite direction from which she had come. This way she would cover the next valley from north to south. The rain which had slacked for several minutes, started to come down from the leaden skies.

Minutes later, she heard over the deadening rain a sound. Could it be the cow was close? She stopped and listened. Sure enough, a cow was bawling. Riding in the direction of the sound, she found the cow in the process of nudging her newly born calf. She watched as the new mother attempted to clean her baby in the undergrowth.

"Well Bossy, I believe you've had an unexpected addition to the family. At least, we didn't know about it." Sarah Susannah dismounted her horse and ran toward the drenched calf which lay on the ground—not stirring. One thing she remembered about a newborn calf, it must start moving, and if it didn't move, the little one could soon die or never be normal. There was only a short time for the baby to breathe, and she intended to help the cow and her new baby to make it.

Running toward the mama turned out to be a big mistake!

Even though the protective mama was tired from giving birth, she snorted and summing up her strength, she started toward Sarah Susannah. To her, this human was an intruder, at least to Bossy.

When the mama reacted as she did, Sarah Susannah remembered her father's admonition from years back—'*don't turn your back to an angry bovine,*' she moved backward slowly, although every nerve in her body said run. The cow covered half of the ground toward her, pawed the dirt, and then took one deliberate step after another in her direction. Sarah kept moving backward.

As if in answer to prayer, her horse nudged her arm. In an instant, she turned, jumped into her saddle and rode to the top of the hill. The angry cow stood still for a moment and returned to her motionless calf. She nudged it gently. Sarah Susannah could not tell if the baby calf moved.

Sarah Susannah sat for a few seconds, looking over the situation.

The cow had won the first battle. It wasn't likely she could outsmart the old girl with any kind of strategy and waiting wasn't an option. If the baby was alive, she needed to get help immediately. She spurred her horse back toward the herd.

Thomas was the first person she came upon. "Thomas," she yelled as she rode swiftly toward him, forgetting the first rules of droving cattle—no loud noises, no quick movements. "I found the cow and she's got a newborn calf," she shouted.

Thomas turned in his saddle, vigorously shook his head, and put his finger to his lips.

Sarah slowed her horse to a walk, as he rode in her direction. "I'm sorry. I forgot, but we have to hurry," Sarah said as he approached. "The baby …"

Thomas interrupted, "You could have stampeded the whole herd for a cow and a calf." Thomas scolded. He turned in his saddle to make sure the herd was safe and waved at the other drover.

"I said I'm sorry."

"All right. What's this about the cow? She has a calf?"

"Yes. Two valleys over." Sarah thrust her finger in that direction. She was hurt at his reprimand, which was evidenced by her shortness of words and jerky actions.

"We need to go get her. Ride over and tell the other drover. I'll follow your tracks and head that way. You catch up." Thomas urged his horse forward.

Sarah Susannah sat watching him go. "Who does he think he is, ordering me around," she said out loud, momentarily forgetting her mission to obey. But she quickly did as she was told and then walked her horse to the top of the hill until she was out of sight of the herd. She spied Thomas in the valley below. Kicking her horse, she caught up with him at the top of the second hill.

"Where is she?" asked Thomas with his hand over his eyes, trying to peer through the pouring rain. Droplets ran from is hat onto his slicker, and down on the horses rump.

Sarah Susannah pointed to a clump of scrub brush. "She's on the other side."

Thomas thought out loud, "Can we approach her from the front? Scare her away from the calf. I'll jump off my horse, grab the calf, and we'll hurry back to the herd."

"I tried that," said Sarah. "It didn't work. Can we shoot a gun?"

"No. And spook the herd?" Thomas said and asked, "Who has a gun? I don't," he patted his bare leg and saddlebag.

"If we can't approach to get the calf, maybe we can ride swiftly toward her, scare her away, and take the calf with us," suggested Sarah Susannah.

"Yes. Good idea. We'll pull off our hats and wave them and shout as loud as we can. Come on. Let's see where her head is turned."

Thomas rode around a rock and motioned for Sarah Susannah to follow. "There," he pointed. "See her head. Are you ready to ride?"

"What if she doesn't run?"

"Then we'll stay out of her way and try to think of another plan. Ready?"

"I'm right behind you." Sarah Susannah took off her hat. She let out a piercing yell, waved the hat and rode behind Thomas. He did the same.

The cow stood for a moment looking at the shrieking twosome. As expected, she turned and high-tailed it into the brush and didn't quit running until she was out of sight.

Sarah and Thomas reined in their horses and halted at the motionless calf.

Before he could stop Sarah, she dismounted, hurried over, and bent down to look at the newborn baby. Was it dead or alive? Its eyes were closed. She nudged it with her toe. The eyelids fluttered. "Thomas, the calf's not dead."

Thomas had dismounted and now stood beside her. "Looks to me like it's about as close as it can get to being dead." He bent over the calf and pulled the head toward him. "I'm going to open the mouth and stick my finger inside."

"Won't it bite you?"

"Not likely. The interior should be warm, and I hope the baby makes a sucking motion."

At Thomas's intrusion into its body, the calf's eyes fluttered again. There was no other response. He shook his head. "I remember something else my father did. Find a straw in the grass and bring it to me."

"What?" said Sarah at this silly request, wiping water from the back of her neck as the rain continued to fall.

"Just do it. Hurry!"

This did not take long. She hurried back and handed the thick grass straw to Thomas. He carefully stuck the blade of grass up the calf's nose and moved it around.

The calf sneezed and emitted some spray from its mouth and nose. It sneezed two more times and moved its feet a little.

"Good," exclaimed Thomas. "The lungs will be clearing and that's a good sign. We need to get it to some warmth. Every moment with this little one is precious. "Sarah Susannah, we need to leave. Mama may be back any minute. Help me get the calf on my horse."

They picked the small calf up, carried it to Thomas' horse and hefted it onto his saddle. Thomas wasn't far behind. "Get on your horse and let's get out of here," he ordered.

"What about the cow?"

"Don't worry about her. She'll follow us. You can bet on that." Thomas started up the hill. "In fact, I think I hear her bawling."

~

Sarah Susannah and Thomas headed straight for the chuckwagon and people experienced at handling weak, almost dead calves. They got there at just about noon, the cook fire was already built at the edge and under the tarp.

The arrival of the small calf caused a stir of excitement in camp. Someone ran and retrieved a warm horse blanket from Gracie's wagon and the newborn was placed on it near the campfire.

The two young people scavenged some empty wooden crates from the wagons, stood them on end, and made walls to the sides and back. More blankets covered the top of the area where the sick calf lay. Thus, they made a warm and toasty, but small, makeshift stable for their new responsibility.

When this was done, Thomas said goodbye and headed back to his drag position.

Sarah Susannah squeezed into the tiny space, pulled the calf into her lap, and started rubbing the legs and body of the calf with cloths dipped in warm water from the washing kettle. She cooed to the little animal and saw the weak calf slowly respond to the warmth and the soothing stroking of its body. A song sung by cow-boys and crooned by the Stockton family around the fire at home came to Sarah's mind. She started singing it to the little calf in a low, sweet voice:

As I was a-walking one morning for pleasure
I spied a cowpuncher all riding along
His hat was throwed back and his spurs were a-jinglin'
As he approached me, he was singin' this song:
Whoopee ti yi yo, git along little dogies
It's your misfortune and none of my own'
Whoopee ti yi yo, git along little dogies

You know that Wyoming will be your new home.

Gracie squatted down and looked in. "Poor thing probably thinks you're her mama," she said smiling, remembering Wooly who kept her warm on her trip West. "I hope the cow hasn't rejected the little one."

"I don't think so," replied Sarah Susannah. "She was trying to tend it. Since it wasn't moving, I was afraid it was going to die. Maybe I shouldn't have interfered. Maybe I shouldn't have gone for help.

"You did the right thing," assured her mother, watching the calf's cautious moves. "The baby seems to be perking up." The tiny calf was trying to stand. Sarah Susannah helped it keep its balance for a minute. When it collapsed again, she let it rest on the warm ground.

"Milk is the most important subject at present," Jorge called from his spot, briefly stirring a pot cooking over the fire. "There's the fresh cow on the drive—one we milk each morning. Of course, the best milk is the mother's milk. But we'll see if we can get some down the little one until the mama shows up. There's always plenty." The milk was stored in gallon jars and any remainder thrown away at the end of the day. "I'll see what I can find to make a bottle. Here comes Thomas. Guess they didn't need him to help with the herd. I'll get him to help. He's got a good head for making things."

Jorge dug into the chuckwagon and came up with an empty bottle with a long neck—a bitters bottle for his rheumatism. The concoction wasn't working, so he dumped what was left of it on the ground. "Thomas get a piece of canvas or leather out of the wagon you're driving." He gestured with his hands the size to bring.

"I know just the piece of leather. I'll get it."

Jorge called after him. "Maybe Gracie or Sarah Susannah can sew us a nipple and we'll tie it to the end of the bottle neck. It won't be pretty, but I've seen it work."

"I'll be right back," Thomas grinned as he left on his mission, thinking he knew just how his bottle would work. There was an old leather glove …

Jorge chuckled to Gracie and Sarah Susannah as he cleaned the bottle, "Back in the good ole days, I've even seen a cattle horn with a leather nipple used for calves to suckle. They've used the same idea on babies when needed."

While Jorge went to look for needle and thread. Thomas found the leather glove. He thought about the shape the glove needed to make a serviceable form for the nipple. He started working and cut fingers loose with his knife. When Jorge returned with the proper sewing implements, Thomas sewed the glove together, leaving only the middle finger to guide the milk to the calf's mouth. Jorge watched and nodded in agreement.

Jorge brought the milk from the sideboard. "Let's fill the bottle with milk"

Thomas held the glass bottle. A small stream of white liquid passed through the narrow bottle neck until it was full. Some splashed on his hands.

Jorge sat the gallon jar down. "Now, we'll push the glove onto the neck and tie the string around the bottle's mouth."

Thomas helped Jorge by holding the string down for the final bowtie. "So, we can get it back off to clean, if need be," Jorge explained, grinning. He held the milk container at arm's length and gave it to Thomas. "Not bad, for two unexperienced bachelors."

Thomas took the bottle to Sarah Susannah. "Should I warm the milk up?" he questioned, looking around a box at her. She half-cradled the calf in her lap, stroking its head.

Sarah looked up at him. Love for the calf shone in her eyes. She was beautiful. His heart did a *WOW*.

"Hold the bottle in the water for washing the pots and pans. It shouldn't take long. Just warm. No more."

After warming the milk in its bottle, Thomas squeezed into the small stall area, sitting shoulder to shoulder with Sarah Susannah. Getting food down into the calf's stomach wasn't easy, even with the made-up milk bottle. Sarah put milk into the baby's mouth, gave the bottle to Thomas to hold and stroked the calf's throat. This caused a swallowing reflex.

The couple did this over and over again. Once, the strangled baby sneezed warm milk all over Sarah Susannah, but she didn't care. Sneezing was a response to her mothering. She loved this baby calf. She looked up at Thomas. His willingness to help made her forget her anger. She touched his hand. "Thank you." She was beginning to respect this gentle part of him.

Thomas left to help with getting water for food preparation. Water ran down the arroyo in a swift stream.

The drovers came in to noon at the chuckwagon. No one hurried for food. Everyone's attention was riveted on the little calf and Sarah Susannah in the put-together stable. Suggestions, statements, and questions came from all sides.

"Are you rubbing its body to keep the blood flowing? Touch is good."

"Warm cow's milk is always needed."

"Did the cow have a long labor?"

"How's its breathing? Better, huh?"

"Do you know how many hours since its birth? Could make a difference whether the calf lives or dies."

"That calf will never make it—too weak," one commented seeing the exhausted calf on its side and not moving.

Sarah Susannah listened to all the comments. Secretly, in her heart, she knew the baby calf would live.

Jonathan came by. "Sarah Susannah, how's your baby calf doing?"

"Showing some desire to live. Eyes open. Milk in."

"All right, but the calf needs to stand and walk. If it doesn't do this soon, it won't make it. Keep milk to it and get it to walk—the two important actions for today. Hopefully, the cow will let it suck tomorrow—if the calf lives."

"Oh, it's going to live, "Sarah Susannah stated adamantly.

"I hope you're right."

"Has the mama shown up?"

"Yes, and she's bawling continuously for her baby. Doesn't understand what's happened. The mother was a heifer. Sometimes, being a mother with the first birth isn't spontaneous. The first-timer has to learn like we do. There's no older cow to teach it the principles of birthing a calf."

Jonathan mounted his horse. "Remember what I said. Feed and walk." He rode toward the herd and paused. "When she can do this, it's best the calf goes back to her mother, if the cow will take her. Remember the sooner the better."

What would happen if she didn't walk? Sarah Susannah hugged the baby to her. She whispered, "You've got to walk and eat Little Bossy. Don't let me down."

As if the calf understood her, it moved its legs, again.

"Can you stand?" Sarah helped her to the standing position, spreading her legs apart. Seconds later, the calf lost its balance, and Sarah Susannah caught her as she fell. "Good. That's a start. You're still weak. We'll try again, soon."

"Sarah Susannah, how's Little Bossy?" Thomas called. He stuck his head inside the boxes. "I'll spell you if you're ready to eat."

"She's showing signs of life, and I am hungry. I'll ease out and you can come in. When I'm through eating, we'll try to feed her again and help her to her feet."

~

By nightfall, the calf could stand and the bottle couldn't flow fast enough for her to feed. Sarah Susannah and Thomas laughed at the baby's milky mouth and wobbly legs as they sat together in the shelter.

"You know, Little Bossy will have to go back to her mother in the morning." Thomas knew this would hurt Sarah Susannah. In a protective motion, he put his arm around her, resting his hand on her waist.

Sarah Susannah didn't object to his action. She leaned her head against his shoulder. "I'm glad we're not moving tomorrow. She'll have a chance to get stronger."

"There's no way she can keep up when we start moving." Thomas flatly stated.

"Poppa will find a way."

Thomas didn't say anything else—content to sit with a female, one with whom he felt akin, but he hoped she was right.

Sarah Susannah started singing again, but this time she changed the lyrics to her song. When she came to the chorus, she sang:

Whoopee ti yi yo, git along Little Bossy
It's your misfortune and none of my own
Whoopee ti yi yo, git along Little Bossy
You know that Abilene will be your new home.
You know that Abilene will be your new home.

Gracie sat with Press listening to Sarah Susannah serenade Little Bossy with her song.

"I don't remember you singing to Wooly when we were on the trail to The Pinery."

"No. I never thought too. Guess I was always too tired or too busy with chores," returned Gracie. She nodded her head toward the makeshift stable. "What do you think about Sarah Susannah and Thomas?"

"You mean as a couple?" asked Press.

"Yes, sweetheart. Exactly as a couple."

"She's a little bit young don't you think, and he lives so far away. Sounds like a long-distance romance, if you ask me."

"She's not much younger than me when I met you," answered Gracie, as Press gave her a hug. "I wonder about her plans to be a doctor or nurse. She always wanted to take after my friend, Sarah Cobb. Will she give that up?"

"Gracie, we've prayed over and talked about our brood. I think they will make good life decisions. Remember we decided to give them life's basics and let them make their own mistakes. I have faith that God will lead them in His paths, and they will be fine."

"But-t ..."

"No buts, sweetheart. I'm tired. I wish we could sleep together tonight. I want to put my arms around you and leave them there."

Gracie laughed. "Not possible on my cot. It's too small for both of us. We could sleep on the ground near the campfire," she suggested.

"I think I'm too old for that—parts hurt, including my back." Press kissed her and got up from his stool. "I love you, my sweetheart. Have a good night." He disappeared toward his tent.

Gracie whispered after him, "Good night, my love."

Chapter Seventeen

Press and Jonathan Check Out the Way Ahead

The following morning on April 8, the rain had slacked to a drizzle. The camp was slow to stir, but the smell of cooking bacon soon had everyone warming around the campfire, stomachs growling, and ready to eat. A couple of the cow-boys, who were relieving the last shift of the night, ate first and hurried to the *remuda* to request their horses from Cephas.

After breakfast, there was another brief rush for horses from the *remuda,* as the other cow-boys hurried to the day's assignments.

Jonathan stopped Caleb before he left. "Get Cephas and help Sarah Susannah take the calf to its mama. See if the heifer will take her baby back to nurse," he instructed.

"Sure, Jonathan. Are you going to scout for a new trail?"

"Yes, I had planned on going yesterday, but time passed so quickly, we decided to wait and get an earlier start today. Poppa and I will head out in a few minutes. He's gone for our horses now."

The two stood around jawing about the men, the mud, and the progress of the drive until Press walked up with the two mounts.

Press and Jonathan climbed on to leave. "Don't forget about the heifer and her calf. Be careful, there's no telling what she will do. She could be aggressive or gentle."

"Are you talking about the cow or Sarah Susannah?" Caleb chuckled. "I could see both of them as a problem."

Press and Jonathan both laughed. "I think my sister will do what's best for the calf."

Gracie joined them, bringing a metal tin container with bullets filled with bacon and eggs and metal bales for hanging on the saddle horn. "Your lunch," she grinned. "They'll eat good when you noon. Have you got real bullets with you?'

Press laughed. "Now what would we need real bullets for, sweetheart. We're not in the Wild West." He was thinking of a bill for Buffalo Bill Cody's coming show, advertised for Nebraska. The ads were plastered everywhere a billboard could be found in a town. "There's no Comanche or Apache or stampeding buffalo or rustlers that I know of."

"You might run across another rattlesnake," she suggested, referring to P.T.'s recent almost deadly encounter.

"How'd you know about that?" questioned Press.

"Never you mind. Do you have your guns?"

They both patted their saddle bags. No one wore their holstered guns on the drive, but they carried them, just in case.

"I have my new Colt-Burgess rifle. It's always handy." Press reached out his hand to its leather case located to the front of his left knee.

"I'll see you men later," said Caleb. "Have a safe trip."

They watched him head out to get his saddled horse from Cephas.

"Which way will you go?" asked Gracie.

Press looked at his son. "Let's ride to the longhorn you killed. I'd like to see if it has a brand."

"Sure." Jonathan said, turning to Gracie. "Momma, we'll be back before dark."

Gracie watched them ride away. For some strange reason, she wished they were *already* back. *Oh Gracie, you're in the intuition way again.*

Press and Jonathan rode north beside the arroyo for several feet. The ditch was now a flowing stream with a thin layer of sand over a rocky bottom. Grass poked its fronds through the surface in the shallow spots. At no point, as far as they could see, was it dangerous to cross.

They turned east when Jonathan recognized the start of his last ride into the area and followed the water-filled hoof marks he'd left earlier. The riding was easy until the large herd coming from the west joined in, churning up a wide, muddy, grassless path, which was visible to the horizon.

Press sat looking at the muddy area. "I see what you mean, son. We could plant grain in this plowed ground."

Jonathan laughed, "I'm afraid it's too far away from the Glory B, Poppa. How long do you think it has been since these cattle passed through here? Two days? Three days?" asked Jonathan.

"Can't tell, now. Too much mud and pounding rain have washed most of the hoof marks away."

Trying to stay out of the worst of the ruts made by the cattle, they rode away from the hills where Jonathan had shot the longhorn, but they kept going east, beside the same mud-covered route Jonathan had traveled the day before. After carefully riding two hours up the miry path, they found no evidence of the dead animal which should have been easy to spot.

"Looks like we've missed it, Poppa. I'm sure it didn't get up and walk. We need to turn back and check the ground more closely."

The second time they rode closer to the hillside and looked more carefully at the seemly, undisturbed earth beside the wide, muddy route.

Press reined in his horse and stopped. "Jonathan, come here."

On the soil was a large, waterlogged, red stain, filling up the hoof prints of the cattle which were driven in the area.

Press pointed. "Look there." Leading up a short rise was the unmistakable sign of something large being dragged by two people on horses. The creosote bushes were flattened, prickly pear cactus tugged completely out of the ground, and rocks disturbed.

Press and Jonathan followed the trail over the rise. The carcass of the longhorn was there with the ropes still around its neck.

Jonathan looked at his father and then over the terrain around them. A chill ran up his spine. "Why would someone drag a dead animal out of sight?"

"Maybe because they had something to hide. But what?" Press got off his horse and walked in a large circle, looking at the soil for tracks.

Seeing the rain had washed some of the mud from the carcass, Jonathan dismounted and checked the longhorn for a brand. A clear double-bar, II, was easy to see. "Poppa, I found the brand. Does a double-bar mean anything to you?"

"Two bars running parallel to each other and up and down?" asked Press, coming to look for himself.

"Yes." Jonathan pointed to the animal's rump, while his father bent down to look.

"If I remember correctly, the Double-Bar Ranch is in the Davis Mountains. They must be moving their beeves to market. I've met the owner, Jake Rainey, at a meeting of our Texas Cattle Raising Association." He scrunched his eyebrows together and continued. "He's not one to leave a hurt animal by the road. He'd kill it and butcher the longhorn for meat, especially if he's herding a bunch to market."

"I wonder if Caleb would know him, since he's from the general area."

"Probably. We'll ask him when we get back to camp."

"Did you find a trail?" Jonathan turned to look east, scanning the ground on top up the hill.

"Yes. In that direction," Press pointed east. "Looks like the two men on horses are following the main herd that's traveling below. Come on, let's see where it leads us."

Holding his horse's reins, Press walked along the hilltop, checking for horse's hooves on rocks and soil.

The riders didn't seem to be making any attempt to hide their movements.

Press expressed his thoughts out loud, "I wonder why they're sticking to the hilltop. Be easier riding down below—no rocks or cactus."

"Poppa, I'm beginning to have a bad suspicion about this whole affair. And, everything I'm thinking and seeing fits right in with this bad feeling."

"Hopefully, we'll have an answer to *our* suspicions soon, Jonathan."

The two continued to walk the crest of the hill, until the tracks moved down into a ravine, which deepened the further they went. "I'm thinking we'll keep edging forward on the hill—very carefully and not follow them into the valley." Press pointed to what looked like a wider open space dead ahead. "Let's get our horses off the crest of the hill on the opposite side and tie them to that scrubby live oak."

"What do you think they're doing?"

"Nothing good," said Press, leading his horse to the tree and placing his reins around a limb. "Put your gun on, son, and take your rifle." The father dug his out of his saddle bag, making movements to put it on.

Now events were starting to get serious. "So, are you thinking the same thing I'm thinking, Poppa?"

Press nodded his head. "Could be rustlers, son. I don't know, but we aren't takin' any chances." Press buckled his gun belt, giving it an extra tug. "Careful. No loose stones. I'd feel better if Texas wasn't dripping with water."

"Rustling might explain them not shooting the longhorn. The shot would be heard for miles and alert the drovers on the drive from the Double-Bar Ranch to their activities—the taking of their cattle."

"If they take very many, the Double-Bar people will know it. Course from the looks of the ground, their herd was twice or three times bigger than ours." Press looked at his son. "Remember, you knew only one longhorn was missing, but a good rustler might get several, especially if the drovers are tired or slack in their duties. And, who knows how long they've been in the area?"

"I wonder where they were when I shot the longhorn? Could they have seen me? I didn't look around for a human while I was here—never thought to." Jonathan's skin had chill bumps, as he spoke, and it wasn't from the cold wet drizzle.

"All we just talked about is guesswork. Let's find out if it's the truth." Press drew in a deep breath and let it out in a gush—not relishing what they were about to do. Grabbing his rifle, he started up the hill, not letting Jonathan go first but leading the way. They topped the hill and threaded their path down the other side about ten feet.

Following the line of the crest but walking just below it, so they would not be silhouetted against the sky, the two headed in an easterly direction. The ravine they were following from the ridge grew deeper and soon led them to a sheltered area between two hills. At first, the bawling of longhorns was faint, but the sound increased as they grew closer to the depression or what turned out to be a small canyon ahead.

~

Press and Jonathan sat for several minutes in the misty rain, observing through the scrub brush the movements of the six or eight men they could see below. The deepening ravine had opened up into a makeshift canyon hideaway with clear-running water probably from a spring at the head of the depression. Green buffalo-grass grew along the stream, and tents were pitched at the same location for the men running around below tending the cattle.

The cattle, those which could be seen, milled below the camp, their bellowing could be plainly heard from where the two men sat watching the activities going on below their perch. A small grouping of longhorns was herded near a fire which burned near the stream.

Two men, one in a large black hat with a red ribbon on it appeared to be in charge. The other tended four branding irons heating in the fire. Others roped cattle and threw them to the ground, preparing them to be branded. Plain as day what these men were doing—rustling cattle. Press and Jonathan's fears had been affirmed.

"Why four branding irons?" whispered Jonathan, as the one tending them chose one and headed for a longhorn who lay roped and tied on the ground.

"Depends on which one will adequately obscure the original brand. They're only pieces of iron made to alter what's on the longhorn."

Jonathan gave a huff, understanding immediately his father's words.

The mouth of the valley evidently ran at right-angles to the herds of cattle passing to the northeast. As was the thirsty cattle's habit, several would stop and bunch up to drink the water, and this would cause them to spread out, up and down the stream.

A wandering longhorn or several being driven to market could easily be picked off if they moseyed further up the creek and into the canyon. The rustlers would have quickly hidden their tracks to prevent being observed.

Press uttered his thought. "Quick action by the rustlers and a few animals would disappear up the stream. Nabbing a few in this way would be a quick and easy accomplishment for savvy rustlers. Even sounds coming from the canyon could be drowned out or mistaken for the noise of the passing herd. And a rancher, owning the herd, wouldn't be any the wiser."

"And Poppa, I've been thinking the unsuspecting drovers might overnight here since water is available."

"Smaller herds for sure," agreed Press. "Not likely we'll lose any, because we will keep our longhorns tightly packed, and they won't need water at this point in time, if we don't have to wait too much longer in camp for the rain to quit."

"The Glory B's longhorns will not be close enough for them to rustle if we scout out a different route."

"What a perfect setup," Press murmured quietly to himself, still observing the rustlers who were branding the longhorns. "They've had to wait until the rain's slackened to brand."

"What are we gonna do Poppa?" asked Jonathan, matching his father's low tone. "We can't let them continue to rustle cattle."

Press shook his head. "One thing we're not gonna do is ride down into their camp and try to arrest them." Press gave a low nervous chuckle. "We need a

Sheriff and a posse, or the Texas Rangers, and the only law close is at Fort Stockton—two days riding to get there. The Cattle Raising Association has inspector's set up along the trail, but I don't remember where the closest one is located. I never thought I'd have a need for one. Shoulda paid more attention."

"Where do you think they're from?"

"There's lots of bad men up and down the Pecos River. They don't call murder a *Pecos* for nothing or the thievery that goes on there a *Pecos Swap* without a cause."

"I've never heard of rustlers in our immediate area."

"I'm guessing going the shorter route to Fort Worth or Abilene, instead of into Kansas, has brought them south toward the Glory B to raid herds."

"I've not once heard you mention those two terms—*Pecos* or *Pecos swap*."

"There's never been a reason to use them. Our part of Texas has been mostly calm since the Civil War and the depression that followed. The bad men stayed to the north of and on the Pecos River. Looks like that has changed."

The two men sat silent and continued to watch the activity below.

Finally, Press made a suggestion. "Let's ease down where we can get a better look at their herd. I'd like to find out how they're altering the brands of the cattle they're stealing."

Jonathan asked, "Do we need to get the horses?"

"No. Less chance of being seen or making a noise, alerting the outlaws to our presence. We'll come back for them."

Being led by the noise of the cattle bawling, Press picked his way along the hill and down the side. Every few feet, he stopped to observe the area, looking for movement in the rocks and bushes. No sentinel was posted. *How long's this been going on,* he thought. These men seemed pretty sure there was no danger of being discovered. One other piece of information he noted, the canyon was about out of room for more cattle.

"Poppa the canyon's just about full of cattle," observed his son as soon as Press had his thought.

"I'd just realized it was, and they'll need to move the herd soon."

"This means they will either be behind us or before us," stated Jonathan.

"Yes, some way we'll need to find out which." Press moved on forward.

Walking to find the herd wasn't necessary. One of the longhorns found them as they rounded a rock at the bottom of the hill.

"Make a mental note of the brand, Jonathan."

It snorted, and backed up, turned tail and walked away.

"I'll do better than that." Jonathan pulled out pencil and paper and drew the design—a double-bar with a bar at the top and bottom.

Another longhorn came ambling into their area.

"Look!" whispered Jonathan. "There's the Johnston J with a bar on top and bottom and another running up and down, mimicking the other brand change. I see what you mean by branding irons of different sizes. Didn't you say the Johnstons went through here earlier?"

"Yes. So, this has been going on for over a month." He and Jonathan noted two other altered brands from the area.

"Have you got all the identifying marks written down, son?"

"Yes." He flipped the pages so his father could see.

"Then let's go back to the horses. There's one more thing I want to do."

~

Following the hoof marks of the previous herd, Press and Jonathan rode to the narrow entrance of the rustler's canyon.

"Doesn't look like this draw would open up to the wide space beyond," observed Jonathan.

"Stay here, Jonathan and hold my horse's reins," Press said and dismounted.

"What are you going to do, Poppa?"

"I'm going to see exactly how a person gets into the canyon, just in case we need to come back with a posse."

"Be careful, Poppa. I'll be waiting."

Press walked up a deep trench to the small opening—so small they'd attached cut creosote bushes and mesquite trees to movable tree logs in a good attempt to cover the entry. The wet, mesquite fronds were dead and fell off with his touch. From where he stood, the faint sound of cattle calling could be heard.

He walked back to Jonathan and mounted up. They started the long ride back to the camp.

"This gang is experienced in rustling. They've covered all the bases, and they're dangerous."

"Poppa, what time is it?"

Press pulled his watch from its pocket. "It's five o'clock! Where has the time gone, and we haven't eaten our biscuits."

"I haven't even thought about eating. Too much excitement. What are we going to do about the rustlers?"

Press shook his head. "I don't know. I'll have to think about this problem. You think, too. Let's head for the chuckwagon and the herd. We'll stop and eat our bullets after we get past where the longhorn was killed. Is that plan all right with you, Son?"

Press saw Jonathan nod. They rode without comment until a cottonwood tree, next to a shallow depression, afforded cover from the continuing mist. At least, the rain wasn't pouring.

Both men dismounted. Press took the tin of food and canteen from his saddle horn. He went to the base of the large tree. With his boot, he scraped the top wet foliage away and the two men sat on dry leaves from last autumn.

Opening his tin with the biscuits inside, Jonathan, blew out a sigh in a loud rush and asked, "Poppa, do you think they know we're here?"

"When they went to the trouble of dragging the longhorn away from the very route we're taking, so we wouldn't see it, I think they might."

"My shot to kill the animal didn't help either, did it."

"Just let them know a little sooner. Actually, son, you've done us a favor. We wouldn't know about them if you hadn't seen the longhorn and shot it. *The good Lord works in mysterious ways…"*

"Now, we have to figure out what to do about what we know, right Poppa. I don't relish the solution." Jonathan was thinking gunfight.

"I think I've figured out a plan of action. I think the plan is one of inaction."

Jonathan shook his head, puzzled, "What do you mean action and inaction."

"Here's what we're going to do. You've got a good drawing of each illegal brand. Make sure you keep it safe. The rustlers are going to have to move soon, because the canyon is full of beeves. Where will they take them, do you think?"

"The closest place—the railhead at Abilene."

"Sure enough. Who'll be in Abilene?" Press pointed to himself. "We will. We'll alert the Sheriff, or Texas Rangers, and we'll stay long enough to identify the herd as it comes in, probably through Buffalo Gap."

"Why Buffalo Gap?"

"Because, it's a small town and a narrow valley in the mountains below Abilene, where the longhorns would be close together. They aren't going to want their herd spread out over all creation. Keeping them together would help hide their dirty work. Because of this need, we will find it easier to spot and identify the altered brands."

"But Poppa, that means we'll have to be in Buffalo Gap when they drive through."

"Yes. We can spot them, but the law can catch and arrest the rustlers after they leave the town and before they get to the railhead. I'm pretty sure we have an inspector for brands on herds before you get to Abilene. The area is open and flat and if the situation should erupt into gunfire, those involved are less likely to get hurt."

"I don't like the idea of a gunfight. Someone—some of us might get hurt."

"We'll stay out of the way. Let the law do their job. Our position is to pinpoint the herd and not shoot guns."

"I see." Jonathan nodded. "Maybe, we should accidently lose a few of our herd. They'd be easy to identify with the B brand on their sides."

"Good thinking. We'll add a few longhorns as bait. That means we'll need to come this way and not attempt to find a new route past them. I think we'll take the southern drive into Abilene—miss Buffalo Gap. It's a little longer and over a low hill, but there'll be no way to interfere with them. Depending on which herd gets to Abilene first … No, we must arrive first. That's the easiest way. We need to be there when they come through the Callahan Divide and Pass, and start across the plain heading for the railroad and cattle lots in Abilene. Going through the settlement at Buffalo Gap will slow them down, whereas we will have a straight shot."

Press got up and walked to his horse. He put the empty tin can back on his saddle horn. "We'd better mount up and ride to the chuckwagon. Your Momma will be sending the Texas Rangers for us."

Jonathan followed, looking up at the sky. "Poppa, do you think the sky is lightening up?"

Press followed his line of sight to the west. "You're right. The clouds are breaking up. Tomorrow, the rain will be gone. I just hope the sun shines."

"I'll keep check on the muddy ground. Thank goodness the Texas soil is a thirsty one. It will drink up the water."

"What do you think, Son? Will we be on the move after an early noon meal?"

"I certainly hope so."

~

During the night the misty rain of the day before quit. Although the morning was chilly, the sun's brightness warmed them up and dried them out. The intensity of the light and the rain-cleaned air, made those on the drive squint and pull their hats down over their eyes to shut out the glare.

Jonathan called them all together at breakfast. "We'll be checking out the trail this morning. If there's any way we can move, we will after our noon meal. Stay close and be ready for my orders." He waved them away to their morning's work.

As if on cue, a slight wind came up, ruffling the tarp over the campfire.

Golden came over to talk to Jonathan. "This wind will help dry the ground," he suggested to his boss.

Jonathan nodded his head. "Do you want to ride with me to check out the muddy trail?"

"Sure, you know me. I'd rather be moving than sitting around doing nothing."

"Poppa and I found out something yesterday, I'd like to let you in on. I'm going to need your help to execute a plan we've made."

"I'm ready. When?"

"Okay, then it's settled. We'll start out soon after breakfast. Tell Cephas to saddle our horses and be ready to ride."

"Okay, boss."

Golden watched him walk over to talk to Press and Gracie. Press nodded his head and looked over at him. The older man waved as if agreeing to whatever Jonathan had said. Golden headed for the *remuda,* wondering what plan Jonathan needed to set in motion.

Chapter Eighteen

The Drive Continues

After Jonathan and Golden left, there was the rattle of cleaning the morning pots and pans in a big dishpan. After drying the cooking containers, Sarah Susannah helped her mother place them in the chuckwagon and stood looking at the stack of dirty tin plates, cups, and utensils.

"Momma, I'd like to go see how Little Bossy is doing when we finish."

"I don't have a problem with that, but let's find out what Jorge is doing for our noon meal. Should the muddy trail prove to be passable, Jonathan may move out as soon as we eat, and we'll need to prepare a quick meal for noon and leave soon after to stay ahead of the herd. In other words—less food and less mess is the best answer."

"Where is Jorge anyway? He just disappeared after breakfast," asked Sarah Susannah, looking around the camping area and across the sun warmed earth.

"I'll be honest with you. I don't know. He said something about talking to Press, and your father went to talk to Cephas. So, he must be on his way to the herd or on his way back."

Gracie walked to the water barrel which was attached to the chuckwagon. She opened the spigot and poured clean water into a pot and then refreshed the kettle which hung over the campfire. "We'll have more hot water in a minute," she said, grinning at her daughter.

The young girl dropped the tin plates, cups, and utensils into the still hot cleaning water, letting them soak while she waited for the hot rinse water.

Emptying a second dishpan, Gracie filled it with clear water poured from the hot kettle water which hung over the fire. She cooled it with a dipper full from the water barrel.

Scrubbing each with the dish cloth, Sarah Susannah took a bit of clean sand brought by P.T. and Thomas from the arroyo to scour stubborn spots.

Gracie helped with the cleaning process by rinsing the dishes, putting them to air dry on the wooden sideboard of the chuckwagon.

Turning to come back to rinse more, she saw Jorge coming toward them. "Here comes Jorge." She waved.

"We've been missing you," stated Sarah Susannah as he drew near. "You weren't here to inspect our work," laughed Gracie's youngest.

"I'm back now," huffed Jorge—out of breath from his brisk walk. "Whew, they've moved the herd again. If I'd known, I would have had Cephas to saddle my horse."

"Did you find Press," asked Gracie.

"Yes, I wanted to know what to do about our noon meal and talk to him about something I heard Jonathan talking to Golden about as they left this morning."

Both subjects piqued the lady's interest.

"What do we do about the noon meal?" asked Gracie, wanting to get this out of the way first.

"We'll need the iron skillets, and Gracie you'll need to mix more biscuits. Try to do two for each drover."

"I can do that. No problem."

"Off the cured and smoked ham, which hangs in my wagon, Sarah Susannah and I will cut slices and fry them in the big skillet. We'll make ham biscuits for noon. This means we'll have nothing to clean up after the men eat except the coffee pot."

Sarah Susannah groaned. "We'll have to clean the iron skillets again."

"We can wipe them out with a rag since we'll only have grease to contend with," suggested Gracie.

"Sure," said Jorge, pouring himself a cup of coffee from the pot hung over the campfire. He stood sipping it, taking a breather after his rushed trip.

"What was the other thing you went to ask Press about?" asked Gracie.

"I heard Jonathan telling Golden there was a problem up the trail as they rode out, and I wondered what it was, since we'll be in the forefront of the drive. Seems to me, we needed to know."

"Well, I reckon," said a surprised Gracie. "Wonder why Press didn't mention it to us—or at least to me?"

"After he explained the situation, I can see why they didn't."

"Okay, Jorge. You've got my attention. What's the trouble we should know about?" Gracie looked at him expectantly.

Jorge sidled toward her and lowered his voice. "You have to promise you won't tell," He said this although Press did not specifically tell him the information should be held close to the vest.

Sarah Susannah's ears were ready to hear. What was going on? Was there danger involved? She stepped around her wash table and closer to the cook to listen to the details.

"Press and Jonathan think we have rustlers on the trail ahead." Jorge waited for this bit of information to sink in.

"What!" exclaimed Gracie, jerking back and shaking her head at this unimaginable news. "We've never had a problem with herding our cattle, and I can't think of anyone in the area saying they've had trouble either."

"I think there's evidence which may support their assumption," he said matter-of-factly.

Jorge went on to explain the scant details which Press had given him.

"Well, I declare. I can't believe it. Rustlers." Gracie stood, hands on hips, looking at the *remuda* and Cephas.

Jorge followed her glance. "I guess we'll know whether we move or not when Jonathan gets back. For now, we need to start fixing our biscuits and hitching the wagons so we'll be ready to move. Have either of you seen P.T. or Thomas?"

"They went walking up the arroyo. Said they might go fishing," she laughed, knowing they were joshing her, since fish couldn't live in a normally dry arroyo. "Do you want me to go get them?" asked Sarah Susannah.

Gracie interrupted, asking, "Jorge can't we manage the biscuits and ham? Sarah Susannah wants to go see Little Bossy."

"Oh, by all means, go on. Your mother and I can handle this."

"I'll go get Thomas and P.T. first," she suggested, heading toward the *remuda* to get her horse. Under her breath she said, "Wait until Thomas and my brother hear about the rustlers," totally forgetting Jorge's admonition not to tell.

~

P.T. looked over at Thomas. "Here comes your sweetheart."

"What do you mean?" said Thomas who was trying to skip a rock on the moving water in the arroyo.

"Here comes Sarah Susannah—my sister."

Thomas threw his last rock, brushed his hand on his britches, and turned to look down the arroyo. "Hey, she's not my sweetheart." He declared, but he had a wide grin on his face which he put up his hand to hide.

A smiling Sarah Susannah rode up to the two, giving Thomas an extra glance. "You're both wanted at the campsite. Mom and Jorge are preparing food for the noon meal, and Jorge wants the horses and wagons hitched up ready to move out at noon. That is if Jonathan makes the decision to continue today."

She turned her horse and waited until the two walked over to their horses and mounted up. Sarah Susannah led the way as they headed slowly back down the arroyo. The two young men caught up and rode alongside her. She noted that Thomas stayed as far away as possible.

Sarah Susannah listened to the chatter of the two friends as they went back to the campfire. She loved their distinctive voices. P.T.'s was changing with each passing month, getting deeper and more defined. She was sure Thomas's was probably doing the same, although she hadn't known him long enough to say with certainty. Both were growing up as they participated in this drive to Abilene.

She was changing too. She couldn't help but attach herself to Thomas. The more she was in his presence, the closer she felt to him. Her thoughts were mostly of him. Was it love? How could she know? She'd never been to this place before. She looked over at him. Her heart skipped a beat.

These thoughts were interrupted by Jorge's "Hello, about time you three arrived."

The two young men dismounted while Sarah Susannah remained on her horse—her eyes following Thomas as he went to hear Jorge's instructions. How would she ask for Thomas to accompany her to see Little Bossy?

She didn't notice her mother observing her look. "Jorge, do you think we could spare Thomas for a few minutes to escort Sarah Susannah over to the herd to see her calf?"

Jorge stopped and put his hands on his hips. "Of course. How about an hour? By then we should have our noon meal cooked and ready to eat. We could even spare P.T. for that long, if he wants to go. When they come back, we'll complete loading and hitch the mules to the chuck wagon. At that point, we'll need Thomas and P.T. both to help."

"Aw, I'll stay here," said P.T. with a grin and a wink at Thomas, continuing to tease him about his former statement regarding his sister as the other's sweetheart, making Thomas more uneasy about the whole situation.

Gracie saw this hidden act and grinned.

That was enough for Thomas who didn't intend to wait for anymore joshing. He quickly mounted his horse and grabbed one of Sarah Susannah's horse's reins, riding away from the wide smiles behind them. "Come on," he commanded, leading her horse behind him as he galloped away from the campsite, irritated at his friend's hints.

Taken completely by surprise, Sarah Susannah hung on and grabbed at her rein. She finally yanked it from Thomas's tight clutch. Even though she was upset, she followed him across the prairie to where the longhorns were at pasture.

When he slowed down, she caught up with him. "Why did you do that?" she asked in an annoyed tone.

"Sometimes your brother discomfits me," said an embarrassed Thomas, his head down as he spoke.

Sarah saw a large red spot on the nearest cheek to confirm this fact. Did that mean he liked her as much as she liked him? Her irritation quickly evaporated—replaced by different emotions.

Instead, she said, "Well, Thomas, sometimes you upset me, too."

Thomas could hear the tears in her voice. She wasn't angry, just hurt. He stopped his horse and turned toward her, "I'm sorry, Sarah Susannah. I hope you'll forget my urge to leave so quickly. I didn't mean to trouble you." Not wanting to answer any additional personal questions, Thomas changed the subject. "Let's go find Little Bossy. Are you ready?"

She was more than ready. Her feelings were a jumble of emotions, and if she opened her mouth, she might declare them. Better to let Thomas control that discussion as he had when he'd just led the way out of the campsite. "Yes. Why don't you lead the way?" she agreed.

They rode the rest of the path to the herd in companionable and quiet calm.

Thomas was the first to see the little calf. "Look at her." He started laughing at her antics.

Little Bossy was kicking up her hooves when they saw her, running around her mama and having fun. When she saw Sarah Susannah and Thomas she stopped and stared at them. Then she walked over to her mother and started nursing.

Little Bossy's mama turned her head and licked the hair on her offspring's rump which was already clean and shining. Meanwhile, her big brown eyes checked out the two humans on horseback, who were watching her and her newborn calf. They looked vaguely familiar—non-threatening. She made no attempt to protect her little one. Unlike before, she felt no animosity from them.

The two former nursemaids dismounted and stood observing the hungry calf, as she nudged her mother.

"See, I told you she'd live."

Thomas laughed. "My pa says, 'never doubt a determined woman.' He was talking about my ma.

You're a lot like her," he acknowledged, paying her a compliment.

Sarah Susannah turned a smile as bright as the sunshine on him.

Hearing their voices, Little Bossy turned and walked over toward Sarah Susannah. "She has a ring of milk around her mouth," laughed the young girl. "Do you think she knows me?"

"She knows your smell and mine, for sure. Let's sit on the ground and see if she comes to us. Animals don't like it when you tower over them." Thomas went for his rain slicker tucked in his saddlebag. Spreading it on the ground, they seated themselves and waited.

"Little Bossy," Sarah Susannah called to the calf. "Come here little girl." She kept calling in the same voice she'd used in the makeshift stable by the campfire. She started humming the tune to 'Git along Little Bossy,' her version of the cow-boy ballad which drovers sang on the cattle trail.

The calf walked slowly toward the two sitting on the ground. She stopped, deciding to run around and look silly on her long, wobbly legs, before coming closer.

Sarah Susannah and Thomas sat very still, hardly blinking an eye. Sarah continued to hum.

Little Bossy stopped, taking a few steps toward the two sitting on the ground. Getting close enough, she nudged Sarah's forehead, dripping a few drops of milk on her arm. Sarah Susannah ignored the wet drops and touched the calf with her hand.

The calf nudged Thomas' arm.

"She knows both of us." Sarah sounded as happy as if she'd been given a birthday present or the money to get one.

The calf backed off and gave a couple of happy leaps.

Accepting of the two, Little Bossy returned and came close enough for Sarah to rub her back and legs. Her mama chomped grass not far away—a watchful eye on the goings on.

"Sarah, have you and your father decided how she's going to travel during the drive? Not many newborns make it. Most are killed to keep from slowing the other beeves down."

"How horrible. No one's going to kill Little Bossy." She hugged the little calf tightly to her chest.

"What arrangements have you made?" insisted Thomas. "Your wagon is full."

"Jonathan says during the day she can ride in the wagon with you and P.T., and at night she'll be let out to nurse her mom." What Sarah Susannah didn't say was how she'd worked on her older brother to make this happen, even calling in her father for the final call.

"She'll be hungry between, won't she?" asked Thomas.

"We can give her a pan of milk at noon. If she can drink water, she can drink milk."

"I shoulda known you would work things out," said Thomas grinning. "Your brother and I'll take care of your little calf at noon. He gave Little Bossy an extra pat.

~

The herd did move at noon. Jorge had orders to go four hours and then make camp for the night.

"What's Jonathan thinking?" he asked Gracie before they mounted up to the wagon seats. "It's not far to Fort Stockton. If we went a few extra hours, we could make it."

"I don't know. And Press is gone," she responded, looking around the camp which was now deserted, except for Thomas and P.T. The two boys were waiting for Jorge to take action so they could follow.

"It's bound to still be muddy, so what's two or three more hours." Raising a muddy boot, he scraped it against the hub of his wagon wheel.

"Are you complaining, Jorge?"

The cook rarely let anything bother him. He took out his pocket watch and looked at it.

"No. Come on. Let's get our four hours in and try to find a nice, unmuddied spot to camp." With that he mounted up to his wagon seat and chirped to his mules. "Come on you gray soon-to-be muddy, red-clay-covered mules," he grumbled under his breath, because no one could hear.

As Jorge passed her heading toward their starting place, Gracie teased him with a grin on her face. "I declare, you are complaining. Admit it. At least, it's not raining now."

Jorge just threw up his hand, gave her a gentle smirk and drove on. Gracie fell in behind him, and the boys followed with their horses tied to the back of their wagon. Cephas soon had the *remuda* in line, tagging along.

~

Sarah Susannah was glad to see the three wagons as the drovers stopped the herd for the night. They'd been riding their horses in mud and next to a hill for several miles. This kept the cattle in a long line and almost single file. From where she sat on her horse at drag, the smell of manure, urine, and sweaty, stinky cattle was beginning to be nauseating. Although she felt hungry, she wondered if she would be able to eat her supper meal.

Along with the rest of the drovers, she helped to herd the cattle into a position where they could be watched by the first two men on the night shift. These two would already be eating their supper and resting a few minutes before riding to the herd. Sarah Susannah would not be riding night herd. Press had put his foot down on this prospect.

After bunching the cattle with the rest of the men, she rode with them toward the campfire, noticing that Golden appeared to be one of the men heading back to the herd. He usually took one of the early morning shifts. She'd heard him say more than once, he liked to get up early rather than stay up late. This puzzled her, but anxious to get out of the perfume of the day's drive, she dismissed her bafflement.

Approaching her mother, she whispered, "Momma, I don't feel so good. Can I be relieved of helping with the supper meal?"

Gracie looked quickly at her, coming over she put her wrist on the girl's forehead. "You're not hot. What's wrong? Are you hurting somewhere?"

"It's the smell, I …"

Gracie interrupted her; forehead wrinkled in a frown. "Yes, you have a rather peculiar odor coming from you. Why don't you go wash up and rest on the cot in the wagon? You'll feel better. Jorge and I can take care of this meal. In fact, most of the work's done already. Skedaddle. Go. I'll get Thomas to take care of your horse."

Sarah Susannah took her time washing up at the water barrel. She went to her mother's wagon and started to climb inside. A hand caught her elbow and helped boost her into the back.

"Are you all right?" asked Thomas, a look of real concern on his face.

"Yes. I just need to rest for a few minutes. Riding drag today wasn't much fun," she managed a weak smile. "Thanks for caring, Thomas."

"Why don't you ride with P.T. on the wagon tomorrow, and I'll ride drag for you."

"I don't know if Jonathan will go for that."

"I'll clear it with him as soon as he gets here. Go ahead and rest. I'll let you know."

Golden looked at the stream coming from the mouth of a ravine. He was sure it was the same one Jonathan had told him about. His orders were to see that around ten of the Stockton's longhorns got lost in the narrow opening. Looking down the creek, he saw just the ones he needed.

He rode toward them, separating them out from the herd. Checking around, there was no one to see his actions. The other drover was far enough away, and his attention was on a wandering longhorn so he wouldn't be a problem.

Golden quickly followed Jonathan's instructions. Guiding the longhorns, he shooed them up the creek and returned to the herd. There, it was done. He breathed a sigh of relief; glad he hadn't run into the rustlers he knew were close by.

He rode over to the other drover. "I'm going back to camp."

"You aren't helping with this shift?" asked the man.

"No. Jonathan will send one of the other men to help. Everything looks quiet and peaceful. I don't think you'll have a problem until my replacement shows up. See you later."

Before the man could ask more questions, Golden spurred his horse and headed for camp. Jonathan was going to give instructions for tomorrow as the men ate their supper, and he wanted to be there to hear them.

Jonathan was talking to Thomas when he arrived. "Yes, you can take Sarah Susannah's place at drag tomorrow," he agreed.

Thomas left and headed for one of the wagons.

Jonathan came over to Golden. "Did everything I asked you to do get done?"

"Yes. No problem. The longhorns are in place."

"Good. Let's go to the campfire and assemble the others so I can talk about tomorrow."

Press, Gracie, and Jorge leaned on the sideboard of the chuckwagon, waiting for Jonathan's instructions. P.T. and Thomas sat on stools pulled from the inside of the wagon they managed. Sarah Susannah stuck her head out from where she rested on the cot, while the others stood or hunkered down near the fire.

Jonathan stood in the midst of the group near the fire warming his hands. "How many of you are glad it's not raining?" he asked.

There were plenty of nods and choruses of yes from his audience.

"I wanted to talk about tomorrow, so you will know what to expect. We will be going through Fort Stockton. We'll stop at Comanche Springs and let the longhorn's water, and then we will move on past the settlement.

"Jorge, you will leave early as usual, go into the fort, and quickly replenish any supplies you need at the Sutler's store. As soon as you get that done, you will continue on past and set up for our noon meal beyond town and at our regular time to eat."

Jonathan turned toward his point man. "Caleb, our longhorns will bypass the town. We've lost so much time because of the rain; we can't stop and visit the area."

Turning his attention back to the drovers, he continued, "I'm sorry. I hope all of you understand. The next few days, we'll try to make up some of the time we've lost. We have at least a month or more before we get to Abilene. After we sell the longhorns, you will be paid there, and we'll take some time to celebrate and relax, before we head back home. So, you can look forward to our visit. I don't have anything else. Any questions?" he asked.

"I hope we don't have any more trouble before we get there," one of the cow-boys commented. Several agreed with him.

"Anything else?" Jonathan waited. He couldn't promise to make life easy. There was nothing but silence. "Is anyone hungry? Let's eat."

The cow-boys crowded the chuckwagon, jostling one another in friendly comradery to be first at the supper meal.

With Thomas's help, Sarah Susannah climbed down from the wagon and headed for the sideboard. She was hungry and ready to eat.

Chapter Nineteen

Abilene and Ruby Eliza

Ruby Eliza walked down the boardwalk in Abilene, wondering where her Momma and Poppa and the longhorns were at present. Because of the steady rain falling from the skies, she doubted if they'd passed Fort Stockton. Pouring rain made driving longhorns undesirable and dangerous. Now, at least the sun was shining. The constant rain of the last few days had let up.

She twirled her white umbrella as she walked down the rough, uneven wooden planks. The parasol was an extravagance, since she was mostly a careful woman when it came to money. Her one luxury was made of wood, cotton, and supposedly Irish lace in Europe and shipped to America. Months ago, when she saw it down the street in the mercantile store window, she had had to have it. On impulse, she walked straight into the store and bought the lovely thing.

Doctor Sarah had chided and teased her about her extravagant purchase, wondering out loud, "How did such an exquisite item get to Abilene,"

Ruby Eliza knew this was anybody's guess. She used it to shield the glare of the sun and dim the brightness of its rays.

"Hello, Ruby Eliza," called someone across the street.

The nurse stopped, turned, and looked up into the glare of the sun. Squinting in its bright rays, she recognized one of her girlfriends from church.

Rachel Woody stood in the open, office doorway of the train superintendent. The office was in one end of the new train station which housed the headquarters of the Texas and Pacific Railway. The ticket office was in the other.

"Hi Rachel," returned Ruby Eliza, wondering what her friend was doing at the train station office. Her first thought was maybe she was taking a trip. Nope, wrong end to buy a ticket.

She asked instead, "Rachel, are you planning a trip?"

Ruby Eliza grinned. "No, I'm just going in to visit our new superintendent."

Ah-h, thought Ruby Eliza. Rachel was single like she, and the news circulating at church said the new man in charge of the Abilene office was too. Rumors were that he and his father would be at church tomorrow.

Rachel was on the hunt for a husband, and everyone knew it. Could she be there asking to escort the young man to the service in the guise of introducing him to everyone?

Not wishing to have a conversation, Ruby Eliza couldn't wave goodbye. Besides her parasol, she grasped in one hand two canvas bags of supplies from the mercantile store—mostly food items for the coming week. They were beginning to get heavy. "See you at church Sunday," she called to Rachel, nodding her head, and continuing to walk.

She resumed walking down the boardwalk, being careful to lift her skirt, with thumb and forefinger, in-between stores where the boardwalk ended. Mud and mud puddles were the norm until she came to another store and stepped on the wooden walk again.

~

Once vacant prairie, Abilene was new—everything in the town.

Established by the railroad company in 1881, the management had made the decision not to veer close to Buffalo Gap, an already established town in the area, which afforded the amenities for living in the west.

Thirteen miles south of Abilene, the Gap was the county seat of Taylor County with a post office and jail.

Instead, the company made the decision to head straight west and across West Texas, maybe even to El Paso.

Entrepreneurs, realizing an opportunity for making money, quickly put-up buildings around the new headquarters on the prairie. Even now, hammers and saws were heard at several places on both sides of the railway tracks.

The new hotel stayed full of construction workers framing buildings, and drovers, bringing cattle to be sold and shipped by the railroad.

Feedlots for cattle to be sent back east had been established on the outskirts, causing a need for fencing around acres of grassland. These were set up far enough away so the smell wasn't offensive for the permanent settlers except when the wind blew a certain way.

Because of the swiftness and expansion of the growing town, there was a movement to make Abilene the new county seat of Taylor County.

~

Ruby Eliza continued to the front of a building where a sign read—*Sarah Cobb, Medical Doctor*. Saturday dinner break and shopping over, it was time to get back to work. Emergency patients arrived at all times of the day and night.

"Hey, Miss Stockton," came from across the street behind her.

I'm really popular today, she thought as she turned around. Leaning over, she put both canvas shopping bags on the sidewalk and waved at the young pastor of Abilene's only church. He sat on the top step at the front of the building's doors, stirring the air with a fan.

She laughed at the sight. "It's hot, Pastor Gridley."

"Yes. I've been moving the pews around so we can get more people inside—using my muscles." He moved his arm into an L-shape, trying to show the bicep muscles in his upper arm. This was a mistake, because the Reverend was not known for physical labor. He did preach a good sermon based on the Holy Bible. "Guess my muscle decided to rest too," he stated, when none showed up. He continued, "Last Sunday, as you know, we had standing room only."

"Yes, I do know. Abilene is growing with leaps and bounds, isn't it? Did you get more pews inside?" She knew there were a few in the church storeroom which were reserved for future growth. "Did you not have help?"

"No. My help couldn't come. You should have seen me dancing around with the pews. But I made it, and we have more room for Sunday. You'll see. Where have you been?"

"Had a few minutes to catch up on shopping today, and I ate out."

Eating out was something the two often joked about.

Like the new superintendent of the Texas and Pacific Railroad, Grider Gridley was single. Joshing Ruby about going to eat was always on his menu, but he didn't have the pluck to actually ask.

"Did you have something good to eat at Cowboy's Victuals?" No one in his congregation ate anywhere else.

"Yes. Always my favorite on Saturday—thinly sliced beef and gravy, mashed potatoes and Ernie's barbeque beans. Yum! You can't beat his famous beans. I was glad not to have to cook today."

"If I'd known you were going, I'd of gone with you." Pastor Gridley avowed, smiling broadly and coming down a couple of the church's steps.

"If I'd known you were hungry, I'd of asked you to go," ventured Ruby, who normally teased right back. She sorta liked the Reverend. He wasn't the most handsome man she'd known, but his heart was in the right place, and his smile was open, toothy, and infectious.

"Are you coming to church tomorrow?"

"Yes, of course, unless the infirmary fills up with sick people. I think Doctor Sarah sent the last one home this morning. She let me take the morning off and catch up on our supplies." Ruby Eliza motioned to the two canvas bags stuffed with grocery items and other necessities which were now sitting on the office's porch. "They're heavy," she commented. Would he help? She waited to see if he caught her veiled suggestion. He didn't. "Guess I'll go inside. See you tomorrow morning."

"Have a good afternoon," said the Pastor, still fanning.

Tilting her umbrella against the side of the building, Ruby Eliza leaned over and pulled her drawstring purse out of one of her canvas bags. She opened it and rummaged inside for her skeleton key which opened the door to the hospital and office. Finding it, she held it up for Pastor Gridley to see. She didn't wait for him to respond, but unlocked the door, picked up her bags, grabbed her umbrella, and quickly went inside.

~

Doctor Sarah had converted, of all things, an abandoned, two-story saloon into her medical office. The building hadn't been vacant but a few days when she came from Nashville, Tennessee. Thinking she might have to build a building; she was pleasantly surprised to find quarters she could renovate.

Before leaving her successful practice in Nashville, she'd sold her part to her assistant.

Gracie Stockton had kept up a correspondence with her Tennessee friend for years. She'd sent glowing letters of life in Texas, encouraging her to come, and finally the wanderlust of moving to the growing city of Abilene on the diminishing frontier was more than Doctor Sarah could resist. She convinced herself of the necessity of a good doctor, packed up her medical equipment and personal possessions, boarded the train and set up her office in Abilene.

Because of the expected and dramatic rise of the new railroad town, the previous saloon owners had miscalculated the size needed for their watering hole. Picking out available acreage to the west and south of the railroad tracks, toward Buffalo Gap, where the newest stockyards were located, they built four times larger than the one Doctor Sarah bought.

Ruby Eliza was glad the new drinking and gambling establishment was far away. On the occasions she was close, the raucous music, loud laughter, and voices vying to be heard, made her even happier to be on the other side of town.

"Doctor Sarah," she called as she stepped through the open doorway. Her boss did not answer. She deposited her umbrella in the nearest chair for waiting patients and continued toward the back of the building.

Part of the downstairs was a small office with chairs for patients to use while waiting, and two private examining rooms which also functioned as surgery, if it was warranted. Behind those three rooms ran a narrow kitchen which served as a scrubbing area for surgery and cooking-eating area. This narrow space had been storage for the saloon. The area was open on both ends for easy access.

Through a door to the right side of the office was the infirmary with four uncomfortable cots. A makeshift mattress of straw and feather pillow with case covering lay on top with a sheet and blanket.

Ruby Eliza stood for a few seconds looking around. It always amazed her how her boss was so organized, thinking of everything.

No one was in the office and the doors to the examining room and infirmary were closed. Where was the doctor?

Putting her bags in a convenient chair next to her umbrella, Ruby Eliza rang the hand bell alerting anyone inside the building of visitors in the office. No one came. She opened the doors to the examining room and infirmary—empty, as were the rest of the rooms.

Going back to the office, she folded her parasol and tucked it under her arm. Grabbing her bags, she went to the kitchen, placing them on the counter. The kitchen was small but serviceable. There was a scrub basin with heavy-duty lye soap for washing your hands, and a kitchen sink for washing dirty dishes.

Ruby Eliza busied herself with shelving her grocery items and took the toiletries back to the office.

Opening the door to the infirmary, Ruby Eliza looked around. The four cots, covered with a thin mattress and linens, were placed at intervals in the room. A fireplace, positioned in the center of the outside wall of the building, was used for heat when the room was occupied. A stack of wood was placed on the brick hearth ready to be used.

An old cow-boy named Chester, who hung around the place for food and shelter in a makeshift room he'd built out back, did diligence as janitor each day. Dependable and trustworthy, his family had died of the fever on the wagon train trip West. He'd adopted the medical practice, those attending patients, and the patients themselves, as family. His cheerful whistle was often the only thing which brightened the day in the hurried and sometimes sorrowful atmosphere experienced within the building's walls. His whole aim in life was being a servant—a Christ-honoring man, he often said. He was that, if nothing else.

Ruby Eliza carefully shut the door to the infirmary and headed for the living quarters. Her steps led her out of the office and down a hallway with windows. The stairs led up to the old boarding house rooms over the old bar and table areas. These had been converted into nice bedrooms for Sarah, Ruby Eliza, and visitors.

Ruby Eliza paused at the bottom of the stairs. A recently installed note board held a single piece of paper. *Gone to Jason's to check on his broken arm. Be back soon.*

So that's where Sarah had disappeared. She thought back to his first visit to the medical practice.

Jason Dunn was a middle-aged man, who bought longhorns from ranchers. He put these herds in feedlots to wait for shipment on cattle cars to the east. He and his family had moved from Fort Worth when the railroad had advanced to the West. Not happy with what he considered a demotion from the city atmosphere of the larger town, he and his family grumbled at the meager amenities found in Abilene. There wasn't enough society for them.

When asked how his accident had happened, he explained a noise had sent a herd running within his most western feedlot. He'd just climbed on a fence to make a final count before driving them to the rails to be shipped. Veering away just as they reached where he sat, several hit the fence, knocking him off with such force, he broke his arm when he fell.

Ruby Eliza grinned, remembering the next scene in the office.

At that point, he'd emitted a large groan. Ruby Eliza had noticed that Doctor Sarah, head down, had a lurking grin on her face.

His wife standing nearby had said, "I've told him a thousand times not to climb on his fences. He can count just as well standing on the ground outside the feedlot. But no. Does he listen? For some reason, he has to tower over them. This is what you get for not being careful." She waved her hand in the air and rolled her eyes in his direction.

Jason's reply to his wife, "I've told you a thousand times I don't need your advice when it comes to my business and how I run it."

Ruby Eliza and Doctor Sarah had exchanged glances. Once he was patched up, they were glad to see the quarreling couple leave the building.

The nurse sighed as she paused to look out of the windows as she passed down the hall. The alleyway wasn't very wide, but distant enough for the afternoon sun to shine into the waiting room and brighten everything inside.

"Oh," she said out loud, remembering her umbrella. She turned and retrieved her treasure. Retracing her path, she went up the steps to the upper floor, walked through their communal parlor, and to her bedroom.

Placing her parasol on her bureau, she looked at her bed, thinking, "Yes, Saturday afternoon is a nice time to take a nap." She knew Doctor Sarah would be home soon, and they would cook supper downstairs.

After the last meal of the day, it was customary for them to take a walk or sit on the porch in their cane back chairs or read a book on the upstairs settees in their communal sitting room. They would talk about the week's happenings and then make a sincere effort to clear their minds of anything to do with doctoring.

Taking off her skirt and blouse, Ruby Eliza stretched out on her bed in her shift. When she woke, Doctor Sarah was standing over her.

"Just checking to see if you were alive or dead," she joked.

Ruby Eliza yawned and responded, "Only dead tired and happy for a nap."

"Here," Doctor Sarah handed her an envelope. "I stopped by the post office on my way home and checked the mailbox."

Nurse Ruby looked at the handwriting and grinned, "One from Poppa—postmarked Fort Stockton." She sat up on the side of her bed, tore at the paper, and pulled out the message inside.

"Where are they?"

Poppa says by the time I receive this letter, the herd will be past Fort Stockton and to look for them in about a month, barring more rain or other trouble."

"Hum-n, about May tenth, I'm guessing." She walked over, wrote a note, and pinned it to the note board.

"Poppa says Momma came with them on the drive, and Sarah Susannah stowed away in one of the wagons, and she's coming too. What do you know about that?"

"Imagine that girl," exclaimed Doctor Sarah. "She's not afraid of taking a step out on her own. She'll make a good doctor."

"Don't set your hopes too high. Poppa says she's formed an attachment to Caleb's young son. They've adopted a newly born calf and named it Little Bossy. He and Momma are wondering how far their relationship will go—Sarah Susannah and Thomas."

"Surely she won't go back on her dream. Doctoring is all we've heard for years."

"Listen to this! Poppa thinks they've identified rustlers on the cattle trail! Can you imagine? Oh, I hope they're not in danger." Ruby Eliza looked up at Doctor Sarah.

"I've heard rumors of gangs in the upper Pecos River area, but as far as I know, no sightings. This is something new. Should we tell the Sheriff?"

"There's a long description of the sighting and the reason he thinks so, and the rustlers have been rebranding the longhorns so no one will know. He's had ten of his cattle implanted in the rustler's herd. He doesn't think they'll be able to disguise his animals. He says there's only two sensible places they can drive their herd—here or Fort Worth. And yes, he says to inform the Sheriff."

Ruby Eliza put down the letter and looked up in amazement at her friend and boss. "I can't believe what I just read."

"I wonder if there's more to the story, and how much your Poppa will be involved in it."

"Are you thinking he may want to help with cornering and apprehending the rustlers?"

"I've never known your father to shy away from trouble or to ask for it. He doesn't like deceit or law breaking. Your Poppa is one of a kind. Not many children can claim a heritage like yours."

"I don't want to even think about him getting mixed up in catching the rustlers. Someone might get hurt." Ruby's eyes filled with tears.

"We'll see the Sheriff tomorrow at church. Why don't you make an appointment to meet him to discuss your Poppa's letter?"

"I will," Ruby Eliza nodded "Are you hungry?"

"I'm starving," Doctor Sarah said moving toward the bedroom door.

Nurse Ruby got up and started to follow her. Stopping, she grinned. "I think I'll put my skirt and blouse on. As sure as I don't, we'll have an emergency."

"Good. Come on down when you're dressed." Doctor Sarah walked outside into the parlor, but stopped after three steps and called, "Did you get the sliced ham, canned beans, and corn at the mercantile store?"

"Yes, and a loaf of bread. You'll find them in the normal places." She heard her steps on the stairs, and then silence.

Chapter Twenty

Ruby Eliza Meets Grant Bailey

Although she didn't know it, church the next day would change Ruby Eliza's life forever. She dressed up in her most beautiful dress. The outfit was ordered from a clothing manufacturer out of New York and made of dark purple silk which shimmered in the sun's light. It had beige silk ruffles on the end of the sleeves and hem—a gift from her parents on her twenty-fourth birthday last August. Her bonnet, gloves, and string purse matched the color of the dress's ruffles. With multiple petticoats underneath, it stood out from her body and swished when she walked. She loved the swishing sound and always felt like a queen when she wore her outfit, holding her head high, and walking regally wherever she went.

Unlike most women on the disappearing frontier, where at least the sharpest boundary was vanishing in Texas, her parents had supported her dreams of a profession. She hadn't needed to get married as soon as she'd come-of-age. She often thought, *what was this phase in a person's life? This age of maturity, or boundary, or stage was changing year-by-year for women.* If they could afford to wait, they got married later in life. Doctor Sarah had proved this, but she had chosen, at least for the moment, not to get married.

Her Momma had encouraged her to go to Nashville and learn the occupation of nursing and while there, Doctor Sarah had offered her a position with her staff. When the doctor had moved West, so had Ruby Eliza—happy to get back to her home state of Texas—back closer to her family in the Glass Mountains.

~

After locking the front door of the office, she and Doctor Sarah crossed the dirt road, heading for the Baptist Church in Abilene, which was almost across the road from their office.

They stepped carefully, bypassing the stirred-up mud puddles caused by carriages and horses heading into and out of Abilene.

On the top step, where he was perched yesterday, Pastor Gridley stood, welcoming each attendant with a handshake. "Good morning, Mr. Mayor," he said as he greeted the newly elected official. The man nodded his head and disappeared inside the church with his wife and children. Doctor Sarah and Ruby Eliza advanced up to the top step.

From inside the soft notes of a piano could be heard, playing the majestic hymn for worship, *Holy, Holy, Holy, Lord God Almighty.*

"Good morning, Doctor Sarah, and good morning, Ruby," Gridley said, winking at the latter. "Happy you could come. Is the infirmary empty this morning?" When there were bedfast patients in the office, one of them didn't make the morning service on Sunday.

"Yes, Grider, our patients recovered during the week. We had some well-deserved hours of freedom yesterday, didn't we, Ruby Eliza? Did Jason Dunn make it with his broken arm?" Doctor Sarah asked. "He was having some pain yesterday, and I made a house call."

"I shook hands with him a few minutes ago. He's here with his family, and we have a visitor, the new superintendent of the railroad here in Abilene. I managed to talk to him before more parishioners showed up. I believe we're close in age, and I plan on us being close friends while he's here."

Hearing a noise behind them, Ruby Eliza tugged at Doctor Sarah's arm. "There's someone behind us. We'd better go on inside and find a seat."

Ruby Eliza's interest was piqued, and she wondered if Rachel had managed to finagle the superintendent into bringing her to church. Finding out the answer didn't take long. There was no need to scan the auditorium.

Rachel Woody stood beyond the church's doorway in the central aisleway, blocking the walkway and introducing the new railway employee to each church goer. There was no route around the couple to the pews except to greet them first.

The newcomer looked a little embarrassed as Rachel, eager to introduce him, pulled the man by the arm to meet the two women as they entered through the door of the church. Ruby Eliza realized immediately he wasn't accustomed to having a woman lead him around.

"Doctor Sarah, this is Grant Bailey. He's the ..."

"Let me finish, Rachael. He's the superintendent of the Texas and Pacific railroad here in Abilene."

"Yes," said Rachael. "How'd you know?"

"Not much that isn't known here in town, especially if it has to do with the main reason for Abilene being a town. Glad to meet you, Mr. Bailey." Doctor Sarah extended her gloved hand.

Grant reached out and encompassed her hand, bowing his head slightly and with raised eyebrows he asked, "You're a medical doctor?"

Before the doctor could reply, Rachael answered. "Yes, she is, and this is her nurse, Ruby Eliza Stockton. She's my best friend." Rachael was glowing with pride at her escort.

Grant Bailey turned the bluest eyes Ruby had ever seen in her direction. "Miss Ruby Eliza," he said. "Pleased to meet you."

"Happy to meet you, Mr. Bailey."

The Reverend Gridley came through the door at that moment, eliminating any small talk. "Shall we all be seated?" he suggested, mounting the platform he stood behind the podium.

Everyone scattered in all directions. Although Ruby Eliza and Rachael usually sat together, it seemed to the nurse her friend decided to sit as far away as possible—protecting her new territory. There was a short song service led by the pastor and afterwards a short session of mentioning those who needed prayer.

Mr. Dunn stood flaunting his broken arm. A couple of others mentioned people in their families. Grant Bailey stood to ask for prayer for his father. When no one else spoke up, Pastor Gridley asked one of the deacons to say a prayer.

Several went forward to kneel at the altar. After those regained their seats, the pastor got up to speak.

"Today, if you will turn to Philippians, chapter two, and verse five, we will stand and read together from verse five to eleven."

When everyone was standing, Pastor Gridley led them in these words …

> *Let this mind be in you, which was also in Christ Jesus, who being in the form of God, thought it not robbery to be equal with God. But made himself of no reputation, and took upon him the form of a servant, and was made in the likeness of men. And being found in fashion as a man, he humbled himself, and became obedient unto death, even the death of the cross. Wherefore God also hath highly exalted him, and given him a name which is above every name. That at the name of Jesus every knee should bow, of things in heaven, and things in earth, and things under the earth. And that every tongue should confess that Jesus Christ is Lord, to the glory of God the Father.*

And as was Pastor Gridley's custom, while the congregation was standing, he offered a prayer for God's word to be divided in truth.

Everyone sat down, got comfortable, and waited for the pastor's sermon to commence.

Ruby Eliza let her mind wonder for a minute. She couldn't deny that the pastor had a deep commanding voice and manner when he spoke. His pronunciation of some words was peculiar at times, bordering on not being understandable.

She guessed this may have come from his Rhode Island upbringing and education under a Principal Greenough, whom he often mentioned. This gentleman taught at a college in his home state where he took religious studies. Grider often talked of his family back east, but now he told her his family was here in Abilene. There were times she was sure this family specifically included her—more intimately than she wanted it to. She chose to ignore this feeling, as they kidded each other back and forth. She loved sparring with him, and that was all.

Pastor Gridley broke through her musing.

"What does it mean to be humble?" asked the pastor, identifying the theme of today's sermon. He immediately got everyone's attention with this question. Raised eyebrows, nodding heads, and inquiring eyes meant his parishioners were in thought.

"Look at our passage of scripture. *But made himself of no reputation*. Sometimes it means to lower ourselves, to be in submission to others. So, being humble means giving up yourself to help others. Our savior, Jesus Christ is a perfect, and I mean *perfect*, example of being humble. Now I ask you another question. Why would anyone who is God want to become a man?"

Several in the congregation chuckled and shook their heads, acknowledging this was a mystery they couldn't solve.

"He didn't have to, *did He*? The answer to that question is yes, He did. Why? Because from Genesis to Malachi, the Bible tells us this was in His plan, to come and give each of us an option—to believe in Him or not to believe—to go to Heaven or hell. All of the Old

Testament points to a coming New Testament, and Jesus Christ was that coming. He came to fulfill the Old one and write the New one."

Some in the audience were now scratching their heads, not understanding his words. Some were grinning from ear-to-ear, because the pastor was making a lot of sense.

The pastor went on. "Jesus gave up a lot to walk the earth, didn't He? He left Heaven, a place we can only imagine with all of its glory and privileges."

Pastor Gridley went on to explain what happened when Jesus voluntarily and humbly came to earth. He noted a person couldn't believe just one part of the story. A person must believe, in faith, all of Jesus. There was another discussion of his sentence. He said, "Have you ever heard of a virgin giving birth?" There was a vigorous shaking of the women's heads in the audience. "No, and I'm sure Doctor Sarah hasn't either." Dr Sarah shook her head, also.

"Have you seen anyone come back to life? Doctor Sarah?" Pastor Gridley looked at the doctor and then scanned his audience. "Only through faith can we believe these things."

Pastor Gridley walked off the platform and gave a poignant description of Christ's death on the cross, the two thieves, and His magnificent return to the Father. He walked back and forth as he explained, "Jesus didn't have to suffer the humiliating death of the Roman cross. The Bible says He could have called ten thousand angels to protect Him. But He didn't. The original plan from the creation of the earth was followed, and now we have a choice, don't we? Jesus humbled Himself and followed His plan. What is your plan?" He mounted to the platform again.

As the pianist came forward to play softly the hymn, *I Surrender All,* Pastor Gridley looked over his audience. "I want to give each of you an opportunity to humble yourselves, and to come forward to accept Jesus as Lord and Savior. I know it's not easy to step forward, but I'll be here to support and pray with you."

"Come, kneel at the altar, anyone needing to say a special prayer. Confess your sin to Jesus, or ask for forgiveness. You are welcome here." He waved his hand over a backless bench placed before the platform he stood on. Stepping down to the level of his audience, he waited as the pianist continued to play.

A young man went down, whom Ruby did not know. The pastor met him at the altar, throwing his arms around him. With his head on the pastor's shoulder, the others in the audience realized the talk with the pastor was emotional and earnest. Two or three others went to kneel at the altar to pray. After several minutes, the respondents went back to their seats.

The pianist stopped playing.

The sermon and invitation time was over. Pastor Gridley asked one of the men in the audience to give a final prayer. While the man prayed, he walked to the front door. When the prayer was finished, he stood wishing everyone a safe and blessed week as they departed.

As Ruby Eliza watched those leaving the church, Doctor Sarah lingered to talk to former patients. The nurse noticed her friend Rachael and her escort were approached by several people, who welcomed and exchanged a few words before they exited. When the couple approached the entrance, Pastor Gridley stopped them. Ruby Eliza heard him ask, "Grant, would you have dinner with me tomorrow or supper tomorrow night?"

Doctor Sarah took Ruby Eliza by the arm, distracting her from Grant's reply. "Are you daydreaming again?"

"No," said Ruby, a bit perturbed at being caught deep in her thoughts.

"Come on, I'd like to catch Mr. Bailey before he leaves. Might as well find out what's wrong with his father. We will most likely have to see him if he's sick." She hurried down the aisle, shook hands with the pastor, and flew down the steps of the church and into a conversation being exchanged in the road.

Grant stood in the dirt at the bottom, talking to Jason Dunn about the next set of cattle cars due in Abilene.

"Yes, our schedule on cars is hit or miss. My whole reason for being here is to streamline the company's operation. I'm finding our new branch is competing with the larger areas of Dallas, Fort Worth, and a proposed Niles City. Niles City would incorporate stock yards and meat packing facilities along the Chisholm Cattle Trail—a future dream at this moment, but in the making I think."

Dunn was complaining, "Coordinating cattle and train movements is my biggest headache. I wish our communications were better in the cattle business. Even the telegraph hasn't solved it."

"Our whole organization is working on this problem. We'll get it done. I promise you. America is changing rapidly and a new century isn't far off. The Civil War and the depression which followed are now behind us. Cattle prices are rising, and for those who were resilient enough to withstand those two cataclysmic happenings, their fortunes are waiting to be made."

Jason Dunn nodded his head, agreeing with the superintendent. "Will you be coming back to our church next Sunday?" he asked.

"Yes, I thoroughly enjoyed Pastor Gridley's message. He reminds me of another preacher I know—a dear friend of my father, who recently passed away. In fact, his name was Jason—Jason Douglas. He was my teacher for many years."

Ruby Eliza listened carefully to this conversation. She was impressed with Grant Bailey's management and knowledge of words. His familiarity with the English language and conversation while using the same was unusual in the West. Where had he gone to school? She must remember to ask this question in the future. What future? Would he be part of it? He was a good-looking gent, and certainly worth a second look. But then there was her friend, Rachel.

How would this affect their friendship? And Pastor Gridley? A relationship with Grant might cause drastic changes in her life. Thank goodness, Doctor Sarah was too old for the new man in town—or was she? Maybe she should just write off any attempt at knowing this man better. So many questions, and no answers, but she had to admit she was attracted to him. *There I go daydreaming again*, she thought.

Jason Dunn was speaking. "Mr. Bailey, I'll see you next Sunday." Jason Dunn walked over to his wife, and children who sat waiting in their buggy. Using his good arm, he pulled his body up onto the seat. His wife flicked the reins, sending the buggy down the street.

The superintendent turned and focused his attention on the women who surrounded him. "Ladies, I see a lot of questions in your eyes. Why don't we all go to Cow-boy's Victuals and eat dinner. I hear they have the best fried chicken on Sunday you've ever put in your mouth. I'll consider it a privilege to buy every one of you a meal. Today, I prefer not to eat alone." He looked at each woman, drawing them into a warm, friendly circle. His bluest of eyes lingering an extra moment on Ruby Eliza, who quickly averted hers.

Rachael, seeing the look, immediately reclaimed his arm. "Of course, an extremely chivalrous offer to three single women," she said rather too loudly, not exactly happy to have two extra women invited into her handy twosome.

Ruby's thoughts went to her friend's choice in reading material. She was reading too many English romances from the library of one of the matrons who'd moved from Dallas, Texas. Ruby had read all the books from the Glory B's collection and had looked over the Dallas lady's assortment, borrowing those on travel, and biographies of famous people both in the United States and elsewhere. She did read romances, but not often. Reality was better than fantasy. But Rachael often escaped into this unreal world, looking for her Prince Charming.

"Ruby Eliza, are you with us?"

"Huh, what?"

"Do you want to go?" asked Doctor Sarah, catching her nurse daydreaming for the second time within the hour. She'd taken some steps down the boardwalk when she realized her nurse wasn't following.

All eyes were on Ruby, who blushed at being the center of attention and responded, "I'd love to go." She flicked her eyes in Mr. Bailey's direction.

He, in return, was looking back and smiling in amusement at her discomfort. "If *Ruby Eliza* is ready," he said, emphasizing her name, "Then let us go. I'm really hungry."

Rachel Woody hung onto his arm, while Doctor Sarah and Ruby Eliza walked behind the couple. There were chatter and questions as they walked the short distance to the eatery. On the way, Mr. Bailey asked them to call him Grant, and they found out he was from the Black Hills of South Dakota.

After eating and over their final cup of hot coffee, Doctor Sarah asked about his father.

"My father is in his middle seventies and most of his problems are related to his age. He's tough, but he walks with a cane. Not because he likes it, but because he has to. Of late, I've noticed a persistent cough. I'll bring him by your office for a checkup. When's a good time for you, Doctor Sarah? Do I need to make an appointment?"

"Tomorrow, at any time. Ruby Eliza and I haven't any patients at present. We'll probably be cleaning up the office and infirmary, getting ready for the next ones."

"I'll try to get by, but Mondays aren't good days for a business. All the problems of the weekend need to be solved."

"Our Monday may be the same," laughed the doctor. "But you come anyway. Ruby Eliza and I'll work you in, won't we nurse?"

Everyone had finished eating. "Are we ready to go?" asked Rachael. "My mother asked me to come home. We're going to visit my grandmother. I have to go, or she will worry about what happened to me."

Ruby Eliza spoke up. "I'm going to stay a few minutes and order some chicken for Chester. He usually eats dinners with us during the day. He'll be waiting for his repast."

"Who's Chester?" asked Grant.

"He's our self-appointed janitor," replied Doctor Sarah, going on to explain the man's duties.

"I was going to order a meal for my father. I'll wait with you two ladies for the food to be prepared. Rachael, it has been my pleasure to escort you to church. I'll walk you to the door." Grant rose from his chair and taking her by the arm saw her to the entrance. He helped her outside, and they exchanged some words which Doctor Sarah and Ruby Eliza couldn't hear.

When he came back to the table, he sat down. "You ladies aren't typical of women in the big city. In my experience, very few of them work. Are you two related?"

"No," replied Ruby Eliza. "My mother and Doctor Sarah are good friends."

"Speaking of your mother, Ruby Eliza, I promised her a letter this week. I believe now's a good time to make good on my assurances there would be a message from me. Thank you, Grant, for the great fried chicken. See you tomorrow."

Grant went to hold the door for her and came back to the table.

"I didn't get your last name, Ruby Eliza," he said.

"My last name is Stockton. My father is Press Stockton, and my family's ranch is The Glory B in the Glass Mountains—several miles north of The Big Bend."

Grant took a sip of his coffee. "I've studied maps of this section of Texas. Isn't there a Fort Stockton down that way?"

"Yes, but we are not connected to the Stockton the fort is named for—a military man. My family's originally from Louisiana. At least my Poppa is from there. My Momma, Gracie, was a Tipton. Her family was part of the Tipton family from the mountains of East Tennessee. But she was born in Nashville. She and her pa headed west from there in the summertime, 1858. He was to man a station on The Butterfield Overland Mail route in the Guadalupe Mountains that went all the way to San Francisco. I'm sorry, I'm hogging the conversation," she apologized.

"Oh, no. I'm finding your family history fascinating. How did you become a nurse with Doctor Sarah?"

"I was never one for lounging around doing nothing. Pastor Marshall, and then his successor Pastor Ormand, taught me and the rest of my siblings. My Momma was a reader and I read all her books. Seeing my interest in learning, my parents offered to send me to Doctor Sarah in Nashville to finish my education, and I realized working with her was something I liked to do. I applied myself, learning to be her nurse." Ruby stabbed at the air with her hands, finishing her words. "So here I am in Abilene, only two days by stagecoach from home."

"Are there any plans to be a doctor in the future?" Grant asked.

"No, I'm content to work as her helper. And anyway, I know almost as much as she." Ruby paused, but continued before he could ask another question. "Enough about me. What about you? How did you end up in Abilene? Where were you born?"

"Excuse me, Sir and Miss Stockton. Your order is done," offered the waiter who'd been patiently standing there with two plates of food completely unknown to the two who were in deep conversation. He placed them on the table, explaining, "Miss Stockton, since you have a ways to walk, I put napkins over the plates and pinned 'em here. It'll make sure the food stays inside the metal rim, and it'll be hot or warm when you get home." Smiling, he pointed to a safety pin holding all corners of the cloth together on top. He pushed one plate to her and one to Grant.

"Oh, thank you. I won't have any trouble getting the food to Chester." Ruby pulled out a dollar bill and handed it to the waiter. With her hand up, she explained, "No change, and I'll bring the plate and a clean napkin back the next time I return."

Grant took care of his bill, offering to do the same.

The two left the building and stood on the front boardwalk in the afternoon sun. "Do you want me to walk you home?"

"No, I live on the quiet side of Abilene. I feel safe going home alone."

"My side is not so quiet. I guess we'll have to continue our conversation tomorrow when I bring my father to your office.

"I'll look forward to it." Ruby stepped off the boardwalk and proceeded across the alleyway. She gained the next wooden porch along the street, wondering if he was watching. *You'll just have to wonder*, she told herself. *You're not turning around to see.* Each step echoed as she walked away from the eatery.

Grant stood watching her go, thinking she was a very interesting woman, and that he'd like to know her better. Unlike Rachael, who was obviously looking for a squire or husband, Ruby Eliza was not a clinger. He wondered why she wasn't married. She was a beautiful woman in the purple dress, with dark brown hair and expressive blue, or was it green eyes? Yes, her eyes were what caught his attention, very expressive, lovely. Maybe they were light brown.

He gave a chuckle, turned and headed home. His pa would love the fried chicken. He'd have to cut it in small pieces, because Henry Bailey's teeth and his eyes weren't as good now.

Chapter Twenty-One

Grant and Henry Bailey

Grant pulled up to the front of Doctor Sarah's office. He hopped down from the seat of the buggy, wrapped the horse's reins over the hitching post rail, and hurried around to help his father off the other side. Henry Bailey was apt to try this on his own, and suffer the consequences.

"Be careful, Pa," exclaimed the son, as he caught Henry just in time to keep him from 'biting the dust,' as his father often described his encounters with the ground. The older man could no longer walk with the assurance he once had of not falling.

Grant started to complain, but in all the years he'd known Henry, complaining had never made a difference.

"Is this the doctor's office?" asked his father, who couldn't read the sign over the door.

"Yes, and it looks like they're busy," stated Grant, as he observed four other horses whose reins were tied to the long hitching post rail. He barely had room to get his buggy out of the road.

"We can come back next year," suggested Henry, who wasn't too keen on the idea of visiting a doctor.

Grant laughed at his comment, and thought silently, *wait until he finds out the doctor is a female.*

Instead, he gently tugged on his father's arm, urging him up the steps and into the waiting room. Only one chair was empty.

They both stood for a minute, examining the rooms occupants—a man, woman, and child. The absence of sitting space was one problem to them, but the other was the sound coming from a room where the door was shut—the rigorous noise of loud bawling. Obviously, a child was not happy, and if this young girl with the tears running down her face was a sibling, she wasn't either.

"April, your brother will be all right, admonished the older woman. This wasn't your fault." The lady drew the girl to her side and comforted her as best she could.

Grant indicated his father should sit down. "I'll get Ruby Eliza to find another chair. You get comfortable."

He headed for the door where the screams seemed to be coming. Should he knock or not?

At that moment, Ruby Eliza, who must have had a sixth sense, opened the door.

So swift were her actions as she hurried through the entrance, she almost crashed into Grant, who caught her arm and steered her away into the waiting room. Her entrance was followed by another loud sob from the room she had just exited.

Grant caught a quick look at the young patient who sat on the examining table. He quickly shut the door, and scrutinized his father's expression.

The look on Henry's face was not one of assurance. He sat down in the empty chair, but his eyes looked at the door to the street. He might bolt at any moment.

Neither were the Stephens content, and April now sobbed outright.

"Oh, I'm so sorry. I was hurrying to tell Mr. and Mrs. Stephens of Doctor Sarah's prognosis concerning their grandson." She turned to the older couple. "The doctor's going to put Jefferson to sleep to remove the mesquite thorn. He rammed it in and broke it off. She can't get it out, and it needs to come out now because an infection has started. There's a chance it might work its way out, but we don't want blood poisoning to start. And, the longer it stays under his skin, the greater chance of a worse diagnosis. Do we have your permission for this operation?"

Mrs. Stephens spoke up, "Will he feel anything, if she puts him to sleep?"

"No, not a thing. He may have a headache when he wakes up, but he won't remember a thing."

"Yes, please go ahead. We trust Doctor Sarah." Mr. Stephens gave his permission.

"April, your brother will be all right. I promise you," said Ruby Eliza, going over and giving her a quick hug, trying to assure the crying sister. She turned to Grant. "This will probably take about one hour. Do you want to wait?"

Another loud bawl came through the closed door of the examination room.

Without consulting Henry, Grant said lowly, "We'll wait, or I'll try to get him to wait. Do you think I can help calm the boy? I've been under anesthesia, so I can tell him about its effects."

"Come in, and we'll ask Doctor Sarah. I think she'll say yes."

Grant waved at Henry who'd already started a conversation with the older man and woman. *How long would this last?*

He heard Henry ask the Stephens man as the couple opened the door to exit the room, "How did your boy get hurt?"

Grant whispered to Ruby, "He'll know everything about them by the time I come back outside your examination room."

Jefferson sat on the examining table, his legs swinging off the side. The eyes he turned on Ruby Eliza and Grant as they entered the room were red and watery. He jerked from his deep sobs.

Doctor Sarah stood beside him, speaking comforting words and rubbing his back, in an effort to calm the unfortunate youngster. The doctor looked at Ruby Eliza and acknowledged Grant with a smile.

The nurse nodded her head, confirming the operation would go on.

The young lad started crying again—louder if this was possible.

"Doctor Sarah, I've been under anesthesia myself. Let me tell Jefferson about my experience," suggested Grant.

"Sure, you do that while Ruby Eliza and I get ready." She and her assistant left to wash their hands and retrieve sterile equipment to be used in the coming procedure.

While they were gone, Jefferson quieted down as Grant explained what had happened to him when he was under anesthesia.

Doctor Sarah appeared, scrubbed, and carrying a tray covered with a cloth and holding the sterile sharp scalpel, pinching tweezers, and curved stitching needle, plus the material to stitch the wound closed.

Jefferson's eyes grew wide.

Ruby Eliza came into the room with the apparatus and gas to put him to sleep.

Jefferson panicked. He started crying and fighting any attempt to start the operation. Obviously, he would have to be restrained by force—not an exciting prospect. Since the table had restraining straps, this could be done.

So much for Grant's attempt to calm him. But he had one more possibility. As the men in the saloon often said *he would play his trump card*.

Grant went and stood in front of him. "Jefferson, have you ever ridden on a train?"

"No-o," came the muffled reply, since his head was down and his mouth was wrapped tightly with his hands.

But, the word *train* had gotten his attention. Only the well-to-do rode the iron horse as some called the steam engine. Every boy dreamed of this possibility, but none of the poorer class had the money.

"Would you like to? Your sister and parents and even your grandparents could go with you. We'll do it on a weekend. How about that?"

The sobbing had quit, with the possibility of such a journey, he couldn't imagine ever taking. "I'd like to." He looked up at Grant, wondering who was this man, offering such an adventure?

"If you will lie back quietly and let Miss Stockton put you to sleep, I'll see that you go as soon as your foot heals. Do we have an agreement?"

"Yes-s."

"Shake on it?"

Jefferson offered a tear-stained hand. With Grant's help, he stretched out on the table with his red, swollen foot exposed. He was still shaking from fear, his eyes following the activities in the room.

Smiling at Grant for his quick thinking and help, Ruby Eliza grabbed a folded woolen blanket from a nearby shelf.

"Here, I'll cover him," offered Grant, taking the coverlet and shaking it out. He placed it over Jefferson and tucked it in securely, remembering the cold nights in South Dakota when Henry had done the same. He felt like shivering himself. "Keep looking at me, Jefferson."

The women hurried around the room, preparing for the small surgery, pushing two metal carts close to the table to hold their supplies.

Ruby Eliza prepared the metal anesthesia contraption which would fit the boy's face, and came near the table.

Jefferson kept looking up at Grant—so much for being strong and facing what was coming like a man as his father often said. A large tear rolled from one of his eyes as he said, "Mister, will you hold my hand?"

Grant looked at Doctor Sarah, who nodded her approval.

"I sure will, cow-boy." He moved to the opposite side of the examining table from where Ruby Eliza stood ready to administer the anesthesia and caught the hand which slid from under the blanket in both of his.

"Just keep looking at Grant," advised Ruby Eliza as she put the cup to his face and turned on the gas. "Breathe deeply," she told him, watching as his chest heaved up and then went flat. She put her hand up and gently stroked the child's hair from his eyes and forehead.

After four or five breaths the young boy was asleep. She nodded at Doctor Sarah, and Grant put Jefferson's hand on the table. "I'll go see what my father is doing. We may have another emergency there."

Doctor Sarah observed, "When we have another crisis, we'll call on you. Thanks for your help, Grant." She leaned over the foot, and picked up the scalpel.

Ruby Eliza walked Grant to the door. "Thank you for offering the train ride. I might take you up on one too. Fort Worth or Dallas might afford more shopping for me and my Momma to enjoy, if she makes it to Abilene before the Stephens go on theirs."

"I might also go with you," he returned, looking deep into her eyes and realizing they were light brown. His admiration for Ruby Eliza Stockton and Doctor Sarah had increased tremendously in the last few minutes.

"I have to get back to my patient. Will I see you when this is over?"

"Yes, I think so. Hopefully my father will still be in the waiting room."

"Good. See you then." Ruby returned to keep the gas flowing when needed, realizing her relationship with Grant Bailey had changed in the operating room.

How many females could say that? Not many, she was sure.

Grant left the room. His father was still chatting with the grandparents and barely acknowledged his son's presence when he entered. Not stopping, he slipped out the front door, walked to the end of the boardwalk, and stretched his arms. He needed to think.

A man, he assumed was Chester, came from the alleyway, carrying a bucket of water and something else. "Good morning," he greeted. "Are you Chester?"

"Yes, I'm bringing water and eggs for the ladies' supper."

"They're performing an operation at present—a young boy," explained Grant.

"I heard his loud cries." He chuckled and continued, "I try to stay away most of the time. I faint at the sight of blood. When that happens, they have two patients to tend." He made a move to head for the door. "I have chores to do. Doctor Sarah depends on me to keep things tidy."

"Oh, don't let me stop you. I came outside for some fresh air." Grant heard the door close behind him. He paced back and forth on the boardwalk. Once when he looked up, he saw Grider Gridley, the pastor of the Baptist Church, standing on the top step of the worship center.

The pastor waved and called, "How are you, Grant? When are we going to get together?"

Grant called back, "I'll let you know, but I'm thinking before Sunday, pastor."

When he went back inside, he'd made a decision. If Ruby wasn't busy with another patient, he would ask her to eat dinner with him. She and his father needed to meet. Between them, she would learn the story of the Baileys meeting and life. Almost before his thought was through, a man came running into the office. Henry got up and headed for the door.

Due to another emergency, Henry didn't get examined. The dinner didn't come to pass.

Chapter Twenty-Two

The Cattle Drive Continues

Press looked over at Gracie—beautiful as always and tall in the saddle. They straddled their horses, sitting side by side on a small hill where they could see the cattle drive in the distance. Squinting their eyes, they could barely make out Sarah Susannah and Thomas who were driving her wagon.

She returned his gaze. "Are you thinking the same thing I'm thinking?" she asked.

"Probably not exactly," he responded, nodding at her. "I'm remembering a young girl with a head full of curls who took control of my heart and never let go. I loved you the minute I laid eyes on you, and that love has grown with the years my dear wife."

Gracie smiled, "My heart and life are full, and you are the reason. I love you." She leaned over, so they could exchange a tender kiss. "Surely, God knew what he was doing when He put the two of us together. Although I never knew them, I'm thankful for your mother and grandmother who insisted on a church and a house before stepping a foot on the Glory B Ranch. Your parents did a good job of raising you. I hope we are doing the same for our brood." She waved her hand at the continuing herd of longhorns, where some of their children were working as cow-hands.

"Are you thinking of Sarah Susannah and Thomas?"

"Yes, they're so young."

"We can't live their lives, sweetheart," noted Press, smiling at this older and matured woman of the person he'd married. "I'm sure your father said the same of you, when he let you live your life and make your own decisions. You were young then. People must make their own mistakes, mustn't they?" he asked, remembering another instance in his wife's life.

"Yes," nodded Gracie, remembering too. "That was a long time ago."

There was a lingering silence as they enjoyed each other's company.

"We'll soon be in the same territory where I, Jorge, and the trailhands left you and your father on your way to The Pinery."

"A sad day for me," she said, recalling the struggle in her heart over two men in her life.

They sat watching the herd pass by below until Press suggested, "Let's see if we can find Jonathan. I wonder if he's located a place to water the cattle. Amazing what the weeks can change. Floods to no water." He shook his head at the amazing transformation. The land soaked up rain like a rag wiped up a spill.

Press laughed and nudged his horse in the direction he'd last seen his son.

~

Four days had gone by since the Glory B drive had passed Fort Stockton. The huge spring near the fort ran clear and cold, and they'd filled all the water barrels. The cattle had their fill, and some of the men had stopped for a few minutes, jumping into the cold water to clean off. The next place to take a dip would be the Pecos River about a day away.

Not a drop of rain had fallen since the downpours of the first days of trailing the cattle. It was as if the sky's spigot had been twisted shut. Since the rain had quit falling, the arroyos and wet-weather springs were drying up.

After the Pecos River, they would be lucky to find water until they came to the Middle Concho River. This was before they arrived at San Angela, a distance of over one hundred miles on the dry, now dusty trail.

For miles, after leaving the fort, the drive had gone by high mesas and buttes, the only vista breaking the monotony of the road. The long hills which made up the cattle trail, slowly and gently went up a rise and down the other side. Vegetation consisted of tiny-leaved creosote bushes and prickly-pear cacti, plus a lonely, olive-fronded century plant with its long-stemmed, snowy-white blooms silhouetted against the sky. The elevation had risen slowly as the herd went forward.

~

Jonathan rode up to his father. "Are you looking for me, Poppa?"

"Yes. Are you heading through Castle Gap after we cross the Pecos River?"

"That was my plan. Do you agree?"

"Yes, I was concerned about the fact our rustlers might be heading for the same area, since it's the easiest place and quickest to get through the Castle and King mountains. They'll head there for sure."

"I'd thought the same thing. Should you and I scout ahead and see if we can find any evidence of their herd? We can look for recent hoof marks before our herd gets to the river which should be plain in the soil. Then, if we don't see their trail, we'll climb one of the higher plateaus at the Gap and look for the dust of their drive."

Gracie had gone to get a drink of water out of the water barrel on Jorge's wagon. She joined Press and Jonathan. "Are you talking about the rustlers?" she asked to their surprise.

Two heads turned quickly in her direction. Press asked, "How did you find out, Gracie? Very few know, and we've tried to keep the rustler's presence from most of the wranglers."

"Well, sweetheart, you have failed. And I'm not telling. Might need to use my source again," declared Gracie.

"To answer your question, Momma, we're trying to ascertain if the rustlers' herd is anywhere near us. We want to try to stay ahead of them."

"Should we tell her our plan, Jonathan?"

"Why not, Poppa. She'll probably find out anyway. Our intention is to get the new Sheriff of Taylor County to arrest them when they arrive close to the town of Abilene. That is after we identify them as rustlers."

Gracie's arms were instantly covered with chill bumps—an ominous warning to her. "So that's your plan. Why do you two have to be the ones to identify these men? Couldn't someone else point them out to the police? I have had a bad feeling about the whole affair from the first I heard of it."

Press answered, "As far as we know, no one else knows of their thievery. We have to do it. They have altered several brands on the cattle we saw in their hidden canyon. There may be as many as five hundred head they've rustled—a few here and a few there. That's quite a haul at twenty-five dollars apiece." He looked over at Jonathan for his approval.

Jonathan nodded at his father. "Even so, robbin' a stage with cattle money on it would net them more and easier money. Since the money comes by train, gettin' at it is harder to do. Think we'll get our longhorns back, Poppa?"

"What!" exclaimed Gracie. "They have our longhorns?"

"Only ten, Gracie. We let them rustle a few of ours, so we can identify them when they come through Buffalo Gap. We'll get them back after we point out the men to the officers. You have to realize anyone driving cattle to market in Abilene or Fort Worth will lose some of their herd. We can't let that keep happening, sweetheart."

"I understand, but why us each time?"

"Because we care," was her husband's short answer.

"Yes you, both of you, taught us to be responsible and obey the law. It's all your fault, Momma," chuckled Jonathan, starting his horse toward the moving herd.

Gracie grinned at her tall son. He was right of course. She knew it.

"We'll soon be to the Pecos, and after that we'll start up the steep side of the Edwards Plateau. You should remember that area, Gracie. Your pa and you drove through here in your covered wagon twenty or so years ago."

"Yes, it looks familiar. Even if where we're riding isn't exactly the same place our wagon went through. The vista doesn't change, and you can see the same thing for twenty or thirty miles. Is Fort Chadbourne on the other side of Castle Gap? I especially remember it. We overnighted there."

"Sure is, but it's several days away. We might stay close for our night. But we'll go through San Angela before we get there. It didn't exist in 1858. Twenty years makes a lot of difference."

Gracie smiled at Press and continued, "Don't forget, I should have a letter from Doctor Sarah at San Angela. That's where I told her to send it. We'll need to pick it up at Fort Concho, since they have no post office."

"I'll remember."

"Where will we stay tonight?" asked Gracie.

"On the western side of the river," he said, pointing off to the distant horizon. "Jonathan, isn't that the Pecos River I see far ahead of the herd?"

"Yes. We'd better go if we plan on checking out the territory before our herd gets there, and destroys the tracks.

"I'm with you. Doesn't look like they've latched onto the smell of fresh water as yet. I know they're thirsty." Press squinted in the bright sunshine.

Jonathan observed, "There's no faster movement at the front of the herd."

"We need to hurry. Come on Gracie."

"Go ahead. I'm right behind you."

Soot, the lead longhorn, smelled it first. He licked his dry upper lip with his tongue. He could already taste the water ahead.

This was the third time he'd led the Stocktons' cattle on its drive to a railhead. Ranchers tended to spare a good lead bull, especially one who recognized the route and instinctively knew the job required of him.

Soot had come out on top in the aristocracy of the *survival of the fittest* on the plains. He had attitude, and used it to manage his herd of longhorns. Having a natural resistance to just about every pest of the lowly eastern cattle, being brought west from the Atlantic states, he and his ancestors had roamed the Southern Plains for hundreds of years.

Being of Spanish ancestry and especially the Black Andalusian longhorns of the plains of Sevilla in the Old World, his breed had sailed to and weathered the West Indies, including the isles of Hispaniola and Jamaica, before being brought to the Spanish dominated *Tejas* area, via sailing ship and land trails.

While the Spanish invasion of the Southwestern part of the New World whirled around them, the *Tejas* longhorn was establishing a home and a breed of their own.

Yes, he had a long history and an attitude to match. He tossed his head and focused his black eyes on the lead drover, wondering if the man they called Caleb was getting antsy in his saddle over the lack of water. If he could have chuckled, he would have.

Instead, he gave a loud long bellow, meaning hold your horses to the herd walking behind him. This was followed by a second saying, we'll get to the water eventually. Only the longhorns understood him.

The Pecos River flowed a little swifter than usual with leftover water from the floods of the first rains in the higher mountains or from rain which hadn't fallen on the cattle drive. Although the Stockton animals did not stampede when the smell of fresh water reached their nostrils, herds sometimes did. The drovers let the longhorns linger in the knee-deep water, drinking their fill.

When Caleb figured the beeves had had enough, he pushed his lasso into the sky and yelled, "Wahoo," his signal for the drovers to move the cattle ahead.

Slowly the cow-boys pushed the stubborn animals up the east bank, with lumbering Soot in the lead, and pointed them toward the gap in the distance.

Instead of remaining on the Western side of the Pecos, as they had planned, they pushed one mile toward Castle Gap and spent the night.

Jonathan's check of the trail and riverbank up to the Pecos had revealed no recent cattle in the area and because the drive was making good time, he had given Caleb instructions to move the cattle across the river to make night camp. Tomorrow they would head on through the gap, and set up night camp on the other side. This would be as far as they would get in one day after funneling the longhorns through the narrow break in the Edwards Plateau.

Golden rode up to him. "Do you think they've found evidence of the rustlers from the plateau?"

"Good question. They didn't here."

"Sure, would make it easier on us if we were ahead of the thieves. We wouldn't have to drive the beeves in a grueling march to get ahead of their herd. I find it hard to believe there's a group of them this far south."

"Yes. We don't have rustlers in the Davis Mountains. Things are calm in my neck of the woods."

Golden nodded. "Opps there goes a couple of longhorns heading back west to the river. I will return." He rode off after the disappearing troublemakers.

Caleb watched him maneuver the long-horned animals back to the herd.

The following day, Jonathan and Press headed to the top of Castle Mountain. There was no dust indicating a trail drive, coming behind them, nor one before them. Satisfied they were ahead of the rustled herd, they rode off the high elevation and caught up with the drive.

Five days passed until the Glory B's longhorns arrived at the upper reaches of the Middle Concho River. Days of one hill after another, but with the appearance of buffalo grass and other grass which fed the cattle. Press was riding on point with Caleb and Jonathan when they spotted the deep ditch the river ran through.

"I'll be so glad to see water in a ditch," exclaimed Caleb.

"Yes," said Press. "The Concho never lets you down."

The upper reaches of the Middle Concho were dry. In astonishment and frustration, the three men sat on their horses looking at the dry hollow of the Middle Concho River.

Over the last days as they'd ridden along, each draw they'd come to had promised water. Everyone was dry. Even the deeper creeks had no water, but to see the Middle Concho dry was very, very disappointing. The men discussed their options.

"Poppa, should we just trail the herd down the bank and walk in the riverbed until we come to water? We'll come upon it for sure that way."

"No, Son. I'm afraid we might find rough, rocky areas where the cattle could not walk, if we hold to the bed of the river. I believe it would be best to turn the herd now and head farther downstream. Then pray when we come up to the riverbank further south toward San Angela, the river contains water."

"Jonathan, we do have maybe two more days before the cattle run into real trouble." Caleb rode closer to the edge of the ravine, dismounted, and looked over. He shook his head and turned back to the others, leading his horse.

"That's all the days we have," agreed Press. "After that, the longhorns will start dropping like flies. They're slowing down now."

"I'm sorry, Poppa."

"Jonathan, no rain is not your fault. We must have faith that we'll find water in time."

Caleb looked up at his trail boss. "Boss, do you want me to ride back and divert the cattle more to the south?"

"Yes, Caleb. Maybe we'll hit a tributary which has water in it."

Press and Jonathan watched him mount up and ride away.

"Son, why don't we ride down the river bank's edge until we find water? We could catch up with the herd and lead them to our discovery."

"I'm with you, Poppa. Going back to the herd won't accomplish anything at present and finding water will save our longhorns. Are you familiar with this territory?"

"Yes, your mother and I often took off across the prairie as the wagon train made its way to The Pinery, which was her father's station on the Butterfield mail route. Me and the trailhands rode with them for protection, since there weren't many wagons. The Apache or Commanche could have wiped them out in one swoop. After Gracie and her Pa came from Nashville, Tennessee, I couldn't let Indians get that curly headed girl so close to their goal." Press grinned remembering their rides through the cacti. He gestured and continued, "There were no mesquite trees along the way then, only ocotillo, creosote bushes, and lots of prairie grass, waving in the wind—more than you see now. At that time, not many people were herding cattle, and the Western gold rush had just started."

"Weren't you getting back from a cattle drive to Missouri, when you met Momma?"

"Yes, our first, and me and the boys were tired. You may not have realized it, but we've just followed the Butterfield Trail the last few miles. We'll keep close to it until we get to Abilene. Once the serious cattle movement started, this area became home to the Goodnight-Loving Cattle Trail. They herded cattle to New Mexico and the gold fields of Wyoming where they got top dollar for their animals."

"I hope we have longhorns to sell when we get to Abilene," stated Jonathan, looking unhappy, and long of face.

"Son, you do believe in prayer, don't you?

"Yes, Poppa. I do."

"Why don't we stop right now and ask for our Father's help."

"I'm with you."

Anyone looking at the two men from a distance, who appeared to be looking at the ground, would have guessed prairie dog holes for the bowed heads. Instead, the two men kept riding and praying to the One who created water in the first place, firmly believing He would provide the same again.

Five miles later, holes of water appeared in the bed of the river. Finally, a trickle of water ran in the stream bed. Making a good guess this would increase, the two men topped a hill and looked for a cloud of dust, indicating where the herd could be found. They rode toward the dust cloud with good news. At least on this part of the drive, the cattle would have water, and they wouldn't lose any of the herd.

~

"Gracie, we're half-way to San Angela." Press informed his wife that night as they sat around on the back of her wagon for a private talk. Tonight, they listened to the lowing of the well-watered cattle. "Five more days to go, but plenty of water on the way."

She laughed. "I've got to tell you something. One of the animals wasn't at a loss for water."

"What are you talking about?"

"Remember your talk with Jonathan and Caleb about water around the campfire, after the skies closed up?"

"Yes. We talked about what the lack of water could do to a longhorn if it was withheld for many days—a required discussion."

"And you talked about cows needing plenty so they could have milk for their calves, remember?"

Press was beginning to have an idea of where this conversation was going. He laughed. "Bossy and Little Bossy?"

It was Gracie's time to laugh and nod. "Three days ago, after dark, I caught Sarah Susannah carrying water to Little Bossy's mother. I wanted to discourage her from doing this, but didn't say a word, except to tell her not to take too much, that we needed water also."

"I'm not surprised at her. She loves that little calf. What's she going to do when we leave it in Abilene with its Mama?"

"I don't know. Guess we'll find out in a month or less, won't we?"

"I reckon. Did you notice how low the water was in the Middle Concho? I've never seen it this low, although the droughts we've been having the last three years have reduced its flow severely."

"You were blessed to find water, weren't you?"

"Jonathan and I prayed for water."

"The Lord provides," stated Gracie.

"Let's pray he keeps remembering us, sweetheart. How about now?"

After the prayer, they exchanged their usual goodnight kiss, and Press headed for his cot in Jonathan's and Caleb's tent.

Chapter Twenty-Three

The Trail to Abilene

While the drovers and the herd remained a few miles outside the town, Jonathan, Caleb, Gracie, and Press headed into San Angela. The four stopped to take in the fort which was built of limestone and wood and composed of many buildings, some two-story and all positioned around the parade ground. The town was across the river from Fort Concho.

"This is the sister fort to Fort Davis where I live. It could almost be my fort except mine is in a box canyon in the mountains and not on the plains. They both have the famous Buffalo Soldier Regiments on their grounds," stated Caleb.

"I remember the Buffalo Soldiers at the fort," agreed Gracie. "I also remember Pastor Ormand sometimes held church services in one of the buildings."

Caleb nodded. "Yes, he did, and I went to those with you, Cephas, and your pa. There's still someone who has services. A few years back, one of the Negro officers of Fort Concho came to work as quartermaster at Fort Davis. I had a chance to exchange some words with him before he left because of put-up charges by the commanding officer, which most of the soldiers said were false. Did you know he grew up as a slave in

Georgia? After the Civil War, he showed great promise, and was appointed to go to West Point. He was the first dark-skinned man to graduate from the military academy at West Point. I liked him."

"Really? Going to West Point is quite an accomplishment for any man." Gracie agreed. Then she added, "I remember the camels, too, corralled in that box canyon. How strange they looked in the state of Texas."

"I don't remember much of anything, except asking a curly-haired woman to marry me," contributed Press, giving his wife a hug. "Should we get on with our errands?"

"Poppa, we'll go on to the town," suggested Jonathan, not wishing to wait on his parents to get his mother's mail from Abilene. He had a list of supplies Jorge had written down. He and Caleb would collect the items on the list and head back to the herd with a loaded mule from one of the wagons.

"Go on. We'll find post headquarters and see where the letters are kept and be on soon."

Gracie and Press watched as the twosome forded the river, with droplets from their horse's hooves flashing in the air. Finding Gracie's letter did not take long.

She came out of the building waving her mail. "Doctor Sarah sent two letters. I'm surprised."

She mounted up, and they crossed the river, passing through the outskirts of San Angela. After riding by numerous framed or adobe houses, they caught up with the *boys* as they came out of a store advertising, *The newest guns sold in the West.*

"Fancy meeting you here," observed Press, looking at the sign.

"Aw, Poppa, we just wanted to see the new models."

"Sure, sure," said his father, smiling.

Continuing on down the street, the group passed a saloon where loud piano music filled the air.

"Hey, wait a minute. They have a newspaper here." Press looked at another sign above a door which said *Concho Times*. "I'll be right back." He dismounted and disappeared inside.

While he was inside, the others dismounted and looked around at the town center, considering places where they might purchase supplies. On one end of the street, a church stood.

Press came back out with a folded paper. He tapped the paper in the palm of his hand, indicating he was satisfied with his purchase. "Have you found a place to buy your supplies?" he asked.

"Poppa, Caleb and I'll head for that mercantile store down there." He pointed to an advertisement saying apples, cabbage, carrots, onions, hats, clothes, boots, and other items. Bushel baskets sat tilted on the boardwalk, showing some of the items which could be bought. "They seem to advertise the staples we need for Jorge. If we don't find everything there, we'll keep looking. I see more stores the length of this street."

"Jonathan and I don't want to hold you up on your look around town. Why don't we go our separate ways and meet up back at the herd?" suggested Caleb.

Their boots loudly announced their steps on the boardwalk as they walked away.

"Come on, Gracie, I'm going to treat you to a store-bought dinner. Then if you want to, we'll see if there's a store to buy dresses." Press took her by the arm. "Let's go."

~

The table was clean but well-worn where Gracie and Press sat at a window in the eating establishment. Gracie was exploring a gap in the wood with her finger as they waited for a menu.

"Sweetheart," said Press. "I'm thinking fried chicken if they have any. What about you? What are you craving today? Something we don't get on the cattle trail."

"Yum. Fried chicken with biscuits and gravy sounds good. Not saying my bullets are bad, but someone else's bread besides mine … well, you know. I don't have to cook it."

"What kind of vegetables do you want?"

"Hum-n, guess it'll have to be canned corn and buttered potatoes. Here comes our server."

The server asked, "What do you want to drink with your meal folks?"

"Coffee, Gracie?"

"Yes, that's fine."

"And we'd like two orders of fried chicken, biscuits with gravy, plus corn and buttered potatoes," said Press, noticing that the server wasn't writing his instructions down.

"I'm sorry, sir. But our special today is on the board over the door," he pointed to a black board where stew with vegetables and cornbread was scrawled.

Press had to laugh. "Well, Gracie. Does stew and the trimmings suit you?" He didn't wait for her to say yes, but told the server to bring their meal.

After the server left, Gracie laughed, "I did so want something different than a one-dish meal. We have those all the time on the trail, because they're the easiest to fix."

"Maybe in Abilene. We're only ten days away."

"I'm going to hold you to it, dear husband."

Press opened his paper.

Gracie looked at the date of Doctor Sarah's letters. She chose the oldest, opened it with her table knife, and started reading.

"Listen to this Press," she said, reading about the meeting with the new train superintendent, Grant Bailey, and their lunch after church.

Press looked over the edge of his paper and questioned, "Huh, do you think she's interested? She didn't say how old he is?"

Gracie checked the letter for the second time. "No, she didn't. Wouldn't it be interesting if she found someone who became important to her? She's been so busy starting two new practices, she hasn't had much time for men in her life, and the one she did have some time for turned out not to last."

Press grinned at his wife. He'd let the women decide the women things. He turned the paper back to a page he'd just read. "Let me tell *you* something interesting which *I* just read. The Post Office has indicated they will put an office here if the town will change its name to San Angelo. It says San Angela is not grammatically correct Spanish. Can you believe that?"

Gracie shook her head, opened the second letter, and started reading the only page. She looked up as Press turned the last page of his *Concho Times*. He put his hand on hers, getting her attention.

"This is disturbing, and may mean trouble for us ahead. Someone by the name of Harris has fenced thousands of acres near here, and others are threatening to do the same. The article says the ones putting up barbed wire are ignoring boundaries and are enclosing property which isn't theirs. There's already been instances of fence cutting, by a group called the Owls, who cut them at night. The article goes on to say the Governor or state legislators must take up the issue before many are hurt or killed."

Press put down his newspaper as the server put bowls full of stew on the table and a plate of cornbread. Nothing was said as he poured more hot coffee in their cups.

After the man left, Gracie asked, "Do you think we'll run into barbed wire fences?"

"I certainly hope not. We haven't before." Press picked up his spoon and started eating.

Gracie couldn't read the expression on his face. She ate a couple of bites while looking at Doctor Sarah's second letter. To Press, she read the description of the surgery on the lad, Jefferson, grinning at the sight and sound he must have made before the operation. "Doctor Sarah says that Ruby Eliza has had dinner with Grant Bailey twice lately." Gracie looked at her husband, her eyes wide. "Is it possible we were wrong and that *our daughter* has a man friend?"

Press raised his eyebrows and shook his head. The happenings around his family were progressing faster than he liked.

Gracie and Press finished their meal, and sat afterward discussing the news they'd exchanged. They were in no hurry to get back to the trail drive and relaxing on chairs at a real table was a welcome change, especially with someone waiting on their every need. Gracie pulled out a blank piece of paper and pencil from her cloth purse. She flattened the paper out on the table, and set about writing a return letter to Doctor Sarah and Ruby Eliza.

"We'll have to take your message to the military post office before we leave," said Press.

"Do you mind, dear?"

"No, sweetheart. Not a bit."

The server appeared with two dishes. The smell of sugar and pecans wafted in the air.

"On the house," he said, setting the plates on the table with a flourish.

The saving grace of the whole meal was the pecan pie made from the trees growing along the different sections of the Concho River—the sweetest nut ever.

Gracie wiped her mouth with the table napkin and sighed. "I wonder if they have more of that delicacy? I'd like to have enough to take to our drovers—treat them to something wonderful and sweet."

Press went to pay the bill and inquire about the pies. He returned with three encased in a wooden box. "We'll have to send someone back with the tin plates and box before we leave tomorrow. I promised."

"The slices will be small," observed Gracie, after looking under the cloth, covering the top pie.

"Don't worry. They'll eat," assured Press.

During the ride to the herd, he balanced the pies on his pommel, holding his horse's reins loosely with his right hand. He remained strangely silent.

Gracie glanced at him once, and then settled down to ride while watching the cacti go by.

Press was thinking, *barbed wire.*

❧ Chapter Twenty-Four ❧

Barbed Wire Fences

The following morning, May 1st, Caleb and the drovers headed up the longhorns and moved them toward Abilene. The sky was clear of clouds and the air already warm. Beads of sweat formed on his forehead. At least, the wind was blowing, cooling him somewhat. He pushed his hat back on his head, pulled his bandana up from his neck, and mopped his face. The distant whistles of the men driving the herd, and the resistant mooing of the cattle, being roused from their night's rest, sounded in his ears. This was music to the point man. All was well.

He and Jonathan rode ahead of the herd, discussing the next watering place.

"The Colorado River of course," said Jonathan. "We should find plenty of water there."

"How long?" asked Caleb.

"Poppa said no longer than three or four days. And then a day or two to the next fort. We won't have to worry about the cows from here to Fort Chadbourne, which will put us a few days out from Abilene. When we get there, I'll take you to Cow-boy's Victuals to eat. Ernie has the *Best fried chicken in the West.*"

"My stomach is growling already. Sometimes Jorge's bullets and eggs just don't stick to my ribs." He pulled out an extra biscuit from breakfast and started to munch away.

"Where's mine?" asked Jonathan.

Another one appeared. "Aw shucks, I was saving it for later," complained Caleb, but he was smiling at his friend.

"By the way," Jonathan managed to say between bites, "the day after we leave the Colorado, Poppa and Momma may wish to take a roundabout way to Fort Chadbourne. I wouldn't be surprised if they ride ahead, so they can spend a few hours there. I'll probably drive Momma's wagon when they ride out."

"I'll remember. We'll be short one hand." Caleb changed the subject. "Jonathan, do you think we'll have trouble with the rustlers when we get to Abilene?"

Shrugging his shoulders, Jonathan said, "I hope not, but if we have to identify them, we'll be close by when the Sheriff goes to arrest them. There's always danger, even when you mount your horse in the morning," suggested his trail boss, realizing each day had its own problems. "We'll try to stay out of the way and let the authorities do their job."

Caleb nodded his head and kept riding.

Press chose to ride on the wagon with Gracie as they started northeast toward Abilene.

After the noon meal, he took the reins of the mules and drove the wagon giving Gracie a rest. "The view's always the same in this part of Texas—one arroyo after the other, and if it's not a dip, it's a high mesa or butte." He pointed off in the distance where the high ground abruptly appeared, pushed from the earth, on both sides of the trail drive.

"My dear, you can't discount the mesquite trees we sometimes drive through." Gracie put her arm around him and gave him a hug.

"Have you noticed they grow in the areas where cattle were and are trailed to market?"

"The longhorns like the tree's seed pods. Many times, there's nothing else to eat.

"At least, the high seat of a wagon lets you see more of the lay of the land ahead. From a horse you feel boxed in unless the area is grassy."

"Makes me appreciate the view from the Glory B—so expansive and beautiful and safe."

"Yes, Gracie, it's really more of the same, but you are towering over the scene and looking down onto the prairie. The world is passing by in front of you." Press chirped to the mules. "We're falling behind Jorge.

"Husband, you just aren't a dreamer like me. I see all sorts of things in the far distant plants and clouds and rocks." She pointed to a cloud. "See that cow-boy hat?"

Press laughed, "Yes, like I see that spindly cactus off in the desert which looks like a pitchfork." He pointed to the one he was describing.

Now, it was her time to laugh and give him a kiss on the cheek. "No, my dear. That's a W for wonder what's next?"

Press changed the subject. "Sweetheart, do you know we're four or five days to Fort Chadbourne. It's one-half the way we have left to our final destination."

"Yes. I'll be glad to set my eyes on the fort. I wonder if it's changed since we were last there?"

"With the passage of time, nothing's ever the same." Press stated with firmness. "I hope we don't run into any more trouble on the way."

Press no more than got his words out, when he noticed Jorge had stopped ahead. Soon the other two wagons were piled up behind the cooks. Press jumped down from his wagon seat and went forward. Jorge met him. All he said was, "Barbed wire and no gate."

Press strode to the fence and looked around. There were four strands on wooden posts as far as he could see. He turned around and yelled at P.T., "Son, get on your horse and head for Jonathan and Caleb. Tell them to stop the herd wherever they are now. Ride there as quickly as possible."

"What about Cephas and the *remuda*?" asked P.T. coming off his wagon and jumping from the wheel to the ground.

"Tell him what's happened, but he and the horses can come on and join us here."

"Okay, Poppa." He headed for the back of the wagon to release his horse's reins.

"Hurry P.T."

Gracie climbed onto the front wheel of her wagon, put her foot on the hub, and jumped to the ground. She walked to where her husband and Jorge stood. "Maybe we should have asked for directions at San Angela. There might be a way through," she suggested.

"Too late for that," stated Press. "We're miles away, now."

"Boss," called Jorge. "Look over here."

The pathway through the prairie wasn't a clearly defined route, because herds of driven cattle spread out and made their way over several acres of land, leaving the earth and grass trampled under multiple hooves, both longhorns and horses. Since there was nothing left to do but wait, Jorge had walked down the fence row for several feet.

Press and Gracie set out to join him.

Press looked where he pointed. "The night Owls have been here, that's for sure," he said as he checked out the mangled fence wire.

"Someone's cut it before, and it's been patched. And look over there," suggested Jorge

Being absorbed by the fence, Press hadn't noticed the many acres of burned prairie. "Burning a man's pasture is grounds for a fight. And what good is it? Even those driving cattle to market need grass." He shook his head, examined the twisted wire, and headed back to the wagons.

"Was this fence across the trail when you took the cattle to Fort Worth last year," asked Gracie.

"No, it was open land," he exclaimed. "But landless cowmen, who owned no property but raised cattle on the open range, were here. Harry Johnston and me stopped to talk to a group of them. They were gathering up and branding a bunch of longhorns to drive to market. We saw them later in Fort Worth with their herd."

"That's right, Boss. I remember talking to them." Jorge turned around to sounds of riders coming. "Here comes Jonathan and Caleb with P.T."

Dismounting their horses, the two men came to the fence.

Caleb spoke first. "Somehow, I knew when I read your paper, Press, we were headed for this. He shook his head, put out his finger to touch the metal wire, and immediately brought blood from one of the sharp points of a barb. He put his finger in his mouth.

"I'm at a loss unless we cut this fence or unwind the patch job Jorge found down yonder." Press gestured toward the area where his cook had discovered the splice in the fence.

Jonathan was thinking. "Poppa didn't we pass a new house around here, if you can call one of adobe and sticks with no windows a house. It was before the large dip where we watered the cattle last year. Remember, we were amazed at ditches dug so crops could be grown in some cleared fields next to the dwelling. The man called them irrigation ditches. He'd seen them back east along the Mississippi River in Arkansas."

"Was there a line of cottonwood and pecan trees along the arroyo?" asked Jorge.

"Yes, that's the one. The man had dammed up a small lake of water so he'd have enough for the growing season. We tried to avoid it, because he asked us to, but a few stragglers took advantage of the pool anyway."

"How far was the house from here?" asked Press, still not sure if he could recall the place. "Did this man have sheep? I do remember some sheep in this vicinity."

"Yes, there were sheep—a field full of them, being herded by a dog."

Press nodded his head and looked over the barbed wire into the fenced area. "I sorta remember, Jonathan, but I don't see any evidence of the place in the distance."

"It was downhill. You couldn't see it from here."

"Who's going to go with me to talk with this man? We need to get this solved as soon as possible and drive our herd on into Abilene. We can't wait too long because the rustlers and their herd will beat us. I hate to even lose a day, but it looks like we may do so."

"Well, Poppa, the rustlers will just cut the fence. They're not going to stop and be nice."

"That's just exactly what I mean. Maybe for the information on the rustled herd and a heads up on what may happen, the rancher will help us through his land, and we won't have a problem. Who's going?"

After a further brief discussion, Caleb stood back while Press, Jonathan, and P.T. took the splice apart, rode through, and put it back. The three mounted up and rode in the direction of the hut.

Caleb headed for the herd with instructions to bring the cattle on close to the fence.

Gracie and Jorge watched until the delegation was out of sight. She looked at Jorge. "There's no telling when they'll get back. Should we set up camp and start fixing the night meal?"

Jorge pulled in a large sigh and let it out with a huff. "I'm thinkin' fried chicken, buttered potatoes, and corn." He looked over to see how Gracie was taking his words.

She made a face at him. "Who told you I wanted fried chicken?"

"Your husband said he's taking you to a place in Abilene which fixes you the best you said you've ever had."

"Since we're *not* going to have fried chicken, what are we going to have?"

Jorge looked down the path they'd just come with the wagons. "I think the answer to our problem is on the way here."

Golden rode his horse up close to Jorge. "I heard about the trouble and felt like we'd be here a while, maybe even for supper. I saw a herd of antelope off in the distance and decided to go fetch us one. It was far enough away so as not to disturb the longhorns. Does freshly roasted antelope whet your appetite, my friend?"

"Sure does. We were just talking about what's for supper," replied Jorge. "Slide off your horse, and I'll help you pull your fresh kill from behind the saddle, skin and dress it. There's enough for supper, and we'll slice the rest to make bullet biscuits in the morning. Gracie, will you and P.T. let down the side board on my wagon. We'll cut our antelope up in chunks, and roast it over a mesquite fire. Thar's plenty of wood around here to make that happen."

"Here comes Cephas with the extra horses. I'm goin' to help him set up his corral."

"Gracie, we've never helped set up the stakes and ropes for the *remuda*. Let's help Cephas, and then we'll all pitch in and fix supper."

Once the horses were safely contained in a grassy area, the supper crew headed in all directions—getting wood, building a fire, setting up a spit, and then standing around with their mouths watering at the smoky-smell of sizzling, roasting antelope.

~

There were five men on horses when Press returned.

The group rode close to the campsite and dismounted near the spliced fence, tying their horses to the posts where the barbed wire was nailed. Press climbed through the barbed wire and headed for the water barrel to get a drink.

The others took the fence apart and strode over to Gracie and Jorge where they were introduced.

"Momma, this is Isaiah Benson and his son, Abraham. They're goin' to help us with the herd. We're headin' through his property tomorrow on the way to the Colorado River."

"Pleased to meet you, Mrs. Stockton. Something sure smells good," commented the older man, sniffing the air.

"It's antelope, roasted on the spit, and we have vegetables to go with it." Gracie nodded in the direction of the smell.

Press returned and asked Jorge, "Has Caleb shown up with the herd?"

"We don't know where he is. He usually comes to check in when he's in sight of the chuckwagon to let us know they'll soon be ready to eat."

"Jonathan, we'd better go check on him."

Press turned to Mr. Benson, "Isaiah, would you and Abraham like to ride with us?"

"Sure would, Press," said the older man.

The group went to get their horses. Even P.T. mounted up to ride with his new friend.

~

The talk was lively around the campfire in the evening. The moon was bright overhead. The fire's coals under the iron bar where the antelope had been roasted spit sparks in the air. Press and Gracie sat in their usual place on the back of her wagon. He whispered, "How about a walk in the moonlight, later?"

She giggled. "With pleasure, my dear."

The talk had been ongoing, but during a lull in the conversation, Gracie asked, "Mr. Benson, have you been to Fort Chadbourne lately?"

"Not this year. You know they closed it up, don't you? The Indian trouble has moved mostly north and west into the Dakotas and Rocky Mountains. The military is long gone and only the family which owns the place lives there. They farm longhorns mostly."

Press gave Gracie a little squeeze. "We're sorry to hear that. Before Gracie and I were married, over twenty years ago, we came through here and overnighted at the fort."

"Yes, I wanted to visit when we went by on our way to Abilene."

"You can still visit. Thomas Odom and his wife, Lucinda will gladly welcome you. They own thousands of acres."

The friendly conversation continued as the flickering fire danced on the faces of the people hunkered around it. Some sat on the ground or empty wooden boxes pulled from the wagons. Gracie punched Press and discreetly pointed. Sarah Susannah and Thomas stood at the edge of the firelight. Her parents watched as they walked quietly out into the shadows.

"Great night for a walk under the Texas stars. I bet they're going to see Little Bossy," Press whispered to Gracie.

"One can only hope," Gracie whispered back.

One by one those around the warm fire headed for their cots—some placed under the stars in the open. Others slept in their blankets on the ground or under the hastily erected tents. Soon snores were heard coming from the sleeping men. Tomorrow was another day on the trail, but their final destination was only days away. Sleep came peacefully.

"Are you ready to go for our walk, sweetheart?" Press said sliding off the wagon gate.

"Yes, which way?"

"Let's just follow the moon," suggested her husband, holding out his hand.

"Silly man," whispered Gracie, grasping his hand and jumping to the ground. "I think the moon is heading that way," she pointed, still holding his hand.

"Come on, and we'll see where it ends."

"Are you flirting with me?"

Jorge grinned at their banter from his blanket under the chuckwagon. He didn't hear Press's answer. They had walked too far away.

Thomas and Sarah Susannah slowly rode their horses toward the milling longhorns, seeking Bossy, so they could check on her calf. They waved to the drover who was riding the sidelines of the herd and continued on, until they spotted the calf. She stood in the moonlight, her eyes on them.

"Little Bossy's really growing, isn't she," stated Sarah Susannah as she dismounted her horse near her pet. As was his custom, Thomas took his rain slicker for them to sit on.

The little calf knew these two humans and came immediately to them. She nuzzled them for a treat, like a piece of greenery they'd pulled during the day or something acceptable from the night meal. Sticking out her wet tongue, she'd pull the delicacy from a hand and then ask for more. She loved getting her back scratched, but don't touch her head. She'd throw it high in the air and kick her heels as a no.

After sitting for several minutes, scratching, patting, and showing their affection for Little Bossy, the calf headed back to its mama.

Thomas stated the obvious, "When we get to Abilene, Little Bossy will have to stay with her mom." He didn't elaborate on his words, but they were enough.

Suddenly, Sarah Susannah started crying. "Y-yes, I know. I'm not looking forward to it," she sobbed. She could have continued, *I'm not looking forward to saying goodbye to you, either.*

Thomas's arm went immediately around her.

She turned to Thomas and encircled him with hers.

He held her until the sobbing stopped, not knowing what else to do. Or rather, knowing what he wanted to do, but not knowing how she would accept his kiss.

Sarah Susannah solved the problem. She raised her lips to kiss him on the cheek.

And then their lips met, only once.

Thomas stood and helped her to her feet—shaken by his feelings.

"We'd better go, Thomas."

"Yes, you're right," he echoed. "We'd better go."

Chapter Twenty-Five

Abilene!

Isiah Benson and Abraham guided the Glory B's longhorns across their property. They made one quick stop at the adobe and stick hut about half-way through to tell his wife what he was doing. Upon hearing a woman was with the herd, she hurried out to greet her. But Gracie was far ahead with the chuckwagons. The Benson men mounted up, and the trek across his property continued.

"My property's so big, whole herds can go across without me knowin' it until weeks later, especially if we're plantin' crops or tendin' fields in other areas," he told Press, as he let them through another place where the barbed wire fence had been cut and spliced. This was at the border of his property.

"Thank you, Isiah, for your help."

"Anytime Press, you are welcome to go through my place. There are more fences around San Angela, but none between here and Abilene. I do think fencin' is coming across the Texas prairie, so trailin' cattle is goin' to end, especially if the railroads keep growin' and expanding. The state will mark out roads and cattle will be driven to the railroad trailheads on established roads and not across owned land."

"Texas is growin' up, for sure. I'll keep your words in mind."

"Here's a little present for your wife from mine." He handed a cloth bag to Press, walked to his horse and mounted up.

Press waited until the Bensons were out of sight in the midst of the mesquite trees. He opened the bag. It was full of pecans, the sweetest most tasty nuts grown in Texas. He tried one just to make sure.

Later in the week, the longhorns were herded through the Colorado River. Fort Chadbourne was only about a day away.

~

Press and Gracie did not go visit the Odom's at Fort Chadbourne. They did take Jonathan up on his offer to drive Gracie's wagon and use the opportunity to take a detour and ride by to gaze at the fort from the mesquite forest surrounding the buildings.

From the rise where they sat on their horses, they could see several children playing on the old parade ground, which was surrounded by several of the buildings, showing some age but still serviceable. While they were there, a woman appeared in a doorway of one of the long limestone buildings. She must have called the young ones in to eat, because they ran apparently to see who-beat-who to their repast.

Gracie shook her head. "Press, let's go."

"Okay, Gracie. The scene does sadden you. But just think, we'll see Ruby Eliza and Doctor Sarah in five days and eat fried chicken in Abilene."

"Why do things have to change?" she asked, not deterred from her thoughts. "Abilene didn't exist until the railroad came to town. Pa and me drove our Conestoga from Fort Phantom Hill to Fort Chadbourne without encounterin' a soul. The Fort was alive with the military men, hangers on, and settlers heading West."

Press just laughed. He didn't answer the question, because he'd pondered the same matter and wasn't sure he'd come up with the right answer. He wasn't sure he was happy with growing old. Instead, he said, "We all grow older, my dear, but as we grow older, we should always keep growin' up. And, Sweetheart, you are so lovely as you grow up."

"How do you always say the right thing?" Gracie looked at him, love showing in her eyes.

Although his comment helped, Gracie still had her thoughts. She'd been insulated from the changing world in the Glass Mountains with her family around her. The inevitable was staring her in the face, and it was called change.

Two days out of Abilene, Steamboat Mountain rose from the edge of the high hills which were split by the Callahan Divide. The separation of the distant mountains could clearly be seen from each rise the Glory B's longhorns topped.

The old town of Buffalo Gap was located to the north, at the opening nearest the cattle town of Abilene. Once the seat of the Taylor County area, it had been rooted out by the new railroad town which took over that honor. The stage still went through the Gap, picking up passengers and dropping off mail.

The chuckwagons of the Glory B trail drive were now being driven through terrain which was rough with multiple shallow arroyos, cacti, and mesquite trees. One deeper arroyo had water for the cows to drink, but did not appear clean enough for humans. With rain, it probably flowed as a stream.

Press pulled alongside Gracie's wagon and pointed to the right at the low section in the mountains ahead. "Gracie, do you see the dip to the left in the hills ahead?"

She turned her head to peer off into the distance, letting the mules set their own pace. "Yes, is that Buffalo Gap?" she asked, swaying on her high perch, and trying to remember the place from her last hurried trip by stage to Abilene to see Doctor Sarah's new office. "Aren't we headed there?"

"Yes, it is the Gap, but we aren't goin' through it. We'll go to the southeast." He pointed to another higher gap, a break in the ridge to which they were headed.

"I see it," she said with no passion.

"When we get to our gap, we'll be a little more than one day away from Abilene. We'll arrive early the next day, in time to wash up, and eat fried chicken at noon," said Press, grinning. Looking up at her, he tried to lift her mood and soothe her spirit.

She is so beautiful, he thought, not changing much from their trip on this same trail when he'd first fallen in love with her so many years ago. How many times had he ridden beside the Tipton's wagon just to gaze up at this lovely woman, hoping one day she'd be his wife?

"Why aren't we goin' through the gap at Buffalo?"

"We believe the rustlers will go that way, so we're goin' to steer away from there."

"Rustlers. I don't like the sound of the word." She shook her head, faster than usual to make her point. Pulling in a lungful of air, she let it out in a rush, her chest heaving with the effort.

"It'll be alright, sweetheart. We'll identify them and let the Sheriff take care of the problem. Won't you be glad to see Ruby Eliza?" asked Press, ever mindful of her concern over those she loved. He wasn't without apprehension himself about the coming confrontation.

"Oh yes. I can't say I won't be glad to see Abilene."

"Gracie, are we getting too old to travel?"

Now she gave a small chuckle. "I love the travelin' part." Suddenly, an idea came to her, "I wonder what it's like to travel by train? Press, do you think we could go east and visit Nashville and your old home town in Mississippi? We might even go to New York—take a really long train ride."

Even in her eagerness, she sounded sad. Was it a leftover from the day before? "Sweetheart, do you want me to drive the wagon for you?" he suggested, trying to cheer her up.

"No, but thanks. I'll be alright. The sun will cheer me up."

"Oh, one more thing. We'll set up our night camp in the gap where we can see Abilene in the distance. Jonathan sent me to tell Jorge. I'll see you when we noon."

Gracie waved at him as he left. What was this feeling she was having? Sadness? Not really. Misfortune? Maybe. Trouble? Yes. The feeling meant trouble. But what? After the noon meal, she felt somewhat better.

~

In the late afternoon sun, Gracie stood looking across several miles of grassy plain, wondering what she expected to see from the night camp. As they'd topped the gap, she saw briefly what she thought were buildings. But in the glare of the afternoon sun and the smoky, hot haze which greeted the drive, she couldn't be sure about the images. The smoke hugging the ground might be the only indication the cattle drive was nearing its destination.

They'd continued on about one mile beyond the gap, where cottonwood trees indicated a low depression in the ground and the possibility of water. Although the ground looked damp, no water was found. The dry, hot air stirred the grassy plain ahead with waves indicating its movement.

She and Jorge were cooking the night meal. *Only one more to go,* she thought. The next one would be on the flatter land near the town in preparation for locating a feedlot on Elm Creek and a buyer for their longhorns. This meant circling south and heading back west around the town.

"Ouch!" she exclaimed.

"What's wrong, Gracie?" Jorge came over to check out a red place on the hand she was slinging vigorously.

"I wasn't watching and splashed some of the hot stew broth out of the kettle. Need to keep my mind on what I'm doing," she was disgusted with herself.

"Are you all right?" he questioned, dropping her hand. "You've been quiet lately. Is something worrying you?" Not waiting for her answer, he headed for the chuckwagon and came back with a tube of ointment. "Some of Doctor Sarah's wonderful salve, according to Cephas. Everybody needs a tube."

Before she realized what was happening, Gracie told her best friend the whole problem. "Jorge, I have to admit I've been down lately. That's unusual for me."

Rubbing the ointment on her outstretched hand, Jorge nodded his head in agreement and waited for her to go on.

"So many things are changing, in the world around us. I guess I've just realized *all* my children are growing up and will be heading out on their own. Soon Press and I'll live in an almost empty house, and be back to where we started. Then there's this rustler business. I have a bad feeling about what may happen when they identify those men. I wish none of our men had to be a party to it."

"Gracie, you and Press have raised some fine children. Your Pa, Mr. Tipton, would be so proud of all of them. I know you and Press are happy, because as the Bible says you've got your quiver full. With grandchildren on the way, your house will be chock-full again."

"That's what Press hopes, and I'm sure you're right. My Pa never settled down enough to enjoy his grandchildren. I think my husband will."

"The rustlers are a different story. Why don't we stop right now and say a prayer?"

Jorge said a short prayer, ending with the words, "Thy will be done, in Jesus' name."

Turning, Gracie gave him a hug and a quick peck on the cheek. "You always make me feel better. I guess that's why I often complain to you." She gave him a smile.

Embarrassed by her show of affection, Jorge's face turned red. He immediately changed the subject. "How's the stew coming?"

"We'll be ready when the drovers get here, and I think I hear the longhorns bawling now."

"I believe you're right. I'll start fryin' the cornbread."

Chapter Twenty-Six

The Arrival

Doctor Sarah finished checking the dressing on Jefferson's foot. "I believe your foot is healed enough to go barefoot again with your sister," she advised, giving him a couple of taps on his knee as affirmation of her words. "Just stay away from mesquite trees and their thorns or you'll be back here in this room, and I don't think you want to go through the last few days again, do you?"

"No, ma'am, I don't. Thank you for makin' me better. Dad says it's now time to start plantin' crops, and he hopes I'll be able to help. Grandpa tries, but he can't bend over like he did in his younger days."

"No problem helping with planting and hoeing and anything else needing done around the farm," Doctor Sarah advised him. "You may go. Oh, bring me some fresh vegetables once they're ripe."

Jefferson jumped off the table and went out the door. Doctor Sarah could hear him telling Ruby Eliza, his *newly found girlfriend,* and his grandparents the good news.

"Will you be at church on Sunday?" came Ruby Eliza's muffled question back to her new admirer. She had asked him before.

Doctor Sarah listened for the answer.

"Yes. Can we sit together?" was the reply.

"If you come, we *will* sit together. I promise," replied Ruby Eliza.

The last words Doctor Sarah heard was a promise by the grandparents to bring him. The good Doctor had to chuckle. The bench at church was changing, because the relationship between Grant Bailey and her nurse had deepened over the last weeks. They were going on buggy rides and horseback rides to places for picnics, or enjoying the scenery which was new to the train superintendent, such as a whole day's trip to Fort Phantom Hill just north of Abilene.

The changing bench would have been just great, but Ruby Eliza had managed to upset her good friend, Rachel. Rachel, considering her best friend had stolen her boyfriend, had moved as far away in church as possible. Although Ruby Eliza had begged her not to be upset, she refused to return.

Even the pastor seemed troubled when she showed up one Sunday on Grant's arm for services. His broad smile was now a tiny, thin line—joking and teasing a thing of the past. The doctor hoped time would heal all wounds, which was exactly what her nurse was hoping.

Still thinking, Doctor Sarah chuckled and shook her head. Because of their attraction for each other, she wondered if she needed to train a new worker in her expanding medical practice. Should she ask or was it too early in their relationship?

At this point in her thoughts, she heard the outside door of her office close.

Ruby Eliza appeared in the examination room. "Jefferson is a changed little boy," observed the nurse.

"He was so-o happy to learn he didn't have to come back to see me. I think he has a fondness for you though. He might be back to see you."

"Yes, he promised to come to church Sunday." The nurse pulled a sheet off the examination table and started folding it. "There's no one else in the waiting room," she explained.

"Ruby Eliza, *someone else* may be at church this weekend."

"I hope you're right and Poppa and Momma do make it. What day did she say in her last letter to you?" The daughter had received one earlier with a note at the bottom, saying Doctor Sarah would get her last letter.

"I'm looking for them tomorrow or the next day. She said she's looking forward to eating fried chicken at Cow-boy's Victuals. If there's no one in the office, I think we should all go together. We'll have one big celebration of their first successful cattle drive to Abilene."

The duo continued into the washup room, so the Doctor could clean her hands.

"Great idea. Maybe Grant can come and join us. I'd like Poppa and Momma to meet him."

Doctor Sarah dried her hands on a clean towel and peered at her nurse. "I need to ask you a question. How *do* you feel about Grant?"

Ruby Eliza stopped folding the sheet and placed it on a shelf with others. "Sarah," she dropped the Doctor, because this was very personal and not business related. "I really like him. I think he's the one I'd like to marry, but he's not said a word to make me think he feels the same way. He acts like he does, but there's something holding him back, and I don't know what it is. I've wondered, and I continue to study his every word. I can't figure it out. Not only that, he hasn't introduced his father, Henry."

"Is Henry very old?" The one time she might have seen Mr. Bailey, she'd had an emergency, and Grant had taken him home.

"I think he said mid-seventies. From what he's said, he is too feeble to come to church. Falls a lot. Grant says he can't handle the steps. Sarah, I think he's too old to be Grant's father. There's something strange about the whole situation. I keep hoping he'll tell me, but so far, he hasn't."

"Does he plan on staying in Abilene with the railroad? I hear they move people around to different places as the railroad expands."

"I don't know the answer to that question either."

"Would moving to different places bother you?"

"I don't think so. Not if I loved the person."

"Then let me caution you to get all these questions answered before you become deeply involved—too far to get out without being terribly hurt."

"I may be there already. Sarah, what am I going to do?" In her voice, there was pleading for an answer to her dilemma.

"There's no way I can help you. I've told you my story, and as you know mine didn't end well. So, I'm not the right one to ask. Just keep praying. Your love for him will work things out. When you involve your heavenly Father, difficulties always do. Although maybe not the way we want, but always the way we need." Sarah thought a moment and added, "You might ask your earthly one, too. Your Poppa always gives good advice. I'm so glad your Momma married him. They are perfect for each other. Have I said this before?"

At the mention of Preston Stockton, Jr., Ruby Eliza grinned. "You're right. Poppa gives good advice, too. I'll do that."

"Come on, I'll buy. It's Cow-boy's Victuals for an early dinner. How about it?" She held open the door.

"I am sorta tired of Chester's chicken eggs. Think he'd want to come with us? I'll go see."

Before Doctor Sarah could say anything, Ruby Eliza hurried out the door of the doctor's office and around the back of the building.

Chester wasn't there, but his garden was starting to show serious green and his expanding brood of chickens were scratching at the grass in their large wire pen and perched on their egg-laying hen house.

Ruby Eliza didn't give this much thought. She turned and headed for the main Abilene street, meeting her boss on the boardwalk. They set out for the center part of town.

Grant Bailey looked over the papers on his desk. They contained the numbers of passengers, loads the station had received and sent, and the amount of money he'd collected in the past few days. He pulled the sheets together and placed the information in an envelope which he would give to the conductor for safekeeping to Fort Worth headquarters. He'd counted a stack of money to be deposited in the bank in Abilene, and placed it in another envelope. Because he didn't like dealing with other people's money, he'd take care of this before the day was out.

Placing the information in a wire basket on his desk, he stood up and went to the window of his office which looked south over the train tracks. The heat shimmered and simmered on the plain toward Buffalo Gap, the sun making waves of heat which distorted the view. The smoke from myriad chimney fires in Abilene didn't help the scene. It lay on the ground like a blanket, barely moving. Surely this heat wouldn't last.

Everyone he'd talked to had insisted the last few years had been cold, and this was just a fluke which would end. It was the middle of May and where he was from the weather should still be cold, or at least cool, and certainly rainy. He wasn't used to heat like this until late June, when the overhead sun beat down on the Black Hills of South Dakota, or the deep valleys of the Ozark Mountains of Missouri. He opened the window and headed for the opposite one, thinking he'd cause a cross current in the room.

Opening the second window did help. A puff of air mixed with the smell of wood smoke went through the room. Looking outside, he noticed the streets of Abilene were empty—unusual for this time of day, when movement of people around the mercantile area and eateries was a given. The business places were bunched up around the train station for easy access of residents and ticket holders.

Turning he went back to his wooden desk, picked up the two envelopes, and walked to a rack on the wall situated next to the door leading to the platform for boarding or loading the train. The conductor was required to check here as the steam engine used the turntable to head back to Fort Worth. Pushing the one envelope into the holder, Grant put the other in the inside pocket of his coat and walked out onto the platform. He stood, arms crossed, looking at the metal rails of the train track—seeing nothing.

These days his thoughts were often of a woman he was beginning to love with all his heart. But how could he tell her? He had no roots. He did not know much about his early life.

True, Henry had taken him in while he was very young to raise and love, and Jason had instilled in him a love of God and an education. The three had moved to Missouri where both men had taken jobs, assuring he learned the business end of manufacturing. He'd been hired by the first company he'd approached. The Texas and Pacific had great plans for expansion. But it was a well-known fact, many railroads on the frontier were just flash-in-the-pans. Some did not survive long because of poor management practices or overreach by the owners.

He loved his occupation, but it might take him out of Texas in the future or far away from the lady's family. Her roots were firmly embedded in the southwest Texas soil—a subject she often talked about on their trips around the area.

He walked to the end of the platform. On the opposite side of the street, the object of his thoughts was coming down the boardwalk with Doctor Sarah. He watched as they approached—Ruby Eliza with her parasol over her head which she twirled in her hand. His heart immediately went out to her.

The two were talking animatedly. Ruby Eliza looked his way and waved.

He threw up his hand, noticing she was gesturing for him to join them. Making that decision didn't take a second as he quickly took the steps to the street and walked across. They stopped on the boardwalk and waited for him.

"Good morning, to the two most beautiful ladies in Abilene," he stated. His eyes and grin mainly for Ruby Eliza.

"Thank you, Grant. Have you had a busy day?" Doctor Sarah asked.

"Just finishin' up paperwork to send to Fort Worth and needin' a quick trip to the bank. I'm glad it's over with."

Ruby Eliza, realizing his eyes were on her as he talked, joined the conversation with a comment she knew he'd be interested in hearing. "Doctor Sarah saw Jefferson for the last time this morning. He doesn't have to come back, and this made him so happy."

Grant laughed, "I can imagine. The last time I saw him he was fightin' getting the thorn removed from his heel. Where are you ladies going?"

"We're tired of our own cookin', and goin' to eat over at Cow-boys. Do you want to go with us?" said Doctor Sarah, motioning a short distance down the boardwalk where a sign for the eatery hung under a porch.

"Sure. Today, I'm an observer, inspector, and avid fan of Cow-boy's for the rest of the day. May I?" He offered the two women an arm each. "I will take timeout for food."

"Jefferson may be at church Sunday," Doctor Sarah offered with a quick look at Ruby Eliza to see her reaction. "He's asked to sit with my nurse. Seems he's taken a *liken* to her."

"You mean we'll have company on Sunday," exclaimed Grant, looking at Ruby Eliza. He hadn't asked her, so this was his way of saying, I'll come by and get you.

She laughed. "Yes. It looks like we will, and there may be more than Jefferson, if my Momma and Poppa get here with the longhorns."

"A bench full is what we're thinkin'," stated the Doctor, as the boards creaked precisely with the weight of the humans as they walked. Three sets of footsteps added to these sounds.

"We're hoping to celebrate their first cattle drive to Abilene and wanted to know if you'd join us for dinner after church."

"I surely will, whether they get here or not. I can't wait to meet the people Ruby Eliza has talked so much about." He grinned at her.

The three had stopped under the sign on the boardwalk.

Grant asked, "Are you ready to eat? Because, we're here?"

"I know I'm ready." said Ruby Eliza as Grant ushered her inside, hand on her waist for a moment. Doctor Sarah stepped through the door after her. "Is there any place else in Abilene which serves such great food?"

Actually, there were a couple of noisy saloons where buffalo or longhorn meat sandwiches were served. And a smaller dirty place outside of town, closer to the feedlots, where the cow-pokes and other wranglers, unwashed and smelling of cows, ate beans and cornbread.

Ruby Eliza turned her head and listened. "Isn't that Chester talking, Doctor Sarah?"

"I believe so. Wonder what he's doing here? I'll go find out." She scooted out of her cane back chair and went to find him.

After the doctor left, Grant said to Ruby Eliza, "I was just thinkin' of you when you waved at me." He was smiling.

"I was thinkin' of you too," she said without thinking, but her eyes said it all, and there was no time to go into detail.

Doctor Sarah appeared from the back of the diner with Chester in tow.

"He was delivering chickens to the owner. I've told him he's joining us for dinner, because there may not be much for supper."

There were hellos as Chester sat down to join the others.

He explained, "I brought some of my chickens for the cook to fry tomorrow. He asks those with more'n they need to bring 'em for his use. He offers me more money, because I kill, clean, and dress them. All he has to do is cut 'em up, roll the pieces in flour, sprinkle on salt and pepper and cook."

"Chester sells his excess eggs, also, and he grows a garden full of tasty vegetables. He makes money off of their surplus. He's quite a businessman," offered Ruby Eliza, looking over at her helper and nodding her head.

Chester, while she was talking, had grown six inches taller, soaking up her kind remarks.

Soon the group was eating, not chicken, but a delicious concoction of aged, diced, floured longhorn steak and onions stirred together and fried. This was combined with potatoes boiled in water and butter along with cooked, sliced carrots, seasoned with sugar and spices. Fried apple pies with coffee finished the meal.

~

At times, the newly established bank in Abilene was the busiest place in the town. At least for now, the street outside was full of Glory B's drovers waiting to be paid after the long walk from the Glass Mountains to the feedlots outside of town.

Before daylight, this morning a delegation from the drive had gone in the general direction of a feedlot where they could sell the herd. In a letter which included a rough map, Ruby Eliza had mentioned a member of her church congregation—a Jason Dunn who could help them. Taking her map in hand, Press and Jonathan had found him on Elk Creek.

Coming back to the herd, they had headed out with the longhorns for Elk Creek, and the transaction was done in record time. Press had gotten top dollar for his herd—being around twenty-five dollars a head.

The depression after the Civil War meant cattle selling for five dollars a head, but over the years the price had increased. *Hum-n – twenty-five times around two thousand head.* Press thought, as they counted the herd going into the large pens.

Boarding the *remuda* and the three wagons to pick up later, he headed the drovers on their horses toward downtown Abilene. Jonathan would purchase rooms for his drovers' stay at the local hotel. Of course, they could eat there, but he would set up a tab for food at Cowboy's. If they ate anywhere else, they paid for it. His decision to supply food for his hands was mainly because the other places dealt in hard liquor and other vices, and bailing his crew out of jail was not something he did.

By early afternoon, his business was done at the bank. Pay for cow-boys depended on their importance within the drive, but Press was always generous with his men, giving good wages for their work, both on the trail drive and at the ranch.

~

Gracie, along with Jorge, sat on their horses, waiting for Press and Jonathan to appear with the funds for the workers.

"Are you happy the drive is over, Gracie?" asked Jorge.

"I never thought I'd say this, but I sure am. I'm glad to get to Abilene, and I'll be glad to pile into a bed tonight. I might even skip the fried chicken. Where are you going to sleep?"

Before he could answer, a ruggedly handsome and well-dressed young man walked from the bank, tipped his hat, and headed up the street. Gracie watched his progress until he climbed the platform and went into the train station door. She turned her attention back to Jorge.

"I'll stay at the hotel tonight and take a hot bath. Maybe tomorrow, Press will let me bring the chuckwagon into town and find a place to put it. Then I'll sleep under it—save him money," he grinned. "Here he comes now."

Press had an envelope. He counted out several bills and gave them to Jonathan who continued on towards the bunched-up drovers, sitting on the wooden boardwalk across the street.

Walking toward Gracie he handed Jorge one hundred dollars. Several more of the cow-boys would get the same, with a caution to be careful of how they spent it. He walked over to Gracie and handed her the same as Jorge.

Gracie started laughing. "You're paying me?" she questioned.

Press looked up at her and nodded his head, "Of course, sweetheart. You were just as much a part of the drive as the rest. You know, I think I smell fried chicken. Shall we go tell Ruby Eliza and Doctor Sarah we're here, or eat?" He was joshing her about the fried chicken smell, being it was too early to eat.

Gracie rolled her eyes at him. "We'd better tell Ruby Eliza. Do we want to invite the cow-boys to join us?"

"I'll ask Jonathan. He might invite Golden, Cephas, Caleb, and Thomas, but the others can get a good meal at the hotel. Let's plan on being at Cow-boy's Victuals at 2:00 o'clock. That'll give us enough time to clean up. Get some of today's trail dust off, and rest a bit."

"Okay, go tell Jonathan, and round up our youngest two. They can come with us now."

Press walked off, and Gracie looked over at the group he was headed toward.

Strange, she thought, wrinkling her brow. Sarah Susannah was sitting on her horse with her brother at one end of the board walk while Thomas sat on the other end with his father. *What had happened to the two? Only days ago, they'd been inseparable.* She shook her head as Press bade Jonathan goodbye.

The trail boss was still paying the hands on the drive. He would join them later after seeing the drovers were comfortable in their hotel quarters and informing them of the arrangements for returning to the Glory B.

Press went to Sarah Susannah and P.T. to tell them the plans for food. They followed him as their father returned to Gracie.

Chapter Twenty-Seven

Talk of the Rustlers

"Poppa, when will we go and see the Sheriff?" asked Jonathan who sat across the table from his father. He wiped his mouth on a cloth napkin, and took a sip of his warmed-up coffee.

Gracie sat beside her son opposite her husband. This was exactly what she didn't want to hear, but her ears perked up over the din of several people at the table talking back and forth.

"What happened?" asked Ruby Eliza who sat closest to her father, a curious look on her face. She hadn't heard anything after the letter with his mention of rustlers. She had stopped the new Sheriff on the street some days later, telling him the contents of the letter.

Press started explaining the events surrounding their drive to Abilene. The more he talked the quieter it got in the dining room at Cow-boy's Victuals. Even the waiter who poured fresh coffee stopped to listen to his comments.

"We think they are two or three days behind us, so I plan on going to the Sheriff's office in the morning. Jonathan, you and I will give him a head's up on the situation and offer to help. We did get a good look at some of the men, even in the drizzling rain."

"Yes, I feel sure we can recognize them, and I have a drawing of a few of the brands to look at—the ones they were changing." Jonathan patted his shirt pocket.

"Sheriff Collins was just elected to his office. He knows Doctor Sarah very well, because she treats his prisoners for gunshot wounds and other medical problems. I told him days ago you would be in to talk to him."

Grant sat on the other side of Ruby Eliza; his arm draped over the back of her chair. He leaned forward to ask a question. "Mr. Stockton, I thought I'd heard that the rustlers and robbers were mainly on the western end or at the headwaters of the Pecos River. What are they doing down your way?"

"First, call me Press, Grant. And you're right, but for some reason they're moving farther south. Jonathan and I think it's because cattle are no longer driven to Kansas for points east. Now they can be shipped from Fort Worth or even here in Abilene. To rustle cattle, they have to follow the herds. They're here because our cattle drives are closer to their home."

"That makes a lot of sense," Grant nodded his head. "How do you think the newly fenced areas will affect longhorn drives? I've heard this from some of the people riding the train to Fort Worth. They say there may be trouble."

"Well, if the railroads keep expanding into areas where longhorns are rounded up, probably not much. But if they lag behind, I can see skirmishes between the ranchers, fencing their property and independent or free range cattle growers—maybe even deaths. I hope it doesn't come to pass. I know the railroad is in

Marathon, but what about Fort Stockton? Any plans for the Texas and Pacific to head our way?" Press asked of Grant.

Gracie's thoughts had turned from the conversation. She was looking at Grant and Ruby Eliza. *Another budding relationship?* It was obvious, although nothing had been said by the two.

She'd guessed at this from Doctor Sarah's letter, and when her daughter had gone across the street to get him to join the group. Curious that his name was Bailey. No. There wasn't any way he could remotely be any relation to her old father-in-law, Hurricane Bailey—this man was young. She wondered if Press had caught his last name when they were introduced.

She rejoined the conversation. Press was talking. "Grant, you will have to come see the ranch. The Glory B sits in the Glass Mountains, high on a hillside where you can see for miles. We'll show you around Mountain City, and introduce you to lots of longhorns."

"Yes, and our Maria can cook fried chicken as well as Cowboy's," added Gracie. "And her soups … yum."

Grant's smile was charming as he replied, "I'd love to come, but I don't see a way of getting loose from my job at present. If Abilene traffic builds up, they may send someone to help, and this'll give me a chance to travel outside the area. Ruby Eliza and I have already explored much of the area close in to town." He patted her hand which was lying on the table, letting his linger for a few seconds.

"Momma, we went to Fort Phantom Hill," advised Ruby Eliza.

Gracie nodded. "I suppose Grant heard the stories associated with the old fort. I haven't been there since Pa and me rode through with the Conestoga on the way to The Pinery, in the Guadalupe Mountains."

"Maybe we could take you, Mrs. Stockton," suggested Grant. "It's an all-day trip, from sunup to sundown."

"Momma might rather go on the train trip to Fort Worth with Jefferson and his family," said Ruby Eliza.

Press spoke up, "We'll be here a few days, so a trip might be something we can plan. Jonathan will be returning to the Glory B in a week with the drovers, horses, and wagons. Can't leave the ranch unattended for long. There's not enough hands to run the place when we drive cattle to market."

Jonathan added, "Yes, we have a large garden to tend, water holes to look after, and a marriage to plan."

"What?" said Ruby Eliza.

The conversation turned to the coming marriage.

At the mention of returning to the Glory B and marriage, Sarah Susannah shot a look at Thomas. He'd be heading back with his father. Would she ever see him again? She looked down at her empty plate on the table, so no one could see the tears in her eyes.

~

Press walked to the hotel to pick up Jonathan for the meeting with the Sheriff of Taylor County. "Who have we here?" he asked when he saw P.T. sitting outside with his brother. "Are you goin' with us, Son?"

"I told him we were on official business, and he would have to ask you."

Press laughed. "Sure, he can come."

The three set off down the boardwalk, talking about the night's happenings. It seemed some of the cow-boys had had a late night, and there was plenty of noise when they returned.

"I hope the Sheriff won't know us when we get there," laughed Press.

"No, nothing as bad as that. I'd informed the desk clerk if he needed me, I was in charge. He came up and knocked on my door to complain. I went with him to caution the boys to be quiet, and that was it. They were playing cards."

"Who was winning?" asked P.T.

"I didn't ask," said Jonathan.

The sign saying 'Sheriff's Office' was new and the door was open. "Come in, men," a man with a badge called, when he looked up and noticed their pause outside the opening.

The room inside smelled of freshly sawn wood. It was sparse with a desk and a few chairs. Pictures of wanted men and even a woman were nailed or pinned to one side of the room.

A curious P.T. went over to look at the array.

At the back, behind the desk, an open door revealed parts of a couple of cells with bars to hold prisoners—none could be seen.

"Are you Sheriff Collins?" asked Press, walking up to the man and offering his hand.

"Yes, I am. Who are you? I don't believe I've seen you around here," he said with furrowed brow and narrowed eyes—his eyesight was not as good, as he had aged.

"No, I don't usually come into Abilene unless it's to see my daughter, Ruby Eliza, and Doctor Sarah."

Press was grinning at the man, thinking this would give him an introduction.

"Why, you must be Preston Stockton from Mountain City," exclaimed the man, grabbing Press's hand and shaking it vigorously. "Your daughter talks about you all the time. Glad to meet you. The last time I talked to her outside Cowboy's, she said you were driving a herd of longhorns from the Glass Mountains. She said you might have trouble on the way? Is that why you're here?"

"Interesting, you'd ask, because we think there may be trouble headed for Abilene. We think a gang of rustlers are herdin' a bunch of stolen and rebranded longhorns in this direction."

"Rustlers herdin' a bunch of longhorns here? Couldn't they be headed for Fort Worth, also? I hope." Sheriff Collins shook his head. He'd not been the chief law officer long, but increased violations of the law as Abilene grew made it necessary to provide someone to enforce the state, county, and city rules.

"It's possible. If not, they are right behind us, and they should show up here in a matter of days. Jonathan and I can identify some of the gang and the rebranded cows. Son, give him your drawings."

Jonathan pulled two or three pages of folded paper from his pocket and spread them out on the Sheriff's desk. The men bent over the drawings which showed plainly how the original brands were altered.

The Sheriff was ecstatic as he looked up from the table. "Son, this is great. We can use this to identify the brands on the cattle, especially how they were altered."

At that moment, a man wearing a green visor came through the front door waving a paper. Everyone turned at the sound of his hurried footsteps.

Not acknowledging the others in the room, he went straight to the newly elected lawman and exclaimed, "Sheriff Collins, you need to look at this." The man's eyes were wide, like he'd seen a ghost.

Collins took the note from the messenger runner.

From where he stood to the side of the room, P.T. could see Western Union Telegraph Company as the header on the paper.

The Sheriff held the paper close to his face and quickly read through the telegram. "It's from San Angela," he said and handed it to Press, shaking his head.

Press sucked in his breath as he read, and then he recited the note out loud.

To the Sheriff in Abilene. Stop. Please be advised. Stop. Rustlers headed your way. Stop. Wanted for murder of rancher and son. Stop. Other information by stage. Stop.

"Oh, Poppa," P.T. exclaimed, coming close to his father. "You don't suppose it was Isaiah Benson and his son, Abraham, do you?"

Press shook his head. "I hope not. When's the stage due, Sheriff Collins?"

"Tomorrow afternoon. I'll be waiting on it, and as soon as I get the letter, I'll be over to see you, Press. Where are you staying, at the hotel?"

Press, Jonathan, and the Sheriff walked outside the door to the boardwalk.

"No, Gracie and I are staying at the doctor's office."

While the others were talking, P.T. eased to the desk and looked intently at the papers lying on top. He hadn't seen Jonathan's sketches. He memorized the penciling and stepped back from the desk thinking, *there must be a way I can help father catch the rustlers. Abraham, he was about my age.* Walking outside, he joined the others. Press put his arm around him.

The discussion continued until Sheriff Collins asked, "Since you can identify the rustlers, would you be comfortable in goin' with me to Buffalo Gap. We may have to stay a night or two, since we don't know when they'll be coming through. But I know the hotel keeper there, and I don't think it would cost us anything, since we'll be on official business."

"Sounds fine with us. We intended to go and help you. Let us know." Both Press and Jonathan nodded in agreement.

"Dependin' on the letter, we'll make plans after I receive it. So, I'll definitely look you up tomorrow. Sorry about the trouble."

"What can you do? We just don't want these bad men doing more harm than they've done already. See you tomorrow, Sheriff Collins."

~

"Gracie, please don't worry. Jonathan and I'll be alright. The Sheriff will be with us at all times. If there's any shootin', we'll let him and his deputies take care of it."

"I don't like it," she stated firmly. "I haven't since I first heard of these bad men.

"Would you like it any better if the rustlers went free and killed someone else?"

"I know. I know. I won't say anything more." Gracie turned away, pulled in a lungful of air, and let it slowly out her nose. "I'll be praying for your safety," she said, turning back to him with tears in her eyes. She watched as he buckled on his gunbelt.

Press went to her and drew her into his arms. "It's okay, sweetheart. You do know I love you with all my heart." He put his hand under her chin to bring her face to his, so he could kiss her.

"That sounds like a goodbye." She sputtered, resisting briefly, but letting her lips meet his, melting against him. "I love you so much. But I think, never as much as right at this moment. Be careful."

The office door at Doctor Sarah's opened. Jonathan walked in with Sheriff Collins. "I mighta known," he said, as his parents parted from each other. "Poppa, are you ready to go?"

"Yes. Let's get this over with. Have you heard any more from San Angela? How about who was shot?" Press asked as he picked up his saddle bags and canteen, and went out the door, blowing Gracie a kiss as he exited. She went to the half-open window to watch him leave.

Gracie heard Sheriff Collins answer with, "The people's name *was* Benson. I guess it's your friends. I'm sorry. And yesterday, trail dust from the cattle drive was spotted near Steamboat Mountain."

"So, the killers are less than a day away from the Gap," responded Press, looking grim. "They could arrive in the afternoon or the darkness of night."

"I'm guessing after dark. Wouldn't you opt for nighttime if you wanted to hide from prying eyes? And, coming through the Gap after dark means they'll arrive in Abilene under the cover of darkness—early morning. It's hard to distinguish flaws in brands by candle or lamplight."

Gracie didn't hear anymore after this exchange. With tears streaming from her eyes, she could hardly perceive anything. All she saw was the backsides of the horses riding away—the Sheriff, his deputies, and her two men headed for what? She immediately sat in one of Doctor Sarah's office chairs and said a heartfelt prayer for Press, Jonathan, and the others.

A noise from the hallway to the upstairs caused her to look up. P.T. came into the room, dropping his saddlebags on the floor.

He went to his Momma and hugged her. "I was watching from the upstairs window. They'll be all right, Momma, *you'll see.*"

Gracie wiped her eyes and cheeks with her fingers and nodded a yes. She didn't read anything into his comment, although maybe she should have. "Where are you goin', Son?"

"Momma, I'm going to see Grant. He wants me to pal around with him today. Is that okay with you? We'll eat supper at his house, and I'll come home." He was telling a little white lie, but he felt the results he had in mind would be an excuse for it.

"I don't see any problem with you visiting with Grant. Did you ask your father?"

"No, he was already downstairs when I got up. Grant said it may be late when I come home. So, don't wait up for me."

He picked his saddlebags off the floor and headed out to saddle up Star in the stable at the rear of the building.

Gracie wondered why the leather bags, but dismissed them as necessary for his visit. No telling what her son had in there. Certainly not the frogs and lizards he used to as a young lad. She grinned at the thought.

Chapter Twenty-Eight

The Confrontation

After picking up several more people from the Sheriff's office, the posse from Abilene rode hard to arrive in the late afternoon at Buffalo Gap. Sheriff Collins guided them to the local hotel. It was two-story and located next to the saloon. The men rode around back and put their horses in a fenced area where they would be fed and watered by a local man hired by the boarding house.

The saddles were not taken off so they were ready to ride when the longhorns and rustlers showed up. The time of their arrival was anybody's guess, but the general thinking was this would not be long.

All afternoon from Abilene, the riders had bucked the wind with dust flying through the air. Feeling grit on their skin and in their mouths did not help their impressions of disquiet. Everyone was feeling the emotion of the coming confrontation—words were few and smiles even less.

Back in the foyer of the hotel, after securing rooms, they assembled for instructions. The Sheriff asked, "Press shouldn't some of us ride out and locate the herd? We might be able to decide on a time for their arrival and devise a plan. At present, I'm thinking let them drive the longhorns on through the Gap and challenge them on the flat prairie outside of town. We don't want to get any of the townspeople hurt."

Press nodded in agreement, feeling the excitement along with the tension of the moment. "Jonathan and I will ride out to help you check on the drive. I hope we can get close enough to recognize two or three of the men."

"We don't want to spook them," warned the Sheriff, shaking his head. He turned to his posse and said,

"The rest of you take an afternoon nap so you'll be fresh tonight."

There were grunts of approval, but not a man headed out of the parlor area.

After picking up their horses, Sheriff Collins led Press and Jonathan up into the hills. The progress was slow through the rocks and cacti, but the three men did not ride very long to find the herd. The rustlers had paused far enough out of town so as not to raise suspicions of the residents.

Even from the distance where Press and Jonathan sat on their horses, the man in the black hat with the band of red ribbon could be distinctly seen, along with two others.

"That's them," said Press. "Look, Jonathan." He pointed to one of the cow-boys standing in the shade of a mesquite tree talking to others. The rustler was jabbing a finger in the direction of the Gap and talking animatedly.

Jonathan nodded his head. "Can't miss the hat and the men who were rebrandin' the cattle. This is the herd, for sure."

"I wonder what he's talkin' about?" asked Press, watching the black-hatted man's actions.

"No telling, and I'll bet we were right. They *are* waitin' for darkness. Why else would they be paused here?" said Collins, looking up at the sky, where a few clouds were starting to gather. "It might rain and that would be a blessin' and a curse," he observed as he turned his horse, heading back the way they had come. They needed rain, but not tonight.

~

To be precise, P.T. had done exactly as he'd told his Momma—up until early afternoon.

He and Grant had spent most of the day together. They'd eaten dinner at Cow-boy's, where he'd insisted on paying for his own meal out of the money from the trail drive. At that point, he'd made an excuse, telling the station superintendent he was supposed to meet his Poppa at Buffalo Gap.

In the stiffly blowing wind, he had headed down the road toward the break in the mountains or Buffalo Gap. The dust obscured the view until he could barely make out an outline, especially since he was constantly clearing his eyes of the fine powder. He pulled his bandana up to cover his mouth.

He had had to say something, because Grant had a clear view of the prairie for several miles, even in the dusty wind. If he went to the window to look out, he'd wonder why P.T. wasn't headed for the doctor's office where most of the rest of the family was staying.

P.T. nudged Star into a trot, because there were several miles to cover. Later, in the deepening gloom at twilight, he'd slowed her down to a walk, so she could rest a bit.

Sitting easily in his saddle, he pulled his canteen loose from his pommel and took a drink. The town wasn't too far away. He could see a faint light from lamps positioned on porches.

At this moment, Star started acting up, lifting her upper lip and smelling the gusting wind—tossing her head and stepping unevenly.

"What's wrong, girl?" he asked, bending over to give her a pat on her shoulder and replacing his canteen. "Is it goin' to rain?" he asked her as he noticed a flash of lightning to the west of Abilene.

P.T. knew a horse can literally smell danger, because of his trouble earlier with the rattlesnake. His father had explained that the slightest breeze, bringing a dangerous scent, puts a horse into flight mode. Tails go high as a signal and the horse is off and running in a flash.

Star's ears were pricked forward toward Buffalo Gap. The horse was giving extreme attention in that direction. Whatever the problem was, it wasn't behind him or to the west.

P.T. stopped in the middle of the road and strained to see what might be spooking her—a wolf, coyote? In the growing darkness, he couldn't see a thing.

He urged Star on and covered another mile when a muffled shot rang out from Buffalo Gap. This shot was followed by a rumbling sound. P.T. didn't know it, but the loud bang of the shot had stampeded a herd of longhorns. The roar said they were running straight toward him.

~

The rustlers headed the longhorns toward Buffalo Gap. When they entered the Gap, they intended to drive the herd quietly out the other side under the cover of darkness toward Abilene, just as the Sheriff and Press had guessed. But their plans changed.

The cattle walked easily at first, but the further they came through the town the narrower the streets became, crowding them together, pushing them by trees and fences, and making them uneasy. Flashes of noiseless heat lightning, lit up their progress, making them cautious and uncomfortable. The slightest provocation would unsettle the longhorns.

A child chasing another one, playing hide and seek in the darkness, let out a blood-curdling yell as he found his hidden prey. The beeves in their vicinity were positioned behind the longhorn leader. Spooked, they pushed the cattle in front, prodding them with their horns, and the whole herd started moving faster and faster, taking out fences and protruding porches as they started running through the narrow, one-lane street of Buffalo Gap.

An angry homeowner, whose front porch and fence was demolished, shot his gun as a good riddance over the disappearing herd. One of the rustlers, riding toward the rear of the stampeding animals, returned fire, making a bad situation worse. The homeowner spun backwards, wounded in the shoulder. He fell to the ground in the street. Other town members rushed to help him. They carried him to the hotel, where they'd last seen the Sheriff, and went after the doctor.

Panicked, the longhorns dashed out of the town, leaving it in their dust. Some of the rustlers, thinking they could save the herd, rode ahead of the running longhorns, trying to turn them into a circle. This would stop the headlong rush of the animals, which was headed toward Abilene at breakneck speed.

By this time the posse had mounted up and started in pursuit of the disappearing cattle and the rustlers, eating dust as they headed back the way they came. The cow-boys at the rear of the herd realized they were being chased by someone, probably the law. Pulling their guns from their holsters, the shooting started.

This only aggravated the running beeves. They ran faster, if this was possible, catching up with the point men, who were trying to turn the herd. Continuing flashes of heat lightning, from the piled-up clouds, lit up the whole bizarre scenario. All was pandemonium.

Not noticing the rustlers coming toward him as they stayed beside the herd, P.T. rode Star away from the stampede.

He saw the flashes from the muzzles of the Colt .45 revolvers as they came closer. Forgetting his purpose to come and help his Poppa, he sat watching the scene play out in front of him. From the clouds came flourishes of lightning, exposing him on his horse. These were followed by gunshots.

He felt the sting in his leg, but the excitement and noise from the moving cattle, running gunplay, and lightning, caused him not to take much notice of the hurt.

Not realizing a stray bullet had found its mark, he put his hand down to scratch the burning itch, his fingers came up covered with a warm substance. Touching one of his fingers to his tongue, he realized it was blood. Within minutes, he was dizzy. *How much blood was he losing*, he wondered? This became his last thought as he went into shock. He slouched over the pommel of his saddle and quickly passed out.

~

If it hadn't been for the lightning flashes, Press would never have seen P.T. He spotted a horse that looked a lot like Star actually sitting on the prairie after the mass of cattle, rustlers, and posse went through. As he'd told Gracie, later, he and Jonathan were letting the Sheriff and his posse handle the rustlers, but he was riding along behind to help if needed, and Jonathan was riding some feet away.

Mystified, he pulled his horse up and waited until the lightning flashed again. Someone was slumped over in the horse's saddle. Riding toward the motionless rider, he dreaded what he'd find. As he neared the two, he realized his worst fears were confirmed. What on earth was P.T. doing out here on the prairie?

"P.T." he called as he approached. He jumped off his horse just as Jonathan arrived, leaping to the ground behind him.

Press ran to his son. Another flash revealed his leg covered with blood. Even Star had splotches on her. Taking his knife out of its holder, he started gently cutting P.T.'s bloody pants leg apart. He had to find the source of the blood. "Here, Jonathan, hold one side. Be careful. We don't want to pull him off Star.

"Are you going to cut this far enough up the leg to see where the blood is coming from?"

"Yes, it looks like he's lost a lot of blood. We'll need to stop the flow."

Another bolt of light revealed a seriously jagged wound from which blood still oozed.

"Let me have your bandana, Jonathan, and I'll make a tourniquet to stop the bleeding. I wonder how long he's been passed out." Press started tying the piece of cloth around the bloody leg.

"I wish we weren't so far from Abilene, so Doctor Sarah could look at him. Taking him back to Buffalo Gap is our only option, Poppa."

Not knowing if the bone was shattered, Press was thinking and talking out loud when he decided, "I don't know what's safest, but leaving him on Star for the trip back might be best—not moving him from his horse. Think we can use your rope and tie him on Star to keep him from falling?" The bandana was tied. He turned around. "See if you can find a ..."

"A stick," said Jonathan, offering one he'd already searched for and found on the ground.

Press put the stick into the tourniquet and twisted it. The blood quit flowing. Jonathan and Press teamed up to secure him to Star.

"Poppa, I'll lead Star. You ride beside P.T. and help hold him in the saddle and make sure the bandana holds. It's not far from Buffalo Gap. Maybe the innkeeper can tell us where to find a doctor."

"Yes, Jonathan, he needs one immediately. He's lost a lot of blood. I just hope ..." Press didn't finish his sentence. He didn't have to. Jonathan understood.

At Buffalo Gap, the doctor was at the hotel, but one look at P.T.'s wound and he advised Press to take his son on into Abilene. "The doctor there has more medical knowledge than I do," he insisted.

The owner of the hotel sent for his delivery wagon. Soon, Press and Jonathan were heading back to Abilene with P.T. on a rental room mattress tossed into the back. The stableman drove the wagon, while Press rode in the back with his son. Jonathan came up the rear, riding his horse and leading his father's and Star. All thoughts of the rustlers and the stampede were erased by the events of the last hours. Dawn was breaking as they headed down the streets of Abilene.

~

Leaving Jonathan to wait with his brother, Press hurried upstairs with the news. His loud thumps and cries of help coming up the stairs woke everyone, which is what he planned to do—wake the sleepers.

"It's P.T.! Gunshot wound! Outside in the wagon," exclaimed Press to Doctor Sarah, heading for the room Gracie occupied.

Doctor Sarah, barefoot and holding up her long gown to keep from falling, rushed down the stairs and out to the wagon. Jonathan helped her into the back. She knelt down on the mattress where she did a quick preliminary exam. She loosened the tourniquet. The blood from the wound still oozed slightly. She handed the cloth to Jonathan.

Shaking her head, she whispered to Jonathan, "It looks like he's lost some blood." She felt his wrist. His pulse was shallow, but there was a heartbeat. "The wound will be hard to suture, but with the ragged skin and all the dried blood, I won't know the extent of his injuries until I can clean him up." Privately, she thought, *it may take a miracle to save him.*

Doctor Sarah climbed out of the wagon just as the others came running out the door and down the steps to where the doctor and Jonathan stood.

The hue and cry had woken Chester, who came flying around the side of the building in his long johns, rubbing his sleepy eyes.

Another early riser, who slept upstairs in a store next door, roused by the hullabaloo, came hurrying over to the group in his britches and suspenders.

Everyone hung over the sideboards of the wagon, looking at the wounded young man who was still unconscious.

Doctor Sarah went to Gracie, as she hurried down the porch stairs from the office. "It's P.T.," she said, holding her friend by her arms.

"How bad is it," said Gracie, before she approached the wagon, fearing her foreboding on the trail had come to fruition.

Doctor Sarah avoided telling her exactly what she thought. "I'll do everything I can to patch him up, but he needs surgery immediately. We must get him inside, to my examining room."

Activity whirled around her. Gracie wasn't reassured by this comment, and seeing her son and the bloody mess on his leg, didn't help. She was in a daze. She didn't even feel Press's comforting arm around her.

Hands appeared from everywhere. They decided to leave him on the mattress and curl the edges to get him through the door. This worked very well—not jostling him.

In shock, Gracie now opened her mouth and kept cautioning them, "Be careful and be gentle." There were no tears. She was numb. This couldn't be her son. He was asleep. He was upstairs in his bed—but she *was* following someone who looked like him into the examination room.

At the same time, Doctor Sarah was remembering the reports in the medical journals she'd read. Depending on what her extensive examination found, she might need every bit of the information to save P.T.

Once in the room where the operation would take place, she and Ruby Eliza pushed the wooden table to a window where the morning sun streamed through. The doctor held the damaged leg as P.T. was moved off the mattress and placed on her examination table which would also serve as the place where he rested for surgery.

"Everyone out," she commanded, as she headed for her wash up sink. She grabbed a bar of red soap and started scrubbing her hands.

Press pushed everyone out of the room and prepared to close the door. Gracie was the last to leave. "I want to stay," she demanded.

"No," said Press, escorting her through the door and shutting it.

The room was now empty except for doctor and nurse.

"Ruby Eliza, will you get the box of sterile gauze, the extra bottle of carbolic acid, and other supplies for repairing the wound. Heat water to sterilize any utensils you think we'll need for surgery. Guess what we may need, boil it, so it'll be ready to use. Then you scrub up. I'll need you to help."

"Are you going to clean the wound first?"

"Yes, starting right now." Doctor Sarah, still in her nightgown, approached the table. She took a piece of gauze and poured the carbolic acid on it. Next, she started gently rubbing P.T.'s skin, loosening the red layer on his leg. Her decision on how to proceed would depend on what was under the dried or clotted blood. At least the bones in his lower leg didn't appear to be broken.

She had adopted her standards of cleanliness years ago because of a Scotsman.

Of course, the use of carbolic acid in soap and the cleansing of skin, and sterilization of instruments was initiated by Scottish surgeon Joseph Lister in the English journal of medicine *The Lancet*, in 1867. She always read his articles with great interest and followed his ideas.

The idea of "Germ Theory" was just an idea. But his paper backed up this notion and claimed the use of carbolic acid and cleanliness killed whatever was causing the infections and deaths of patients. He proved this because his patients didn't die.

Because amputation was the result of most operations, his own words said that many wounded limbs, *"may be retained with confidence of the best results."* She had found this to be true.

As the cleaning of the wound progressed, Doctor Sarah saw some major blood vessels which needed suturing. Here again, she would be on the revolutionary edge or forefront of medicine. There *were* some articles on sewing blood vessels back together. She would pick one and try, using silk thread. There was nothing else she could do.

P.T.'s bone was chipped by the bullet. She would remove the chip, knowing the bone would repair itself. This gave her some relief. But he wouldn't be able to put pressure on the limb for several weeks.

The final problem concerned his loss of blood. Articles on intravenous injection were not encouraging at all. She would leave this thought alone, but months earlier she had ordered the parts involved in the infusion of salt and sugar to hydrate a patient. Saving P.T. would depend on her cleanliness and this technique. After the operation, she would consult her medical books and papers on the mixture for this injection into his body.

P.T. was not alert, but, "Ruby Eliza put the ether close by. If he starts to come to, we may need it. Are you ready?"

Her nurse shook her head. No. She wasn't ready. The person on the table was her brother, whom she loved dearly. She felt helpless.

Doctor Sarah patted her sterilized hand. "Pray," she said. "Because I'll be praying all the way through." Saving P.T. would push the limits of her knowledge and use the trailblazing edge of medical science.

Ruby Eliza nodded in affirmation. She *could* pray.

Doctor Sarah prepared a large blood vessel, picked up a small, curved needle with silk thread from the sterilized tray, bent over and started to reattach the first blood vessel.

The attempt to save P.T. had started. Three hours later, the operation was over, the wound closed, and the infusion pump with the salt and sugar installed.

Not wishing to move her patient, Doctor Sarah left him on the table with the noonday sun shining through the window. Now the waiting started.

~

Press and Jonathan had brought more chairs from upstairs and each one was being used.

All the family in Abilene sat mostly silent in the waiting room, along with Thomas, Caleb, Golden, Grant, and Jorge. Any talk was whispered or spoken very low. Some eventually went outside for some fresh air. They milled around and walked up and down the boardwalk. In the afternoon, Pastor Gridley joined them.

Finally, someone got hungry. Chester was sent to Cow-boy's for food.

Press and Jonathan went across the street to talk to the Lord in the Baptist Church. At least, this was Jonathan's aim. Once at the altar, he noticed his father was crying. *Can sobbing be a prayer? Yes, it can,* he thought. The Holy Spirit will understand each sob. He moved over to comfort and put his arm around the man who'd taught him all he knew.

~

When some of those who were waiting inside had gone outside, Thomas followed Sarah Susannah to the boardwalk. He and his father would be leaving soon to head back to Fort Davis. They would follow the route of the stagecoaches which would take them almost home.

"Let's take a walk around the square, Sarah Susannah," he suggested, taking her hand and leading her to the corner of the street, where they turned left.

He did not give her time to say no, because he wanted to talk to her in private. Some things needed to be said.

The few sprinkles of last night had dried up, and they walked on grass unless a boardwalk appeared in front of a business or home.

"Sarah Susannah, I've enjoyed being on the trail drive with you … no that's not what I want to say," Thomas shook his head. He stopped walking and turned to her, plunging into his subject. "What I want to say is I really like you, and I wonder if you feel the same way about me?" There he had it out in the open—his feelings for her, but what would she say back to him. He couldn't smile. He almost couldn't breathe.

"Thomas, I like you too, but you live so far away. I don't know how we can see each other again, since the trail drive is over." She looked at him with tears in her eyes.

Putting his arm around her, they continued their walk. "Things will happen. There has to be a way." The walk was almost over. "Will you be my sweetheart, forever?"

"Yes, I will—forever."

The front boardwalk was only steps ahead.

"Thomas, do you want to seal our forever with a kiss?"

He didn't answer but leaned toward her as their lips met.

Chester, hearing the exchange, grinned in his little shack.

~

Without a break, Gracie had remained by P.T.'s bedside for two days. He had been moved yesterday into the infirmary where she could easily hold his hand. She would lean her head on his pillow as she dozed in her chair. She even ate in her chair. As evidence, her breakfast tray was on the floor close to where she sat.

P.T. was showing signs of waking up.

Doctor Sarah had tied his arm to a board and then attached it to his bed so the intravenous injection would not be disturbed. The whole apparatus was attached to a tall coat and hat stand beside his bed. Much of the solution going into his arm had been guesswork, gleaned from recent articles she'd read. But he hadn't expired, as would have been expected.

Doctor Sarah came into the room. "How's my patient?" she asked.

"I'm wondering, myself," returned Gracie.

The doctor took P.T.'s vital signs, checking his pupils and feeling his arm and leg, both of which were warm, meaning blood was flowing in his extremities.

"His color is back," she observed.

"Yes, and his fingers are twitching on the tied down arm," Gracie told her.

Could he be noticing he couldn't move his arm because she'd made it stationary? If so, this was a good sign, thought Doctor Sarah.

Suddenly, his eyes opened. He looked around the room. Noticing his mother, he asked, "What's wrong with my arm?"

Both Doctor Sarah and Gracie burst out laughing. The laughter soon turned to tears as P.T. tried to lift his arm.

"No, no," exclaimed the doctor, pushing back. "Don't move your arm or your leg."

His next question was expected. "What happened? How did I get here?"

Gracie wiped her face with a piece of his sheet. "That's what we'd like to know. You were supposed to stay the day with Grant and come home afterward. Instead, you wound up shot at Buffalo Gap. Now it's my turn to ask *what happened*?" Grant had stated to her that P.T. had left after eating dinner at Cow-boy's.

P.T. shook his head. "I don't know. I'm hungry."

The two ladies laughed once more. This led to more tears.

Doctor Sarah advised him, again, "Don't move your leg. You've had surgery to repair a large gash where the bullet went through."

"Bullet?" exclaimed P.T., looking puzzled.

"Yes, bullet! We may let you sit up on the side of the bed this afternoon, but that's it. I'll get you some soup to eat." She bent, picked up Gracie's tray, and headed for the door.

"I want stew and cornbread," P.T. sent after her.

"No way," she called back and disappeared through the opening.

Chapter Twenty-Nine

The Recuperation Continues

Because P.T. needed Doctor Sarah's constant care, Press and Gracie made a decision. She would stay in Abilene to help with his recovery. He would head back to the Glory B with the wagons and men, including Caleb and Thomas. As soon as P.T. was out of danger, the rest of the family would come home on the stage. Both of them were sure this would take several weeks.

The drovers with the *remuda* left Abilene with Soot in the lead. After all, he was the point longhorn. Seeing he was in command, he gave a toss of his head and a bellow. His way of stating this was his rightful place.

Press had been gone three weeks when Gracie decided it was time to explore the new cow-town as stations which moved cattle to market in the east were called.

P.T. was sitting up in bed and showing signs of great progress. Of course, Doctor Sarah had insisted he not put pressure on his injured limb.

He hadn't had an infection in his sutured leg nor very little pain associated with the bullet wound. The intravenous *contraption* as he called it was long gone, and he was eating everything in sight.

For a week he'd asked to be carried in a chair to the boardwalk where he could observe the traffic in the road and talk to the people passing by on errands. Those passing were beginning to expect him, and some actually drove their buggies and wagons close enough to chat with the interesting young man on the doctor's porch.

Putting her bonnet on, Gracie walked outside where he sat in his chair. "P.T., I'm going to take a walk. Will you be all right? Do I need to get you anything before I leave?"

"Momma, I'm out of water," he said, holding the glass out to her.

"Yes, it is hot today. I'll fill it up for you."

Ruby Eliza was in the downstairs kitchen. "Momma, are you going somewhere. You have your new hat on."

"Heading to town. Do you want to go with me?" She asked as she filled P.T.'s glass up with water.

"No, not today. I have to strip the sheets from the beds in the infirmary, and take them to our laundry lady. She has others ready for us to pick up and put on. Otherwise, I'd join you. Have a good time."

"Will Grant come by tonight?" She held the full glass, wiping off the outside with a towel.

"Yes, we're going to take a late afternoon drive, and then go to Cow-boy's to eat."

"I'll see you later. I'd better get on the way."

"Oh, Momma. Doctor Sarah said she may let P.T. try crutches later today. She's thinking she'll let him walk back to his bed in the infirmary."

"Does she think the chipped bone in his leg is strong enough?"

"Possibly, but she won't let him put pressure on it at present. Like everything else he needs to start walking a little at a time."

"That's wonderful news." Gracie was thinking—*home to the Glory B. Yeah!*

"Don't tell P.T. He'll want to get up and go right now. Doctor Sarah isn't here. House call on a patient from last week. She wants to make sure he follows instructions.

"I'll keep silent. See you later."

~

Although the Texas air in late June was hot and the early sun beat down on her head, Gracie was thankful to have a chance to get out into the sunshine. She'd been beside her son for four weeks, at times sleeping with her head on his bed. Her muscles were tight and aching. To unwind, she needed a good walk and something else to think about—like clothes and shoes. Woman things.

Crossing the street, she waved at P.T. and strolled toward the middle of town.

Checking out the windows of the businesses as she went, she soon arrived at an interesting store she'd passed before the shooting occurred. The sign said Abilene Haberdashery. The store brought back memories of Memphis and the store she and her Pa had visited on the way to The Pinery. He'd broken all the rules and bought her men's clothes, because he knew she'd be more comfortable on the days and miles ahead. She'd worn them out many years ago.

She went in and walked around. After greeting the owner, she exchanged a few pleasantries and left.

"I'll be back. I see some things I like," she assured. She wasn't in the mood to buy anything—just look. She was happy to be out, breathing the fresh air after the antiseptic smell of the infirmary.

Down the street she went, going into interesting stores and enjoying her new freedom. She passed the open door of the train's superintendent, peeked in, but Grant wasn't there.

One long boardwalk later, she crossed the dusty street, intending to walk back home on the other side of Abilene's main street. The smell of coffee from Cowboy's Victuals was strong, inviting her to visit. She entered the door. Grant Bailey sat at a table near a window facing the street.

He motioned and called, "Gracie, I saw you pass the station earlier. Come sit with me."

Although she was still in the mood to enjoy her day of aloneness and not be social, she joined him.

Smiling, she said, "Good day, Grant. I'm out for a stroll after being nursemaid to P.T. for so long. The smell of coffee was just too much to resist."

He gave a chuckle. "I understand. I can sit here and watch the office door down the street. If anyone comes, I see them. The train's arrival and departure are posted outside. If anyone goes in, I know there's a question to be answered. My waiter thinks it's funny to see me jump up and rush to leave. Here, let me order your coffee." Grant summoned the water. "How's P.T. doing?"

"Sitting in a chair, outside on the boardwalk. And Doctor Sarah plans to let him use crutches today, to see if he can walk with them. Then he can move around on his own."

"That's great news. My father has a pair he used when he sprained his ankle in Missouri several years ago. You can borrow them if you need some."

"I'll tell Doctor Sarah." A question approaching the subject which was nagging Gracie came from her lips. She needed to know more about this man. "Are you from Missouri, Grant?" she decided to manage the problem slowly.

"Raised in South Dakota—the Black Hills. We lived with my father's friend, Jason Douglas, a pastor from Minnesota. He taught me to read, write, and use numbers. Then he and my father moved to Missouri so I could go into the higher classes of learning. I worked for another railroad before applying to the Texas and Pacific. My father wanted to come back here."

"What's your father's name, Grant?" The answer to this question had plagued Gracie since she'd heard the young man's last name was Bailey.

"His name is Henry, Henry Bailey."

At least it wasn't Hurricane, she thought. Not quite satisfied, she opened her mouth to ask another question. "Why was he …"

"Oh, I'm sorry," said Grant, holding up his hand. "Someone just walked through the door at the office. I'll have to answer your question another time. Better skedaddle and see what they want." He stood up, put his hat on, and hurried out the door.

As he went across the street, Gracie heard him call, "I'm coming."

She continued to sip her coffee, why was she so nervous about his last name. Of course, Bailey was the last name of her first husband—Ruby Eliza's father.

Shortly after they were married, Press had adopted the baby. She'd always been known and loved as a Stockton. They hadn't told her of her parentage because it wasn't important. Still, if this old man was Hurricane, then Ruby Eliza and Grant were stepbrother and sister. She realized there could be no marriage between them.

What a mess! Gracie shook her head. Surely the good Lord wasn't putting the family into the place of breaking her child's heart. And what about Grant?

After running her fingers through the curls, escaping her bonnet, she placed the money for her coffee on the table. There was no way to solve the problem, unless she met Henry Bailey. She needed to ask Grant and his father to lunch. Somehow or other she must lay eyes on the older Bailey man. Taking another sip of her coffee and with an almost imperceptible nod of her head, Gracie got up and resumed her walk down the street. She decided not to wear the bonnet, carrying it by the strings.

She'd passed several establishments before coming to one which said, ***"Cow-boy Hats and Boots."*** P.T. had lost his hat in the melee of the stampede and shooting. She stood looking at the selection displayed in the store window. The morning sun at her back made a shadow of her body on the store window. She had decided to go in when another shadow joined hers.

She turned. Her passage was blocked by a large, impressive Indian, wearing brown britches held up by a belt and large buckle with a buffalo stamped on it. His blue shirt, which was open, showed his bare chest.

He wore a white cow-boy hat on his head with an eagle feather stuck in the band.

"How-dy," he said grinning.

"Good morning, to you," she returned, a frown on her face and wondering why he stood before her.

"You no remember me," he said, still with a hint of a smile. This wasn't a question. It was a statement.

Drawing her eyebrows together, Gracie looked at the tall man. Something did seem familiar. His eyes? She frowned. Where had she been in the presence of an Indian up close?

Suddenly, the exact place dawned on her. The raid! As she and her pa came West. Years ago!

"Oh!" Her hand flew to her mouth. "You!"

The tall Indian grinned again. "Me. You no worry." He nodded. "Me, different." He kept nodding his head, trying to reassure her.

That was an understatement. "You certainly are. Why are you here in Abilene?"

"Me, guide. Business Indian. Take customers on trips. Very successful." He said this with pride, waving his hands.

Gracie looked down at his pair of expensive cow-boy boots. He must be doing well to afford them. She wondered if he missed his moccasins.

Following her gaze, he continued, "Like moccasins much better. Buy boots and hat inside. Good merchandise," he pointed to the door.

Gracie gave an incredulous smile and turned to check out the store again, quickly understanding why the man was here. A smaller advertisement on the door said, ***Check out our trips into the Wild West.***

Inquire inside. "Land's sakes, I would never have believed this in a million years."

"Mutual scratching of back. Good business, owner says."

Gracie shook her head and started laughing. "I guess so."

A bell jingled as the door of the shop opened. Four people came out. The gentleman in newly acquired cow-boy attire spoke. "You must be Flying Eagle?"

"Yes, need ticket." Flying Eagle held out his hand and received a square piece of paper. He spoke. "We go."

Gracie stood and watched as the group headed down the sidewalk. At the end of the block, Flying Eagle turned and waved. She waved back. Taking a deep breath and shaking her head, she wondered at this chance meeting. People can change and be totally different. Flying Eagle was the perfect example.

Before, he and his braves had raided her pa's wagon train. They'd taken her and another girl hostage. Without food for two days, he'd finally offered her a chunk of roasted meat.

When her Pa and the others showed up to rescue her and the other girl, there was a fight to liberate the two, and braves were killed. Some of her Pa's group were wounded. The other girl, an arrow in her back into her lung, did not survive.

Gracie opened the door and went inside. She wanted to buy a hat, but she needed to know more about Flying Eagle's story.

Later that day, she wrote Press about the encounter and the fact that P.T. had walked for the first time on his new crutches, but without putting pressure on his injured leg.

~

The air had cooled after a hard rain and the Texas darkness was setting in as Gracie sat in the chair P.T. had vacated. He was in bed, complaining that it was early, he wasn't sleepy, and demanding something to read or do. She had taken him the latest edition of the *Abilene Reporter* which she picked off a chair in the waiting area. Moving a table with a lamp to the head of his bed, she hoped he'd find something inside to interest him.

Leaving a kiss on his forehead, she quickly left the infirmary, before he could ask for something else.

From the kitchen area, she heard sounds of dishes being washed, dried, and placed back in the open cupboards. Sarah Susannah and Ruby Eliza often did this duty after the supper meal, especially after the heat had abated in the small cooking room.

After being closed most of the day, because of the rain, every window in the building was open, taking advantage of the cooler air.

No, Gracie didn't intend to help. Tonight, she was tired. She had headed for the covered front porch or boardwalk, and now she was relaxing to the sounds of busy Abilene at night. There was always a faint humming sound, mixed with the scratching of hidden animals, and chirping of a few night birds. She sat with legs outstretched and eyes slowly closing. She looked forward to a delicious night's sleep.

She missed Press—his strong arms around her. At home they would be sitting on the porch swing, her head on his shoulder. She pulled in air and let it out slowly. She wanted to go home. She had to admit, she was homesick. Could she and the rest of her family soon head for home on the stage? Time for a discussion with the doctor—tomorrow for sure.

The street was dimly lit by lights from the stores along the side who hung lanterns on posts supporting the porch which overhung the boardwalks. Because of the rain, those on horses or driving buggies had to tend with the muddy streets and potholes.

Occasionally, a screech from the street meant an especially deep mud puddle, as hands grabbed for holds to control the wild shifts on the unbalanced buggy seat. The light wasn't enough to illuminate the holes or the flailing occupants. Only shadows moved in the darkness.

Sometimes, Gracie walked the square around the doctor's office. But tonight, she had blown out the lantern on Doctor Sarah's porch, and she was content just to sit and rest.

She heard Sarah Susannah before she saw her.

"Momma, I need to talk to you," Sarah Susannah came out the front door of the doctor's office, closing it behind her.

"Come on over. The rain has stopped and the cooler air feels wonderful."

Gracie watched the shadow of her youngest daughter walk to sit in a vacant chair beside her. Sarah Susannah stretched out her legs and let her arms hang beside the chair. "I'm glad the dishes are done. Doctor Sarah feeds a lot of people each day," she commented.

"Yes, maybe you ought to stay here and help out. You could learn a bunch about being a nurse," suggested her mother.

"Are you trying to get rid of me?" asked the daughter. Then she added before her mother could answer the question, "I'm just joshin' you, Momma."

"I hope so, young lady." Gracie didn't say this sternly. "What did you want to talk about? You'd better hurry. My eyelids are slowly going down."

"Momma, you must know that I like Thomas Carter. I can't stand the thought of not seeing him or being around him again. I think of him all the time. You and Poppa were married at a young age, weren't you? I'll be seventeen in two weeks and …"

Gracie was now wide awake. She interrupted her headstrong daughter. "Sarah Susannah Stockton, I don't know what your Poppa would say, but you've always wanted to follow in Doctor Sarah's footsteps. I think you would be disappointed if you didn't follow your dream."

"You may be right, but I'd like to know Thomas better, be around him, and see if we could become a couple—like you and Poppa."

Gracie's mind was racing. What could she say? Finally, she made a decision. Press needed to be involved. After their conversation on the cattle drive, she wasn't sure that he wouldn't be on her daughter's side. "Sarah Susannah, why don't you write your Poppa. P.T. is still on crutches. Maybe Caleb will let Thomas come and take your brother's place until he gets to the point of being able to work again. After all, he is your father's shadow, and Press will miss him not being around."

"Huh, I hadn't thought about Poppa needing a shadow. I'll start the letter tonight." Sarah Susannah stood up. "I'm heading upstairs to bed. Good night, Momma. I love you."

"Wait, my dear. I'll go with you, if I can haul this leaden body off this chair and toward bed. I'll be asleep as soon as my head hits the pillow."

Both mother and daughter went into the waiting room. "You go on Sarah Susannah. I'll go check on P.T. and follow you. Sleep tight. I love you, too."

"Night, Momma."

Gracie heard her steps down the hall and up the stairs. Going into the infirmary she saw P.T. was sleeping soundly. Gracie removed the newspaper from his chest and blew out the light.

Quietly, she went into the dark waiting room, as the distinctive rattle of an approaching carriage sounded outside on the road. The noise stopped. She waited for it to move on. There was no sound so she went to the window to look out onto the street.

She saw the unmistakable silhouettes of Grant and Ruby Eliza, who stood on the boardwalk, talking in muted tones. Suddenly, he took her daughter into his arms and kissed her. Feeling as if she was an intruder into a scene of some emotion, Gracie immediately headed for the hallway and stairs. She undressed, put on her nightgown, and got into bed. Minutes later, she heard her daughter enter her room, and close the door very quietly. With so many thoughts running through her mind, Gracie did not go to sleep immediately.

~

Early the following morning, Sheriff Collins appeared at the doctor's office. Gracie was downstairs in the kitchen fixing breakfast for herself and Chester, who'd delivered his customary eggs. Ruby Eliza showed the officer into the eating area, and waited to see what he wanted.

"Good morning, Sheriff. Will you have a bite to eat? The cured ham is fried, and the biscuits are almost done. All I have to do is cook the eggs to order." Gracie stood with the egg turner in her hand, poised to start cooking.

"Thank you, Mrs. Stockton, but I've had breakfast at home. I need to talk to you for a minute."

"Oh, is this a private conversation or can you talk here?" she asked. "We can go into the waiting room or outside.

"No, not private. I'm going to need your husband and son to come to Abilene next week to testify in the rustlers' trial on Monday. I'm sorry this is such short notice, but Judge Abbott just telegraphed me he's coming. Can you get word to Press by the next stage, or do I need to get in touch with him?"

"I'll write him for you and see that the letter gets on the stage this afternoon. I'm sure he'll be here by Monday. He's as anxious as you to see those men locked up for years. Are you sure you don't want some more eggs?" Gracie asked, still waving her egg turner.

The Sheriff laughed. "No, thank you. I'd better get back to my office. If you get a reply, let me know. Otherwise, I'll expect Press to come by to see me when he gets into Abilene. How's your son?"

"P.T.'s much better—using crutches."

"Glad to hear he's making progress. I need to go." The Sheriff turned around and headed out of the kitchen. Everyone heard the door close.

Sarah Susannah came bouncing into the room. "Good morning, everyone."

"Sit down, and I'll fry you some eggs. Chester, will you get the biscuits from the oven? And Sarah Susannah, you won't have to write your father. He's coming to town to testify in the rustlers' trial. You can ask him in person."

"Ask him what?" ventured Ruby Eliza, who hadn't left the room.

"Oh, really nothing," responded Sarah Susannah, sitting at the table and looking at her mother as if they had a big secret. "Is it, Momma?"

Gracie only laughed and shook her head. Life was getting so complicated. Her husband's arrival wouldn't be too soon for her.

Chapter Thirty

The Measles Comes to Abilene

The trial took two days and it was over. Press reported the rustlers were given several years in the new Wynne Unit of the Huntsville facility in Southeast Texas. The Sheriff would leave on the weekend to take the prisoners there by train and stage.

"Gracie, are you ready to go home?" asked Press, who'd only arrived Sunday in time for the trial on Monday. They were in bed, breathing a sigh of relief from the last two days. He was propped up on his elbow as he asked the question, looking down at her.

Gracie realized the time had come to discuss things which were close to her heart. She sat up in bed, pulled her knees up, and put her arms around them. "I've been ready, sweetheart, but there's something we need to talk about, actually three somethings we need to talk about."

"Uh, oh. I feel a serious discussion coming on. What happened while I was gone?" Press lay back to listen, watching his wife carefully.

Gracie pulled in a lungful of air and plunged on, "You've seen P.T."

Press nodded his head. "What bothers me is the fact he hasn't put pressure on his leg."

"Me, too. Most of the time, his whole life, he's pushed the limits and surged ahead."

"Just like his Poppa," agreed Press, giving Gracie a little love pinch.

"Ouch. This is a serious discussion, my dear." Gracie pinched him back and then continued, "I'm wondering if he's tried. If so, he hasn't said anything."

"You think he's tried and not said anything on purpose?" asked Press.

Now, Gracie nodded her head. "I think there's a problem, and he knows it. He's not telling anyone."

"Let's talk to Doctor Sarah tomorrow morning at breakfast. Ask her to let him try to take some steps, and see what she advises. Then we'll make our decision to go home from there. What else?"

"Sarah Susannah is in love with Thomas Carter."

"Sweetheart, that was obvious on our cattle drive. You've known this all along."

"I know," Gracie waved her arms in the air. "But she wants to be around him to see if he's the one she …"

"Thomas is at the Glory B. Caleb. I had a talk with Caleb about P.T. He's agreed to let his son stay until Christmas. He'll take P.T.'s place, be my shadow, and help around the ranch. Then he'll go home."

"Why didn't you tell me?" asked a surprised Gracie.

"I wanted it to be a homecoming present for Sarah Susannah, and I didn't want to cause you concern, since you had your hands full taking care of our son."

"I wonder what P.T. will think of Thomas taking his place"

Press thought a minute, "We'll cross that bridge when it happens. P.T. may be fine tomorrow when he tries to walk. If so, he and Thomas can be working buddies as they were on the trail drive."

"Press, do we solve problems just to create more?"

Press gave a low two-chuckle laugh and shook his head. "Sometimes, we do. But we've always come out ahead. What else? There's one more something." Press waited for the last problem, thinking it must be a doozy.

Gracie sat wondering how to begin. She decided to start at the beginning.

"Sweetheart, do you remember when you adopted Ruby Eliza and gave her the Stockton name? We decided telling her about Jedediah wasn't necessary, since she would never know him or his father."

Press sat up beside Gracie in the bed, looking intently at her. "She was *my* daughter, and I love her as such. What is it?"

"You know I have this intuition, and I have a tendency to be right."

"Gracie, sometimes I'd like to bury your intuition in a hole," stated Press forcefully. "What's the problem concerning Ruby Eliza's name?" Press wasn't happy with the way this part of the conversation was going.

"It's not Ruby Eliza's name. It's Grant *Bailey's* name."

"Oh? What's wrong with his name?"

Gracie wrinkled her forehead and replied, "The Bailey part."

Press fell back on his pillow, putting his hands behind his head. Even he'd been a little concerned about Ruby Eliza's attachment to Grant.

Gracie continued, "I wonder about Ruby Eliza's relationship with Grant Bailey. Should there even be one, because of what we may know?"

Press took a deep breath, blew it out, and pulled his mouth down into a thin line. He thought, *this could be a mountain or a molehill.* "Do you think Grant's father, Henry Bailey is Hurricane?" There the question was out in the open.

Gracie was on the verge of tears. "I hope not, but if he is, then Ruby Eliza and Grant should part immediately. And what about Ruby Eliza? We haven't told her about her father."

Press sat up, putting his arms around Gracie. "Sweetheart, we didn't set out to deceive anyone, if that's what you're thinking."

"No, but we didn't tell the whole truth. That's what got P.T. into trouble—almost got him killed. I just didn't believe I'd ever see Hurricane Bailey again. He vanished into the night," she said, recalling the circumstances of his leaving.

"Didn't you tell me Grant was born in the Black Hills of South Dakota?"

"No. He said he was raised in the Black Hills. He didn't say where he was born." Gracie had to admit. "So many things need to be discussed, and quickly."

"I agree with you there—on both sides. Wonder how this older Bailey ended up in such a deserted part of the Northwest? Do you think he was looking for gold?"

"I don't know, but we need to meet him to determine whether my thoughts are correct or wrong. And we need to meet him *soon*." Gracie emphasized the soon.

"What do you suggest? Should we just go over there and bang on the door?"

"Let's think about the problem and decide on a course by noon tomorrow."

"Okay, Gracie. Go to sleep." Press turned over onto his side, back to his wife.

Togetherness this night had flown out the window. Tossing and turning in the bed, neither went to sleep immediately.

~

When Grant Bailey came home with the name Ruby Eliza Stockton on his lips, Henry Bailey wondered how anyone in Abilene had come up with the exact first name of his deceased wife. In fact, he'd asked again and gotten the same name. He couldn't remember telling anyone about her, except his son's wife, Gracie.

And that was when he'd come back from Arizona to The Pinery after his son's death from an Apache arrow. Henry wouldn't have told her then, but Jedediah, his son by Ruby Eliza, had loved Gracie enough to leave him, *if only for a short time.* The old schemer had made sure of that, knowing that blood is thicker than water.

He'd played his old trick on his son. As a drunken sot, he'd say, "You must come with me, or I may die." He meant of drink, or an altercation in a saloon. He did this every time Jedediah showed any inclination to leave. When his son left to marry Gracie, this took Henry by surprise, and he was determined to rectify his son's attempt at independence.

The story of his former life he'd never completely told Grant, although his former partner, Jason

Douglas, knew the whole sordid truth of his younger days—of drinking excessively, abusing his son, and women.

With Pastor Jason's help, Henry had done an about face, turned from his former life, and started believing in God's Son, Jesus. Although he regretted them, he knew the exploits of his youth were forgiven, erased by the cross, and the shedding of the Savior's blood. He had found more than the peace he'd sought. He'd found, through faith, eternal life.

In his old age, Henry was slowly becoming an invalid—something he wanted to avoid— being a burden to anyone. He felt his strength ebbing each year. Still able to hobble around, he was losing mobility each month. Heaven was getting closer, and he knew it.

~

He was sitting in his favorite chair by the open front window of his and Grant's home, the loosely woven white curtains with flowers waving slowly in the afternoon breeze.

A shadow on the porch and an insistent knock on the door, caused him to struggle to his feet and move in its direction.

"Mr. Bailey, please open up," exclaimed his next-door neighbor who was a widow with a young child of twelve years old.

"I'm coming, Betsy. Hold your horses," replied Henry, who moved slowly to the door. He fumbled trying to get the door open with his arthritic hand. One look at her agitated face, and he knew something was terribly wrong. "My goodness, what's happening?" he exclaimed.

"It's Judith. She's burning up with fever and very sick. Will you come and stay with her while I go get the doctor?"

Henry had always been available for his friend when needed. She had returned the favor by bringing him a little something for the noon meal. They would regularly sit for a while on his front porch and exchange their experiences of daily life while Judith played nearby with her dolls—by herself or with one of her friends.

He had no way of knowing his son, Grant, helped pay her bills in exchange for this service, and Betsy was sworn to silence.

"Of course, I'll come." He reached for his old, misshapen hat which hung from its peg by the door. He pushed it down on his head. He never went anywhere without a head cover.

Betsy had informed him days earlier of Judith's cough and runny nose. They'd decided she had a summer cold. Now, she had a fever. "I don't want to move her until the doctor comes to see her."

Henry followed Betsy through the front door of her home. Even from the entrance, he could hear the child's deeper breathing. Judith lay on her mattress in her dimly lit bedroom. She had the coverlet pulled to her chin. "Mama, I'm freezing," she said, turning her fever-stricken eyes on Henry with her lips quivering—an arm, almost lifeless, on the quilt top.

Just as he'd done for Grant when he was a young lad, Henry went to her and put his hand on her forehead. From this touch, he knew immediately she had a high fever, and from the sound of her breathing, she might have a touch of pneumonia. "Go Betsy, hurry. I'll sit with her."

"I shouldn't be long, Henry," advised Betsy, practically running from the room.

Henry pulled off his hat. He placed it on the top of the spoke of the ladderback chair and sat down by the young girl's bedside. He took Judith's hand, noticing her face was flushed. He looked again. Flushed or spotted? Hard to tell in the darkened room. He placed his face closer to hers for a better look. Even with his fading vision, he could see the answer. Spotted. She had spots of red all over her face and on the hand, he now held close to his face to inspect.

The child coughed and let out a faint moan.

He pushed the hand and arm beneath the coverlet, thinking, *could this be the measles*? Like the cholera, flu, and typhoid fever, this disease usually infected everyone who came in contact with the sick one. Many died.

Too late now, he thought. He'd felt the air brush his face from her continued coughing.

Doctor Sarah and Betsy arrived some minutes later. Bringing in a lamp, the doctor took one look at Judith and ordered Henry and Betsy out of the room.

A few minutes later, she emerged, wiping her hands and thermometer with carbolic acid on a piece of gauze. Turning her attention to Betsy, she said, "Your daughter is very sick." Then she asked, "How many people have been here since Judith became sick?"

"The widow across the street and Henry. No one else."

"Is it measles?" asked Henry, thinking he knew the answer.

Trying to remember everything about the new idea of Germ Theory, the doctor replied, "Yes, I'm sure it is. Betsy, you run across the road and see if the widow has had visitors. Find out their names. Write them down and where we can find them, and tell the widow not to see anyone else. Tell her I'll be over soon to talk to her. We'll have to set up a way to get food and other necessary items to each of you. We don't want this to go another inch from here."

"I'll be on my way," said Betsy and went out the door, calling back, "I'll hurry."

"Henry, are you Grant's father?"

"Yes, I am." Henry had found a seat in Betsy's living room. He needed to ease his arthritic knees.

"Do you know anything about the measles?"

"Yes, enough to realize I stand a good chance of gettin' them, and my chances of beatin' them ain't good at my age."

"We'll have to set up an area here where those who might be infected will stay without visitors. This means if Grant doesn't have any symptoms, he'll be staying at the train depot and not coming home. First, I'll have to see how your son's feeling. I'll stop by and see him as I go back to my office. Do you know how long Judith has been sick?"

"Betsy came over to tell me, on Sunday, I believe. Grant wasn't here. He was at church. Judith only had the sniffles and cough. I haven't seen her all week, but Betsy's been to the house since then. Grant works during the hours she comes over."

Doctor Sarah nodded her head. "That's good. Maybe he hasn't caught them. Here comes Betsy." The doctor opened the door for her.

Betsy rushed into the room. "The widow said her family hasn't been to her house since Sunday," Betsy ventured, out of breath. "She fixed dinner for them, and they stayed until nightfall. Here, she gave me their name and address." Betsy held out a piece of paper with the information scrawled on it. "What can I do to help my daughter?" she pleaded. "She's all I got in the world."

Doctor Sarah put an arm around the distraught mother and suggested, "Wipe her down with cool water every hour, and I'll give you some laudanum to quiet her and write out how to give it. She needs liquids. Try to get her to drink water or lemonade with plenty of sugar and you might add a pinch of salt. Warburg's Tincture will help with the fever. I think I have some at my office. I'll see that someone brings it by. The instructions for dosage is on the bottle."

"Where will I get lemons?"

"I saw some at the mercantile store. They probably came on stage from El Paso. I'll send Chester for a dozen, and he can bring the Tincture. He'll knock on your door and leave the items on your porch. He can't come in, and Betsy, no one else should enter your house. Do you understand?"

"Yes, Doctor. I'll get some soft cloths and water. You'll see, I'll take good care of my little girl." Betsy left the room with tears in her eyes."

"Come on, Henry. I'll walk you home. The same goes for you. No visitors." When the older man got to his steps leading up to the porch, the doctor reached out a hand to help him.

"No, I can manage," he said, struggling with raising his weak legs until he finally accomplished his task and walked inside his door.

Doctor Sarah realized Henry was right. If he caught the measles, the disease would not go well for him. She headed across the road to the widow's house with the same instructions—no visitors. She left for her office.

After making a detour to talk to Grant Bailey to explain the circumstances and instructions pertaining to the measles, she arrived back at her office. Standing in her waiting room, she wrote lists and made arrangements for food, medicine, and any other thing Henry, Betsy, and the widow needed. Ruby Eliza went to get Chester.

After describing the problem to her handyman, Doctor Sarah said, "Chester, I'll need you to go to town to buy the supplies which the households need. Here's the list and the money for your purchases. When you come back, I'll give you directions on their delivery." She intended to use him as a good go-between. Chester would mind her instructions to the letter.

Hearing the shutting of doors, tramp of feet, and talking downstairs, Press and Gracie entered the waiting room, expecting multiple patients. Doctor Sarah gave them a nod and smile. She continued on with her instructions to Ruby Eliza and Chester.

Chester left for town, list in hand.

"What is going on?" asked Gracie.

"The measles," was Doctor Sarah's two-word answer. Then she turned back to her nurse, with more instructions. "Ruby Eliza, we'll go gather up any medicines needed."

After they disappeared into the adjoining room, Press spoke to Gracie in a low tone, "Haven't you had measles?"

"Yes. Both Sarah and I had them, years ago, back in Nashville as younger children."

"Why don't you volunteer as another go-between? That way you can help and check out Henry at the same time. You would make a perfect doctor's assistant," suggested Press.

"I agree." Funny, he would say just what she'd been thinking.

"Also, I'm thinking I should load up P.T. and Sarah Susannah and go back to the Glory B. If there's an outbreak of the measles here in Abilene, they would be much safer on the ranch."

"Do you think Doctor Sarah could take a minute to check out our son's walking ability?"

Press had hoped this would happen, but he expressed doubt. "She's so busy with the families and the measles, I don't think she would have time to see how P.T.'s doing."

"What's that about too busy for P.T.?" asked the doctor coming back into the waiting room, expecting an answer. She held an open box which contained several small bottles.

"We were wondering if P.T.'s ready to head back to the Glory B. Especially what you thought about his walking without crutches." Press walked to the door of the waiting room, opened it, and looked out. His son sat on the porch with his leg propped up in front of him on a second chair.

P.T. looked around at his father and waved.

Doctor Sarah looked at Press and Gracie with a slight smile and continued, "Yes, I think he can go home, but he will have some difficulty walking. He can recuperate in the Glass Mountains as well as here, and maybe being home will give him an impetus to get moving faster. Here's what I think you'll find when we go outside. His leg will be weak, and his muscles sore and stiff. The bone is fine by now, but he will be leery of putting pressure on it. Whoever works with him will need lots of patience. Massages with horse liniment or salve and hot water to loosen the muscles, that's what I recommend."

She put the box down and went outside, where the doctor gently suggested to P.T. they needed to test his walk without the wooden crutches.

P.T.'s face showed excitement, but there was fear in his eyes.

As P.T. leaned forward in the chair, Press put his arms under the young man's shoulders, helping, almost dragging, him away from where he sat.

Upon standing by himself, P.T.'s leg immediately gave way, and his father caught him before he fell.

Gracie wanted to rush to her son, put her arms around him and comfort him, but she held back, letting Press handle the situation. This was a man-to-man thing.

Press helped him back toward his chair, saying, "Son, Doctor Sarah says you can go home. We are heading for the Glass Mountains on the next stage. Do you want to go back to the Glory B and see Winky and

Star?" Star had gone home with the *remuda* and the cow-boy drovers.

Hanging on and hopping to keep from falling, an exhausted and disappointed P.T. answered, "Yes, Poppa. I'm ready."

"Thomas will be there," volunteered his Momma, now leaning over him like a mother hen. She added a hug and a kiss on his cheek.

P.T. brightened a bit. "Good," he said, although he was thinking their relationship wouldn't be the same with him on crutches and unable to walk. The attempt had proven to him completely what he'd guessed all along. His leg felt like jelly and his muscle had collapsed without the aid of a crutch.

"Don't be discouraged," reassured Doctor Sarah. "Most muscle injuries take a period of time to heal."

Later, in a quiet time with Gracie, she said, "Press will have to keep encouraging him—keep his spirit up. And I'll give P.T. some exercises for the family to use in loosening up the muscle and getting him up to walk. Your front porch with its railing at the Glory B will work wonders for a place to hold on to, exercise, and walk—to slowly put weight on his leg. And what a view ..."

~

Gracie got busy packing clothes. A couple of days passed while Gracie got her brood ready to head back to the Glass Mountains. By the time her loved ones left, Henry Bailey had started showing some symptoms of the measles.

In the flurry of packing, Gracie made one trip with the doctor to meet Betsy and find out where Henry and the widow lived.

In the end, Sarah Susannah, P.T., and Press were to leave on the stage.

Press stood whispering in Gracie's ear before he entered, "I love you, Sweetheart. I'm sorry to leave you with *our dilemma,* but I know you'll take care of it with kindness and wisdom as you always do." There was a brief kiss, and he was gone.

On the way back to the doctor's office, Gracie told Sarah she would be nurse to all the sick who had measles. But Gracie didn't tell Sarah she had an ulterior motive. She didn't want anyone to know of her findings until the results of her search were clear … not even Sarah.

~

Earlier, when making the hurried trip to meet Betsy and Judith, and find out where they lived, Gracie had rushed out of Doctor Sarah's office without a hat.

Henry Bailey was standing inside his house in front of his window, sipping his second cup of hot coffee, when the two had walked by and entered Betsy's next door. He'd gotten the shock of his life. Even with his bad eyes, the woman with the doctor was familiar, very familiar. The curly, blond hair had darkened and straightened somewhat over the years since he'd last seen her, but he was sure she was Jedediah's wife. So, Gracie had remarried and had children, because Grant had said so.

In a strange quirk of fate or a God thing, they were close again, but this time he was different. Even so, there was no need to expose the truth of who he was. Henry determined Gracie would never know. He didn't look the same, but her curly hair and manner had given her away.

Memories rushed back. First, he was sad, and then the question came quickly. Ruby Eliza, could she be his granddaughter? Grant had talked so much about her. He counted back and the years worked out. Was that where the name had risen? How interesting. The son he'd raised, and maybe the granddaughter he never knew he had, now loved each other. He was happy knowing of the twosome's attachment. Then he remembered a phrase Jason often quoted, *God works in mysterious ways his wonders to perform*. Henry laughed and shuffled away from the window.

Chapter Thirty-One

Gracie Becomes a Nurse

Doctor Sarah came back from her normal visit to see Betsy and Judith with some news. "Gracie, I think it's time you started nursing the sick people full time. The widow has shown no symptoms of the measles, but Henry and Betsy may be coming down with them. Betsy can't manage her daughter and herself."

"How do you know if Henry's sick?"

"Like Betsy, he's got the sniffles and a slight fever. I'll know about them in a couple of days when the red spots start. Why don't you go and sit with Betsy? She's worn herself completely out, and if she's coming down with the measles, I can't think of anything worse than being tired. She needs nourishing food and moral support right now. You're the perfect person to feed and cheer her up."

Gracie grinned. "And you're the perfect doctor. How is Judith, today?"

"I think she's better. After four or five more days, she should show enough improvement until I can say she's on the way to recovery, but I don't want to give her mother hope unless this is true. There's nothing worse than giving mistaken information to a parent."

"I certainly hope you can give her this encouraging news. I'll pack a bag." Gracie turned to go.

Doctor Sarah called to her, "Gracie, I want you to stay at Betsy's house and don't go to Henry's until I'm sure the measles is involved in his diagnosis. According to the latest in Germ Theory, you might spread the disease."

"Germ Theory?" Gracie was frowning.

"Yes. Take my word for it. If this thing Henry has is only a summer cold, you might actually carry the measles to him. So, stay away."

Shoot, thought Gracie. How was she going to talk to the elderly man? She needed to find a way, but she would follow Doctor Sarah's instructions until the opportunity presented itself. She climbed the stairs, packed a bag, and headed to Betsy and Judith's home.

Hefting her bag, she couldn't help but think she'd be glad to pack it for the last time when she'd be going home to the Glory B.

Press and their children were there, waiting for her return.

Next year, she'd stay at home. This trip on the cattle drive had turned into an unwanted nightmare.

~

Doctor Sarah was right about Betsy. She was exhausted.

Upon arrival, Gracie ordered her straight to bed and took over her duties. "I'll see that Judith is wiped down every two hours," assured Betsy's replacement.

When she went in to see Judith and felt her forehead, the young girl wasn't hot. Her fever had broken. Judith was on her way to recovery. Gracie just knew it.

Upon looking around the frame house, Gracie found Chester's store of chopped wood and kindling for cooking food on the iron stove and supplies in the cabinets of some canned goods. When needed, she knew he would appear with a dressed chicken or a piece of meat from the mercantile store's supply.

She set about tending to the chores of the household and making sure Henry had food also. Her instructions were to set his cooked food on his front porch and knock on the door.

Since she wasn't showing any symptoms, the widow could now fend for herself or ask her family to help.

~

A night or two later, Gracie sat on Betsy's front porch in a rocking chair, thinking about the last few hours.

On doctor's orders, she had stopped cooling Judith down with dampened cloths. Because of her mother's loving care, the young girl was on the way to recovery, but on bed rest.

The doctor promised if she obeyed her orders, she would get out of bed by the end of the week, if she continued to improve. This assurance had produced in Judith a smile as bright as sunshine.

Tending Judith had brought back memories of Gracie's girls at this young age. When they were alone, she'd given Judith an encouraging hug. "You're going to be alright."

An earlier conversation had produced this question, "Gracie, does my Mom have the measles?" It was asked in alarm at overhearing talk surrounding her mother's sickness.

The caregiver had answered, "Yes, but as soon as you are able, we will both take good care of her." This seemed to assure Judith concerning her mother.

A slight breeze hastened the chill of the Texas night, and brought Gracie back to the present. She crossed her arms to turn aside the wind.

Under doctor's orders, Gracie had switched to Betsy, who now had a high fever and spots on her face. Doctor Sarah had left with the suggestion that tomorrow Gracie might have another patient, meaning Henry.

"I'm almost positive he has the measles," was the doctor's last comment before she'd left in the morning.

How long ago was that? Gracie pulled in a deep sigh and pushed it out in the gathering darkness. She wondered how Sarah could take sick people on a daily basis, week-after-week. She never seemed to be depressed even with the worst cases coming into her office. Gracie chuckled, thinking *Sarah was the perfect doctor.*

Gracie moved the rocker in a slow arc and watched as Abilene embraced the night. Other residents, who lived up and down the street, were now coming out and taking advantage of the cooler night air. The late summer crickets kept up a constant chirp. Gracie preferred no light, because a lamp would attract mosquitos, moths, and other insects.

In the darkness she was alone with her thoughts.

Carrying a lantern, the widow across the street came out to her porch. Peering into the darkness she noticed the rocker's movement. She waved to Gracie, and called, "How's Betsy and Judith?"

"Judith is much better, but Betsy has a fever and spots. I'm giving her the cloth rubs and the medicine which Judith took."

"Oh, I'm so sorry about Betsy." The widow crossed her arms and rubbed her hands up and down. "It's chilly out here. I'd better go in before I get my death of cold." Not realizing the content of what she'd just said might apply to Gracie's patients, the widow disappeared into her house. Soon the light of the lamp shone through a window.

In other circumstances, Gracie might have chuckled at the truth in the statement, but in this case the cold wasn't the culprit. The people she was nursing weren't out of danger. Death was not a word she wanted to hear. She rocked in the chair, resting for a few minutes, and clearing her head of thoughts of sick people. Leaning her head back against the wood, she closed her eyes, and dozed off.

A noise woke her.

She looked around and saw slow movement on Henry's front porch. The older man bent over and put his dinner dishes and utensils in a wooden box, placed there so she could retrieve them. She heard the rattle of the knife and fork as they went onto the metal plate. He always washed them so she could fill them with the next meal.

In the gloomy night, all she could see was a dark form, but she did notice the slight limp. Or, was she just imagining it, because she knew Hurricane Bailey had one?

She squinted her eyes, hoping to see better.

The dark form turned, slowly walked back through the door, and shut it. He must have picked up a lamp from his front room, because the light slowly disappeared from view.

Gracie grasped the arms of the rocker, got up, and went to retrieve the tableware. Back on Betsy's porch she paused to glance around one last time. Tiredness settled over her like a blanket. She walked inside with leaden feet and placed the dishes in the small kitchen for filling tomorrow.

She looked at the cook stove. No, she didn't want to take the ashes out and place them on top of the smoldering coal, but she did. In the morning, she would poke the embers and add more chunks of coal.

Her bed was an old cot from Sarah's infirmary, but it felt good as she stretched out in her day clothes—too tired to change into her gown. A light sheet and she was fast asleep.

~

Doctor Sarah woke her early the next morning. "Gracie, are you dead or sleeping?" she asked, grinning and shaking her shoulder. "I looked in each room. No one in the place is awake."

Gracie blinked in the daylight. "My goodness! What time is it?"

"Time to get out of bed," said Doctor Sarah, looking at a watch on a long chain hanging around her neck. "Seven-thirty to be exact."

"I knew I was tired last night. I guess I didn't know how tired." Gracie jumped up and headed for the wash basin. She splashed water on her face and wiped it off with a towel hanging on a wooden peg nearby.

"I brought supplies, including eggs and bacon for breakfast. You'll have to make the biscuits though." Doctor Sarah went to the cabinet in the kitchen and placed the canvas bag filled with items on the cupboard.

Gracie rummaged through the bag and pulled out the brown paper wrapped bacon and the bag of eggs. Her stomach gave a big growl at the sight. "Now that wasn't very ladylike," she mumbled quietly to the offending organ, knowing this was standard procedure for it. Press would have laughed.

"I'll check on Judith and then Betsy. Why don't you get breakfast ready for everyone, including me?" Doctor Sarah left the room.

Gracie poked at the leftover embers in the stove.

After the appearance of the measles, Grant had obtained permission from the railroad to share coal to the infected households. This burnable material was heaped up for the steam engine's trips back and forth to Fort Worth. He had built a small shed in Betsy's backyard and at Henrys and stocked a small pile of coal for their use.

From the coal bucket, Gracie placed several pieces of coal on top of the live coals and waited for the stove to heat up. After washing her hands, she put coffee grounds and water in the coffee pot, and set it to the back of the stove. Taking flour, baking powder, and other ingredients, she stirred up several biscuits—enough for the day. After they were in the stovetop oven and the temperature set, she put the iron skillet on a removable eye. Hearing a noise behind her, she turned as Doctor Sarah came into the room. "Did you look at Judith?"

"Yes. She's doing well, but I don't want her out of bed for two more days. You'll be hard pressed to keep her there, but getting up might mean a setback. We don't want her to get sick again."

"How about Betsy?" Gracie put thick slices of bacon in the hot iron skillet. They immediately started to sizzle.

"Betsy has the measles."

"I thought so." Gracie turned the bacon.

"The next five days will be the worst for her. Keep dosing her with the medicine. I have more coming on the afternoon train from Fort Worth. We'll need it for Henry, because he has the measles also. I checked on him first this morning."

"Does that mean I'll be taking dinner and supper to him?" Gracie pulled some bacon out of the pan, placing it on a platter.

"Yes. He had something for breakfast. Looked like biscuits with ham. He wasn't feeling so bad this morning, but my guess is by supper his fever will spike. He doesn't need to be moving much either. Being one who doesn't want to admit his age, I'm sure he will try not to take to his bed. I'll go by and tell Grant as I go back to the office. Do I smell the bread?"

"Yes, yes!" Gracie grabbed a pot holder and put the pan on a wooden trivet. They hadn't burned, but they were definitely brown. She removed the rest of the bacon from the pan, got rid of the extra grease into an old coffee can, and started cracking and frying eggs. "Would you set the table?" she asked of Sarah.

"Yes. Fix our eggs, and I'll help you feed our sick ones," suggested Sarah.

After eating hurriedly, they filled plates and cups for the sick in their bedrooms. Gracie headed for Judith's room.

On returning to the kitchen, Gracie's plate and cup were empty, but Doctor Sarah's didn't look like it had been touched. "I tried feeding her to no avail. She kept shaking her head. She did take a few sips of coffee, and I left it just in case she would want more. Hopefully she will eat better at dinner."

"How is her fever?"

"Up, more than yesterday. Keep rubbing her with a damp cloth and giving her the tincture. That's all we can do for the fever, except pray—like we did for Judith. Do you have any questions, Gracie?"

Gracie shook her head.

Chapter Thirty-Two

Henry "Hurricane" Bailey Rejoices in Heaven

Gracie soon found out her life was to become more hectic. Cooking three meals a day, wiping down two patients, especially one who wasn't cooperative, with wet cloths every two hours or so, and administering medicine was a full-time job. She took a calendar and started marking the times and making notes on each day.

"Doctor Sarah, do you think we could move Henry over here?" she asked on day two of her frenzied work.

"What will you do with Judith?" said Doctor Sarah, noticing her friend's haggard look and realizing the house had only two bedrooms.

"Maybe the widow could keep her for a few days. Will you go and see and also talk to Henry?" Gracie hadn't had time to sit down and talk to the man. He answered her questions in one or two words, and usually didn't sit up to eat until she went back to Betsy's house. Why? She didn't know.

"I'll do that. I can see where having them both here would make your life easier."

Gracie followed Doctor Sarah to the front porch and watched her walk across the street. She walked back inside and went to prepare the wet cloths for wiping down her patients.

When the doctor returned, she said, "The widow will gladly keep Judith, but Henry won't budge. I think he's now upset that we asked. Of course, I think he's getting too weak to move, although he tries to hide his frailness. After checking in on him with his high fever, I'm not sure changing his surroundings is a good plan. I just wish he'd mind what I say."

From Judith's bedroom came, "I'm not going anywhere either. Gracie promised me I'd be able to help my Mom."

"Eavesdropper," called Gracie to the girl. She was answered with a snicker.

Doctor Sarah shook her head. "Guess that answers your question."

"She's feeling so much better." Gracie indicated Judith's bedroom by shoving her finger in that direction.

"I've been thinking, Grant's wanting to come see Henry. Maybe he could stay for the night and help you with breakfast the following morning—if he keeps his distance from Henry, washes his hands, and does his best to not breathe in the air surrounding the older man—hmm." She was thinking. "In fact, I just got these in from Nashville." Doctor Sarah opened a sack and held out a white covering with strings.

"What is it?" asked Gracie, reaching out a finger to feel the cloth.

"It's called a mask and it's to reduce the danger of infection from germs floating in the air. Here I'll demonstrate." She placed it over her face and pulled one set of the strings back over her hair. "See? You tie the back."

"Is that part of the Germ Theory you've been talking about?"

"Yes. I'm beginning to believe in it. Every time I follow the principles I've read about; they prove to work."

Gracie nodded her head. "Has Grant had the measles?"

"He doesn't know for sure, but he's willing to take the gamble. He's strong and healthy, and, if he insists, I don't have the authority to stop him. He's been honoring my wishes. But with this mask …"

~

Seeing Grant, in the mask at the first light in the morning, caused Gracie to grin. He smelled of soap and looked freshly shaven on his face's exposed parts.

"I know. I know. I look ridiculous," he agreed, touching the cloth addition to his face. "But if it keeps me or someone around me from getting the measles, it's worth the aggravation. I've washed my hands so many times last night and this morning, they'd be turning white, if they weren't so red from the carbolic acid." He held them out, turning them over.

"How's your father, this morning?" Gracie indicated the coffee pot and the supplies for making the dark brew.

Grant proceeded to open the coffee can and started making coffee.

Grant answered her question. "I'm no doctor. He seems the same. Hot to the touch and lethargic." He handed the full pot to Gracie. "But no worse," he continued. "I've been praying he'll get well."

She placed the coffee pot on the back of the stove near the stovetop oven where the biscuits were already baking.

"That's Betsy, plus she's not eating," said Gracie in a lower voice. She put her finger to her mouth and gave a low, "Sssh," nodding toward Judith's bedroom. "She has big ears."

"I did too when I was her age." Grant smiled and started putting plates on the table for the food to be served.

"I think Doctor Sarah will let Judith get out of bed today." The bacon started to sizzle in the iron skillet.

Gracie walked to the wooden countertop and picked up a basket of eggs. She handed them to Grant to hold. "The smell of bacon is a good start to the day," she observed.

"How long has Judith had the measles?" Grant was wondering about his Pa, who wasn't inclined to stay in bed very long.

The bacon was done, grease poured into the can, and Gracie started cracking eggs into the skillet. She answered, "Over two weeks, while her mother and I've nursed her."

"You said Betsy's fever is high?"

"Yes, and she's lethargic like Henry. Doctor Sarah says older people have a tougher time. She's losing weight rapidly, since she has no appetite."

Gracie put the bacon on the plates. This morning she had four plates to fill. Soon she had scrambled eggs to go with the bacon and the baked biscuits.

"Gracie, I won't be back over here after I feed my Pa. I'll leave the clean plates on the porch like he's always done. Maybe I can leave work a little early this afternoon. Why don't you rest for the night meal, and I'll get stew from Cowboy's for supper? Also, I'll buy some of Ernie's apple butter to go with our meal tomorrow morning."

Gracie nodded in agreement. She had enough biscuits to eat with stew, unless he brought Ernie's cornbread from the eatery also. She thought about suggesting the bread, but decided against it.

Grant left with two plates, and she went to Judith's room to feed her. Instead, the young girl sat up in bed and reached out her hand for the plate.

"You're feeling much better this morning, I see," commented Gracie, handing her the plate and pulling up a wooden stand to rest her glass of water with lemon and sugar in reach of the bed.

"Yes. I think I could get up after breakfast." Judith was nodding her head and *please* was in her eyes. "Gracie, I want to see my Mama. I miss her." The last was said with a hint of a tear.

"We'll see when Doctor Sarah comes this morning. Since you can feed yourself, I'll go help your mother. I'll come back and give you an update." Gracie left the room and went into Betsy's.

At first, the caregiver didn't think Judith's mom was breathing. This scared Gracie who started shaking her, causing Betsy's eyes to fly open.

She stared at Gracie and gave a weak grin. "I'm so tired," she said weakly and in a low, almost hoarse voice.

"I know you are. I've brought breakfast, and I need you to sit up in bed to eat."

They both struggled to get her into a sitting position. She leaned forward to take a sip of her lemon-water and then fell back against the pillows which Gracie had hurriedly pushed behind her as she tasted the liquid.

One bite of bacon and one fork of eggs and she was finished eating. "I'm just not hungry," she explained. "Nothing tastes good."

"But you need to eat. Remember Judith? How you insisted on her eating?"

"How is my sweet daughter?"

"She's just about well and wondering about you. I think Doctor Sarah will let her get up today. Maybe she'll be in to give you a hug and kiss."

This perked Betsy up a bit. "Maybe I'll have another bite of bacon and egg," she agreed. Gracie made sure these were big bites, but that was all she would eat.

Gracie went by Judith's door, "Mom's moving around." She picked up the girl's dishes and headed back to the kitchen. Well, she consoled herself. Her comment wasn't a total falsehood.

She was eating her breakfast when Doctor Sarah came in the door. "Do you have enough for me?"

"Yes, on the counter. Help yourself."

When the doctor left, Judith could get out of bed with restricted activities for the following days. She immediately went in to check on her mother. She crawled into bed with her and put her arm over her chest, kissing and patting her on the face—murmuring, "I love you, dear Mama." That's where Gracie found her when she went to wipe Betsy down with the wet cloth. Both mother and daughter were fast asleep.

Getting them back together might be the best thing to happen to Betsy, thought Gracie. Gracie looked at the cloth and the sleeping two. Shaking her head, she left the room. There would be time later for this activity. Gathering her pan of water and another cloth, she headed for Henry's house.

He was either asleep or possuming. She could almost guess the latter. She decided not to disturb him either. For her, a morning rest before fixing the noon repast sounded good. Potato soup was on the agenda, along with a rubdown for her patients.

~

After two days of varying his normal movements, Grant was tired. He'd gone to see Ruby Eliza at dinner and they'd walked to Cowboy's Victuals for fried chicken. He missed their times together of long rides in his buggy, walking the boardwalk in the cool of the afternoon, or sitting in the intimate darkness on the office's front porch, while watching the buggies and people go by. He wanted to talk about their future, but with Henry so sick, he realized the time wasn't right. He'd dispensed with most of his usual activities, and after work he always headed home.

Arriving at the frame house where he and his Pa lived, he walked in and closed the door. He could hear his father's labored breathing as soon as he walked into his room. Something was really wrong. Before he could check the older man out, there was a knock on his front door.

"Hello there, Judith," he said, surprised to see her.

Judith stood with two plates of food, stacked on top of each other. The lower one was protected from the other by turning a metal one on top and placing the second on it. "Are you allowed to be outside?" The young girl's hands clamped the two together.

"Oh, yes. Doctor cleared me to go outside, but not to get hot or run. I can walk. What's that noise?" Judith peered around him at his father's room.

"I was just going to check. You stay here."

Judith walked into the kitchen and sat the plates down on the table. She heard a weird noise as if someone was talking … calling her name … "Judi … Judidi." Curious, she walked to the bedroom door.

"Jededi …" came from Henry's mouth. And again, "Jedediah."

"Pa, wake up," pleaded Grant, who was standing over his father. He had a hand under his Pa's chin, gently moving his head.

"Who is Jedediah?" asked Judith of Grant.

"I have no idea," said the railroad superintendent. "If he comes to, I'll ask, but I think he's taken a turn for the worse."

Suddenly Henry threw up his hand and yelled, "Oh! No! Jedediah," and then he groaned.

Judith jumped back at the sudden outburst, putting her hand to her open mouth.

"Pa, wake up, wake up." Grant moved his hand and shook him by the shoulder.

Henry didn't open his eyes.

"Hurry, Judith. Let's go over and talk to Gracie." With that, he turned, leaving the plates of food and headed for Betsy's home.

Judith opened the door and hurried inside.

Grant followed, making noise as he entered the door at the heaviness of his step.

Gracie came from Betsy's room, basin and cloth in hand. One look at Grant and she asked, "What on earth's happened?"

"It's Pa. I can't wake him, and he's mumbling something about Jededi or something like that. I'm going to Doctor Sarah's. She needs to come immediately. I wanted you to know."

He headed out the door with Gracie following. "I'll go over and check on him." Then she went back indoors for more water and a cloth rag. "Judith, I'll leave you to take care of your Mom. If you need me, you know where to find me."

"I'll take good care of her," promised Judith, her eyes wide at the swift pace things were happening. She vanished into the safety of her mother's room.

Gracie disappeared out the door and walked quickly to the Baileys' porch. Filling her lungs with air, she blew it out in a quick burst, straightened her shoulders, plunged through the door and inside the house. She went immediately to the sick man's bedroom. She placed her hand on his head. He was burning up with fever, but what scared her was the rattling sound in his chest. His breathing was irregular, and when he did take a deep breath, the funny sound came out with it.

All the days she'd tended Henry Bailey, she'd wanted to talk to him, but the right time never happened. There was one way she could find out if he was Hurricane Bailey. The scar. The scar on his left shoulder when he'd helped rescue her after the Indian raid on the wagon train as she and her father went west so many years ago. Chief Eagle Feather had been her captor.

Henry hadn't let her rub his arms down, preferring her to wipe his abdomen and legs. Even then, he mumbled and shuddered at her touch. She unbuttoned his pajama top and gently raised it to expose the ragged scar from an arrow. It was there—a thin white uneven line, just as she knew it would be. It was Hurricane. Hurricane Bailey in the flesh.

She staggered back as her unruly legs gave way. Luckily, she fell into a chair, as some of the water in the basin splashed into the floor. She sat the container down and wrapped the wet cloth over its edge. Leaning over, she placed her elbows on her knees, and buried her face in her hands.

Glancing at Hurricane through her fingers, she realized he didn't look like the old hostile man she once knew. Something must have happened after he left The Pinery over twenty years ago. But what? And who was Grant's mom? How come they were in South Dakota? Ruby Eliza and Grant? And …

She shook her head vigorously. Before she had time to think more of the consequences of her discovery, she heard noises from the front of the house. Doctor Sarah came quickly into the room. "Has he said anything?" she asked, popping her thermometer into his mouth and checking his pulse with the watch hanging around her neck.

"No, he hasn't said a word." Gracie, still suffering from her discovery, didn't elaborate on her findings. She sat in shock and disbelief at what her conclusion meant for some of the people she loved the most.

Doctor Sarah pulled out her stethoscope and listened to Henry's lungs, moving it around in different places. She shook her head. "Grant, he's definitely developed pneumonia in his left lung, and I think I hear something in his right. Getting this infection started in his lungs is a very bad development. I don't have any medicine to treat it."

"Is there nothing we can do?" Grant looked at the man who'd been his Pa for over twenty years. He'd said goodbye only this morning, not realizing he might never speak to him again.

Doctor Sarah continued, "Some doctors will do blood-letting and some would blister his chest and place a cup there to draw out the illness. But I don't believe in either one of them. There just isn't any combination of chemicals or treatment as yet for this lung infection, and your father is old—a major case against his recovery."

"What can we do? Will he be conscious again? What is your prognosis?"

"I don't know, except to pray. I can give him more laudanum. He's been taking a bit to let him rest at night. This will keep him comfortable. I don't know if he'll ever be conscious to talk to you again."

Grant nodded at Doctor Sarah, his face knotted in anguish at his distress over his father's illness.

"I'll stay with you for a while, so I can monitor his progress, if you wish."

"Please do. Maybe he'll get better." He went to bring two more chairs from the kitchen—one for him and one for the doctor.

The three sat with Henry for a while, listening to rattling sounds coming from his chest.

Finally, Gracie stood up. "I'd better go check on Betsy and make sure Judith is okay."

Doctor Sarah nodded at her, and turned back to the bedside. Grant sat on a chair opposite her, holding his father's old arthritic hand in both of his.

"Gracie, I'll need to go to the office in late afternoon. I'll get Chester to come and spell me then. We'll need a messenger, and he can be one. Watch Betsy. Let me know if there's any change in her breathing."

~

Gracie headed straight to Betsy's kitchen. Shaken to the core over what she'd just learned, she paced up and down. She knew the truth would have to come out, but when? And how?

She didn't have time to dwell on a solution because muffled sobs came from Judith's room. Walking toward the sound, she saw the young girl stretched out on her bed, her face buried in her pillow.

"Judith, are you okay?" Gracie asked, heading toward her.

Judith sat up and hurried to Gracie, throwing her arms around her waist. "Oh, Gracie. Will Mama be like Mr. Henry? Will she breathe so hard? Will she die?" sobbed the young girl.

Gracie realized her first priority was to Judith, Betsy, and the Baileys. The other problem could wait until the present crisis was solved. "Judith, I can't respond to your question. Only God knows the answer to Henry and your Mom's difficulty. Maybe we should pray and ask His opinion and His help. Come on, let's kneel beside your bed. You go first, and I'll finish your prayer."

Judith hesitated, "But Gracie, I don't know how to pray. Mom and I don't go to church."

"Come on. I'll teach you."

The two walked to Judith's bed and knelt on a rag rug beside her bed.

Gracie put her arm around Judith and asked, "What's your biggest fear right now, and what do you want done about it? These are the reasons you should be praying. God is listening. Just open your mouth and pour out your heart. He has big ears. Just remember, He will decide what's best. After you do this, you could thank Him in advance for His help. Then, I'll finish with my prayer."

~

Just before noon the following day, Henry "Hurricane" Bailey breathed his last. Gracie was standing in the kitchen at Betsy's, stirring a large pot of vegetable soup when Doctor Sarah came in the front door with the news.

"He's gone, Gracie." She looked exhausted as she leaned over to grasp the kitchen table to steady herself. "Grant is devastated."

"What happens now?" asked Gracie, turning from the stove and using her apron to wipe and fan her face.

"Chester has gone for the undertakers. I've told Grant I'll come over when they get there, and give instructions on handling the body. Chester will come here for me."

"Is there still danger of the measles spreading?"

"I don't really know, but it's always better to be safe. We don't want anyone else to get it. I'm really amazed someone hasn't. We must've done something right, Gracie." She ran the palm of her hand over her forehead. "I'll step in and look at Betsy. Where is Judith? Is she in her bedroom?"

"No. You'll find out soon enough, and I think you'll be pleased with Betsy's progress. When you come back in here, the soup will be ready to eat. I'm sure you could use some nourishment."

"I am hungry," the doctor stated without enthusiasm. "Are you doling out naps too? I think I might need one of those worse than the food."

She disappeared into Betsy's bedroom, and Gracie turned back to stirring her soup.

Judith came into the room. "Doctor Sarah says Mama is much better, Gracie.

"It's all of the good nursing she's been getting from someone we both know," said the woman stirring the pot on the stove, holding out her arm to receive the young girl's hug.

"And a lot of prayers we've been praying," said Judith, craning her neck to see what was cooking in the pot. "I'm hungry. Something smells really good."

"Vegetable soup, young lady. Sit down, and I'll get you a bowl to eat." Gracie went to the cupboard, got a stack of bowls, and filled one up for Judith. "When you finish your bowl, here's one for your Mama."

She had removed the soup from the stove when Doctor Sarah came from Betsy's room.

"I can't get over how much she's changed. She's weathered the worst of the infection. There's no fever, and her lungs are clear." She shook her head in disbelief.

"Will Mama be alright?" asked Judith, brightening at the doctor's comments.

"A few more days of good nursing, and she will be back to cooking meals, mending clothes, and playing games with you, dear child."

"Whoopee," exclaimed Judith, getting up. She grabbed the soup bowl and ran to her Mama's room.

They could hear her telling her Mama she would soon be playing hide and seek with her and a child who lived next door.

"Sit down, Sarah. I'll get you some soup.

Doctor Sarah did as she was told. She sat thinking, *one in heaven and one on the way to recovery. Such is life on the frontier of Texas*. She ate her soup with Gracie, pushed back her bowl, and put her head on her crossed arms on the table. "Gracie, I'll rest my eyes for a moment."

When Chester came back with the undertakers, he found both of the friends fast asleep. He put his hand out and gently shook Doctor Sarah's shoulder.

"Doctor Sarah the men are here to take Mr. Bailey back with them. You wanted me to tell you." He stood, hat in hand, waiting.

Doctor Sarah arose, stretched her arms, and tugged her skirt back straight. "I was so tired, Chester. But just a few minutes of sleep and I feel much better. Gracie, do you want to go over with me?"

Something in Sarah's voice told Gracie she needed her support. "Sure." She peeked into Betsy's room as they left. Judith sat reading to her Mama from a book. "I'll be back soon," she called to the young girl.

The two undertakers, dressed in black, stood on the Baileys' porch with the hearse and horse on the road out front. They waited for instructions.

The doctor held out her hand as she approached them.

"Doctor Sarah, it's good to see you," the tallest one stepped forward and shook her hand. He was the one in charge. "Chester said you wanted to talk to us."

"Yes," and Sarah proceeded to explain the cause of Henry's death. "I wanted you to know what we were dealing with and that we need to be careful when he's moved. It's like the original case we had when I first met you. Do you remember?"

"Yes, Ma'am. I'll get the extra sheet from the hearse and bring it to you. Then we'll get the casket and place it in the house where you indicate."

The next few minutes ensued like a ceremony and were accomplished with dignity and solemnity and according to Doctor Sarah's instructions. She was given the extra sheet to hold.

Grant stood looking on at the preparations. The three chairs were placed in a row outside the bedroom. The wooden casket was positioned on them.

Doctor Sarah went to Grant. She put her arm around him and steered him into the old man's bedroom. "This is the hard part for you. It's time to tell your father goodbye."

Grant nodded his head, knowing he'd been doing just that for several minutes with so many memories running through his mind. Here was the man who'd raised, educated, and loved him—his earthly anchor for many years. From now on, he'd be alone and on his own. How would life be without Pa? He nodded again at the doctor. His tears fell on the sheet which they wrapped the lifeless, shrunken body within—the one under him on his bed. With one last look, he placed the end over his father's face and wiped his own with the back of his hand.

Instead of the undertakers coming in to remove the body, Grant gathered his Pa in his arms and walked to the casket. The men helped position Henry Bailey within and placed the lid on without fastening it down. "Will this afternoon at four be acceptable for the burial?" the tall one asked Grant. "We'll have everything ready by then."

"Yes, I'll be there."

The two undertakers, Grant, and Chester removed the body from the house, walked to the hearse and pushed the coffin inside. The men mounted to the seat of the horse-drawn hearse, and with a flick of the reins, Henry "Hurricane" Bailey was driven out of sight.

It seemed everyone breathed a sigh—some in relief and some in sorrow.

When Grant went back inside, the new, clean extra sheet had been placed on the bed. Gracie went to him and gave him a hug. "I have some soup on the stove. Right now, you need strengthening for what's coming later on today." She did not take no for an answer, but took his arm and steered him out the door. Everyone else followed.

After eating, the company got up to go their separate ways until the afternoon.

"Doctor Sarah, will you tell Ruby Eliza I'd like for her to accompany me to the burial?"

"We'll both come, if there's no one in the office," assured the doctor.

"Me, too," agreed Chester, following his mentor out the door.

Chapter Thirty-Three

The Truth Comes Out

After the short service by Pastor Gridley on the hilltop, everyone who attended hurried back to Betsy's home. Gracie still had to make sure her ladies were doing well.

On the way to the funeral, Doctor Sarah and Ruby Eliza had gone by Cowboy's and ordered stew beef for everyone along with cornbread and pecan pies. Ernie was gracious enough to deliver the repast after it was cooked and ready. The food sat on the kitchen cupboard.

Gracie and Judith poked the coals in the stove and heated up the meal while everyone made themselves at home.

Hats went on pegs in the wall, and Grant and Chester carried chairs from the Bailey house so everyone could have a seat at the table or in the kitchen area.

Grant sat down and stretched his feet and legs out in front of him. He relaxed his shoulders and with a long-drawn-out sigh was the first to speak. "I'm so glad our pastor could hold the funeral, although he'd never seen my father but once. Pa wanted to come to church. He couldn't sit through a long service. Too many aches and pains from arthritis. Too much hard work in his past."

"Yes, I wish the pastor could have stayed for our meal," offered Doctor Sarah. "We have plenty."

"He apologized, saying he had to go and work on his sermon for Sunday," added Grant, running his fingers through his hair, pulling in a lot of air and letting it out in a rush. He sat in the place of honor in the rocking chair from the front porch which everyone had left vacant. His stress over his father's death was obvious.

Ruby Eliza, who had settled beside Grant, put her hand on his arm and asked, "Did your Pa always go to church with you when he was younger?"

"Yes, especially when we moved to Missouri while I went to school. Before that Jason always taught us on Sunday."

"Weren't there churches in the Black Hills?" Ruby Eliza asked, not understanding how remote the area was in the late 1850's.

Grant smiled. "No, not wooden structures with steeples. The church was the beautiful tall spruce and pine forests, and the warmth of Jason and Pa's cabin with a fire in the fireplace. We sat around the kitchen table while Jason taught us from the Holy Bible. No, there were no churches in the Black Hills back then. No other people either, only Flower." Grant seemed transported to the site as he spoke—remembering.

"Flower?" questioned Gracie, thinking this may have been Hurricane's second wife.

Grant smiled again. "A grizzly bear, Gracie. She visited at times with her cubs. Our horses and mules went crazy when she was around."

"Oh." Gracie nodded her head, understanding.

Judith ventured a question. "Were there Indians in the Black Hills?"

Everyone grinned. "Yes, dear. My father once saw Crazy Horse running some beautiful wild horses in an arroyo."

"Crazy Horse!" Judith exclaimed. "I wonder if your Pa was scared. I would have been."

"My Pa wasn't afraid of anything," stated Grant, his face again showing sorrow.

Doctor Sarah asked, "You said you moved out of the Black Hills."

"Yes, so I could go to a school of higher learning. Jason got work as a teacher in the grade school where we lived, and sometimes he laid stone on occasion for fireplaces or homes. Pa worked shoeing horses and blacksmithing. He was good at it."

"What was Jason's last name?" asked Gracie. This wasn't *the* question she wanted to ask, but it was a starter.

"His name was Douglas, Jason Douglas. He was a pastor to the Indians in Minnesota. While there, his wife disappeared and was never found. He came to the Black Hills to find peace. He did, and so did my Pa—find peace, that is. I never knew what happened to Pa to cause him unrest. Seemed to be a closed subject, if mentioned."

"What about your mother?" asked Ruby Eliza. "You never talk about her."

This was the one question Gracie wanted answered. Putting down her stirring spoon, she leaned a little closer across the table to hear the response.

"I don't know anything of my mother." Grant stood up to help serve the hot food.

"No, no. We'll serve the food," indicated Gracie by holding out her hand and pushing it up and down in a please sit-down gesture. She started filling plates, thinking of what he'd just said.

His answer was not what Gracie expected. The words took her by surprise. "How can that be?" she asked. "Surely Henry talked of her."

"He didn't know my mother," stated Grant, receiving his plate of food from Chester.

Gracie's eyebrows furrowed. She wanted to laugh, because that wasn't possible if he was Grant's father. Suddenly a glimmer of hope ran through her mind. Maybe her next question would solve her dilemma. But she didn't get to ask it.

Doctor Sarah did. "Was Henry not your father, Grant?"

Gracie held her breath for the answer.

Grant's face looked pained, as he explained, "I don't know who my father or mother were." He went on to explain how the military found him by himself, in an old log cabin they assumed was his home, with no indication of what had happened to the rest of his family. "Before that, I don't recall. I guess I would have died if they hadn't come along. But, knowing they couldn't leave me there alone, they put me on a pony they found in a shed at the homestead. "I left with them to complete their mission—looking for Indians who were renegade in Nebraska Territory."

He had paused when Ruby Eliza asked, "You don't remember anything about your parents?"

Grant looked at her and shook his head. "No, nothing." He squeezed her hand. He would have preferred telling her these details in an intimate setting, but he continued on. "One afternoon a few days later, the patrol had camped a bit early. Henry rode into the area and was taken to the commanding officer. The Captain asked Henry to take me with him, because the patrol had several more weeks of travel and searching the area. Any day could be filled with danger, and I presented the possibility of getting hurt or of slowing them down. Henry refused. Later, he told me he didn't want me as a responsibility for the same reason. He was on a search for peace."

"If Henry didn't want you, how did you happen to go with him," asked Doctor Sarah, as everyone sat intrigued by Grant's story.

"It's very simple. Henry was worn out by his long day. He slept soundly, snoring in his tent which he'd positioned at a few steps from the main camp next to a large tree. The patrol mounted up before sunrise. A junior officer took me to Pa's tent and placed me inside. They left as quietly as they could. When my Pa woke up, he had a new responsibility—me." Grant paused again, this time smiling at another fond memory.

"Please, this is fascinating," said Ruby Eliza, leaning toward the man she had grown to love and feeling his hesitation at telling the story of his life.

Gracie had *almost* relaxed during Grant's talk, especially after finding out Henry wasn't his father. "How did you get the name Grant?" she asked.

"Granted by God as a second chance was what Jason told my Pa after we showed up back at his cabin in the Black Hills. I remember Jason winking, and my Pa laughing at the comment. He said, 'That's surely true.' And they called me Grant. The rest you know."

There was chatter among them as they sat eating the remainder of their cold stew and cornbread. Gracie was wondering if she should finish Grant's story with a confession. This wasn't necessary because the problem of marriage between Grant and Ruby Eliza was solved. Still … wouldn't Press want her to tell *all* the truth. Not telling the facts had gotten P.T. into trouble which wasn't finished even now.

In the midst of the conversation, Judith solved her problem. "Mr. Bailey, what was your Pa saying when I came to bring you food yesterday. I thought he was callin' for me. Judi …"

"Yes, or Judea. I couldn't hear clearly, so that's a question I can't answer."

Okay, Gracie, here's your chance. Her mouth opened and, "I think I can answer the question." All heads and eyes turned in her direction. "Was he saying Jedediah?" she asked of Grant.

"Yes," his brow furrowed as he looked at her intently. "That's exactly what he said. How would you know, Gracie?"

"Because his only son, Jedediah, was my first husband and Ruby Eliza's father."

There it was. The whole truth, out in the open for everyone to hear. Gracie watched her daughter to see what her response would be.

Ruby Eliza and Doctor Sarah were the only ones who weren't amazed! Doctor Sarah knew because of letters written to her years ago. She was sworn to secrecy after the adoption. But Ruby Eliza …

Gracie was flabbergasted. It was obvious this wasn't news to her. "How did you know, Ruby Eliza?"

"Grandpa Tipton told me. And Momma, you have to remember, I'm a nurse. I can count on my fingers." Ruby Eliza was nodding as she spoke—almost a *shame on you* action.

Gracie sat laughing at the table while shaking her head.

"Momma, you might as well tell Grant and everyone else *the whole story*. I'd like to hear it too."

"Shouldn't we clean up the dishes first?" ventured Gracie, looking at the mess in the kitchen.

"No!" came from the group. "We want to hear," several said, nodding their heads.

Then Gracie told the assembled group the rest of Henry "Hurricane" Bailey's history as far as she knew it.

Chapter Thirty-Four

Back to the Glory B Ranch

Two weeks had passed since Gracie's return from Abilene. Just long enough for her to settle into her old routine, and feel comfortable in her surroundings. Taking a break from the day's chores, she sat in the shade from the early September sun. It shone on the familiar valley below as Gracie rested on the front porch swing at the Glory B in the Glass Mountains.

Down below her the clinking sound of horseshoes being thrown broke the stillness of her surroundings. The cow-boys had had chores close to the bunkhouse today. They'd eaten their food, and were taking a brief respite to relieve the monotony by a friendly game. Occasionally, a distant yelp of triumph could be heard.

She and Maria had spent the morning peeling apples and making apple butter for the approaching winter. She'd had an extra morning-baked biscuit coated in butter along with a sampling of the mixture just before the noon meal, saying she needed to taste the new batch to make sure it had enough sugar.

"I shouldn't have eaten the extra biscuit," she said to a yellow butterfly which flitted amongst some late summer flowers planted near the steps to the ground. She blamed the browned flour concoction as an over indulgence and the cause of her willingness to nod in the sun.

She had closed her eyes for a few minutes after the noon meal. Her brief nap wasn't long.

Disturbing her rest, Press and P.T. came out onto the porch. Press came over and sat beside her on the swing. He put his arm around his wife, pulled her to him, and kissed her on the cheek. "Gracie, P.T. and I've decided on something."

"Uh, oh. What's going on," replied wife and mother, blinking in the bright sunlight, and noticing the letter she'd just read from Ruby Eliza still lay safely on her lap.

"P.T. and I are going to take a trip."

Gracie sat forward in the swing and turned to ask Press, "Where are you going?"

"Momma, we're going to the Big Bend and camp out." P.T. stood at the porch railing, leaning on his crutches.

Gracie turned toward her son. "Why? I'm barely used to being back home, and I'm enjoying your company."

Press explained, "We want to go before the snow falls, see the sights, and visit the Boquillas Hot Springs on the Rio Grande. The Spring is supposed to have curative powers."

"So, when is this journey going to start?"

"In the morning—the sooner the better." Press looked at Gracie, his eyes asking her to agree.

Gracie didn't immediately answer, but she knew Press was right. Their son needed to address this physical problem now. Finally, she nodded her head in agreement. "Is there anything I can do to help?"

"No. We've been packing our saddlebags, and we'll take a pack mule to carry the necessary things like tent and stools. We've thought of food …"

Gracie interrupted here. "I'll get the food ready. Do you have a list?"

Press nodded his head. "It's not complete, so you can add to the items. And we'll take the campfire kit we keep for spending the night when we travel and overnight at the far reaches of the Glory B."

"How long do you plan on staying?" Gracie dreaded the answer to this question.

Press discussed the issue with himself as he answered. "We'll need several days to get to the Big Bend and several days coming back—plus at least two weeks to roam around." He looked at Gracie and said, "We may be gone more than a month, sweetheart." *Maybe sweetheart would soften the blow*, he thought.

"Sweetheart, huh." Then Gracie laughed. "Take your time. If the Boquillas Hot Springs help, don't come back until they've done as much to restore P.T.'s movement as possible. If you're leaving in the morning, I'd better get busy." She leaned over and gave Press a peck on the cheek. She grasped the letter, and rising from the swing, got up and walked to her son. She gave him a big hug. Then she disappeared into the house, calling as she left, "By the way, Ruby Eliza is engaged to be married. They're planning on a late November wedding."

"What?" called Press, his eyes open in surprise. He jumped up and followed her through the door. P.T. heard him ask, "When and how?"

Gracie and Press had talked about their son's lack of motivation in addressing his left leg's problems. He complained because working his muscles hurt, and seemed content to walk with crutches for the rest of his life. They both felt he could do better, and the longer the problem wasn't addressed, the more likely he'd be assisted by the wooden supports forever.

~

"It seems we've stood here and done this before," stated Gracie, looking around at the group below the front porch steps which included in-laws and siblings. The sun wasn't up, but it's coming light lit the gathering as dusk faded into sunlight. "This time, we have more people to see you two off." She walked down the steps to greet Press and P.T., who waited with their saddled horses.

"Yep, Mrs. Stockton. Thomas and me can't wait to see him leave." Winky nodded at P.T. He was kidding of course. His concern had been great when his wounded friend had come back from the trail drive, and Press had told Gracie, he'd hovered over P.T. like a mother hen.

All eyes turned to the porch. Sarah Susannah moved daintily down the steps and went to stand by Thomas. He blushed at her obvious choice of him, but they immediately joined hands.

"I think we're ready to go, aren't we, Son?" The father clapped his son on the back.

"Yes, Poppa." Going to the wrong side of the horse, holding and pulling on the pommel, and using one crutch, he balanced while putting his foot in his father's hand and letting his father elevate him so he could sling his damaged leg over the saddle.

Getting on his horse was awkward this way, but by now, Star was used to this strange act, and accepted this odd method of mounting her. She turned her head to watch her owner's movements.

Press strapped the crutches to the pack mule. He turned, and embracing Gracie gave her a quick kiss and mounted up. "We'll see you all in a few weeks," he said, waving his hand as he kicked his horse with his bootheel.

He'd gone only a few yards when Gracie, cupping her hand to her mouth, called after him, "Remember your last adventure to the south, and don't go near any rattlesnakes."

Press threw up his hand, but she knew he'd be smiling.

One hour later, the two were revisiting the old wagon road beside the Glass Mountains with the sun's early morning glow illuminating the vista in an orange foggy haze.

"Poppa, do you think it's goin' to rain?" asked P.T., knowing this color didn't bode well for dry weather.

"I certainly hope not," replied his father, content to ride in silence and enjoy his son's presence, knowing the outcome of P.T.'s escapade in Abilene might have been much different.

Days passed. Going south, they rode through a flat grassland with the high mountains punched from the earth into the sky. These reared from the earth on their right hand side.

Warning whistles from the prairie dog village announced their presence as they went past the Johnston Ranch. Press noted the cattle they were herding now, enclosed in barbed wire fencing. If the opportunity came to drive longhorns south to a railhead, their fencing would pose a problem. How would future Texans solve this problem, he wondered.

Upon seeing the hated strands of metal, Press made the comment, "Texas is changin' and growin' as much as you are, Son."

"Are we goin' to stop and say hello?"

"No, we don't have time. Maybe we'll pass one of the boys as we ride through."

They continued the ride toward the new village of Marathon, established when the Southern and Pacific Railroad extended a line to support the military at Fort Peña Colorada.

On his last visit to Fort Stockton, Press understood there'd be a few houses and a place where he could buy supplies. If not, there was always the sutler's store at the military camp.

The Glass Mountains grew higher and higher with grasslands spreading from the base for miles toward the rising sun. Press kept thinking ranchers would soon be grazing cattle on this range. The one thing they would need was water. Far up on the hillside, he spied a flat area where a house and buildings could be built, reminding him of the Glory B. Getting there would necessitate several switchbacks. He wasn't interested, but the view from the place would be spectacular.

The sky was clear. Looking up, he could see individual rocks and trees in the gray, olive, and beige landscape. Finding a break to go through the ridgeline, if you wanted to cross to the other side, would have been difficult to impossible.

In the daytime, antelope and prairie dogs were the only ground animals they saw. The rest were under the earth in burrows, staying cool. Hawks, eagles, and vultures flew overhead. At night, there were rustlings in the grass and among the scrub brush—snakes or rats or armadillo.

"Poppa, is that the end of the mountains?" P.T. indicated a graduated bluff, sticking out and towering into the sky, pointing toward Marathon and the Big Bend.

"Yes, it is."

"Do you remember being here before?"

"Yes, vaguely, years ago with my father. There were still isolated groups of Apache and Commanche Indians in the area. We avoided them on our trip. In fact, it's not been long since the Apache renegade, Victorio, was captured in the region."

"How far is Marathon?"

"Are you getting hungry, Son?"

"Yes, I was hoping for some home cooking for a change." The words were out of his mouth before he could stop them.

"You don't like my cooking?" Press drew back and feigned surprise.

"I don't mean yours is bad. I was thinking a change ..." P.T. didn't finish. Star finished the sentence with a snort.

"I know what you meant, and I wouldn't be opposed to someone else feeding me tonight either. I hope we'll be there by sundown. Maybe we can find a bed to sleep in, also."

"Now you're talking," said P.T. with a big smile on his face. His sleeping bag didn't do much for the hard ground.

"We'll turn right here and head west into the sun," advised his father, pointing to a noticeable road and pulling his hat down to reduce the afternoon's sunlight glare.

"When we leave Marathon, how far to the Big Bend and the Boquillas Hot Springs?"

"About four or five days if we push the horses, but I don't want to force them during the day. The air is still hot, and the Bend will be very hot. We'll take it easy. There's lots to see on the way."

At Marathon, the only place to stay was surrounded by tents. No Vacancy, the sign read.

"You don't have any room?" asked Press of the proprietor.

"No," said the greasy-haired man who owned the place. "But," he held up a finger, "I do have mats, I'll rent you."

Press went outside and looked up at P.T. "What do you think, Son?"

Sweating in the hot afternoon sun, P.T. was nodding a yes. "Could we rent them for the rest of our trip and bring them back on our way out?" Two rolled up mats soon joined the other items on the pack mule. Press bought them outright.

Looking for a place to stake their tent, Press decided to join the others in the area. He stood by as P.T. got off his horse.

P.T. could manage this by himself, but the crutches needed to be brought to him. He helped as much as possible as his father set up the tent. By now, he was an expert at using his wooden supports.

"Son, let's go eat." There was only one place. They had soup beans and cornbread.

"Poppa, that's the best meal since we left home."

Press laughed and didn't comment. If there was anything else to eat, P.T. rarely ate soup beans. "Come on. Let's make the acquaintance of who's staying in the other tents."

Press found out the tents held an expedition of men who had been studying the area's mineral deposits and water resources. Later, he got into a conversation with the group's leader, a John Love from Austin. They had finished their mission and were headed home.

"The state of Texas has aquifers under the surface of the land. During the driest spells, if wells were dug, there'd be plenty of water," the head man explained. "Also, water for irrigation of crops and other possibilities by drawing water from an aquifer.

"What's an aquifer?" asked P.T.

Press was listening, too. He always had problems when there was a dry spell. He'd taken care of some of it with large hand-dug ponds and dams which collected water when the rain fell. In times of prolonged drought, these went dry.

Love explained, "An aquifer is a large pocket of water under the surface of the land. It can only be reached by digging wells and putting in windmills to pump the water to the surface. This digging of wells has only just begun in Texas. But I think where no water runs in rivers to irrigate the land, windmills will be seen all over the state. The Governor has been interested in maps, detailing where these might be. We've been in several areas working to develop those for him."

"How do you determine where the water is located?" asked Press, awed by this man's expertise.

P.T. also listened raptly to his explanation.

John Love talked about the development of a conceptual model, forming an understanding of the physical geography, climate, and geology of an area. Then the team researched other aquifers located close by.

"Then we blend the two and establish the hydrogeologic setting, consisting of the hydro-stratigraphy, structural geometry, hydraulic properties, water levels, and regional groundwater flow, and recharge. Interactions between surface water and groundwater, well discharge, and water quality are all involved in the information we compile."

By this time, P.T.'s head was spinning with information, most of which he didn't understand. He continued to listen, especially to talk of drilling wells.

"Is there an aquifer under the Glass Mountains?" Press waited for an answer.

"Yes, the Edwards—Trinity Aquifer runs under it. Why do you ask?"

"Because, I live on the northern part, and I have problems having enough water for my herds of longhorns."

"Windmills will solve your problems. My guess is you wouldn't have to dig too deep since there are some springs in the area, maybe fifty to three hundred feet."

"That's great to know. Did I hear you say you have maps of the Big Bend? My son and I are headed for the Boquillas Hot Springs on the Rio Grande. We've heard it has curative properties."

Love had noticed P.T.'s lameness. "Yes, I do have maps. I'll get one of my team to trace the one you need to get to the springs. You'll have it in the morning. By the way, we were just there. Try to follow our tracks for the best way in," he suggested.

"Do you know where I can get information on windmills?"

Love wrote an address on a pad of paper. "Try this for starters. Also, my address is below. Let me know if you need more information. Governor Ireland is always willing to help."

Press looked over the paper. "Thanks, I'll keep windmills in mind."

~

The next day, after leaving Marathon, the two went through miles of flat, grassy prairie with a vista of sharp peaks always in front of them. Press explained they were dormant volcanoes from years ago. He knew this from the map Love furnished and which he checked at intervals in the day.

In two days, they were riding through the area of the volcanoes and seeing dikes. When given the map of the area, Love had explained some of the symbols noted thereon. Dikes were where molten lava had pushed through cracks in the earth, forming long, ragged lines across the hills surrounding the entrance to the park. Love explained they were seen everywhere in the Big Bend area.

On the fourth day, Press and P.T. arrived at Persimmon Gap. Up until they got to the gap, the young man felt like he'd been transported to another world.

He sucked in his breath as he looked across several miles of valley to another peak, Mount Emory, which protruded into the sky.

"It's in the Chisos Mountains," explained his father to P.T.'s obvious awe. "It's another huge volcano top."

The world below where they sat, turned all shades of gray, olive, and beige. In places an arroyo had a few scraggly, green trees indicating water at times—no large towering ones. Even most of the bushes looked gray. The grass was mostly in tufts, not fields.

"Wow, Poppa, can you imagine what was going on in the Big Bend years ago."

"I'm glad I wasn't here," said Press. "I can imagine plenty of fire and fury from the peaks with chunks of rock flying through the air, and ash floating and covering everything in sight." He paused to look at the breathtaking scene. "Do you want to get off Star? I need to spread the map on this rock and get our bearings." He pointed to a flat rock beside the trail leading off the gap.

"Yes, it would be nice to take a break. I sure wish there was a tree to get under." He dismounted and looked around. There was nothing but rocks and cactus, but one tall stone had possibilities. Press handed him his crutches. Threading through numerous rocks, he headed for the only shade in the area.

For the next two days, because of the oppressive heat, Press and P.T. rode in the early morning and late afternoon. There had been enough traffic in and out of the area so a clear trail could be followed, and there was always the wonderfully detailed map.

P.T. made the comment, "Poppa it's almost like we're the only humans on the earth."

Press responded, "Now you know how Adam and Eve felt." He waved his hand over the vastness of the desert surrounding them.

"Yes, Poppa, but they were in a beautiful garden."

Early one afternoon, they located Dugout Wells which was on Love's map. Actually a spring, they watered the horses and pack mule, filled their containers with water, and wandered around under taller trees in the area, taking a rest from constantly sitting in the saddle.

Suddenly, P.T., following an indention in the ground, where he could easily use his crutches, was confronted by a dark-gray, large pig-like animal with ugly looking tusks. He stopped and the hairy animal stopped, staring at each other. His heart started pounding. "Poppa, come here."

Press looked up from checking his horse's hooves, and spotted his son. "What's wrong?"

"I'm not sure if anything's wrong. Can you see this animal?"

Press took a few steps in P.T.'s direction. When he saw the animal, he advised, "Just stand still. I think it will be the first to move.

P.T. stood still and the piglike animal left, in no hurry at all. There were grunts in the brush around the area where it disappeared. "What *was* that?"

"That, my son, was a herd of Javelina. They are native to the area. Usually they aren't a problem, but if small ones are around, they can charge you. The large male did not feel threatened by you."

"Javelina, huh. I'll remember that name." He turned on his crutches and went to mount up.

With their horses and mule well-watered, they continued on, slowly going downhill. They rode through a low area filled with sandbars, obviously where most of the rainwater from the massive Big Bend flowed. The bed was now dry but with a hint of moisture here and there. On the other side they ascended through craggy rocks until they reached another flat dry plain.

Looking at the map on the third day out of Persimmon Gap, Press noted, "We'd better be looking for a trail leading off to the right. We're not far from the springs now." They separated to cover the flat, rocky area—never getting out of sight of each other.

Thanks to Love's instructions, it wasn't long until P.T. called, "Over here, Poppa. I see a trampled area where several horses have walked.

Heading down the slowly developing arroyo, the flat area where they rode turned into a rocky dry ravine with rolling hills on each side. This indention in the earth ended in a canebrake area beside the Rio Grande. Several tall cottonwood trees towered in the air over the area.

"Right here, Poppa," pointed P.T. "This is where I want to pitch our tent." He was indicating the tallest tree whose shade covered a big area next to the river. "In the afternoon this will be the coolest place in the Big Bend."

Press had to agree with him. He started for the pack mule to get P.T.'s crutches when the loudest, harshest bellow came from back up the ravine. Startled, he stopped and listened, hoping he'd hear the noise again, so he could pinpoint where the sound came from and identify the offender.

"What was that, Poppa? My heart jumped in my chest."

Press put his finger to his lips. "Sssh."

There it was again. Looking toward the direction of the noise, he waited to see if there was movement. There was! "Look, P.T., standing on the rocks."

When P.T. followed his father's pointed finger, he started laughing. Two long-eared, wild burros were standing on a hilltop they'd just passed.

Press was grinning. "They'll be down for a drink, but we won't see them," he advised his son. Come on, let's set up the tent and ready our camp, then we'll search out the springs. We'll walk past this stand of cane and go east a few hundred feet." He waved his hand down a disappearing trail near the river. "If I remember correctly, there's sights to see on the way."

When the tent was up and the stakes in the ground, Press threw a rope over the lowest limb of the cottonwood tree and pulled their provisions up off the ground. There'd be no marauding animals into their grub while they stayed here.

Press staked the horses and mule to graze. They were ready to walk to the springs.

"In case you want to go into the water to cool off, empty your pockets." Press emptied his and placed his and P.T.'s on their sleeping mats. In this deserted area, there'd be no possibility of anything being stolen. They hadn't seen another human in the whole of Big Bend.

The walk was level. At first, you couldn't see the river for the cane growing on its banks. Then it thinned out and there were glimpses of the rushing, gurgling Rio Grande flowing majestically by them—the border between the United States of America and Mexico.

Press pointed out pictographs on the rock walls which rose above and over them beside the river. P.T. took a good look but couldn't decipher the etching on the stone. The figures were bleached out from many years of weather.

Farther on, Press pointed to the conical nests of swift swallows, which hung protected from the elements under a rock overhang. "Where are the birds?"

Press chuckled, "Gone south for the winter. They feel the first nip in the air and leave. They'll come back next year to the same nest and lay their eggs. I wonder if we'll be feeling a little nip tonight ourselves, since we're not camped in the Chihuahuan Desert but on the Rio Grande."

Finally, a glimpse of why they'd ridden two weeks—the Boquillas Hot Springs.

P.T. was sorely disappointed. The hollowed-out rock was full of mud and debris. "Poppa the place is a mess," said an upset P.T., being tired from the walk on his crutches.

Seeing the distress on P.T.'s face, his father said, "Yes, it is. Let's get in and clean it out." Press pulled off his boots and eased into the water. He started lifting logs, stones, and limbs, tossing them into the river, waiting on his son to respond.

P.T. watched for a moment. Then he held out his hand, "Poppa." His father helped him with his boots and steadied him into the pool. The rocks in the bottom hurt his feet, but he bent down and followed his father's lead, throwing rocks into the shallow, rippling water of the Rio Grande. The rock bowl, surrounding the hot spring, was only inches above the river.

After working for several minutes, Press sat down on the basin's edge to rest, putting his hand in the river. "Wow, you can tell the difference." He splashed water toward P.T.

"Ouch, that water is cold! Poppa, why is the spring so full of debris?"

"When the rain falls upriver, it causes the river to flood and rush over the side of this basin, rolling in and filling it with trash and rocks," explained his father. "Another factor is the curve of the river. The arc directs the water this way." Press looked at the dirty water which the bubbling spring was trying to clear up. "I'll have to dream up something to get the silt out in the morning."

"Was it this way when you and grandfather came to visit?"

"Yes, it was," Press gave a slight nod of his head. "The river's route may have changed some, and the curve may be sharper."

They continued to clean the bottom of the spring.

One time when P.T. raised up, he spotted a hole in the canebrake on the far bank of the river. The daylight was rapidly turning into shadows, but he thought he saw a bench in the far darkness of the opening. Not saying anything to his father, he'd wait to make sure. Maybe, he was imagining things.

When all the major work was done to clear the spring of debris, Press and P.T. beat it back to their campsite. After changing into dry clothes, Press looked for firewood, and P.T. hung the wet pants and shirts on bushes in the area.

"Poppa, what are we eating for supper?" asked P.T. when his father returned.

"Tonight, we'll open cans and heat food over the campfire. Tomorrow, we'll take time to look for a jackrabbit or a squirrel to roast over the fire."

Chapter Thirty-Five

The Angel on the Rio Grande

The following morning, the alarm clock went off. Press nudged his son and said, "I believe we've been rousted out of bed."

Rubbing his eyes, P.T. sat up and listened to the woodpecker, working away, high in the cottonwood branches. Rat-a-tat, rat-a-tat, rat-a-tat. "Poppa, will we hear that noisy bird every morning?"

"I guess we'll find out tomorrow. I'll start the fire so we can cook breakfast."

The morning meal consisted of the last of the smoked bacon and some eggs from Marathon cooked over the campfire.

The air was cooler under the cottonwood trees, and the two humans lazed around camp, just as others long ago had rested—the Comanche, a thousand of them, looking in expectation across the river at the prospects on the other side. They had raided the Mexicans every year about this time, looking for supplies and slaves to take north to their villages in North Texas and Oklahoma. The United States military had taken care of those raids, not long after the Stocktons had moved into the Glass Mountains.

And last, but not least, were renegade bands of the Apache, who holed up in the Big Bend and raided the unsuspecting, who settled above the Bend in the Texas midlands.

Press sat looking at the map where a Mexican village, Boquillas del Carmen was noted. Love had said several people lived there. They used the river for transportation and food. He had said he often spotted them working on the other side of the river and waved. He always received a responsive acknowledgement.

"P.T., do you think we should plan on a dip in the hot springs in the morning and one in the afternoon?"

"Yes, Poppa, and I'm ready to go." He had pulled from the bushes and folded the wet clothes from yesterday. They would be ready to wear on the afternoon's trip to the spring. "Should I take a bar of soap?

"Why not? I can't think of a better place to bathe, and before we go, I want to cut your pants leg open so we can work on your leg. Better to do it here and now." Press pulled his knife out of his pocket and cut the side of P.T.'s pants up above the knee.

On day two, Press and P.T. set off down the path to the springs. The father was walking behind his son, thinking *what do I expect to gain from this trip? Will the stories we've heard about the water's curative effects be true?* These accounts had been passed from person to person, and there was no way of knowing. Press heaved a sigh. *What does it matter? It matters a lot, because I desperately want my son to walk. But if nothing changes, my son and I will at least get to know each other better.*

Press had carried a bunch of rushes he'd gathered from the canebrake. With twine he'd made something to sweep the mud from the bottom of the spring which this morning flowed crystal clear. He stood mystified by the sight.

~

Alejandro was nodding in the sun on the Mexican side of the Rio Grande. Although he was protected by his canebrake shelter and large sombrero, the reflection off the water, low sound of the ripples in the Rio Grande before him, and the heat of the day made him drowsy.

A resident of Boquillas del Carmen, he was sitting in his favorite place fishing when he was disturbed by voices coming down the trail on the United States side. He jumped up from his small wooden bench and gathering in his fishing line, retreated to the back of his shelter—bench in hand. He placed the bench on the ground and stood in the darkness at the back, watching the two men as they appeared at the hot spring, named after his village.

In the excitement of visitors, he'd forgotten the fish on a string in the flowing water. He couldn't get them out with the Americans on the other side without revealing his presence. Moving onto the trail at the back of the canebrake, he waited.

He noticed the older man's protective attitude toward the younger man—the one using the crutches. He guessed they were father and son. He did not have children, something he and his wife regretted.

Alejandro knew something about disabling injuries because he and his wife had helped boys and men in his village through several devastating gunshot wounds and fractures of arms and legs. Everyone agreed, his wife had miracle fingers when working with injuries. He had buried her two years ago. The hurt of her going was only now diminishing.

Tears gathered in his eyes as he watched the two across the river. He grinned as the father splashed his son with the colder water from the river, and he almost laughed out loud with the son's response.

He didn't normally spy on people, but something about these two made him curious. What were they there for? He decided he'd find out. Maybe he could help. But he would be patient, until he knew this father and son were safe for him to approach.

When they left, he got his string of fish and headed for his village. He would be late getting there, because he had several miles to walk.

He decided he would clean the fish and have them for breakfast the next day.

The following morning, he was at his canebrake retreat early. Wading across the river, he plunged his broom into the water of the hot springs. He didn't work long until the mud was gone from the bottom. He felt sure the water would be crystal clear by the time of the two men's arrival.

Press stood in wonder at the clean appearance of Boquillas Hot Spring. You could see clear to the bottom. "What happened?"

"An angel came overnight and cleaned the rest of the dirt out," suggested P.T., laughing in amazement.

"Well, I'd sure like to thank him. Let's get in."

Since they could see the bottom, it was easier for P.T. to enter. After a brief struggle, he sat down on the rim, and his father came near.

"P.T., we'll use the same exercises Doctor Sarah gave us to help loosen your muscles. She said the warm water should help as I work on your leg. Are you ready?"

His son grimaced because he knew what was coming. He held up his injured leg, pulled the pant's cloth out of the way, and waited for the worst. His father had tried before, but his experience was with cattle. He didn't mean to be, but he wasn't very gentle. P.T. watched him hunker down. He lasted until he couldn't stand the pain, and then he said, "Stop, Poppa. We will have to try again this afternoon."

Press wanted to stop as much as his son. He hurt when P.T. hurt. They stayed in the warm water, relaxing until they both got hungry. Then they went back to camp and ate a light lunch of bread and cheese.

Press took the horses and the mule to the edge of the river to water them. When he came back, he asked, "How about a short ride down the trail beside the river? We'll take the horses and our rifles and see how far we can go."

"Are we looking for our supper?"

"Yes, unless you want more eggs, bread, and cheese and the bread is almost gone."

P.T. nodded his head. "I'd like exploring past the hot springs."

Press saddled the two horses and looped the canteens onto the pommel. He helped P.T. into his saddle and mounted up. Press rode ahead.

When they got to the hot springs, P.T. called to his father, "Sure didn't take long on horses. Maybe we should ride down tomorrow." He also noted that the bar of soap had either swum or walked to a new place. He'd left it on top of a large rock and now it resided on a flat one next to the water. He glanced quickly at the opening in the canebrake. In shock, he realized there was a stool, and in the back, movement.

Again, he did not alert his father. Whoever was there, he felt had no bad intentions.

During his afternoon session at the hot springs, the soap was there, but the stool was gone. They had eggs, cheese, and bread for supper with a small can of beans, because they only saw one jackrabbit, and it went into its hole before Press could shoot it.

~

The following morning, a freshly dressed jack rabbit lay on wide green leaves on a rock by the trail. A startled Press looked in all directions. He soon had his who and where questions answered.

In the canebrake sat a Mexican man in a wide sombrero. "*Hola,*" he called over the ripples of the Rio Grande. He got up, walked carefully over the rocks in the bed of the river, and came to the hot spring. He pointed to himself. "*Me llamo Alejandro.*"

Press knew a smattering of Spanish because of Maria. He pointed to the rabbit. "*Gracias.*" Then he pointed to himself, "*Me llamo*, Press Stockton. *Mi hijo,* P.T."

The Mexican man pointed to himself and then to P.T. "*Ayudaré a tu hijo.*"

Press shook his head. He understood 'your son' but not the rest.

Alejandro grasped his lack of understanding. Instead, he helped P.T. sit down and take his boots and socks off. Then with Presses help, they eased him into the water where he sat down. Again, he said, *"Ayudaré a tu hijo."*

Press watched as Alejandro knelt in the water before P.T. He rolled up and handed the cut pants leg to the young man, gently examined the old wound, and felt the muscle.

Press could have sworn the man's slim fingers *saw* the damage inside. This man had knowledge of how to approach the dilemma. He'd done this exact procedure before.

After testing the area, Alejandro started to massage P.T.'s leg. He felt the muscle and worked in toward the scar, gently at first and finally more aggressively.

The warm water and moving fingers relaxed P.T. Unlike his father's attempts, he let go his anxiety and let Alejandro work on his muscles. When Alejandro was finished, he stood up and said, *"Adiós."*

Both Press and P.T. watched him walk back across the river. He took his cane pole with the fishing line and sat down to fish, waving goodbye to them.

The father and son, amazed by what had transpired this morning, took the rabbit and headed back to camp. Press roasted the rabbit over the campfire. "Dinner's ready, Son."

There was no response. When he turned around, he saw that P.T. had crawled into the tent. He was fast asleep. P.T. slept most of the afternoon. When he woke up, they ate some rabbit and returned to the spring.

Alejandro was waiting.

~

For five days, it was the same every day. Seven days passed. Alejandro motioned for Press to help him.

After the customary hot-water massage, he intended for P.T. to stand up.

"Careful," cautioned P.T as they helped him out of the basin onto the trail. On went his socks and boots.

When Press approached with the crutches, Alejandro shook his head and waved them away. *"No, no,"* he said, shaking his head.

Suddenly it dawned on Press and P.T. This was his stand-alone day. Today he would test his ability to balance on both legs and take a few steps without crutches.

With the two men supporting him on both sides, P.T. stood up. Cautiously, he put weight on both legs. At first, he looked scared, but then a smile appeared on his face.

"Let go," he told his father.

Press stepped away, but not too far away.

Alejandro, understanding what was happening, did the same.

"Well, praise God." said Press upon seeing that P.T. was supporting himself without crutches.

His son, elated that he was standing, decided to take a step. He made the first one and a second, but on the third he became unbalanced and started to fall.

Alejandro and Press caught him.

"No hay problema," said the Mexican, a big smile showing perfect white teeth.

Press understood him, because Maria said this expression at the Glory B. "Yes, no problem," he responded in English.

"Mañana." And then he was gone.

Press and P.T. watched him wade the river again.

By the end of the second week, P.T. could mount up on his horse and take several steps without a problem. Walking long distances would take time and perseverance. Now, it was time to head for home.

"Momma will be so surprised," said P.T., a beaming smile on his face.

"Yes, she will. How will we tell Alejandro goodbye? We don't have anything we can spare for a gift."

P.T. sat thinking. Abruptly, he came to a conclusion. "Poppa, we'll give him my crutches. I don't think I'll need them anymore."

"That's a wonderful idea. Are you sure?" His son was walking—but not far. Of course, not having the crutches would require him to stretch this limit.

"I'm sure. I've been praying at night for God's help. I think he sent Alejandro to help. Remember, I said an angel was near when we first came?"

"I do remember. We'll give him the crutches this afternoon, and head home in the morning."

~

Rat-a-tat, rat-a-tat, rat-a-tat. "Poppa, the alarm has gone off," said P.T., stirring on his mat, punching, and grinning at his father.

Press stretched his arms over his head and yawned. "Yes. I'll miss the old woodpecker." He sat up and sniffed the air. "Do I smell frying food?"

"You do!" P.T. threw back the tent flap and looked out. "It's Alejandro. He's cooking over the campfire." He crawled out of the tent, carefully stood up, and wandered toward the fire.

When they'd left the Mexican yesterday, it was with multiple hugs and the hint of tears in the old man's eyes. There was a bond between them all, not easily broken. He had taken the offered crutches. They were now tied on a burro along with what looked like supplies for a trip.

"Alejandro, are you going with us?" asked P.T. He wished he could speak the Spanish language. Why hadn't he listened to Maria talk?

There was a big smile on the Mexican's face at this joke he'd played on his friends. *"Iré y ayudaré,"* he explained, pointing toward the north. Hoping they would understand, he tried again by pointing to himself, to them, and to the north toward Marathon.

Press repeated his actions and then nodded his head in agreement. He didn't know how far their friend intended to go, but as far as he was concerned, the Glory B could be his stopping point. He would be a welcome addition to the staff at the ranch and to Mountain City.

~

Two weeks later with more than a nip in the air, three men rode up the hill and by the bunkhouse at the Glory B.

Blown in a day earlier during a wind and rain storm, Sarah Susannah was sweeping the front porch of dead leaves. When she looked up and saw the three coming to the house, she stood wondering who they were.

One looked like her father. And another looked like her brother, but who was the other one in a sombrero?

The one who looked like her father threw up his hand—an action familiar to her.

"Poppa!" she exclaimed and rushed into the house, yelling, "Momma, Momma, Poppa's back." She heard footsteps from everywhere in the house, as the people rushed to the front porch to welcome Press home. Even Maria hurried out of the kitchen to greet her favorite Stockton, forgetting her stirring spoon.

Gracie rushed down the steps of the house, hurried down the road, and grabbed the reins of Press's horse. At that moment, there was no one else in the world except the man she loved with all her heart, and his kiss would bring a flood of tears to her eyes. In fact, she was crying so hard, before the kiss, it was through a blur of tears she saw him dismount and hurry to her. She felt his lips on hers.

There was one long kiss and then multiple small ones all over her face. "Gracie," was the one word she heard, "Gracie."

When she got a chance, she blurted out, "I've been so concerned. You've been gone much longer than I thought you would. These separations have got to stop."

"Yes, you're right. We have been gone much longer than I thought we would. But, Sweetheart, you said not to come back if P.T. was making progress."

"I remember those words. I take them back." It was time to recognize the others in the party.

Press suggested, "Let's go on to the house, where we can get off our horses. We've ridden a long way today, and we are all tired and dusty."

Gracie went to P.T.

He leaned over so she could kiss him on the cheek. "This is my angel," he told his mother, waving at Alejandro.

Gracie looked at the Mexican man with a question in her eyes. He looked like flesh and blood to her.

The Mexican man, who couldn't understand a word spoken, smiled at her and touched his hat. He did understand the need for greetings.

At the porch, the scene was pandemonium—everyone greeting each other. When P.T. slid off his horse and walked without his crutches to the porch steps, there were cries of wonder and happiness. Even some, hearing the cries of greeting at the bunkhouse, rushed up the road to greet the travelers. Thomas and Winky waited for their chance to say hello.

Maria looked shyly at the Mexican man in the sombrero. He hadn't spoken a word but stood by watching the celebration. She sidled up to him and said, "*Hola,* who are you?" Realizing she'd spoken the question in English, she translated it into Spanish. When he answered in Spanish, she started peppering him with questions.

The combination of English and Spanish made the conversation at the bottom of the steps more confusing. Finally, Gracie told Press, "Let's go into the parlor. Some things have happened here which I'd like to talk to you about."

Everyone trooped into the house, with Press and Alejandro supporting P.T., because he hadn't mastered steps as yet. In the house, chairs were brought from the dining room and other areas so everyone could sit down. The story of P.T.'s miraculous change was the question the people in the room wanted answered.

Press sat by Gracie, while the others arranged themselves around the room.

"Sweetheart, before P.T tells his story, I need to tell you what's happened here. We've got ..." She didn't get any farther than those words.

A loud "Waa-a-a," sounded from the children's wing of the ranch house.

Press looked at Gracie in astonishment. "We have another baby," he exclaimed.

"No, dear, Mary Elizabeth and Peter have a baby boy. They've named him David Ormand Stockton after our pastor."

Press jumped up, and before Gracie could stop him, he headed toward the sound.

Some of the family followed him and others stayed behind. At the entrance of the largest room in the children's wing, Press and Gracie stopped.

Inside, the cradle Press had brought from Fort Stockton for Ruby Eliza stood by Mary Elizabeth's bedside. The new mother had her hand on the crib, rocking the crying baby to sleep, just like he and Gracie had done with all their brood.

Press walked quietly near, peering at his new, red-faced grandson. "May I?" he questioned, his hand on the clenched fist of the crying child.

"Yes, of course, Poppa," Mary Elizabeth agreed.

Wrapping the blanket around the child, he said, "Little Davey," in wonderment. The baby soon rested in the arms of his new Grandpoppa who bent to kiss him on the forehead. He settled into a rocking chair by the window, setting it in motion.

"How old is he?" asked his Grandpoppa after the baby quit crying, knowing he was nestled in strong, safe arms.

"Five days," was the reply.

Gracie had stayed back, observing the interaction between the two. "Sweetheart, you've added another name to your collection. How does it feel to be a Grandpoppa?"

"It's the *grandest* feeling in the world," replied her husband, grinning up at her.

Chapter Thirty-Six

Life Continues at the Glory B

"Gracie, I've figured out why grandparents like their grandchildren the best," stated Press one month later, after the carriage ride into Mountain City to see Little Davey. Peter, Mary Elizabeth, and Little David had gone home when the mother could fend for herself.

They were in bed and snuggled together under the coverlet. It was cold outside, and the fire from the drawing room had died down, making the sleeping room colder. Press needed to get up and put another log on the embers.

"Why, Sweetheart?" asked Gracie, her voice sounding sleepy in his ear.

"Because, they go home, and someone else tends them most of the time."

"Yes, that's true," was her drowsy answer.

"Are you listening to me?" said Press, turning to look at her.

"Uhm," came the sleepy reply.

Press threw back the covers and padded across the cold floor to replenish the wood on the hearth. The fire blazed higher.

He walked back into the bedroom, and eased under the quilts on the bed. "I love you, my wife," he said, as he turned to look at her.

All he got was another, "Uhm."

He gathered her into his arms and went to sleep.

~

Sometime before Christmas, one early morning, Gracie rushed from the house, her arms full of items for the church in Mountain City. She had red candles, some purple bows, and tape. She put them in the buggy floorboard and using the step hanging below her carriage hoisted herself aboard.

Ruby Eliza and Grant Bailey would tie the knot in the early afternoon. She had just enough time to finish decorating the church, and then to rush back home to get ready. She flicked the horse's reins, and they were off.

~

For days, the house had been in turmoil, preparing for the wedding. The bedrooms were full of guests and family. Ruby Eliza was her firstborn, and as she'd told Press, everything must be perfect for her. She and Grant had arrived two days ago. Her father had taken them in hand, using the couple's early arrival to show her intended some more of the Glory B environs.

Before gathering her supplies, she'd checked in on the couple. Going to her daughter as she sat around the large dining table eating breakfast, she bent to kiss her cheek and asked, "Are you ready for the big day, dear?"

"Yes, Momma. Grant and I are more than ready, aren't we honey?" She patted Grant's hand. He gave her a hug. "Our concern is for you. We've been wondering if you are?" she asked.

Doctor Sarah chimed in. "You're beginning to look a bit peaked. I'll be glad to go and help you, Gracie."

"No, I don't lack much, and I'm particular on the final finishes. I'll be okay. Tomorrow, I'll sleep in and dare anyone to wake me." She turned to Ruby Eliza. "Where's your father?"

"He said something about taking P.T. out for exercise. We didn't hear where they were going."

"P.T.'s done amazingly well," observed Doctor Sarah. "I've talked to Alejandro, trying to persuade him to come to Abilene and help out in my office." She grinned. "But I think there's a reason for him to stay here." Doctor Sarah nodded toward the kitchen.

"They do support each other, and he's helping with the ailing cattle and the cow-boys. He can set bones, but as far as medicine, he has no concept of what's available."

"Maybe he can come with Sarah Susannah, and I can teach them both, until she's ready to head north to Geneva Medical College—especially since I'm losing my nurse."

"Now Doctor Sarah, I've told her to keep working part-time, and she can help in the case of an emergency," Grant asserted.

"How is Sarah Susannah?" Ruby Eliza wondered about her younger sister.

"I have to say she's torn about Thomas. But he insists. He instinctively knows if she doesn't at least try they will never be totally happy. And it's like he told her, they could use a good doctor in the Davis Mountains. I'm so amazed at his clever understanding of her needs. He'll make a fine husband. She cried for days after he left. There was no way I could comfort her." Gracie smiled and shook her head. "The one bright spot is she will get to see Little Bossy."

"The Stocktons seem to form attachments to animals and people," agreed the doctor, taking another sip of her coffee.

"Speaking of attachments and husbands, have Jonathan and Joanna set a date?" asked Ruby Eliza.

"Not a number. But as soon as the house is built in Panther Hollow, they'll get married—sometime next year. He's already started working on it, and Press has made plans to deed him the property. Of course, with winter coming up ..."

"And Benjamin? What's he up to?" Doctor Sarah asked.

"Writing. He loves to read, and he's been studying the books he loves the best, to learn the way of words. I'll be his editor." Gracie smiled at the thought. She couldn't wait. "He assures me, if I don't like them, no one else will.

"What's his favorite subject, Momma?" Ruby Eliza asked.

Gracie laughed. "Texas, of course."

"That only leaves P.T.," said Grant. "I heard him talking about windmills. Something about the Big Bend, aquifers, and drilling wells. What about them?"

"Press knows a man who will come here and help us drill wells and set up windmills on our property. P.T. wants to learn the process and see about drilling on other property—if it's feasible. I think he's convinced his Poppa of the need to set up wells for our neighbors, and even some in Mountain City. Who knows where it will go from there? Press has corresponded with the governor, and the state will help on the first ones. They've ordered the equipment, so they're serious."

"I can see the sign Stockton Well Drilling and Windmill Pumping." Doctor Sarah said this with a flourish of her hand. "Another successful Stockton adventure."

"Yes, maybe so. Right now, I need to leave and finish what I started at the church. If the clouds continue to cover the sun, the candles will provide a warm glow over the wedding. See you later."

"Let's hope it doesn't start snowing cats and dogs," Ruby Eliza threw after her.

~

Gracie stood back, looking at the labor of the last few hours. She'd positioned aromatic juniper in every window of the church. Its blue berries along with her red candles and purple bows looked beautiful on the window sills. At the front of the church, two candelabras, ordered especially for weddings, held red candles. These were entwined with the same juniper. They held streamers of purple and bows at each end. Everything looked great, and she couldn't wait to light them. So she wouldn't forget, she placed a box of matches on the first chair inside the main hall.

Hurrying back to the buggy, she headed for home. It was time to put on her favorite dressy dress and enjoy the rest of the day.

~

"It's about time you got here," exclaimed Press. "I was starting to get worried."

"Sweetheart, the church is beautiful. I had to make sure everything was perfect." She gave him a quick kiss on the cheek. "Uhm, I think I need another one of those." This time she stopped to receive one on the lips. "Is everyone ready?"

"I think we are waiting on you. Do you want to come in the second carriage or should we wait for you?" Press was watching her undress, go to her wardrobe, and pull out her beautiful sky-blue silk dress—the one he loved the best.

"I'll come with Ruby Eliza. You go ahead with the groom and best man. I'll meet you at the church door."

"Jefferson is so excited. He looks really sharp in his suit and tie. And he and I've had fun, keeping the bride and groom apart. Of course, we finally failed." Press helped to secure the tiny buttons up the dress back.

"I'm glad Grant chose him since Henry Bailey isn't here to stand with him."

"But part of Henry will be here when the two exchange vows with their hands on his Bible."

"Go on, dear. As soon as I finish dressing, I'll find Ruby Eliza, and we'll be on our way. I won't be long."

Press waved as he went out the door. She heard his footsteps fade down the hall. How many times in her life had she heard this sound? She sat on their bed and started putting on her hose. When this was accomplished, she found her shoes and a heavy cloak. A little bit of powder and rouge and she was ready.

~

When she got to the church, Press was standing outside. "Hurry," he said. "Are the candles supposed to be lit?"

"Oh, my word! I forgot to tell you. The matchbox is on the first chair inside the door in plain sight."

"No, it isn't. I've looked where I assumed it might be, because I thought you said you wanted the candles lit."

Gracie rushed into the main hall. Someone was sitting in the chair. She leaned over and quietly asked, "Did you see a box of matches in this chair?"

"No," was the reply. "But the others moved down the row so I could sit here."

Gracie continued to ask each person. Heads were shaken indicating a no until she got to the last one. The man held up the box of matches. She hurried back to Press. "Please," she begged. "Do the candelabra first and then the windows."

Once all the candles were lit, she breathed a sigh of relief.

Jonathan came to escort her to her seat on the inside aisle. He walked to the other end of the pew, slid in, and put his arm around Joanna. The rest of the Stocktons were already in the pew behind them.

The groom and his best man took their places at the front of the altar. The Wedding March started being played on the church piano, and everyone stood.

Press held out his arm and Ruby Eliza, looking beautiful in a white dress and veil with lace trim, walked down the aisle on the arm of her Poppa, at least the only one she'd ever known.

Grace heard a muffled sob behind her—tenderhearted Sarah Susannah. She had to admit her eyes weren't dry either.

~

The reception, held in the dining room of the Glory B was full. Ruby Eliza was now a Bailey *again.* After changing clothes, she and Grant snuck out the back followed by Jonathan and P.T. These two would drive them in the buggy to a train stop on the new extension to Alpine, Texas. From there they would eventually end up in Abilene. Their first night together was spent in riding to their new home. Grant had sold the old one and bought a completely new one, telling her the house was hers to furnish.

Epilogue

Pastor Ormand Tells All

Pastor Ormand opened the gate leading to the cemetery. Even though the weather had turned cold, spring was on the way. He'd just officiated at his second wedding since the return of Press and P.T. from the Big Bend, and he wanted to tell the two most important people in this fenced area, of his accomplishment. He often did this during his stroll through, because many of his activities concerned these former friends who lay beneath the green grass above them. In some cases, two generations were here resting.

There was a skiff of snow on the ground where he walked, leaving his footprints plainly on the straight path. He was bundled tightly against the Texas west wind which blew through the bare limbs of the oak trees behind the church. There was no rustling of leaves in the trees. The hullabaloo of yesterday and today, was gone. This afternoon, a quietness was in the air—a waiting. Tomorrow, according to the clouds in the sky, there might be more snow and this time in abundance.

He paused between the Tipton and Stockton graves, because what he had to say concerned them equally.

"I think you both need to know; your grandson Jonathan Tipton Stockton and Joanna Lea Stewart were married today. Because the clouds looked heavy with snow, they left immediately by horseback for Panther Hollow and their new home.

"Mary Elizabeth and Peter's new baby is growing fast. Press was bouncing him on his knee when we assembled at the house after the ceremony, and the baby was laughing at his Grandpoppa's antics. He's such a happy child, smiling all the time. I know it won't be long until Gracie and Press will suggest a night visit, but they must wait until he quits nursing. Although, I also heard a case of baby bottles with rubber nipples arrived at the Glory B. We'll see.

"Jay, you'll be pleased to know your granddaughter, Ruby Eliza and Grant are expecting their first child in November—a before Christmas baby, or as Gracie says, "A Christmas gift." Their announcement almost overshadowed the joining of our couple today. They plan to stay for a few extra days as Grant has a replacement at the train station, and this means time for him to see the Glory B. Although he hasn't been told his next assignment, the Texas and Pacific is sending him on West as the train expands into new territory. He might end up in El Paso. Press and Gracie weren't very excited about that, but this event will be an excuse for them to do more traveling when the baby is born.

"I was laughing the other day, remembering the joke we played on Gracie at Fort Davis. She was so shocked to see the bed we made for her daughter in the large iron wash kettle. I can still see her face as she asked where Ruby Eliza was, and we pointed to the black bowl. We both laughed so hard when she peeked inside at her sleeping daughter. Those were good times.

"Gracie and Press are expected to take Sarah Susannah to Geneva Medical College in New York State in the Spring. They want to visit the area where his mother lived, before she married his father. Sarah Susannah will start school and come back as a doctor. At least, that's the hope.

"When they return, Press and P.T. will drill their first water well. P.T. and his father have slowly moved the equipment into place for the grand start at Bull Elk Hole. P.T. is young, but his father recognizes his swelling ambition. His enthusiasm reminds me of his father when I first met him. I believe he'll accomplish more in life than all the others put together.

"Alejandro and Maria have started a small candle making business in Mountain City. Alejandro uses the candelilla plant for making wax candles. This is a talent he learned in Boquillas del Carmen where he lived. The plan is to sell their product to settlers and visitors at the mercantile store in Fort Stockton. Press has been helping with the details and with the purchasing of supplies from Fort Worth. The next wedding, I officiate, should be theirs.

"I think Gracie has finally come to grips with the change going on in her life. Evidently, she had a hard time on the longhorn drive to Abilene. Press said cheering her up was often a difficult job. She and Jorge have both said they'll not go again. I think Press will turn this trip over to Jonathan and his cow-boys for as long as it can be made. Gracie and Press are looking forward to more grandchildren. I heard her telling

Maria, she'd be glad when theirs were walking. She can't wait to show them the Glory B land, take them on picnics, and horseback riding."

Pastor Ormand stood for a few more minutes, thinking silent thoughts.

He turned to walk away, took a step, thought better of it, and said, "You two men should be proud of your offspring. Texas and the West will soon be full of Stockton and Tipton descendants. Their footprints will spread and be seen and talked about from Longview to El Paso, and from the Red River to the Big Bend. The land of *Tejas* as Alejandro calls it, or 'The Land of Friends,' cannot hold them back.

"Instead, as with other great Texans, the Land of Friends will push them forward into exciting adventures and accomplishments, and this great state will benefit greatly from their sojourn on the Glory B in the Glass Mountains."

Going through the gate, Pastor Ormand walked home with a perceptible limp and rubbing his aching hip. He opened the door of his house, to the mewing of Ticksey's great-grand kittens.

Books of the Tipton Chronicles

In England and the West Indies

The Tipton's of Tybbington, Before and Beyond, Part One - 500 to 1300 A.D.
The Tipton's of Tybbington, Before and Beyond, Part Two - 1300 to 1700 A.D.

In America

Butterfield Station - 1858 to 1859
The Glory B, A Sequel to *Butterfield Station* - 1859 - 1883
Chilhowee Legacy - 1911 to 1930's
My Cherokee Rose - 1930's and Present
Tipton's Sugar Cove—Matthew - 1917 to 1921
The Six at Chestnut Hill - 2008

There will be sequels to some of my books. I can't write but so fast. Be patient. R.R.

The books are available at Amazon.com or may be ordered through your local bookstore. If you like what you're reading, go to Amazon.com/Reba Rhyne, and leave a review for any book you've read.

Ms. Rhyne may be reached at rebarhyne@gmail.com.